W9-BZP-362

KISSING THE GROOM

"Perhaps you should put me down now," Imogen whispered huskily, barely able to recognize the voice that shattered the silence as her own.

"Perhaps," Robert said hoarsely and began to slide her slowly down his body till her feet made contact with the floor. She was not surprised to find that he didn't let her go. She couldn't seem to let him go either. Not just yet.

She felt almost dizzy as the dazzling heat rose through her body. She was feeling things she could scarcely identify, wanting things she should not be able to bear, but if her mind struggled to understand this bewildering new world, her body seemed to know of it already. It knew exactly what it sought, and moved instinctively against Robert in the getting of it.

He moaned in the back of his throat and lowered his mouth to claim hers.

She drew in a sharp breath at first contact, then slowly her hands wound themselves around his neck. It was the first kiss she had ever wanted. She whimpered as she felt his tongue move along the seam of her lips. He answered her small whimper with a demanding growl of his own and she opened her lips in eager response to his primitive demand.

Her first true kiss.

It quickly deepened, taking Imogen to a place she had never known existed inside of her . . .

BOOK YOUR PLACE ON OUR WEBSITE AND MAKE THE READING CONNECTION!

We've created a customized website just for our very special readers, where you can get the inside scoop on everything that's going on with Zebra, Pinnacle and Kensington books.

When you come online, you'll have the exciting opportunity to:

- View covers of upcoming books
- Read sample chapters
- Learn about our future publishing schedule (listed by publication month *and author*)
- Find out when your favorite authors will be visiting a city near you
- Search for and order backlist books from our online catalog
- Check out author bios and background information
- Send e-mail to your favorite authors
- Meet the Kensington staff online
- Join us in weekly chats with authors, readers and other guests
- Get writing guidelines
- AND MUCH MORE!

**Visit our website at
http://www.kensingtonbooks.com**

MIDNIGHT EYES

SARAH BROPHY

ZEBRA BOOKS
Kensington Publishing Corp.
www.kensingtonbooks.com

ZEBRA BOOKS are published by

Kensington Publishing Corp.
850 Third Avenue
New York, NY 10022

Copyright © 2007 by Prue Brophy

All rights reserved. No part of this book may be reproduced
in any form or by any means without the prior written consent of the Publisher, excepting brief quotes used in reviews.

If you purchased this book without a cover you should be aware
that this book is stolen property. It was reported as "unsold and
destroyed" to the Publisher and neither the Author nor the Publisher has received any payment for this "stripped book."

All Kensington titles, imprints, and distributed lines are available
at special quantity discounts for bulk purchases for sales promo-
tion, premiums, fund-raising, educational, or institutional use.

Special book excerpts or customized printings can also be created to fit specific needs. For details, write or phone the office
of the Kensington Special Sales Manager: Attn. Special Sales
Department. Kensington Publishing Corp., 850 Third Avenue,
New York, NY 10022. Phone: 1-800-221-2647.

Zebra and the Z logo Reg. U.S. Pat. & TM Off.

First Printing: January 2007
10 9 8 7 6 5 4 3 2 1

Printed in the United States of America

Prologue

Mary's voice halted abruptly and Imogen turned away from the inadequate fire to face the sudden silence, her eyebrows raised questioningly.

"M'lady, that is all of your brother's message that is fit for human hearing," Mary said slowly as she began screwing up the expensive parchment.

Imogen laughed softly. "Oh, Mary, you know you shouldn't worry about things like that. When Roger visits, he says all manner of things that aren't fit for human hearing to me. By reading the message in full you certainly won't be telling me anything that I haven't heard many times before."

"Well, I've certainly never said such foul things before, and I don't intend to start now."

Imogen tried to smile as she turned her face back to the fire, hoping to hide her rising panic.

Roger had started the end game. She had always known that this day would come. On that small piece of parchment, which Mary refused to read out to her, he was giving her formal notice that the real war had indeed begun.

"Burn it, Mary," Imogen murmured quietly. She shuddered almost imperceptibly when the smell of acrid smoke reached her heightened senses.

"Well, it doesn't sound all bad," Mary said encouragingly. "Those bits about your bridegroom sounded interesting anyway. Your brother did manage to say around the vitriol that this . . . Robert Beaumont is suitably impatient. He seems most anxious to claim his bride if he set out within the week, and I for one think that shows a very pleasing degree of eagerness."

"But I doubt he is racing all this way just so that he can claim the infamous 'Lady Deformed' for his wife, don't you?" Imogen said dryly.

Mary's voice sank with embarrassment. "I didn't know you had heard about them calling you that."

Imogen smiled. "I'm blind, Mary, not deaf."

Mary was silent for a second, then said bracingly, "You're not deformed either, if you don't mind me saying."

"I'd be a fool to mind when you're being nice." She shook her head with a sigh. "But you seem to be forgetting that Robert Beaumont doesn't actually know I'm not deformed. He is racing up here, eager to claim his land, not some gargoyle hidden away in a tower."

Imogen got up and began to pace carefully around the room. Twenty-one paces one way, seventeen the other. Her bedchamber, her world. Sometimes, it felt as if the four walls were pressing in on her, suffocating her with the darkness that had held her so tightly for the past five years. There was a monotony to her days that ate into her, a sameness and isolation that threatened to destroy her.

If it wasn't for Mary's loyal presence, her destruction would have been completed years ago.

Imogen would never know what capricious whim had ruled Roger when he let Mary, their old nurse, stay with her when he had taken almost everything else she held dear, but she was pathetically grateful for that one small kindness.

She swallowed hard and tried to ignore the guilt that always rose to the surface when she forced herself to acknowledge that her gratitude meant she was as complicit as Roger in holding the older woman prisoner.

That Mary bore her exile with an admirable fortitude didn't ease the heavy weight of shame Imogen felt. Abstractly, her acceptance actually added to Imogen's burden till the pressure of it almost consumed her.

Sometimes she longed for the silence of death; sometimes it seemed like the only way to escape the loneliness and guilt, but at other times she longed for life with every fiber of her being. Especially at moments like now, when Roger and his dark threats were worming their way inside her, whispering of endings. When the threat of the end was so real that she could almost touch it, even her blind life became precious.

And no matter what Mary said, Imogen knew Roger's threat was very real.

He wanted her, and he was prepared to destroy her completely to get what he wanted. Robert Beaumont was his weapon of choice. On his last visit, when she had been shivering while kneeling in front of him, he had made sure she knew all there was to know about Robert Beaumont, and now she knew why. Now she knew why Roger had gloated as he had told the story of how the bastard son of a Norman nobleman had risen from obscurity to be one of the best killers in all of England; how he had, with cold deliberation, sold his sword out for hire, not even pretending to fight for such illusory things as honor and integrity, but for cold, hard gold only.

As a mercenary, Robert Beaumont was second to none, and soon only the king himself had been able to afford him, for only he was able to promise the land and position that the warrior craved. Robert fought for the king, and the king was led by his lover, Roger.

Imogen could only too well imagine how her brother had calmly manipulated King William till everything was how he wanted it to be. She didn't doubt for a second that it had been Roger who had seen to it that after four years spent fighting in the bloody border wars with Wales, Robert could claim his just reward only if he took the infamous Lady Deformed as his wife.

The last time Roger had been in the Keep he had bound her hands and hauled her to her feet. He had walked around her like an animal prowling after its prey, he had then stood so close behind her that she could feel the heat of him making her skin crawl and he had told her calmly that he was nearly finished playing games with her. His victory was now in plain sight. He had wanted her to know that, wanted her to know the man he had chosen to destroy her, wanted her to know that she had no way to save herself.

Knowledge, as she had learned through hard experience, was in itself a frustratingly inadequate weapon. After all, she had known his dark, twisted jealousies and brooding hatreds all of her life, but she had not been able to stop them from claiming her sight.

And now he was after her body and soul.

She had to stop thinking, knowing that in those memories lay a strange kind of madness. She turned toward the window, feeling the pale glow of the winter sun on her skin. God, how she wanted to live!

She sighed and raised her hand to her aching forehead. "I can't stop him, Mary. I know what he plans, but I can't see anyway that I can stop him."

"Perhaps this is really the king's plan, like Roger says." Mary's voice rang with a conviction that Imogen didn't dare let herself believe. "Maybe it really is all about the cruel joke the king wanted to play on Beaumont."

"I don't know if I like being thought of as a cruel joke," Imogen said dryly. She heard Mary's embarrassed fluster and allowed herself a small, tight smile. She groped for her dear friends hands and when she found them, she also found comfort in their work-roughened familiarity. She took a deep, steadying breath.

"Mary, you must believe that the threat is real. I can hear the triumph in Roger's letter. He is now a step closer to his goal of annihilating me and he has chosen Beaumont and the king to bring it about. They are ways and means only but never doubt that the threat is real, the outcome uncertain, and I will ask you once again to leave this accursed Keep."

Mary gave Imogen's hand a reassuring squeeze, silently communicating her loyalty and support, but Imogen refused to let herself give in to that offered strength.

"Roger's hatred might not be appeased by merely tormenting me and, if not, it will spread, destroying all it touches. I couldn't bear for you to be caught up in this. It is enough for you to have shared so many dark hours with me. I can't let you end them with me." Imogen drew another deep, shuddering breath. "Mary, please go."

"I'm here because I want to be here and here I will stay. You can't tell me to leave, my girl, because you never invited me to be here in the first place," Mary said gruffly. "Besides, just where do you think I'm going to drag these old bones? No, I'm happy enough here by this piddling fire, thank you very much."

"But Mary . . ."

"No buts. You won't be rid of me that easily."

Imogen smiled, tremulous with tears. "I know it's selfish, I know it's wrong, but I'm so relieved that you will stay. I fear the dark alone."

"I think a little selfishness never hurt anyone much, and remember I'm being selfish too. I love you like a daughter, and I can think of nowhere I'd rather be and no one I'd rather be with."

Imogen bowed and buried her head in the old woman's coarse skirts. A warm hand covered her hair. For a moment neither of them needed to speak, and then Mary cleared her throat, trying to remove the huskiness.

"So, Imogen, what do we do now?"

Imogen rolled her head to the side but let it remain on Mary's knee. "Now, Mary, we wait." Her voice dropped to a whisper. "And we pray."

Chapter One

"You don't mean to tell me that you have dragged me halfway across this frozen wasteland of a country to farm rocks amongst starving peasants? Because, if you have, Boy . . ."

Robert smiled absently, his mind concentrating on the deceptively repetitive horizon, but about two days ago he had stopped listening to Matthew's constant whining.

Ideally, he should have left the old man and his endless steam of complaints back in the London inn that they had been calling home, but he had no idea how such a thing could have been achieved. After all, as he hadn't invited him to come along in the first place, there was no way he could really have invited him to stay behind.

From many years of hard experience Robert had learnt that nothing in the mortal realm moved Matthew one inch unless the cantankerous old man wanted to be moved. Just because the man called himself squire didn't mean that he actually took orders at any point.

Which was also only logical, Robert thought with a wry smile, considering that the position itself was entirely self-appointed.

It had happened in Robert's first battle as a knight when he had been forcefully removed from his horse. He was hacking his way to a certain doom when he had heard a yell from the skies. Matthew had jumped from a nearby tree and cut down the man who had been about to fatally attack Robert from the rear. For the rest of the bloodbath they had fought back-to-back till their retreat had been called.

When they were safe, Robert had tried, clumsily, to thank the man for his timely intervention. Matthew had just looked him in the eye and said, "God may look after the stupid, but obviously he's handed you over to me for a little closer attention."

And so Matthew had become his squire and had stayed with him ever since. Robert couldn't help but view the association as something of a mixed blessing. While he knew that there was no more loyal and trustworthy squire to be found in all of England, that sometimes couldn't make up for the fact that more often than not Matthew treated Robert as a wayward, slightly backward son. Time had taught Robert when to listen to the old man and when not to. As Matthew didn't do anything he didn't want to, Robert felt he could safely ignore his complaining now as an exercise in contrary-mindedness only.

Besides, he had far more important things to dwell on right at this moment.

Absentmindedly he reached down and ran a hand over Dagger's graying mane. He had worried how the old stallion would withstand such a long journey over indifferent roads in the middle of winter, but all in all he was holding up very well. Still, Robert would be pleased to see journey's end even if just for his old friend's sake.

Journey's end—Robert knew he should be looking forward to it. After all, it was the fulfillment of all his dreams, his reward for years of hard labor. If only it was all that simple, he thought, and let out a disgusted sigh.

It had seemed simple enough when he had been making his plans. All he had wanted was land, something that the changing fortunes of war couldn't take away from him. He may have come into this world with nothing, but he would be damned before he left it the same way.

Well, he had that land now, but to claim it, he had to marry Lady Imogen. Robert clenched his teeth as he tried to quash the anger that rose every time he recalled how the king and his lover had manipulated him. Now that the deal had been struck there was nothing to be done about it. He would be married by sunset tomorrow and the very land beneath Dagger's hooves would be his.

The winter snows lay over everything like a blanket and the trees were bare of leaves. It was a spectacle of seasonal desolation, but strangely Robert could feel his soul expanding as he took it all in. The closer they got to their destination, the more entranced he had become with this alien world.

Indeed, everything would be perfect if only Matthew would stop moaning and see the beauty that surrounded him. But Robert knew there was no more chance of that than there was of Dagger taking flight.

The old man sat slumped in his saddle, burying

himself deeply into the enormous pile of furs he had procured from one of the towns they had passed. It left visible only his wizened hands, blue with cold, and his condemning eyes. From a distance, he looked like a heap of rags that had been dumped randomly on a horse.

If only he would be as silent as a pile of rags, Robert thought wistfully. However, the old man showed no sign of stopping his steady stream of spleen.

"So tell me, Boy, why did you drag me up here?"

Robert sighed loudly. "I didn't drag you anywhere. Only the will of the Almighty himself might be able to drag your sorry bag of bones anywhere against your will, and I actually doubt even He can do that."

"But you have to admit that this land seems to be worthless for anything save for the breeding of surly peasants."

Robert ran a hand through his black hair, his heavy brows drawn together thoughtfully. "They do seem to be getting a little less friendly the further north we go, don't they?"

"That is an understatement." Matthew snorted, trying to bury himself farther into the furs. "I thought Lady Deformed was to be your punishment for irritating the king with your excellence, but now having met some of the locals, I'm not so sure."

"Don't call her that. She is Lady Imogen Beaumont." Robert's voice was hard and cold and Matthew looked over at him inquiringly. Robert turned his concentration back to the road.

"She ain't no Beaumont. Not yet," Matthew said

gently. "And why so defensive, Boy? You haven't even met the lady, much less given her your name."

"It matters not why. She is to be my wife and her honor is now mine." Robert refused to meet the old man's eye. Matthew's brow was raised questioningly and Robert couldn't even begin to answer the unasked question when he didn't understand it himself. After all, he'd never been one of those mindless fools who would willingly die in the name of honor. He'd always been too cynically attached to life to worry about such things, managing to brush aside all of the small slights he'd ever encountered.

And yet suddenly, here he was not only prepared to defend his nonexistent honor, he was also attaching that honor to Lady Deformed, a woman he didn't even know. Even Robert could see that it was irrational, and was relieved that for once, Matthew wisely allowed the silence to claim his skepticism. The only sound to be heard was the crunch of the horses' hooves through the crisp snow and Robert gritted his teeth, irritated by his own illogical behavior.

He regretted his terseness. He knew Matthew had meant no slight and they had now been too long together to start being precious about each other's sensibilities. They had always talked without boundaries; been free with their thoughts and opinions.

Until now.

Now, Imogen, Lady Deformed, was something that he didn't want to discuss with anyone, not even faithful Matthew.

Lady Deformed. How he had come to hate that name. To hear it sent a shaft of pure rage through his body and created a creature in him that he barely recognized. A creature comprised solely of pride and honor.

As a bastard and a mercenary, what could he claim to know of personal honor? He had spent the last five years killing for a man he despised. He had always lived his life to his own code and had never cared that the rest of the world couldn't understand that code. And had never felt the need to justify his actions to anyone but himself.

But right now, even he didn't understand himself. He was jumping to the defense of a woman he had never met. More than that, he became a rabid beast, and could only be amazed at his anger, at his protectiveness.

It was the protectiveness that was the most perplexing. He had never considered himself callous, but the life he led never left room for such sentiment, and he couldn't honestly say that he had missed it. Now, strange, dark emotions were raising their heads, emotions he didn't even recognize, and they seemed to have a single focus: the poor creature that was trapped in these cold lands so far from her warm southern sun. To hear her insulted in any way started a battle rage deep inside him.

"I hate to bring you back to the real world, but I think that pile of stones up ahead might be yours."

Robert's mind instantly shifted.

Home.

It stood tall and bleak against the winter sky. It did indeed look a little like a pile of stones thrown together by chance. Robert raised his brows, their earlier conversation forgotten.

"I didn't know that the Conqueror's building program had stretched so far north, but surely the Saxons never used stone."

"I don't think they did," Matthew said thoughtfully. "No, that pile of stones looks new, but also totally uninhabitable."

"Are you calling my new home uninhabitable?" Robert asked with a smile.

"No, Boy, I'm calling that pile of stones uninhabitable. I'm sure your home will be a habitation fit for a great warrior."

Robert threw back his head and laughed. "Don't snivel, Old Man. It doesn't become you."

"Who's sniveling?" Matthew asked derisively. "This is just basic survival. If I compliment you a little, stroke that formidable ego of yours, I just might be able to get out of this blasted cold at some point."

"Then there is no time to waste. Yah!" Robert spurred on his horse and streaked out ahead at a full gallop. Matthew sighed and muttered something about being young again and, with a creak of leather and old bones, tried to catch Robert.

The closer they got, the stranger the lone tower seemed. It jutted out of the forest in a harsh, unnaturally straight line. New, but already it seemed to be falling apart, littering the land with silent, gray stone corpses.

Robert frowned. "This can't be Shadowsend Keep, Old Man."

"No, Boy," Matthew yelled back as he drew even with Robert, "but I can see smoke from those trees. Looks like a fair-sized chimney."

Robert squinted in the direction Matthew had indicated, only just making out the thin wisps of smoke rising slowly and disappearing into the patchy gray winter sky.

"Let's go and talk to more unfriendly peasants, Old Man," Robert bellowed, trying to be heard above the wind in his ears and galloped toward the smoke.

As he maneuvered his horse expertly into the small courtyard of a wooden Keep and swung down in one fluid movement, his eyes quickly scanned the clutter of buildings, trying to take in everything at once. A thick blanket of snow covered everything except where the fires warmed the roof sufficiently to keep it clear. The buildings themselves were dilapidated, but at least they looked lived in.

"Ah, now, this is better. This looks like it just may have one warm corner to rest these cold bones," Matthew murmured appreciatively as he slowly dismounted his horse.

Everywhere he looked, Robert could see where things were in urgent need of repair, where things had been incompetently repaired and where things had been repaired just enough to barely keep them useable. But it wasn't all bad. Three or four brave chickens scratched hopefully through the snow and the smell of wood smoke gave the insubstantial Keep a surprisingly warm air of welcome.

Home.

"It would be impossible to defend, of course," Robert said as he walked briskly to the double doors, trying to keep the excitement out of his voice.

"And whom are you envisioning defending it against?"

"The world," Robert said to himself as he rapped his gauntlet-covered knuckles against the timbers. The two men heard the scurry of feet, but the door remained resolutely shut. Robert tried again, rapping his knuckles harder.

"We've nothing left to give. Clear off!" The screeching voice carried well into the courtyard.

Robert looked at Matthew. The older man's face split into a grin. "Not so badly defended at all, it would seem. Your hallowed portals would seem to be protected by a savage crone."

"Behave," Robert murmured, then lifted his voice to what Matthew called his combat roar. "It's Robert Beaumont out here, freezing on his own doorstep, and he has no intention of clearing off from what is rightfully his."

A satisfyingly comic volley of noise followed the stunned silence inside the Keep.

Within seconds the door flew open to reveal an old woman. She was surprisingly small, considering the amount of noise she had been making. Her hair was scraped back into a kerchief, giving her face a stretched look.

"Sor-sorry, my lord, but we weren't expecting you, and . . . and you can't be too careful nowadays, not with all these Norman brutes wandering about attacking innocent folk." She stared openmouthed for a second, flushed scarlet, and then slammed the door shut.

"Would you like us to storm the door, Sir Knight, or just burn it down?" Matthew asked with an unholy amusement in his voice.

Robert crossed his arms over his chest, exasperation beginning to tell on his nerves.

"Don't tempt me, Old Man." He took a deep breath, preparing to bellow his way to Hades, when the door flew open once more, this time wide enough for them to actually enter.

Neither he nor Matthew hesitated, afraid that this offer of warmth might suddenly disappear again.

They found themselves in the main hall with the doors being shut quickly behind them. It took a second for Robert's eyes to adapt to the gloom. The room had no windows and light came from the guttering candles and the fire that burned sluggishly in the hearth. The enormous stone fireplace took up one entire wall and Matthew let out a groan of ecstasy as he rushed over to it, releasing the smell of stale rushes with every step. He thrust his hands to the small blaze and closed his eyes blissfully. Robert remained near the door, taking full stock of his new home.

It took Robert a moment to locate the person in the shadows who had finally allowed them in.

She stood so that the candles illuminated only one side of her face, leaving the rest in shadow. It was a harsh effect, seeming to magnify the lines on her face and the steel in her gray hair.

By her dress it was clear that she was a servant, but she held her back straight and met his gaze squarely as if they were equals.

Robert had spent years relying on his instincts, and wasn't entirely surprised when his body eased automatically out of its wariness. It was clear that this woman wasn't a threat, for all her apparent severity.

He gave her a small smile, which she didn't return.

"Greetings, my lord, and welcome to Shadowsend,"

the woman said stiffly. "I apologize for Alice, but you did startle her, although we have been expecting you. At the moment, the Keep is only being served by nigh on ten women, but if you ask for me, I'm sure that we will manage to serve most of your needs, Sir Knight."

"What is your name, and what exactly are your duties here?"

"My name is Mary. I'm principally my lady's companion, but I also function as a chatelaine in the absence of someone else more suitable."

Robert nodded, only a little wiser than before. What he knew about the running of a castle, keep or cottage was insignificant, and he had only the vaguest of notions as to the function of a chatelaine. Hopefully it meant that she could run everything without any help from him.

"You may go about your duties," Robert said in what he hoped was a confident manner, feeling large and clumsy in a domestic setting. Give him a meadow and twenty unseasoned soldiers and he moved with confidence. Present him with one self-assured servant and he was almost ready to eat the rushes. He tried to hide that uncertainty by turning his back in dismissal, but changed his mind abruptly, catching the woman midcurtsy.

It was a clumsy return to standing, and Robert felt a little more at ease in the face of this small imperfection.

"Wait. Why isn't Lady Imogen greeting her guests?" Even he was aware that the basic rules of hospitality demanded that the lady of the house see to her guests' comfort.

For a moment Mary looked disconcerted. "My lady, uh . . . sleeps and I was asked not to disturb her."

Matthew snorted, stopping for the first time his fire worship. "They have found you the perfect wife. One who can manage to sleep through your battle bellow."

The woman had the grace to blush at the too-obvious lie and for the first time lowered her gaze.

"We have much to discuss," Robert said gently, "the lady and I, and I think we should start now. If you can go and wake her and tell her that Sir Robert desires very much for her to present herself in the hall."

The woman seemed dumbstruck for a moment before her natural confidence returned. "I'm sorry, Sir Robert, but Lady Imogen never leaves her chamber."

Robert was momentarily nonplussed. Perhaps Lady Deformed was unable to manage the stairs? Perhaps her legendary deformity prevented her moving altogether?

A nauseous feeling rose up in his throat. He had never been squeamish before. How could he, when the battlefield offered so many kinds of death and none of them were pretty? He had seen men ripped to shreds, splattered so far that they were unidentifiable. He had seen retribution, that cold, mechanical murder of the enemy. He might never have relished it; but he had accepted it. It seemed natural to him after so many years and he had learned to live with it, learnt that it was part of his days and, occasionally, a part of his nightmares.

But never before had he seen a female so scarred by her injuries that she couldn't leave her room, so badly damaged that she hid from the world. Warriors wore their scars as a badge of pride, a symbol of their survival. This new kind of pain didn't sit well with him. He longed for escape, longed to leave the lady buried in her living grave, but his newly defined honor demanded more.

He set his shoulders. "Well then, it is only fitting that I go to the lady if she is unable to greet us. Lead the way."

Mary bowed her head and grabbed the candlestick from the great table, using a burning stick from the fireplace to light it. Robert raised his brows. The sun had risen two hours ago. Did none of the Keep open to the natural light? As if she read his mind, Mary shrugged her shoulders, a little apologetic.

"The light on the upper floor is not the best, Sir Knight, and the steps are not entirely sound. After a few nasty falls, you will learn the wisdom of these candles."

She smiled and left the room. Robert paused for a moment but knew the time for delay was passed. It was time to face the lady herself.

The wooden stairs groaned ominously under Robert's foot. He grimaced, and tried to pick a quiet way through the cacophony of noise. It would seem that before he was able to husband the land back into some fruitfulness, he needed to rebuild the Keep first! Even in the dim light cast by Mary's candle up ahead he could see the rising damp and decay.

Mary stopped in front of one of the doors and turned to him. For a moment, her clear eyes looked deep into his, as if trying to find the very source of his being. Robert shifted uneasily but refused to break contact, refused to be the first to give in.

It seemed she reached some conclusion as she nodded. "I think you might be a good thing after all," she muttered enigmatically. She nodded again and went to brush past him, leaving him increasingly confused. She paused for a moment, and then suddenly reached out a hand to touch his leather-covered forearm. "She awaits you within, Sir Knight. She has passed the last weeks in much fear. Please be kind."

He stared bemused for a second as she and her light quickly retraced their steps, leaving him alone in the darkness.

Fear. He supposed his was a reputation to invoke fear and he was disconcerted by the guilt that flared to life inside him. Perhaps he should have tried some other contact first, allayed the lady's fears somewhat before presenting her with a warrior husband. He should have found some way to woo her.

Woo. The word was strange to his mind.

Although, he added defensively to himself, hers wasn't exactly a reputation designed to calm a suitor's fears either. For a brief second he felt some mild justification, but then he flushed as he realized just how clumsy he would appear to his gently bred, soon-to-be wife.

Hells blood! What did he know of home, hearth and wooing? How was he going to manage not terrifying his poor, deformed virgin wife? he thought with despair. He might manage for a while, say an hour or so, but his own nature would find him out in the end.

Bracing himself he knocked on the door, only to be greeted with silence. For a second he hesitated, but impatience won out in the end. His need to get this first meeting over with was too great to dally in a cold hall on a lady's whim.

He pushed open the door.

After the dimness of the hall he was blinded by the brightness of the full sun in the chamber. It was seconds before he could make out the figure on the other side of the room.

When his eyes adjusted, his heart almost stopped. She had stepped forward, and unknowingly revealed to him every exquisite detail. It was like an angel had stepped down from heaven.

Her long black hair hung in waves around her, glowing in the sunlight like an aura. It framed her gracefully, outlining her tiny waist, the gentle flair of her hips, the lushness of her breasts.

Her skin shone a pale ivory, splashed with the redness of her perfectly formed lips and the deep glow from her brown eyes. They were eyes that a man could drown in and never regret the demise.

She stood straight and proud, but still she would reach only his chin. He felt suddenly large and clumsy before her, felt unworthy to see such ethereal, unworldly beauty. A beauty that produced a very earthy reaction through his body. He could feel that reaction in the tightening of his loins, in the pounding of his heart, in the air that suddenly rushed into his deflated lungs, making him almost light-headed.

For the first time in his life he was totally struck dumb and when his mind finally kicked back in, all he could manage was to hoarsely say, "My God, you're perfect!"

Chapter Two

She let out a shrill peal of laughter. The hollow sound hung heavy in the air.

She instinctively closed her eyes, wishing the laughter away. She wished she hadn't given vent to the hysteria she could feel rising from her stomach, but somehow it was a force that could not be denied. The absurdity was just too great.

He saw perfection. She couldn't see at all.

His deep, strong voice created pictures for her, but she could not see him, couldn't tell what kind of man he was, whether he came to her dressed for war or wooing. She couldn't even see to run away from him.

A shiver ran down her spine. It was a creeping disadvantage. She longed to hide, and felt vulnerable when she knew she couldn't.

Roger's dark whispers rose up to taunt her. Robert had both the strength and the determination to devote his life to one goal. He was here to claim his reward from the king, and she doubted that he would allow her to hide, but it wasn't the king that she was afraid of. No, this was all Roger's dark game, for all it had a royal disguise.

If Robert Beaumont was part of Roger's plans, then he must be her enemy, and an enemy that you couldn't see was a very dangerous foe indeed.

Fear squeezed her throat. She wanted to scream, to yell freedom, to fight and claw her way out of the dark, out of this man-filled room, out of her life.

She wished wildly for a moment that she was indeed so hideously deformed that the dismembered voice would run screaming from her, and leave her to her fears.

It wasn't going to be that simple, Imogen realized sinkingly. This was Roger's game. It had to be played out, and she could only hope that when the time for the ending came she had the strength to fight.

She walked stiffly to the chair two paces in front of her and sat down on the edge, clasping her hands tightly. For a second the man seemed to pause indecisively, and then he pulled back the other chair gratingly and sat down heavily.

A big man, Imogen mused. A man whose knees didn't fit in the space she had left between the chair and the footstool, a man who made her solidly built furniture groan.

She had never really thought about his physical proportions, but a knight would have to be big, strong. Small men did not kill easily. Roger had never had the body mass to be a true knight. He couldn't bring down a man with one swing of a sword, couldn't physically control those around him. No, he had to use the more subtle method of fear and isolation. This man he had sent to her won through sheer bulk.

It was hard to say which she found the most horrifying at the moment. Perhaps that was why Roger had chosen him. Robert was a physical threat that he couldn't make himself. Roger could torture her with his little games, but this man could crush her with one hand.

She mentally shook herself. There were smaller things to be concerned about here, like returning the chair to its spot if she wanted to avoid yet another bruise.

"I'm sorry for my rude silence, Lady Imogen," Robert said slowly, "but you aren't quite what I had been led to expect."

He was trying desperately not to stare like some callow youth, and hoping against hope that she wouldn't notice the red heat that had risen and swamped his face.

She smiled bitterly. "Surprise must be one of the downsides of buying without first checking the stock."

He went absolutely rigid. He had expected politeness, been prepared for patronizing, but he hadn't ever thought that she would be openly rude. That wasn't his understanding of how ladies acted.

His first instinct was to return like for like, but some part of his mind whispered about the vulnerability that lay beneath those bitter words and held him in check.

That part of him understood it very well. It was the reaction of a wounded animal to lash out wildly. Instead of getting in range of the claws, he knew it was better to wait till the fear and pain had played itself out.

"I don't think of you as purchased," he said

tightly, "and I would prefer it if you also refrain from such merchant talk."

"I apologize." She raised her chin an inch. "You are right, of course. *I* wasn't purchased. It was my land you were bargaining for. I'm just the sting in the tail: the catch at the end of the bargain. It must be depressing to finally have your Keep, but to also have to take possession of Lady Deformed as well."

She smiled at him silkily. "And what a very brave knight you must be to accept a bargain that binds you in marriage to Lady Deformed."

His lips tightened, and he held his temper with the greatest difficulty. "I do not care for that name, and I will not have it mentioned again."

"What? 'Lady Deformed'? That would be too harsh, Sir Knight. The poor women who look after the Keep lead such dreary lives that they have little else to talk of. Who are we to deprive them of such small pleasures?"

"If their pleasures interfere with my honor, then I'm afraid I will have them stopped." He leaned closer, trying to catch her gaze, but she stared resolutely over his shoulder. "Besides, I see no need for the name. I can see no imperfection to warrant such harshness."

Her hands gripped more tightly to each other, her nails drawing blood.

He hadn't noticed! It seemed incredible to her, the darkness too evident to be hidden.

Perhaps he was attempting gallantry. Perhaps . . . but it didn't make sense any way she shifted it about. Her brother hadn't sent her a lover. He had sent her a punishment, and punishments didn't entice with honeyed words. No, they pulled you apart piece by piece.

There had to be some deeper game being played here, some tactical reason for claiming her imperfections invisible.

Maybe he wanted to hear her declare her deformity. Maybe he was like her brother and enjoyed making her destroy herself. It had always made Roger feel like he was stronger than a god when he had brought her to her knees.

She tightened her jaw. She was not ready to play dead for this man yet. "Knight, I've no patience for idle flattery. My deformities are plain for all to see and I will not be mocked. Our marriage may give the rights to my land and my body, but I will not give you my pride on a platter. So beware."

He raised a hand in supplication. "I meant no offence. I'm a blunt man and the subtleties you speak of are not in my nature. I was stating an honest puzzlement."

"You mean you really don't know?" she asked incredulously. "You mean my brother hasn't prepared you for the role he wants you to play?"

Robert paused, trying to find the diplomacy that was normally lacking in his character. "Your brother and I do not move in the same circles," he said carefully, not mentioning that he thought of Roger more as something that slithered out from under a rock than as a man. That didn't seem to be the kind of thing that you mentioned to a man's sister, however.

Nothing makes any sense, she thought with some agitation. She stood abruptly and began pacing.

"What does it mean?" she muttered darkly to herself, trying desperately to understand this latest ploy of Roger's. In her agitation she forgot that Robert had moved the chair and his shout of warning came too late. She ran into the back of the chair and was beginning to topple over when strong arms grabbed her, steadying her against his firm chest.

For a moment she forgot her fear, and gave herself up to this strange new experience. Never before had she stood so close to a man that she could feel the ridges of muscles beneath the soft spun wool of his tunic.

So Robert had come to her dressed as a suitor after all, with no metal to hide behind. She wasn't surrounded by the acrid smell of sweat-soaked metal; instead her senses were clouded with sandalwood, fresh air and another strange element that she couldn't name, something unique to this man himself.

It was intoxicating, just as was the warmth radiating from his large body. For the first time since she had been exiled to this cold north, she felt a warmth that actually seeped into her bones, warming her to the core. Her limbs felt like they were on fire, but it was a strange fire that excited rather than hurt. It rushed along her nerve endings, causing sensations she didn't understand, but she already knew she never wanted them to end.

It was a moment that seemed to both last forever and yet to end far too soon.

Robert struggled with himself. Every fiber of his body screamed the rightness of this near-embrace. She fit against him like she had been made to rest there. It seemed against nature to let go. He longed to pull her closer; longed to raise a hand along the soft, smooth skin of her throat and cup her face; longed to lower his head . . .

He tried not to think such things. Down that path lay madness. He closed his eyes for a second, but quickly opened them again. He didn't want to lose one moment of this. He stared deep into her eyes, and almost lost control altogether.

Her pale translucent skin was flushed, and her lips parted to reveal two rows of perfect white teeth. It was as if she could hear his lurid thoughts and was responding with a desire that equaled his own. He tried to read an invitation, a rejection or anything to stop this torment of indecision.

Her eyes didn't quite meet his.

He wanted to howl to the moon. He wanted to kiss her till they both lost their senses. He *wanted.* He had never understood want until this moment. He pulled her closer for a fraction of a second. Then he let her go and stepped back, holding his hands ruthlessly to his sides.

The end was cold, abrupt and complete.

For a second she couldn't work out where she was on her mental map. She seemed to float a little above the ground, her carefully crafted realities dissolving around her in the heat of this man. Without the warmth of his body she seemed to have no existence.

She floated for a second but quickly pulled herself back together. She shouldn't stand stunned before this man like some lovesick mooncalf. She wouldn't show him such weakness. Unfortunately, despite her reluctance to show weakness, her knees no longer seemed strong enough to support her.

"Can you please direct me to my seat?" If her

voice broke a little, she could always blame it on the near collision, she decided desperately.

"Sorry?" Robert asked, bewildered both by her apparent calm in the face of his own suddenly burning needs and the question itself.

Imogen could feel the color leave her face. It seemed like the ultimate humiliation.

"Don't worry," she snapped out. "I'll find it myself." She stretched out her hands, groping for a familiar object. She could have cried with relief when she felt the back of his chair.

She moved her hand over the still-warm fabric and reached out to where she should have been able to grab the next chair. She could barely suppress the urge to stamp her feet. He had moved the chair. That was what had caused the chaos in the first place. She stood undecided. The two options before her were both equally unattractive. She either stood till the wretched man left, or she was going to have to crawl to her seat.

Robert stared, stunned by the dawning understanding.

"You can't see?" he muttered, unable to hide his shock.

She let go of the chair and straightened her spine. The simple words belied all the pain of the reality.

Robert was lost for words. He had braced himself for ugliness, had been prepared for it, even—but this, this was somehow more unjust. A perfection that couldn't even glance into a mirror to see itself?

His silence was beginning to grate along her nerves.

"Say something," she said through gritted teeth.

"My lady, I don't know what to say."

She made a frustrated gurgle in the back of her throat and threw up her hands.

"By all that's holy, you can't be that shocked. You didn't think I was called Lady Deformed on a whim did you? You bargained for damaged goods knowingly."

"I asked you not to use that insult," he said carefully.

For a second her mouth fell open. "You really meant it? Why ever not? That is how I'm known the length and breadth of the country. I find it strangely apt and I can't see why I alone should stop using it."

"I care not about the rest of the people on this island, only my small corner of it, and in that corner I expect never to hear it again. Am I understood?"

"No. It's nonsense. And I won't be dictated to this way."

"I'm your husband, and to a larger extent, my word is your law."

"You're not my husband yet," she muttered resentfully.

"Why will everyone keep reminding me of that small, inconsequential fact?" he murmured enigmatically.

"Because, fact it is."

"Well, not for much longer. I shall send word to the priest this night and we will be married by sunrise."

"We are still to be married?" she asked in a small voice, not entirely sure what answer she feared hearing the most. Inside her all was confusion, but the one thing she seemed to know for sure was that she was glad Robert hadn't fled when he had found out about the first of her dark secrets.

He smiled a little and stepped closer. He picked

up her small hands in his larger one, engulfing it
with his calloused strength.

"I have pledged my honor on it. You are now my
honor."

Her brow crinkled in confusion. "I don't understand."

He lifted his forefinger and clumsily massaged the
frown out of existence. "You don't have to understand.
It is fact."

She felt his warm breath on the back of her hand
as he lifted it to his lips, felt the moisture as they
brushed over it, and she realized with dawning
amazement that in the welter of emotions that filled
her there was no repulsion at this man's touch. She
was confused, excited, frightened and bewildered,
but she felt no revulsion. She absorbed that realization with dazed amazement.

"Until dawn, my lady," Robert said with a gravely
voice that played over her nerve endings. Then
suddenly the room was empty, emptier than it had
ever been before.

She raised the back of her hand to her lips and
felt her first kiss.

"Oh, Brother dear, what is it you do now?" she
whispered.

Imogen spent the night before her wedding in
vigil. After Mary had prepared her for bed, Imogen
sat in front of the fire and waited.

She waited for the terrors.

They were almost like old friends, the terrors.
They had always been her companion, even

when she'd had sight. She had always been afraid
of the dark.

Nothing her parents had done could convince
her that the dark held nothing that the light didn't.
Each night she would curl herself into a tight ball
and wait for the sleep of exhaustion to finally claim
her.

Then came the day when a darkness descended
that would never end. The terrors had stalked her
day and night. At first she had been beyond coping,
but time had taught her to keep them at bay, she
had learned to shut her mind away from its own
phantasms.

Still the fears grew, joined by dark memories of
pain and the causing of that pain.

So now she waited alone in her room, waited for
the memories to come. She curled up on the rug,
feeling the fire on her face, smelling the smoke but
remembering a place a lifetime away.

Once more she was sixteen. A beloved child of
loving parents. It seemed to be always summer,
there seemed to be only laughter. Even fear was not
so cold and destructive. Fear was a thing only of the
night. She had been too young to see the dark hate
in Roger's face, too young to comprehend his
twisted soul. She had danced around her dark sibling and had never noticed the threat: never saw
the silent predator waiting in her summer youth.

She hadn't seen him that day as she had raced up
the tower steps. They had been at their estate in
Cornwall for weeks and she had barely noticed his
brooding presence at all. It was too lovely a time to
think about Roger's bad moods and strange, hard,
staring eyes.

She had raced up those steps only to get a better view of the eagles.

He had caught her in the tower room. Trapped her. Suffocated her.

She had at first been too stunned to fight, but soon she had used her claws, used her teeth, to try and get him off her.

He had stepped away enough to allow her air, and she had clung desperately to the cold stone wall. The smell of his blood hung heavily in the air between them as it streaked down his cold, dark face.

"This is not the end, Sister dear," he had hissed. "This will never end."

She hadn't seen the blow before it landed, but she had felt the sickening crunch of her jawbone, felt the rush of air as the stone steps seemed to rise up to meet her, felt the first impact.

Mercifully after that she had felt nothing.

She had awoken to darkness and a fear that echoed with those prophetic words.

It would never be over.

Even now, safely hundreds of miles from him, his dark soul still stalked her. Every visit he came and renewed his vow. He had never yet tried to hurt her like he had in the tower. He was patient. He would wait till she came to him on her knees.

But it would never be over while they both lived.

Sometimes she wished that it would all end. Sometimes just the thought of another day in darkness made her retch into the chamberpot, but tonight her stomach felt strangely calm.

She waited for a dawn that she would never see and tried not to think about the darkness. She found herself not thinking of ends. Instead her mind strayed to the warmth of Robert's arms around her.

It was the first night since the age of sixteen she didn't scream.

"Imogen Colebrook!" Mary exclaimed in horror. "Don't tell me you slept there all night?"

"No, I didn't sleep at all," Imogen murmured as she slowly straightened her cold, stiffened body.

"I can tell that by the violet under your eyes." Mary leaned over, took her face and held it up to the light of her candle, then let out an exasperated sigh. "Not that it makes much difference. You're still an unearthly beauty, maybe just a might more fragile."

Imogen smiled slightly. "Don't sound so disgruntled. You make a compliment sound like an insult."

"Well, I certainly meant no insult. You don't insult a bride."

"Why ever not?" Imogen asked in puzzlement.

"Because it brings bad luck," she said authoritatively, and then ruined the effect by adding, "though God knows, most things seem to. To my way of thinking, what we be needing are things that bring good luck."

"Maybe if you're nice to me, you might get a little bit of good luck."

Mary raised a brow but helped Imogen to a chair and began getting things ready for Imogen's bath.

"Did the priest arrive?" Imogen asked nonchalantly but couldn't stop herself from stiffening.

Mary didn't answer for a second as she scrabbled to find the hairbrush.

"Oh, yes, almost instantly," she said finally. "Sir Robert can be a might forceful when he puts his mind to it. He had that lazy beggar Alice cleaning out the place, and setting up an altar table near the main room, and I don't know what else."

Imogen froze for a second.

"He plans us to be married downstairs?"

"So it seems." Mary's voice was curiously neutral.

"I can't go down there, Mary." Imogen's voice rose in panic. "I've never seen down there. I can't go down there."

She swung in her seat and made a grab for Mary's hands. "You'll have to tell him. Tell him. You must. We can be married here. It makes no real difference. Not to him."

"I don't think he's the sort of man you go telling things to. He's the sort that seems to do most of the telling himself."

"Please," whispered Imogen.

Mary sighed, disengaging her hand. "I'll give it a try once I've got you dressed." She went to the chest at the end of the bed and began foraging for clothes. "But I don't be liking my chances of achieving the impossible," she muttered darkly.

"No. I'm not getting married in some damn bedchamber."

Robert's voice sounded calm enough, but Mary could clearly see the fury in his eyes. Still, she tried again.

"I've told you that Lady Imogen never leaves her

room, and she doesn't understand why where you get married makes that much difference."

Robert stared into the black embers of the fireplace. He had spent his night sitting there near the hearth in his room, watching the fire slowly die. It had seemed like too important a night to just lose it to sleep. He had waited, and before the dawn had risen he carefully got dressed in the clothes he had bought especially for a ceremony that he had never thought to go through.

As he had belted his simple black-and-silver-trimmed tunic, he had felt a peace descending. There was a rightness to this day that had been missing from every other, but that rightness also dictated he take Lady Imogen for his wife in front of her people. Their people, now.

He turned to look at Mary.

"The marriage will take place in the hall in one hour," he said softly. "I will come and collect her just before."

Mary stared for a second, then bowed her head and left. She knew when a fight was lost. The time left would be better spent preparing Imogen.

Today, it would seem, had been set aside for the conquering of fear.

Robert stood and walked over to the small table. He picked up the leather pouch he had placed there the night before and tipped the contents into his palm.

The single gold ring winked at him. He could well remember the strange, inept feeling that had haunted him as he had looked for the right tokens for a wife he had never met. He had never bought such things before, and had been unable to visualize them on his unseen wife.

Now the image of her was burnt with an acid brilliance onto his mind. He had seen her face dance in the fire all night, yearned to feel the satin of her skin against his own. In the long night he had been haunted, but it was by no malignant spirit. No, he had been haunted by a wonderful future he had never expected to have, haunted by a rightness he felt unworthy to possess.

Lady Imogen. His Imogen. His wife.

The ring seemed to burn into his palm as his fingers closed round it.

"Well, Boy," Matthew asked gently from the door, "are you ready?"

Robert felt his back straighten, his chin rise.

He turned and saw his old friend and companion standing near the door, the other man's discomfort clear. His hair was damp and combed back in a scary fashion. He seemed out of place in his good clothes, but Robert could well read the pride in the old man's face.

"Matthew, I'm more ready than I have ever been for anything in the whole course of my life before."

"Then let's go to it, Boy."

The door to Imogen's room stood open. Robert stepped in quietly, wanting to assess the situation before deciding how best to deal with his nervous bride.

She sat on the floor; her knees drawn up to her chest and held tightly by her arms. Her face was hidden by her waves of black hair. He felt a strange warmth in his chest as he noticed that she too was specially dressed for the event. Her pale pink dress swept fluidly over her body and was held taut round her waist by a girdle of gold lace.

Robert still felt a little dazzled by such beauty. It was almost beyond his simple human comprehension. He was smiling as he crouched down in front of her, his knees cracking a little.

Her head flew up.

"Who's there?" Her voice sounded small and defiant. He could now see the trails that tears had left on her face.

Robert mentally castigated himself for not making her aware of his presence before frightening her. The last thing he wanted to do was frighten her.

"Sorry." His voice sounded thick even to his own ears. "I didn't mean to sneak up on you."

She tried feebly to smile. "Everyone sneaks up on me. I've been thinking of giving the servants bells just to stop it."

"I don't think I want to wear bells."

"No, I suppose not." She seemed to gather her strength for a second. "Please don't make me go downstairs."

He looked down at his calloused, scarred hands, trying to sound calm and unconcerned. "Is it that you don't want to marry me in front of your people?"

She seemed stunned for a moment.

"You think I'm ashamed to marry you?"

He shrugged his shoulders. "Perhaps."

She instinctively reached out a hand, trying to find his, but instead she found his knee. It was a warm solidness under her palm.

"No. No, it has nothing to do with you. I don't know enough about you to be ashamed." She ducked her head. "You have been kind enough to me."

"You are easy to be kind to."

"Well, can't you do one more kindness?" she asked pleadingly. "I've never left this room, not since I came North. I've tried, but I can't. Within two steps, I don't know where I am. I panic. It's like . . . It's like being alone in Hell." Her voice broke. "I don't want to be alone."

Robert's vague feelings of rejection evaporated, replaced by a warmth that started in his heart and spread to his whole body, especially the part where her small hand rested. He covered it with his own.

"You won't be alone. I promise to never leave your side for a second." He cupped her face with his other hand, running his thumb soothingly over the damp softness of her cheek. "Let me be your eyes."

"And you won't leave me alone in the dark?" she asked, thinking of that day alone.

"Never," he whispered, thinking of tomorrows stretching into eternity.

Chapter Three

She heard the gathering long before they reached the hall.

The low murmur of many voices sounded like the roar of a multitude in her mind. She had lived in her isolation for so long that the sound of the people from the Keep and the nearby villages gathered to see her was terrifying. The noise clouded her senses and dislocated her from the world. She moved as if in a dream.

And the only real thing in her dream world was the man beside her. The warmth from his body seemed to calm the panic that was trying to form a cold knot in her stomach.

He held her close to his side as if she was made of the finest crystal.

This gentleness was perhaps the most surprising thing about her warrior. Instead of the exasperation and anger at her panic that she had expected, he had simply lifted her from the floor and looped her arm through his, placing his other warm hand reassuringly over hers.

She was enclosed entirely in the strength of his almost-embrace.

He had led her slowly from her sanctuary. It had been only the calm in his deep voice as he had talked softly to her that had given her the courage to take the first step. And the next. But now, in the face of so many others, it wasn't enough.

"We are at the door of the main hall now. You're doing well," he murmured encouragingly, but even his calmness could no longer still the chaos that suddenly swarmed to life inside her. The strength that had got her to the doors of the hall now fled.

She felt rooted to the spot with panic.

"I can hear people. How many people?" Her voice squeaked in rising terror. "There are too many people."

He let her hand drop and wrapped his arm around her trembling shoulders, drawing her more tightly into the cocoon of his warmth.

She lacked the strength to deny the comfort he offered.

She leaned into his warmth, barely resisting the urge to bury her face in his side. He was strong enough to fight off the world, and for the first time in longer than she cared to remember, momentarily she let someone else's strength be her own.

For this one moment, it didn't seem to matter that he had been sent by her brother or that she scarcely knew him. Instead, she concentrated on the peace that radiated from him. The only thing that mattered was that she could feel the long, muscled length of him as he held her securely. The smell of man and sandalwood that filled her mind was at once calming but also oddly exciting.

"It's just the household," he said soothingly, "and people from the villages near Shadowsend."

"It sounds like more." She took a deep, shaky breath. "I've been alone too long."

For a second his arm tightened around her, subtly forcing her to shift her balance into him more completely or risk falling over. She felt him take a steadying breath of his own.

"Well, you are no longer alone."

He couldn't explain, even to himself, the tightness he suddenly felt in his chest at her words. The sensation was so strange that he didn't even try to identify it.

What was easier to understand was the raw anger that accompanied the tightness. It was a wrath being fed by questions that circled his mind, questions whose answers he already knew he wasn't going to like.

Why had this woman been carelessly dumped in an obscure corner of this remote island? Why had she been abandoned to the protection of this motley group of women and old men? Why had she been left so isolated that she was frightened by her own wedding gathering?

It was past all understanding, but a feral smile lit his eyes as he envisioned trying to get some understanding out of the guilty party. Robert quickly tried to dampen down his anger.

The righteous rage that was boiling in his belly was explosive and he didn't want this fragile woman to sense the depths of that anger, didn't want her to be frightened by its intensity.

God knows, he was a little frightened by it himself.

"What is it?" she asked nervously. "You've gone all tense. Has something gone wrong?"

He carefully eased his rigid muscles, kicking himself mentally for not being more careful. She might be blind, but his soon-to-be bride was far from stupid. Of course she could sense the anger that he had let momentarily take hold of him and although the focus of his anger was her enemies, he had fought alone too long to let another know all that he thought.

Besides, there was nothing to be done now about the past. There would be time enough for retribution later. For now he didn't want Imogen to know just how violent a man she was committing her life to.

"It's nothing," he said soothingly. "I just couldn't see the priest, and I'm anxious for the deed to be done."

She nodded, her sightless eyes instinctively trying to scan the room.

If she felt some small disappointment at the coldness of his statement, well, she had no right to, she told herself sternly. After all, this was only an arrangement of necessity. Just because being held in the arms of this man felt right to her, didn't mean she could expect him to pretend a sentiment he was far from feeling.

"Now you wouldn't be looking for me by any chance?" spoke a voice suddenly behind them.

Robert turned and narrowed his eyes at the priest, who simply smiled benignly in return.

"Sorry for the delay," the man said breezily,

straightening already neat vestments, "but I was . . . uh . . . elsewhere when your messenger arrived."

He smiled engagingly up at Robert, who struggled to hide his immediate and intense dislike of the slick little man.

His temper wasn't improved when the man's eyes fairly glowed as they rested on Imogen. "And might I say that I have rarely seen a bride looking as radiant as our fair Lady Imogen?" He lifted one of her hands and grazed his lips along the knuckles.

Robert struggled not to growl his disapproval. He would have dearly loved to hit the man. Instead he settled for a good, all-purpose glare that had been known to set even hardened veterans to flight. The priest ignored it.

The priest's lips lingered over her skin for a moment, but Robert's displeasure must have registered, because he let go of her hand with a sigh. Robert only just stopped himself from grabbing hold of Imogen's hand and wiping it clean.

"It's time to get started, I think." The priest clapped his hands together with some evident relish. "Give me a small head start and I'll have the crowd worked up to a fever pitch of prewedding ecstasy for you."

Robert watched as the little man walked confidently into the room, commanding an instant silence. Robert grimaced a little. It seemed that the priest had everyone in the room already in his thrall.

"Idiot," he growled darkly to no one in particular.

"Always was," Imogen said with a small smile.

Robert raised a brow. "You know that pompous idiot?"

"I remember him," she corrected. "Ian was apprenticed to be my father's squire. He was a real ladies' man till he, uh, got 'his calling.' I didn't realize he was the priest of this parish, though." She shrugged her shoulders. "Roger must have had him installed. Those two were always close."

Robert's brows lowered in puzzlement. He couldn't stop himself from asking, "How do you know it's Ian without . . . you know . . ."

"Without being able to see him, you mean?" she asked, and Robert grunted in reply, more than a little embarrassed by his own awkwardness.

"I just can," she said slowly, for the first time struggling to explain her dark world. "We are more than just our faces and body. A human is made up of so many other little signals that if you wait for them, it's easy enough to recognize them. I knew Ian so well as a child, I suppose. The sound of his voice, the top of his finger missing on his right hand." She smiled her first real smile that morning. "The smooth, arrant nonsense that seems to come out of his mouth every time he opens it. It's all very distinctive."

Robert couldn't help but smile, and some of the irritation he had felt at the sight of Imogen's hands in Ian's eased a little. "Arrant nonsense or not he's going to be the one who marries us."

Marry. The word was like a cold weight in Imogen's stomach.

She turned and placed her hand high on Robert's chest for support. "Are you sure you want to do this? I know you're only doing it to get the land, but there might be some other way, some other arrangement . . ." She could hear the panic in her own voice but wasn't entirely sure whether the panic was because he might say yes or because he might say no.

Robert covered her small hand with his own, trying not to be uncomfortably aware of the callouses and brute strength in his own hands compared to the small softness of hers. "Are you trying to say that you don't want to marry me?" he asked, as if whatever her answer, it would mean nothing to him.

She hesitated for a moment, then shook her head decisively. There would be no escape. If it wasn't Robert Beaumont, then it would be someone else. Roger would never allow her to escape this game and she must never forget that. Nor should she forget that Robert was first and foremost Roger's choice.

Instead of being distracted by the muscles on his chest that she could feel beneath his tunic, she should be thinking of tactics, of survival.

Robert allowed himself only a moment of relief before gathering up his thoughts.

"Good!" he said briskly but couldn't seem to stop himself from dropping a gentle kiss on her forehead, enjoying the feel of her soft skin under his. "Then let's go get married, Little One."

The ceremony passed in a blur.

Afterward, Imogen couldn't seem to recall anything except the moment when Robert's strong, clear voice pledged himself to her forever. For a moment she had felt a quickening in her soul, a sense of rightness.

At that moment she had to really struggle to

remember that her brother had sent this man. Caught up in that struggle, she barely noticed the cheers as Robert bent to kiss her.

He had hesitated above her for a second, bathing her lips in the warmth from his mouth. The tingle of sensation caused her to let out a small gasp of surprise. Robert swooped on the movement, and claimed her parted lips as his own.

Every nerve ending seemed to come alive in the radiance of that kiss. Fire spread through her body, teasing and titillating every part of her.

That kiss was so entirely beyond her realm of experience that her instincts took control. When she felt his tongue trace her lips demandingly, she opened them wider without question. The only voluntary response she seemed to have left was the one that demanded she lean farther into him, opening herself up completely.

His tongue moved questioningly along her teeth in a slow, teasing movement before withdrawing.

Though the touch had been brief, its sudden absence left her feeling bereft. There had been a long moment when she had managed to forget their audience entirely, but as he moved away from her, their voices could be heard once more, penetrating the fog Robert had spun round her. She had been left momentarily stunned by the knowledge that she had forgotten them all and, more than that, she had actually felt safe. In Robert's arms, she suspected, anything could seem safe.

She was still reeling from this shock when Robert had calmly announced that he wanted everyone present to pay their respects to the new master of Shadowsend Keep and to his wife. Robert then led her to a chair near the fire without a word and through everything that had followed he had remained standing stiffly at her side. Mary had stationed herself at Imogen's other side like a silent sentry, but Imogen had felt her trying to give her comfort and strength.

What followed was a hideous confusion. Each person came forward, bowed respectfully, then left the room. There were so many people that Imogen very quickly became confused, but pride wouldn't let her show it.

Through it all she felt their eyes upon her, felt each of them trying to see her fabled deformity. Some of them knew, and soon they all would. Instead of an easily dismissed mystery, she would become a part of their known world, the Blind Lady of the Keep. It would be the death of the little false dignity anonymity had left her.

When Mary softly told her that the last of them had gone by, Imogen could have cried with relief. Instead she had stood briskly and imperiously, and demanded to be taken back to her bedroom. Robert immediately stepped forward.

She felt his warm hand on her arm and was almost seduced by it but her fear was too raw. She refused to be fooled by the comfort he offered. She shook off his hand.

"No. I want Mary." Her voice wavered, but she lifted her chin defiantly.

She clearly heard Robert's breath whistle between his teeth in shock, but he quickly hid his irritation at her public rejection. "Of course," he said quietly, but it seemed to roar through the silent room.

Imogen pretended not to notice and regally walked from the room as she had been taught all those years ago, but once in her chamber she dismissed Mary as soon as she could. She needed more than anything to be alone with the chaos that now filled her.

She collapsed into a chair, covering her face with her hands, feeling more afraid than she had ever before in a life filled with fears. She now had fear about what was real and what was false in this world turned strange.

She had almost believed in that kiss.

For a moment she had almost believed that it wasn't all an elaborate game. She had almost lost herself in the man. Almost.

It was pitiful, really, that she had been so easily absorbed into a dream world of his making. She should be grateful for the prying stares of the guests she had felt pulling away the layers of her skin. They had forced her to return to the harsh light of her reality.

And the reality was that they had all wanted to see Lady Deformed, wanted to feel that vague, tantalizing thrill that came with touching her corruption. Perhaps they had even been a little disappointed that her disfigurement hadn't been more apparent, that they couldn't actually see her ugly darkness. She could never let herself forget that, no matter how tempting it was to do so.

Her deformity was the darkness that only she could see but for a moment Robert had blinded her even to that and she couldn't allow him to have that power over her. She could never allow herself to lose sight of what she had become, of who had made her that way.

She must never forget that Roger had robbed her of her vision, robbed her of her youth. She should never forget that the man who had taken her very life away from her was the same man who had sent Robert to her dark prison. If she forgot, Roger would win.

She sighed. It sounded simple but was so hard. It had been too long since she had been held, too long since she had felt the warmth of another's concern. The forgetting was all too easy. Her reality seemed less real when she found herself drowning in Robert's roughly tender charms.

And losing herself in that charm could prove deadly.

Robert walked up to the large desk in the center of the room. It was dusty from disuse, but the quality of the oak furniture was evident, he thought with some satisfaction, and he was making sure that the dust wouldn't last long.

He had given his orders and he expected them to be obeyed. He wanted the Keep cleaned from top to bottom and he had made it painfully clear that there wasn't one inch of his new home so insignificant that it wasn't worthy of his inspection.

He looked after what was his.

He ran his hands over the oak table, trying to fire a flare of ownership, trying to find satisfaction in all that this morning's vows had brought him, but instead a hollow feeling seemed to have lodged itself permanently inside of him.

That emptiness had flickered into life when Imogen had coldly rejected his help, and it had grown to crowd the day.

He had tried to fight it, tried to deny the sudden hollowness of his victory. He had called everyone in the keep together and issued their new instructions, had sorted out the arrangements for a suitable wedding feast that evening and had set about cleaning up the stables in preparation for the horses he had coming in easy stages from the Welsh borders.

Everything was being done as he had commanded.

Even now he could smell the succulent aromas of the feast being prepared in the great hall. No, *his* great hall, he corrected himself sternly, but the long-awaited concept was stillborn in his mind, swamped by the image of Imogen's cold face as she had told him he was surplus to requirements. He had not been prepared for the dismissal, not after that all-too-brief kiss they had shared.

Just remembering it brought a pulsing heat to his loins. Holding her in his arms, feeling the innocent heat of her lips under his had shifted the universe. He had forgotten bargains, forgotten his name, and forgotten all but the bit of the world that he had enclosed in his arms.

And then she had turned from him, rejected him.

His mind relentlessly circled the memory. He couldn't seem to let it go, even though he knew he was behaving like a half-starved dog with a bone.

"My lord," Mary said quietly from the door that he had left half open.

She was obviously uncomfortable and not sure

how to approach the lion in his den. Good, Robert thought savagely, even as a heated flush of embarrassment climbed his neck at being caught staring broodingly at a dusty table. He sat down on the chair behind the table and held his breath as the furniture creaked ominously, horrified at the prospect of being thrown onto his rump in front of this supremely dignified woman. His luck was in, however, and the chair held.

"What do you want, Mary?" he growled.

"I just thought you might like to know that my lady is having a rest before the feast."

Robert raised his eyebrows in surprise. He never believed for a moment that Mary genuinely thought he needed to know such pointless information. She flushed under his scrutiny and started to shuffle her feet. Her very apparent embarrassment made her look a little more human.

"Is there something more important you have come to tell me, or have you just temporarily lost your mind?" Robert murmured.

It was the opening Mary had apparently been waiting for. She stepped fully into the room and closed the door firmly behind her.

"I just wanted to know if my lady had offended you too deeply."

He shrugged his shoulders with a careful negligence. "No more than she intended to offend me, I am sure."

Mary shook her head and frowned in exasperation. "She didn't mean to be offensive, my lord. Can't you see that she was reacting, not acting? She wasn't thinking about you at all." Her voice pleaded to be understood even as it lectured.

Robert smiled faintly. "I had gathered that much. Her indecent rush to leave the hall was, I felt, a fair indication of her extreme lack of interest in her husband."

"No!" she said sharply. "That's not it. You don't understand. It wasn't a rational thing. She was too afraid to be logical."

"Afraid! What had she to be afraid of?" he snapped out bitterly. "I have yet to do anything to frighten anyone. I simply haven't had time to make anyone afraid." A feral gleam lit his eyes as he added ominously, "Yet."

Robert felt momentarily in control until Mary smiled gently, clearly unperturbed by his playacted ferocity.

"It's not you she fears, my lord, well, not yet, at any rate. Her fears come from a time long before she was threatened with this marriage."

"Threatened! It wasn't . . ."

Mary simply lifted a hand to still his blustering. "This isn't about you, not yet. It is Roger who is the threat."

The words had a chilling effect on his anger. "She fears her brother?" he asked coldly.

"Yes," Mary said flatly. "I can't claim to know all that's between them, but I know that Lady Imogen is terrified of him. Every three months the Keep is emptied of all people while the brother visits his sister. When he leaves we return to find more expensive clothes and fashionable fripperies, and Imogen acting like she has been fatally wounded although there is no blood."

"Why does he come here?" Robert asked calmly enough, but rage burned clearly in his eyes.

"No one but the two of them know for sure. She never seems to be physically hurt beyond a bruise or two, but whatever the truths of the matter, they remain locked together in some evil dance. No, not a dance. That's not what Imogen calls it." She paused a moment as she groped for the right word. "A game. She thinks they are playing a game and I don't believe my lady holds out much hope of winning."

Robert looked down at his hands and was surprised to see his knuckles white where they clenched the top of the table. Carefully he loosened his grip. "That no longer matters," he said with deceptive calm. "I am her protector now and as such I will not let anything happen to her in this . . . game."

"If she will let you. To Imogen, Roger sent you, and that now makes you a part of the game. She's frightened that you are Roger's winning gambit." She leaned forward earnestly. "That's why she fears you."

"She talks to you about this?"

Mary hesitated a moment. "We talked before you came, but since, no. No, now she's holding on to herself so tightly to stop from falling apart that she can't let anyone share her fears. She's isolating herself in her head and it is starting to frighten me."

Robert stared off into the middle distance, not seeing. He took a deep, steadying breath, trying to gain control of the raw anger that had flared to unexpected life inside of him. He had never experienced a rage like it before, and was at a loss to explain its existence. Moreover, he couldn't let it rule him now. He needed to be in control, needed calmness to devise a strategy to defeat the man who had suddenly become his enemy. He tried to remember everything he could about the man, even through his anger, a part of him understanding the vital importance of knowing the enemy.

His knowledge was scant at best.

Roger belonged to the lowest set at the court. He was one of the pack of mindless animals that now surrounded the king. As a group they were noxious and prone to all the vices that money could buy, but Roger's particular perversions could only be surmised.

Robert narrowed his eyes. It wasn't much, but it was enough to feed his rage. Roger Colebrook. That such a man could even think of using him for his private warfare was abhorrent, and Robert never doubted for a moment that it was indeed a war, for all their calling it a game. Anything that claimed real victims was a war as far as Robert was concerned.

Robert smiled savagely as he spotted Roger's first mistake. Roger had faulted badly if he thought to use Robert in the collecting of Imogen's defeat. Robert was not a man to be used by one of the court parasites, not against something he had taken for his own.

And that was the one truth that shone, even through the haze of his anger: Imogen was his, body and soul.

"You've given me much to think on," Robert said slowly. "Thank you for taking me into your confidence. I won't see that trust abused."

Mary let out a long sigh of relief. "I'm glad you didn't see it as an impertinence. I was so afraid that you would, but you needed to understand, needed to see a little of what Lady Imogen sees."

Robert sat and steepled his hands. "Oh, I see a little now, but I intend to see a lot more. Soon."

Robert's easy shouldering of leadership had inspired everyone in the Keep to new heights.

By evening the main hall had been scrubbed till it glistened. Fresh rushes had been gathered hastily and laid, their meadow fragrance quickly masking the mustiness. Enough tables had been located to seat all of the guests, each festooned with holly and ribbons, creating something of a festive air. Over the central dais a canopy of red cloth had been hung and the two chairs that had been placed on it had been decorated with matching ribbon.

The men of the nearby village had spent the morning at the hunt, killing two boars, a young deer and other smaller game, which were given to the cook and some women from the village to dress. The cook had complained bitterly about people expecting miracles, but had still managed to produce any number of mouthwatering dishes with only the most basic of assistance.

Robert felt congenially pleased with the preparations. He should have felt every inch the expansive host as he watched everyone eat, drink and be merry. Everyone, except Imogen beside him, was enjoying themselves mightily, but that omission was the thing that irritated him the most. Imogen was silently fighting him and, damn it, she may even be winning.

Aware of her fear of crowds, Robert had intended

to behave the chivalric knight and escort her, also intending to reassure her as best he could, just as Mary had wanted him to.

Imogen, however, had easily forestalled the small gallantry. As the first guests arrived, Imogen had floated regally into the hall, with Mary discreetly leading her. Even as he felt the heat of irritation flare on his face, the vision she presented nearly brought him to his knees. All rational thought dissolved, leaving Robert with nothing to do but stare like an idiot at a queen.

She had changed from her angelic pink into a red velvet robe, but it wasn't the sultry color that Robert found himself objecting to. No, it was the way the tight lacing made the fabric almost lovingly cling to the curves of her body, and the neckline, which seemed scandalously low to Robert's suddenly puritanical eyes. They had narrowed when he noticed that every male in the hall had focused his attention on the flimsy lace inset that covered the pale skin at the top of her breasts. She had carefully bound her hair with gold thread, and eschewed the mantle worn by the women of the court, leaving the line of her vulnerable throat naked and, for a moment, Robert was struck dumb with awe. It seemed almost impossible that such a being existed outside of heaven.

He had watched as she walked with a calm dignity toward the dais, obviously trying to hide that it was actually tearing her into small pieces. Only when she got closer did Robert become aware of the whiteness of her knuckles on Mary's arm.

When the old woman carefully removed those fingers, Imogen dropped into a very correct curtsy in front of him. He, with ill-disguised eagerness, had got up and helped her up the steps of the dais.

Then she ignored him; ignored them all.

She now sat stiffly in her chair, her hands held tightly in her lap, seemingly oblivious to her surroundings. She had remained unmoving when the sumptuous food had been brought into the hall. When the grunts and murmurs of satisfaction filled the large chambers she seemed to draw into herself more tightly.

Robert could almost physically feel the strength of will radiating from the woman, as she deliberately made no attempt to sample the aromatic food just in front of her, but to look at her she seemed entirely unmoved. It was as though she had been turned into a very beautiful statue, as if she was denying herself out of existence—and that was what angered Robert so much.

Robert didn't want a lady made of stone and willpower; he wanted the blood-hot woman he had kissed that morning. He needed her to be real. He would make her real, he thought with a small, grim smile of determination. Casually he leaned toward her.

"You do know that the food tastes even better than it smells, don't you?" he asked with a lip-smacking, satisfied noise. "In fact the food is amongst the best I have ever tasted."

"I'm sure it is," she said stiffly.

"Then why don't you try some? You might surprise yourself and actually enjoy it." He lifted a fragrant morsel from his plate and placed it near her face. He dropped his voice suggestively. "But if it's not the enjoying that you like, if you find your plea-

sure in pain and denial, well, then, as your husband
I'm sure I can accommodate you."

"I'm sure you can," Imogen said through
clenched teeth, "but I'm not abstaining for my own
personal pleasure. I can't see where the meal is to
eat it." She lowered her eyes and drew in a deep
breath, wincing slightly as she was once more assaulted by the scents rising from the feast. "I haven't
eaten in front of anyone since the . . . accident. It's
not a pretty sight and I can't say I have any desire
to make a spectacle of myself in front of the whole
district solely for your own perverse amusement."

Robert's languid cynicism died. He felt a flush of
shame heat his face as he realized just how great a
mistake he had made.

He hadn't meant the dinner to be a torture. The
hollow feeling of failure opened in his gut. She now
not only thought of him as part of Roger's plan, but
also as the oaf who had brought her into a roomful
of food to starve.

"Why didn't you say something earlier?" he
said quietly, trying unsuccessfully to hide his
embarrassment.

She shrugged her shoulders with a seeming care-
lessness, her hands clasping more tightly in her lap.
"I didn't see the point."

"The point," Robert said with careful slowness,
"would have been that you wouldn't have had to sit
there like a martyr, starving at your own wedding
feast, if you had mentioned it to me."

He picked up his own empty plate and began re-
filling it with the most tempting delicacies and he
reached over and filled his goblet with wine. With
economical, deliberate movements he carefully

loaded a spoon with roast boar and brought it to her lips, trying not to notice the way they seemed to glow rose-red in the candlelight. "Open your mouth, Imogen," he said huskily, and was unable to stop himself leaning a little closer so that he could bathe himself in the perfume from her hair.

"No . . ." she started to stay but he took advantage of the moment and shoved the spoon into her open mouth. He couldn't help but be smugly pleased that he had left her with only two options. She could either spit out the tasty meat and draw attention to herself, or she could eat it.

Robert watched with amusement as she began militantly chewing the meat, grinding it with her teeth as if it was her enemy, swallowing it with exaggerated grimaces.

"I won't be treated like a child." Her voice quivered with irritation and outraged dignity. "It's not . . ." Ignoring the diatribe, Robert took advantage of her open mouth to pop in a small piece of herb bread. He had to hastily pull his fingers back to avoid the sharp little teeth Imogen brought closed with a snap. A blush of anger flagged her cheeks red as she once more began chewing.

"Trust me, Imogen, I will keep feeding you. Eat and we can argue about it later," Robert said soothingly. "It's always a lot more fun to fight on a full stomach, I find. I never meant you to starve, so let me make it up to you so I don't have to feel guilty for too long. That's a good girl, hmmm?"

She opened her mouth to speak, but closed it too quickly for Robert to get any food inside. He let out a deep chuckle of appreciation, even as he sighed in exasperation.

"I'll have to remember that you are no fool. I only got to pull the same stunt twice before you spotted it. You're obviously going to prove to be quite a test on my creativity."

Imogen could well hear the smile in Robert's rich voice, and the open sincerity of it drew a small answering smile from her.

Robert realized helplessly that he was in very grave danger of having his heart snared by the single dimple that danced on her cheek. Never before had he ever worried whether a woman had a sense of humor or not but found himself inordinately pleased that Imogen seemed to.

"Please eat some more," Robert whispered huskily in her ear. "I find I like to watch you eat." It was true. There was no denying the primitive satisfaction to be found in feeding one's wife.

Imogen smiled a little broader. "How can I say no to my lord, when my lord has quite clearly lost some very important parts of his mind?" She opened her mouth and closed her eyes with all the appearance of wifely obedience.

Robert's eyes were drawn to her open lips, to the way they glistened in the candlelight. They looked tempting, lush and infinitely kissable. Lust, pure and compelling, slammed through him, momentarily depriving his lungs of air.

"Well, your lord has certainly lost control of something," Robert growled with awe as he reached blindly for some food.

His gaze never wavered as he slid a piece of spiced apple over her waiting lips. Indeed, he watched in rapt fascination as her pearly teeth closed again, more slowly this time, biting into the soft flesh of the fruit. A little of the juice trickled from her lips, and she licked it away with the tip of her tongue.

Robert could barely contain a groan. By God, he thought with astonishment, he was on fire! He had never felt anything like this intensity, and over so innocent a thing!

He had truly thought until this moment that he had experienced all the shades of lust there were. This white-hot burning, however, was unique to his experience. The simple lust that he had always associated with sex had suddenly taken on a tangled web of other, entirely foreign emotions. They seemed to tighten around him till he no longer wanted to escape them. He was in torment.

No more.

He surged suddenly to his feet, not caring if his advanced state of arousal was evident to all or not. He barely noticed that he had knocked over his chair. Imogen flinched, startled by the suddenness of his movements and by the sharpness of wood hitting wood. She turned quickly toward the noise.

"Robert, what happened?"

"Madam, I'm through with eating," he ground out.

"But I've barely started," she squeaked, her brow furrowing with her confusion.

He reached for her hand, pulling her to her feet and after he had helped her down from the dais, he began to stride from the hall, ignoring the hooting and ribald comments that followed them.

As he pulled on her arm, Imogen had to run to keep up with his longer strides. He slowed down only after the second time she stumbled. Slowed, but wouldn't be deterred from his ultimate objective. She yelled at him and tried to tug her hand free, but could not catch his attention until they were at at the bottom of the stairs.

He turned, despite the demon that rode him mercilessly, and even managed a smile at the innocent bewilderment on her face.

"Sir, this is madness," she said breathlessly, all the while trying to reclaim her hand, which remained resolutely held in the warmth of his. It took only a slight tug for Robert to bring her body up to the burning heat of his. The silent sliding movement of her skirts over his thighs was almost his complete undoing.

"This might be madness," he said hoarsely as he bent and placed an arm under her knees and swung her up to his chest, "but it is a divine madness, Wife."

She let out a small squeak of protest, but as she felt his powerful strides start up the complaining stairs, she suddenly felt calm. Held against the warmth of his broad chest, listening to the steady beat of his heart, she almost dared to feel safe for the first time since her parents died. For this one, precious moment it was as if Roger and his dark games didn't exist.

She was amazed to find herself actually snuggling herself against him. Her mind struggled to equate this strange behavior with the terror of her dark memories. She should be running, freezing, screaming or any of the things she did when Roger touched her, but somehow, it just wasn't the same. Robert surrounded her so completely that he blocked out all of the darkness, leaving her free of it for the first time in her life.

It wasn't to be trusted, she told herself sternly, even as she let herself enjoy the sensation. He wasn't to be trusted. This was all an illusion conjured by Roger. She should be trying, however inadequately, to protect herself. She needed to prepare herself for the pain and fear that Roger always brought into her life, albeit that this time he was using this stranger as his weapon.

Instead, she found her arms tightening around her husband's neck, drawing herself as close to him as she could be.

Robert was right. This all must be some kind of divine madness.

Chapter Four

Robert leaned against her chamber door, panting for a moment. He still held her tight to his chest, his arms like steel bands around her.

"Perhaps you should put me down now," Imogen whispered huskily, barely able to recognize the voice that shattered the silence as her own. She didn't even recognize herself in the wanton who so willingly embraced a man who was essentially a stranger, for all he was her husband, in her bedchamber. But she was. Despite all that Roger had done to her, he had not robbed her of her ability to find pleasure in the touch of this man. The realization staggered and amazed her. It was almost frightening, and a part of her wanted to run away from this strange new sensation, but a deeper, more primitive part had turned to molten lead. That was the part of her that seemed to be making her decisions at the moment.

"Perhaps," he said hoarsely and began to slide her slowly down his body till her feet made contact with the floor. She was unsurprised to find that he didn't let her go. She couldn't seem to let him go either. Not just yet.

She felt almost dizzy as the dazzling heat rose through her body. She was feeling things she could scarcely identify, wanting things she should not be able to bear, but if her mind struggled to understand this bewildering new world, her body seemed to know of it already. It knew exactly what it sought, and moved instinctively against Robert in the getting of it.

He moaned in the back of his throat and lowered his mouth to claim hers.

She drew in a sharp breath at first contact, then slowly her hands wound themselves around his neck. It was the first kiss she had ever wanted. She whimpered as she felt his tongue move along the seam of her lips. He answered her small whimper with a demanding growl of his own and she opened her lips in eager response to his primitive demand.

Her first true kiss.

It quickly deepened, taking Imogen to a place she had never known existed inside of her. She found herself helpless and entirely unable to resist his sensual invasion. Her body longed for this strange new self he was showing her. It was as if she had come alive after a lifetime of slumber, every nerve ending opening to the world in a whole new way.

He invaded her every sense.

Her fingertips buried in his hair, tingling with the feel of his warm scalp. She could hear the scrape of his stubbled cheek against her skin, his roughness against her smoothness, her mews, his half groans, the moist sound of his mouth plundering hers and the shush of fabric rubbing against fabric created the most exquisite music that Imogen had ever heard.

It was the song of Robert making love to her.

Making love. She only half understood what those words meant. She knew of dark deeds to be forgotten in the daylight, but she knew nothing of love between a man and a woman. Somehow, though, her body knew. It knew what it needed, and relentlessly pushed her toward the abyss of the unknown to get it.

It was in the part of her mind where the memories were freshest that a small doubt came to life. That small, rational region of her separated itself, hiding behind a cold wall of fear. It was almost overwhelmed by the sudden need of her body to learn all.

But fear was relentless and slowly froze her body's needs. She lowered her hands to his chest and tried to push him away. It was no more than the fluttering of a butterfly and in Robert's passion-clouded mind it barely registered. His body, however, was at one with hers and was instantly aware that she was no longer following him into the mad sensual realm they had stumbled upon. He struggled to lift his mind free of the lust that had taken hold of him and he couldn't help but groan with frustration as he tore his lips free from hers.

Even though it was what she had silently asked for, she wanted to protest the sudden loss of the warmth of his mouth as she struggled to slow the rapid beat of her heart while she listened to Robert's labored breathing. She found it oddly intoxicating that she could bring him to a state that equaled her own. His forehead leaned against hers, bathing Imogen with the sweetness of his breath.

It was a long moment before either of them could speak.

"I'm sorry," Imogen finally murmured.

Robert lifted his hand to gently cup her face. "You have nothing to be sorry for." He inhaled sharply. "It is I who should be apologizing for my behavior. First I rush you from your own wedding feast without letting you eat properly, then I behave like an animal without control over his lust."

He slowly ran his thumb over the softness of her cheek and she shivered as she felt the rasp of his callouses against her skin. Without any conscious thought she reached up to hold his hand to her face when he made to move it away.

"I didn't really mind," Imogen said shyly, surprising herself as much as him with the truth of that statement. "I'm just not sure . . ."

Robert's sharp laughter cut off Imogen's confused apology. They stood so close that she could almost feel it inside of her as it reverberated through his chest. His laughter almost felt like her own.

"Well, I am sure. You need time and I should be giving it to you," Robert ground out harshly.

He held her tightly to his burning need for a second, then carefully lifted her bodily away from him. Bereft of his support she had to lean against the door to support her suddenly weak legs. In confusion she listened to him prowl the room like a caged lion, his disgust and self-loathing almost a tangible presence in the room.

The knowledge that it was her own fears and confusion that had caused his torment haunted her. She had never meant to cause him pain. She wrapped her arms around her middle, feeling his pain in her own body in much the same way she had felt his laughter. He thought his clean lust had frightened her, when instead it was her dark memories of another's twisted perversion that had forced her to turn from the passion he offered her so freely.

Suddenly it seemed to her that those memories weren't as important as the feelings that had come to life inside her with Robert's touch.

"I don't need all that much time."

She said it so quietly that it took Robert a moment to hear it. His shout of grim laughter caught her by surprise.

"You don't have to lie to save my feelings. Of course you need time to get over the fright and disgust caused by the insatiable animal you have married." He slumped into a chair by the fire. He buried his face in his hands and tried to control the guilt and desire that raged in conflict through his body. Imogen could still feel it like it was a presence under her skin.

It was that new pain that made her decision for her.

Carefully she followed the sound of his ragged breathing and knelt slowly in front of him. She slid a hand up his thigh, partly for support, but mostly because she liked the feel of his coiled strength. Robert lifted his face, startled first by the voluntary touch and then by the look of earnestness on her face.

"Don't say that. I know what fear and disgust feel

like, and I didn't find either in your kiss. It was beautiful and I wasn't exactly fighting you off, if you remember."

"How could you fight me? I'm at least twice your size," Robert said darkly, trying to deny himself the comfort she offered.

"But you never used your size against me." Her hand tightened over the tenseness of his thighs. "You stopped," she whispered, and that knowledge was like a shaft of light into the darkness of her world. He hadn't tried to harm or overwhelm her. He had stopped the second she had wanted him to. He had given her the choice. With that revelation came another, equally startling one; she chose to feel more of the fire he had built in her with just the touch of his lips on hers.

"May I touch you?" she asked, her face flaring with embarrassment at her own daring. She refused to be daunted, however, and took his sudden silence as an affirmative.

Robert's breath stopped as he felt her small hand begin to move caressingly over the length of his thigh. "Lean back," she murmured, and Robert found himself mutely complying, unable to resist the chance to feel her touch on flesh that craved it. She moved till she kneeled between his muscular thighs and carefully moved both her hands to his face. She ran a fingertip over the whorls in his ear, the fine hairs on his brow, the bridge of his nose.

"So soft," she purred as she ran a thumb over the satin of his lips. Robert inhaled sharply as he felt the small tip of her finger trace the moist skin just inside his mouth. He couldn't resist drawing it in even farther and gently sucking on it, all the while keeping his eyes locked on her flushed face. He watched in fascination as a faint shudder ran through her body, and felt an answering quake through his soul.

"It's odd," she whispered with awe, "that such little things can feel so large. I can feel your tongue all the way to the pit of my stomach."

She slowly pulled her finger away, mimicking the action that his body burned for. She trailed the damp tip down his neck, tickling his Adam's apple and the hollow of his collarbone. She mewed with frustration when the silky edge of his tunic stopped her explorations. She tugged ineffectually at the cloth, needing to touch the warm male skin that lay intriguingly beneath.

Suddenly Robert surged forward and all but tore the valuable cloth from his body.

Smiling with satisfaction and with her bottom lip caught between her teeth, she moved her greedy fingers over him. Burying her hands in the springy hair on his chest, she sighed at the decadent plea-sure of the feel of him under her palms. When she found the small masculine nipples that hid there and teased them gently, Robert had to grit his teeth to stop himself from sweeping her up and taking this exquisite torture to its only natural conclusion.

Unaware of just how tenuously Robert had con-trol of himself, Imogen followed the path of his hair down to his navel, and then spread her hands out to cover his lower abdomen.

The ripple of muscle encased by satin-soft skin en-tranced her at first, then her sensitive fingers became aware of other ridges, ones that marred the perfec-tion of his smooth skin. Scars. She felt a kinship to scars and the pain that had caused them, she thought sadly. Gently she followed their lines with her fingertips, feeling the pain that lingered on these badges of his wars.

Some were old, almost indiscernible, others puckered and new. One, just above his hipbone, still gave off the heat of healing. Robert stilled her hand with his and made to move it away from the ugliness of his healing flesh.

"No," she murmured softly, then lowered her head and gently kissed it.

Robert was struck dumb. He stared uncomprehendingly at the bent head of the woman who knelt at his feet. It was a selfless act, meant to both reassure and comfort. Robert had never been the receiver of such an action and found himself swamped by emotions he could neither name nor deny. His vague feelings of protectiveness and concern had crystallized into a solid reality that, he realized with sudden awe, could all too easily be mistaken for love.

She raised her head, her hand still moving caressingly over the heated skin of his stomach. "Now, now I know you," she breathed, leaning forward to press a kiss on the center of his chest and rest her cheek on him. "I know you in my mind; I can see there the lines on your face, the scars on your body."

He raised a shaking hand, and cupped her head with it, holding her to him. It would be so easy now to take her, he thought wildly. She was alive to desire; it would take only a little push to tumble her headlong into the waters of serious passion. God knows he wanted to; his body was swollen and straining with that want.

But suddenly, mere want wasn't enough. Not on its own.

Not when he was newly aware of the complexities of desire. They were complexities that warned he would need far more than an animal coupling on a hearth rug. He needed more than her awakening passion; he needed her mind, her trust, her heart and her soul.

He needed from her all the things she had somehow managed to take from him with just a kiss to his battle-scarred body.

He lifted her bodily off the floor and held her against him tightly, nestling her into his lap. She squirmed for a moment; unaware of how the feel of her body moving against his fractured his control. "Stop moving," he said hoarsely.

A silence descended between them as she curled herself comfortably against him, enjoying the warmth that emanated from him. Imogen sighed her contentment.

An almost-peace had descended over her.

While her body was still tingling with a curious sensitivity, there was a certain serenity to be found in being held in this man's arms. She lifted her hands and tucked them under her head. His arms held her tight, enclosing her within his warmth and she felt so safe that it would be easy to forget the specter of Roger that had haunted her always.

She furrowed her brow as she realized that there were many things she didn't seem to understand in this strange new world that Robert had opened to her tonight.

She didn't understand the fires he built in her, didn't understand the vulnerability she had heard in his voice, didn't understand why he was now just holding her as if she was a child when moments ago he had been reacting to her as if she was in fact a whole woman, not one weighed down by her own hidden scars. She wanted him as if that really was true and it was even more amazing to realize that as he would never force her, she was going to have to coerce him. She had no idea how it should be done, but she would give it her best shot, she thought with a smile.

"Is touching and holding all that is between a man and his wife?" she asked in a small voice. Somehow, it didn't come out sounding as she wanted it to. She wanted to sound knowing and sensual, but instead she sounded awkward and nervous.

Robert had to clear his throat before he was able to answer. "No," he growled tersely and closed his eyes, hoping against hope she would leave it at that, if only for his sanity's sake.

She arched a brow. "But you stopped. Why?"

"Because I was getting carried away and it will be better for you if we wait till we know each other better before I show you all that is between man and wife."

She thought about it for a moment, struggling to find the words. "Aren't we supposed to get carried away?" She ducked her head and added clumsily, "I was enjoying it."

Robert squeezed his eyes more tightly shut as a wave of pure, white-hot longing washed over him. He was on fire. Her words were almost as seductive as her small hand, but he didn't want to be seduced, or to be a seducer.

It wouldn't be enough, he realized, not now when he sensed that there was so much more than a brief, physical pleasure at stake.

"I'm glad you were enjoying it," he said as evenly as he could and rested his chin on her silky hair. He opened his eyes and stared into the orange flames of the fire, searching deep inside himself for the strength he was going to need to turn down what she offered so sweetly. "I want you to always enjoy what we do together and to that end, I think we— I, should go more slowly."

"You think I'll enjoy it more if we go more slowly? You want to go slowly?" she asked doubtfully.

He smiled, more than a little gratified by her obvious impatience. "I want many things, and slowly is the way I'll get all of them, not just some of them. For tonight all I want to do is to hold you for a while, if you will let me."

She gave a small shrug, trying to manifest an acceptable level of unconcern. That her body was still on fire she tried to ignore. After all, if he could, then so could she.

"Does this 'going slowly' mean that after you are finished holding me for a while, you will return to your own rooms?" she asked as calmly as she could.

His arms tightened around her almost painfully for a moment before he was able to deliberately relax them a little. "No," he said firmly. "From now on we sleep in the same room. Always. That is part of the going slow."

She experienced an almost overwhelming desire to slap his dictatorial face at that moment, her passion changing like quicksilver into anger. She struggled to get out of his lap.

"Well, I hope you like the floor," she said imperiously, moving with confidence that she wasn't quite feeling to where she knew the bed to be. She dragged off the top fur and threw it in his general direction.

He caught it easily without conscious thought, momentarily stunned by her sudden flare of temper.

A part of him could laugh at her feeble attempts to control him. Didn't she realize that he was entirely beyond her control? All he had to do to shatter all her illusions of being in control was stride over there and physically drag her into the bed. One small woman could hardly be expected to hold her own in any physical confrontation against him.

But he didn't laugh.

The fear and uncertainty that had fueled her outburst was painful for him to see and that pain killed any desire to laugh, cold. So much had changed so quickly that all she could try and do was to stop it spinning totally out of her control.

He looked at her standing defiantly beside the bed and a wave of protectiveness washed over him. She stood there, trembling like a wild animal caught in a trap to which she knew there was no escape, but at the same time she fought so bravely for that fear not to show.

Fear was the last thing he wanted her to feel. Somehow he knew that she had already known so much of it in her life that he didn't want to create any more for her. He wanted her strong and whole of spirit and if that took letting her think she had him cowered, then so be it.

"As my lady wishes," he said simply, the ghost of a smile playing over his lips. "Although the floor doesn't look too inviting. I think I will stay where I am. The chair might make an acceptable bed," he ended doubtfully.

She listened, with bewilderment, as he calmly prepared to take his rest in the chair. She had been expecting an argument at her angry challenge, and was half disappointed that he hadn't given her one.

In no time the room was settled into silence and Imogen panicked a little. "You're not going to sit there while I change and get ready for bed, are you?" she asked stiffly.

"I can close my eyes if you like," he rumbled mildly, as if the mere idea of her being naked before his gaze hadn't inflamed his senses. He pulled the fur up to his chin, trying to deny his body's reaction, even to himself.

"How can I know that I can trust you?" Her eyes narrowed. "You might look."

"Little One, you're just going to have to learn that I am a man of my word. If I say I'm going to do something, then I do it." He yawned loudly. "Besides, I'm too tired to look tonight. Good night."

She glared furiously into the darkness, trying to gauge if he mocked her or not.

"Robert, are you awake?" she whispered, but silence was her only answer.

She hesitated for a moment before beginning to undo the gown's lacing, clumsy at the unaccustomed task but reluctant to call for Mary's help. There should be no need for help on a wedding night and Imogen's pride demanded that the fact she did need help had to be kept private.

Robert's eyes squeezed tightly shut and his hands clenched into painful fists. This self-denial would surely make him a candidate for sainthood, he thought savagely. He ground his teeth together, causing a satisfying shaft of pain. It was the hardest thing he had ever had to do. The temptation to open his eyes and enjoy the sight of her body almost overpowered him.

The knowledge that she would never know if he looked or not tormented him. The pleasure he would feel at the sight of her would almost be worth the guilt he would feel over his small deception. At least it would if lust was all that was at stake, if he could be satisfied by brief carnal pleasure, but it wasn't and he couldn't.

So instead he listened.

He listened to the sound of her strained breathing as she tried to undo the more difficult fastenings. He listened to the small, satisfied sigh she gave as the dress finally came undone and slid from her body in a quiet whoosh of fabric.

He knew she was now naked.

Sweat broke out on his upper lip and he quickly licked it away as he strained to hear more. He listened as she shook out the dress and threw it over the trunk and was barely able to stop himself from groaning out loud in protest as he heard her slipping a chemise over her tiny form.

He dared open his eyes again only when he heard the bedclothes shift as she snuggled down under the covers. The dying fire cast a warm glow over the room. In it he could just see her head above the furs, her unbound hair spread out in a dark cloud around her head, hiding the pillow from his view.

"Did you look?" she whispered suddenly, breaking into his thoughts.

He felt a glow start in his chest. Despite the strangeness of their all-too-new, arranged marriage, she trusted him to answer such a question truthfully. It proved that his decision to slow things down had been right. By waiting, he wouldn't find himself caught with just a pale shadow of a true marriage.

"No, Little One, I didn't look."

She yawned, her eyes closing as sleep slowly stole over her. The last words she spoke before sleep finally claimed her kept Robert awake long into the night.

"I don't think I would have minded all that much if you had looked just a little."

Robert shifted uncomfortably in the chair. His sleeping mind roamed over battlefields, making him frown.

In the dream, the killing was done, and he'd been sent to count the dead.

He was wounded; blood streaming forth till everywhere he looked was covered with it. The bodies on the field were endless and to count them, he had to reassemble them.

He was covered in their gore, and no matter how hard he tried, he couldn't seem to finish the task. There seemed to be no end to the corpses. There was field after field of the dead.

It was a nightmare he knew well and it always

continued until he managed to shake his mind free from the coils of sleep.

Robert twisted uncomfortably in the chair again; his brow furrowing as the silent battlefield of his dreaming filled with a whimpering. His dream self tried to hunt for the living amongst the dead, but despite his increasingly frantic efforts he couldn't find anything alive in this familiar nightmare world; couldn't find the source of the sound of living pain.

It was a sharp, ear-piercing scream that finally dragged his mind back to full consciousness.

By now, the fire had gone out entirely, and the cold had started to seep its way into his bones. At his age sleeping in a chair was no easy thing, he thought morosely, and he couldn't quite contain the strangled sound that escaped as he tried to struggle upright.

The scream had died and the whimpering returned.

Imogen lay in her bed, tossing and turning, her limbs flailing as she tried to fight off her own night demons. In seconds he was by her side. He pulled her up into his arms as he called her name sharply, his voice infused with a cold panic he had never felt for himself.

Her skin through the chemise was cold to his touch, but a thin film of sweat covered her face.

"Imogen," he called again, more loudly, shaking her as gently as his fear would allow. She moaned, thrashing her head from side to side but remained in the world of her own imagining. Ice clutched at Robert's heart, filling his voice with a desperate need.

"Imogen. Imogen. For God's sake, Imogen, wake up."

She suddenly opened her eyes wide and screamed. She lifted her hands to her face as her body was racked by loud, heaving sobs.

It no longer mattered to Robert whether she slept or woke; her pain was all too shockingly real either way. He gathered her fragile body to his and rocked her back and forth, running his hands up and down her back to soothe her pain. He found himself babbling words of comfort that even he didn't fully understand.

Imogen woke in the sheltered warmth of his fierce embrace.

For the first time in longer than she cared to remember, she didn't shed her night tears forlornly into her pillow. No, they were being absorbed into the blood-warm skin of Robert's chest and matted into the hair there. It was Robert's muscular arms that held her gently tight, the rumble of his deep voice seeping into her bones, dulling her lingering fear.

Robert waited patiently for her to cry herself out but still he couldn't let her go when calm descended.

Now he was holding her for his own comfort and reassurance.

He needed her close, needed to know that she wouldn't break in two if he let her go. The sound of her gut-wrenching sobs had torn into him, leaving him helpless in the face of her raw, open grief. Many moments passed before he dared to move her slightly away from him so that he could look into her face and reassure himself that her demons had indeed fled. Her face was red and her eyes a glassy pink, but the fact that she tried to smile up at him made her the most beautiful being he had ever seen.

He wiped away her last tears with the pad of his thumb. He stared at the droplet of saltwater that beaded on his skin briefly before rubbing them in thoughtfully. He tried to find words of comfort and reassurance, but they eluded him.

He mightn't know how to be softly caring, he thought with a silent sigh, but years of training boys to be men had taught him to be practical in the face of others' raw emotions.

"Do you want to tell me about it?" he asked quietly.

She sucked on her bottom lip and shook her head.

He took a deep, fortifying breath. "Sometimes these things don't seem so bad if you talk about them. They shrink a little if you bring them into the real world."

"No, they don't," she said, her voice roughened with her tears. "Sometimes you talk about them forever, yet they are still big enough to destroy you."

Robert hesitated for a moment, but couldn't push her. Perhaps with time, she would share her scarred soul with him, would give him the chance to kiss her wounds as she had kissed his. Until then, he would have to be patient.

He ran his palms down her arms till he was holding her hands. "Would you like me to stay with you?" he asked in a carefully neutral voice, afraid to show just how much hope he attached to her answer.

For a moment Imogen couldn't breathe. She hadn't even realized that she wanted him to stay until she heard him say the words, and a part of her shrank from the whole idea of letting a man into her bed, especially with the dark nightmare still chilling her skin. That fear was drowned out by her far-greater need right now for the cleansing comfort he offered. Hesitantly she reached her hand up to the middle of his chest. "Yes. Stay. Please stay."

Robert didn't hesitate in case she changed her mind. He wrapped his arms around her back and gently leaned forward till they were both lying on the bed with him outside the covers. It wasn't the way he wanted to share her bed, but he could sense the nervousness underlying her boldness and he didn't trust himself enough to crawl in beside her. When she immediately curled her body into his as though she belonged there, he knew that he was doing the right thing.

He closed his eyes and savored the perfection of their simple embrace. It didn't matter that his body was chilling down rapidly in the cool chamber, not when the warmth of her trust was enough to heat him. It also didn't matter that only an absolute terror had driven her to accept him in her bed. The fact that he was there was a thing he hadn't dared hope for yet. It didn't matter that the closeness of her body was swiftly re-igniting his unfulfilled desires, causing an ache in his body that was as much pain as pleasure. There would be time enough for him to indulge those desires, soon.

All that mattered was that Imogen was curled up trustingly in his embrace and was sleeping peacefully there.

Home.

He was finally home.

Chapter Five

Imogen stood with hands on hips, her face flushed with anger.

"He's gone where, exactly?" she bit out.

Mary raised her hand, but quickly dropped it with embarrassment, realizing it wasn't terribly astute to try and pacify a blind person with hand signals.

"I said, he's gone to the stone tower with a few of the men. They're going to see what can be done with that pile of rubble, if anything." Mary tried to ignore the look of fury on Imogen's face, adding quietly, "It's actually a very sound idea, Imogen."

"Oh, most sound," Imogen snapped. "Everything he has done around here is most sound, most wise or just plain, bloody messianic." She threw her hands into the air, growling with pure irritation as she stalked over to the window. She wrapped her arms tightly round her middle to try and stop herself from breaking something. There was no point breaking inanimate objects when it was his head she longed to crack like an eggshell.

The sunlight streamed cheerfully through the open window and it seemed to have a little more warmth in it today. Perhaps the long, unrelenting winter might be finally coming to an end. Or perhaps it was the lavish fires Robert had insisted be lit in all of the Keep's rooms that generated the added warmth that was causing Imogen's face to flush.

She ground her teeth, angered by something that should have made her happy.

She might have hated the cold dankness of the Keep but she couldn't stand it that all Robert had to do was wave his magic wand and everything was put to rights. This was *her* Keep, goddamn it, and she honestly felt that she had looked after it as best she could.

The Keep had become sadly neglected, true, but that had never been Imogen's choice. It was Roger who decided how she lived in her prison, and he had preferred it to be an all-female prison, forbidding all but two males from serving at the Keep. Duncan functioned as the Keep's groom, come shepherd, come gardener, come anything else that might possibly be required. Really, he did a remarkable job, for a sixty-four-year-old.

The cook's son, Lucas Ross, on the other hand, worked in the Keep itself, trying to do any of the small jobs that defeated the women, and at seven years of age he had become a surprisingly good rat catcher.

Imogen felt a growing sense of justification replacing her feeling of incompetence. Which of these two fine examples of masculine strength had Robert actually envisaged as the master woodsman? Imogen thought snidely. While their wood supplies had never been plentiful, that they had had wood at all should be seen as no mean achievement.

And it wasn't as if Robert was making all these grand achievements in household management by himself, Imogen thought with a scowl. Far from it. The Keep was now bursting with his people. His male people.

Life had changed for everyone in the Keep since their wedding night, but for her most of all.

She had awoken early the next morning and, turning instinctively to Robert, had found only his cold furs. She had tried hard not to brood too much about his desertion, telling herself that it was only to be expected, but feelings of betrayal still lingered.

However, the greatest betrayal was that of her wayward heart and body.

For a moment she had held close the pillow that had cradled his head through the night and had bathed her senses in the echo of scent he'd left behind. Even when she had then put the pillow firmly from her, his scent haunted her.

She couldn't let that show, however. Haunted or not, she wouldn't have people pitying her for being an unwanted bride. She had gone about her days as usual, telling herself that all was as it had always been, but it didn't work. There was now a loneliness to her days that surpassed even that of her years of isolation.

It was a loneliness that bit deepest in the rare moments Robert breezed into her days.

On that first morning he had arrived in her chambers around midmorning and had brought with him all the bracing scents of a brisk winter's day. Her heart had skipped a beat at the sound of his voice, even if it was only mouthing polite nothings, and the wonders of the night before rose up before her, starting her wanting him all over again. So powerful was the feeling, it took her a moment to realize that he wasn't similarly affected.

He stood before her with all the joy of a man facing his executioner.

In those all too precious minutes he found just time enough to tell her that his horses had arrived. They had been traveling in relatively easy stages from Wales, accompanied by the knights that had fought under him in the recent wars on the borders. He had then muttered something about eating in the hall with his men, but understanding that she would prefer to eat in her rooms.

In his eagerness to get away from her, he had all but run from the room. Why he bothered at all remained something of a mystery to her.

That the visit was to prove to be something of a record wasn't improving her temper any.

That evening she had eaten in splendid isolation and the food had tasted like sawdust. Somehow, the sound of raucous male laughter had soured her appreciation of the food that night and every night since.

Each night the laughter was only getting louder as slowly more and more of Robert's men trickled up North to be with their glorious leader, but her isolation remained just as absolute. Loneliness was becoming such a part of her days that sometimes she could almost choke on it, and it was a loneliness that followed her each night into her dreams. She had been alone for years, had lived as if in sleep,

but then so had everything around her. Now the
Keep was waking up. Robert was quickening it,
drawing it into the living world. It was she alone
who remained in the dark world of sleep.

She leaned her head wearily against the
casement.

For one who had been alone so long, loneliness
was suddenly becoming an impossibly heavy
burden to bear. In bed at night Imogen could feel
inertia laying like a heavy blanket on her, suffocating her, and each night she went to sleep with her
cheeks wet with tears.

Strangely, though, she no longer met the familiar
demons in her dream.

No, a new torment had arisen from her mind to
plague her.

Her sleep was now haunted with half memories
of being held close in Robert's arms. As she slept,
her skin was tortured by butterfly kisses, by slow,
sensuous caresses from warm hands. She would
struggle to wake, wanting to know if what felt so
real was only a sad, unfulfilling dream. A part of her
was even traitorous enough to want to believe that
Robert came to her each night under the cover of
dreams.

She tried to wake but failed. Her mind slum-
bered while her body burned, and each morning
she woke alone. Only the scent of him on her skin
gave her a small hope that she did more than
dream her nights away, but perhaps that was nothing more than a desire that it was so.

Hope, she was fast discovering, was as much a torment as anything Roger had devised.

Imogen could feel resentment building inside

her. The more he stayed away, the tighter he seemed to hold her mind. She longed for him yet, perversely, when he was with her, she found herself withdrawing into herself, treating him ever more coldly. She was unable to reach out to him. She lived each day with the fear that if she didn't try something soon he, and the fire he brought to her body and mind, might slip through her fingers.

It really was enough to drive a person mad!

And that would serve him right, Imogen thought darkly. See how he liked being married to Lady Deformed when she was also known as Lady Deranged. At least then he couldn't ignore her.

Strangely it wasn't only the ignoring that irritated her. No, what really made her want to scream was the fact that he dared as well to make decisions and plans about her Keep. She would be damned before she would allow that anymore, she suddenly decided.

She turned quickly from the window. "Mary I'll need some stout walking shoes."

"My lady . . ."

"And a warm cloak too, I suspect. Do I possess such things?"

"I'm sure I've seen some in the south chamber, my lady, but . . ."

"Good," Imogen spoke over Mary ruthlessly. "Well, please go and get them. I have an overwhelming desire to go to Roger's tower."

Mary's jaw dropped. "But, Imogen, that is well over three hours' walk from here."

Imogen raised a brow imperiously. "What are you trying to say exactly?"

"What I am trying to say, Imogen Colebrook, is

that for the last God knows how long, you haven't moved farther than these four walls. One trip downstairs and you think you're up to a stroll across unforgiving country, knee-deep in snow. It's complete madness."

As you would expect from Lady Deranged, Imogen thought with a small smile.

"Possibly," Imogen said aloud, "but if I am mad, I think it would be best if you humored me. A madwoman might not like having accusations of laziness thrown about." Her face suddenly went very serious. "And that's Imogen Beaumont now, I'd thank you to remember."

Mary had the grace to blush a little. In her horror at the suggestion she had momentarily forgotten both the change of name and the rights of nobility. She supposed she should be grateful that Imogen had seen fit only to reprimand her on the former, when the latter was seen by many as the more serious crime.

"Now don't you go changing the subject," Mary said, blustering a little to hide her discomfort. "We were talking about you walking miles in the snow, not what your name might be."

"This fear of me walking isn't just your polite way of saying that I have got fat, is it?" Imogen teased, feeling surprisingly lighthearted for the first time in years.

"You know I mean nothing of the sort. Any extra weight you might carry has always managed to land in all the right places." Mary huffed with evident disgust.

Imogen couldn't stop a blush of pleasure at the old woman's words.

"Do you really think so?" Imogen asked, unable

to keep the eagerness out of her voice. She ran unsure hands over her gently rounded hips to try and feel if there was any truth to the words.

Mary's anger evaporated in the glow of Imogen's pleasure. That such a small compliment meant so much to an awe-inspiringly beautiful woman was a travesty. The older woman sighed silently. Sometimes she was apt to forget just how much Imogen had been cheated in life.

"Aye, I really think so," Mary said gruffly. "I'll just go and get all that you'll need for this expedition."

The glow of happiness on Imogen's face went up a notch. She could momentarily block the whys and wherefores of her "expedition," and just enjoy the pleasure and anticipation of going outside again. Every fiber of her being hummed with excitement and she couldn't stop herself from clapping her hands together and doing a small, excited jig.

It didn't even seem to matter that she would be heading toward the dark tower Roger had built and told her tauntingly so much about. How could that matter when she would be entering the land of the living again after all these years? It was almost too good to be true.

She hugged her arms around herself more tightly, trying to hold in her excitement.

"All right, my lady, I've got some sturdy shoes and a cloak that might vaguely fit. I have also found a hat, gloves and young Lucas," Mary said briskly, dumping everything but Lucas, who stood impatiently near the door, into Imogen's waiting arms.

"Why Lucas?" Imogen asked, sitting down to put on her shoes.

"Why Lucas? Because one of us has to use her

brains and it would seem that the honor is all mine," she said dryly. "You clearly can't go out by yourself and, as much as I would dearly love to be the one continually picking your sorry hide out of the snow all day, it will be one pleasure I will be forced to forgo. You might consider yourself able to walk for hours in snow up to your knees, but I'm not. Your husband has managed to thaw most of me out with his excellent fires, and I'm damned if I'll let you freeze me up again." She paused before adding, "Besides, Lucas was all I could find in the kitchens."

Imogen smiled as she stood, trying to get a feel for the boots. They pinched a bit, but other than that they seemed just fine. "Cheer up, Mary," Imogen said playfully, "and I might even bring you back a snowball."

Mary humphed and grabbed the cloak from off the floor where Imogen had dumped it and thrust it into her hands. Imogen twirled it around herself with a small flourish, then spread her arms wide. "How do I look?"

"Like a beggar with stolen clothes," Lucas said round a mouthful of apple as he wandered farther into the room.

Imogen was momentarily taken aback, then a slow smile lit her face.

Mary scowled and gave Lucas a good-natured cuff round the ear. "Now, don't you be giving Lady Imogen any of your cheek."

He nodded vigorously and gave her a mischievous salute as he stuffed the core of the apple into his mouth and started crunching his way merrily through the seeds. Before he had even finished it he was reaching a hand for more into the food basket he carried. It was only a second stinging slap from Mary that stopped him.

She scowled down at him severely. "And don't you go eating that basket clean of food. That's meant for Lady Imogen's and Sir Robert's lunch." The mere mention of Robert's name miraculously produced the result that any number of cuffs round the ear would never do.

"Now that my noble guide has been given all of his vital last-minute instructions, may we be on our way? Please?" Imogen couldn't stop herself from rubbing her hands together in anticipation.

Mary hesitated a moment. It was a dangerous world beyond the Keep's walls, and Imogen was more vulnerable than most. She might have longed for the day when Imogen started to live again, but it now seemed to have arrived all too soon.

"Aye, be gone with you, then," she said gruffly. She thrust Lucas's hand through Imogen's crooked arm and gave them a shove out the door.

Imogen had to stoop to try and match herself to Lucas's slight stature and even then she stumbled. With a shake of her head she stopped after a few yards. She gently put Lucas's hand down and stepped a half pace behind him and firmly placed her hand on his shoulder.

As Mary watched the mismatched pair disappear down the stairs without any further problems, she reached her hand into her apron pocket and grabbed for a handkerchief. She let out a loud sniff before allowing herself a moment of noisy grief. She then shoved the handkerchief back into the pocket from whence it came and resolutely straightened her spine. Perhaps if she kept telling herself that this was a good thing, then maybe it would be easier to get through.

It didn't seem to work.

Her brows dropped a little as she thought of consoling herself by spending her time blaming Robert for this wonderful misfortune. After all, till he came here, there had been no talk of walks. It helped only for a moment.

Pity, as she had kind of liked the idea of having someone to curse. Instead she marched back into Imogen's bedroom and over to the fireplace. She sat down heavily and began stoking the flames with a will. If she was going to wait and worry for hours, she thought with a self-righteous sniff, then there was no way in hell she was going to freeze while doing it.

Lucas walked Imogen slowly down the last of the stairs and guided her toward the main door. The burden of his new responsibility showed in the seriousness of his expression.

The Keep seemed oddly still after the past weeks of noisy activity.

With Robert gone to the tower for at least the rest of the day, the servants had taken a much-needed chance to rest. After years of near inertia, to be suddenly working for a human whirlwind, even one as respected as Robert had become with everyone in the Keep, was something of a shock. The chance to breathe normally again was too good to ignore.

Imogen smiled broadly, feeling better than she had in weeks—no, in years, she realized with wonder. A bubble of happiness rose inside her and she was gripped by a desire to run, to skip, to dance; just to see if she still could after all this time.

"Can we go a little faster?" she whispered to Lucas, wheedlingly.

"Only if you want us to fall on our faces, m'lady," he whispered back.

She thought about it for a moment. "We mightn't, you know."

"Yes, but if we do, Sir Robert will have me torn into little bits."

"Coward," she said severely, but smiled. It seemed impossible to stop smiling on such a day.

She could feel his head nodding vigorously. "You bet I am. I intend to live to see my eighth year."

Imogen was just about to add something when Lucas came to an abrupt halt. Imogen collided with his small body, causing him to stumble a bit.

"Why did you do that?" she exploded in shock. "If you don't say something when you plan to stop, then falling on our faces becomes an inevitability."

"Sor-sorry, my lady," he stammered.

"It was my fault," came a deep, velvet-sounding voice in front of them. "I stepped away from the wall rather abruptly while you were both whispering."

The sudden arrival of a third person, one she hadn't even sensed, stopped her heart for a second. She could feel the shock lodging in her hands, causing them to shake a little, but she lifted her chin in defiance. This had to be one of Robert's men whose laughter had haunted her for weeks, she thought darkly.

"Well, sir, you are obstructing our path," she said

imperiously, "so please remove yourself so we can continue on our way."

"I'm sorry, but I can't do that until you tell me what you are about. Sir Robert has left me in charge of the Keep, so, Lucas, if we start with who exactly your delightful companion is, I might be able to decide whether either of you represent a threat or not."

"Sir Gareth . . ." Lucas stammered clumsily, but Imogen's alarm was quickly turning to white-hot anger.

"You mean to tell me that you intend to prevent me from leaving the Keep if I don't answer your impertinent questions?" she asked coldly.

The man paused thoughtfully for a moment. "Yes, that would about sum it up. Now, your name—"

"Why, you nasty little toad," Imogen exploded. "Come, Lucas, step around this worm and we will be on our way."

Lucas hesitated for a moment. In the fortnight since Robert had taken possession of the Keep, Lucas had quickly learned to treat both him and his knights with careful respect. The first time one of them had clapped him encouragingly on the back, he had been sent reeling. They just didn't seem to know their own strength, and Lucas didn't want Sir Gareth to feel he had to physically stop them. His innate common sense warned him that it would hurt.

This respect for their raw power was also mixed with a large dose of awe. Until now the only male Lucas had been in regular contact with was Duncan, the old groom. These massive warriors had suddenly invaded his world like a whirlwind, each of them as impressive as the last, and Lucas was thriving in this masculine world. They were all gruffly kind to the small boy who hung around with such obvious devotion. They tried to answer his nearly endless questions, and one of them had even let Lucus try to pick up his prodigious sword. He worshipped both the knights themselves and the world they came from and would rather die than upset one of his new heroes.

He also knew that it was simply daft to just ignore a direct order when it was given with such calm authority.

"Ah, I'm sorry, my lady, I don't think so—"

"I didn't ask you to think, Lucas," she snapped. "I asked you to do." She could feel him hesitate and she gritted her teeth impatiently. "Very well, I will go on myself."

She dropped her hand from his shoulder and without allowing herself time to consider the wisdom of her actions, she moved to step round where she judged the rude man to be standing. She misjudged this by a good couple of inches and ran straight into him instead and at that moment, she had an almost overwhelming desire to stamp her feet with sheer frustration.

"If you would just go away, then . . ." She was stopped by the squeal that escaped her as her world shifted.

The knight had easily picked her up and gently threw her over one shoulder. Lucas's eyes went totally round at the sight of Lady Imogen being carried like a sack of washing. It took a few seconds for him to collect his scattered wits enough to drop the food basket and scurry after the spluttering lady and the amused knight.

Gareth placed her carefully down near the fire in the main hall, then stepped back. He crossed his arms over his massive chest and intently considered the outraged woman in front of him.

"So, may I have your name?" he asked quietly, his deep voice rumbling impressively through the hall.

"You dolt, I'm Lady Imogen Beaumont, owner of this damn, blasted Keep." She stepped forward to just in front of where she had heard his voice coming from, waving her finger wildly. "And you had better grab hold of anything on your person that you might value, because by the time I'm through with you, you will end up being just so many pounds of useless meat for the dogs."

He couldn't quite prevent the small smile that toyed with his lips.

It was just too delicious. So this was Robert's bride. This was Lady Deformed.

Robert hadn't married a gargoyle but a termagant instead, Gareth realized with relish. He smiled with anticipation at the fun that would soon follow as his friend tried to keep control of his life now that this woman had stormed into it.

"I'm sorry for any offence, my lady, but I was just following my orders."

"Your orders were to waylay defenseless woman and children and then manhandle them? How bravely my Keep is to be protected," she sneered.

"No, my orders were to monitor the Keep and its occupants and to maintain security till Sir Robert returned. The 'manhandling' I consider just a momentary inspiration, or perhaps even a personal pleasure."

"A personal pleasure!" she exploded, spots of red flagging her cheek. "You have the impertinence to touch my person at all, then you have the audacity to call it personal pleasure? A momentary inspiration in the line of duty?"

"No, my lady, it had nothing to do with my duty," he said precisely. "Manhandling beautiful women such as yourself is no duty, more one of life's little rewards."

Imogen glared at him dangerously. "Are you daring to flirt with me?" she asked slowly.

Gareth considered this for a moment. "Yes, my lady, I believe I am," he said with a beatific smile. It was the kind of smile that had landed many a woman's heart at his feet. She simply tossed her head and placed her hands on her hips.

"And what would your precious Sir Robert have to say if he found out that you openly confessed to flirting with his new bride?"

"I would hope, my lady, that I'd have the good sense not to mention it to him," Gareth said with all seriousness.

Imogen's sudden laughter was as spontaneous as it was unexpected.

The silliness of his answer seemed to instantly evaporate all of her anger. To Gareth, her carefree laughter appeared a little like a rainbow after a storm.

"I like that. It has a certain vestige of dishonest honesty," she said, the laughter still bubbling up inside her. "I would like to know the name of one so skilled in survival."

"Sir Gareth de Hugues, your husband's second-in-command." He remembered to bow correctly but his mind was becoming muddled by a dawning admiration. He had heard rumors about Lady Deformed and it was those rumors that could be blamed for his unusually slow-witted inability to identify this small, beautiful sprite as the Lady herself. This woman could be thought of as deformed only if exquisite beauty was considered a deformity first.

Robert had been frustratingly tight-lipped about his new bride and after a fortnight of conspicuous absence, Gareth had come to expect the worst. Any woman who was too ugly to come and eat with the rest of the household, Gareth had concluded, was in a very bad way indeed.

However, instead of a repulsive gargoyle, Lady Imogen was a small, delicate woman who possessed the kind of beauty that wasn't the least diminished by the fact that she was dressed a little like a vagrant. The body he had felt draped over his shoulder had been a very tempting one indeed. He hadn't been only flirting when he said he'd enjoyed the manhandling.

Mere flirting had stopped altogether, however, when she had laughed.

With that joyous laughter she went from being a pretty little baggage to being the most beautiful woman Gareth had ever seen. It had taken his breath away and, for the first time in his life, Gareth found himself envying Robert.

And how the man had managed to fritter away a fortnight pottering around the Keep when this woman waited for him was entirely beyond Gareth's

comprehension. The man must be using dung
for brains!

If he ever had such a wife, and Gareth prayed
silently that one day he would, then he would spend
every day, no, every moment of every day, basking in
the radiance of her smile. He'd devote his life to being
her jester just to hear the music of her laugher. And
to think he had always admired Robert's intelligence!

Not anymore. It would take many acts of raw cunning on Robert's part to make up for this total lapse
of sanity.

"Sir Gareth. It is my pleasure to meet you," she
said softly as she dropped into a very proper curtsy.

Gareth bowed again over her hand with a small
flourish, "No, my lady, I can honestly say that the
pleasure is all mine." He kept hold of her hand, enjoying the texture of her soft hand in his larger
one.

Imogen couldn't stop a small giggle from escaping. "I suspect, Sir Gareth, that you might be something of a rogue."

"One does one's humble best."

"I'm sure one does," she murmured. "Well, thank
you for the entertainment, it really has been most
enjoyable. Sadly, however, I have need of that hand
you are holding so tightly, and must be on my way
with it."

"May I enquire as to your destination?"

"Certainly you may enquire, and I may even
answer." She paused a moment, her cheek dim-
pling with humor. "Lucas was escorting me to the
tower. I have a pressing desire to see it," she said finally, carefully avoiding any mention of any similar desire she might have to see Robert. Gareth

heard the need there all the same, and was a little surprised by the small grief it caused. He quickly shook it off, not prepared to waste time dwelling on impossibilities.

"And they send a boy to do a man's job?" he scoffed.

"Actually, they send a boy to do an old woman's job. Mary normally acts as my eyes but she thought the journey might be too great and cold for one of her advanced years, so she nobly nominated Lucas in her stead."

Gareth paused a moment. "Act as your eyes?" he asked gently.

She smiled again, but this time her earlier easy amusement was missing. "To act as my eyes, as my eyes can no longer act on their own."

His own eyes narrowed on her, hoping for a moment that what he thought she meant was a lie. Instead, her empty eyes just missed meeting his.

He recovered from his shock quickly. Well, there had to be something wrong, he told himself rationally, the rumors about Lady Deformed had to have come from somewhere. That it was a gross exaggeration didn't stop it from being some kind of twisted reality.

And what did it matter? Why dwell on such a thing when in everything else she was beyond such sterile concepts as mere perfection?

"Well, let me offer you the use of my own, rather attractive, sky blue eyes. Not only are they exquisitely beautiful, they are also exceptionally keen and you can consider them at your disposal."

"Very prettily said," she murmured, enjoying his easy acceptance of her problem very much.

He leaned confidentially closer, trying to ignore the fact that he liked a little too well just being near this woman. "For you, I will even be pretty. Of course if anyone else said such a thing, I would slice them in two."

"I must remember that. It would make you interesting to clean up after, I must say."

Gareth opened his mouth to reply in kind but was stopped by Lucas's piping voice from the doorway. "But I was told to look out for my lady."

Imogen found it strange that she had nearly forgotten his presence. Normally she kept very firm in her head the mental map needed to see her world. Perhaps, it had been so long since she had last been able to just be silly that she had forgotten all else in the pursuit of it. There was no denying that she also enjoyed the man who shared his silliness with her.

Gareth might not produce in her the rush of strange emotions Robert did, but his simple, easy manner was a balm to her badly battered pride.

"Lucas, you must learn to give up a lady gracefully," Gareth said with mock severity. "Especially when your rival is several times your size."

"But Mary said I was to go with her."

"Well, now I say I have to."

"I'll tell Mary on you."

"Well, I'll tell Robert on you," Gareth countered, flourishing the winning stroke with relish.

"Stop teasing the boy," Imogen said sternly, but a smile gentled the words.

"Who was teasing?" Gareth growled threateningly. "The boy certainly wasn't when he threatened to set that harpy on me."

"Mary's not a harpy," Imogen said with a smile,

"anymore than I am, despite how we both might appear from time to time."

She turned toward Lucas's voice. "Of course you can come along if Mary said you must. How about carrying the basket and making a path through the snow for us to follow?"

"Making a path?" he pondered. "That's kind of like being a scout, for an army, isn't it?" He was still deeply suspicious, but his excitement at the thought of being near food and having a status was evident.

"You bet it is," Gareth said, with the authority of many wars behind him.

"And you can feel free to liberate a titbit or two from what I suspect is one of Mary's overstuffed baskets," Imogen said coaxingly, reluctant to be parted just yet from a man who simply made her smile.

Lucas considered every aspect of the deal for a moment. "All right," he said, then ran to see what exactly Mary had put in the basket.

Gareth smiled as he hooked his arm through Imogen's and they followed slowly.

"Do I get to sample from the basket too, even though I don't get to be a scout? Or do I just get stuck with the beautiful lady?" Gareth asked innocently, his voice full of guile.

"You may sample the delight of the basket only if you are a very good boy," she said with mock hauteur.

"Oh, I'm always a good boy," he said nicely, his face splitting into a decidedly wolfish grin. "Always."

Chapter Six

Robert stepped gingerly over yet another fallen stone.

" . . . or we could always just paint it in your colors and stuff your banner on top . . ." Matthew said gleefully.

And while his face might have appeared serious and earnest, Robert was only too well aware that his eyes were dancing. When he had first suggested this excursion, Matthew had grumbled loud and long at the earliness of the hour, then at the cold, then at the riding required.

Robert had shrugged his shoulders and ignored him just as he usually did when Matthew got into one of these moods, but he had also known that Matthew would manage to extract his revenge at some point, both for being dragged from his warm bed and for being ignored.

Matthew didn't like being ignored.

Robert sighed loudly and cast a puzzled eye over the tower. Matthew's revenge had been too easy, really. No matter from which angle you looked at it, this derelict stone tower in the middle of nowhere was an absurdity, and Matthew was relishing pointing out that fact as the two of them walked slowly round it ostensibly to see if there was any logic to be found on the other side.

" . . . and I really think it is a marvel for a tower to have no entrance, but to have windows near the top. Had you noticed that, Boy? Extremely clever, I think," Matthew yelled, by now almost jogging to keep up with Robert's lengthening stride.

"I can't say that it had entirely escaped my notice," Robert muttered in reply, hoping against hope that that would be the end of it.

"Clever lad!" Matthew beamed with expansive pride. "We will make a builder out of you yet, what with that eye for detail and all. The next observation that I really think you should take note of is the fact that it seems to be falling down," he said as he daintily sidestepped one of the larger boulders.

Robert stopped and turned on the old man, his gauntleted hands crossed over his chest.

"Come on, Old Man, spit out all the rest of your spleen and have done with it. Just what are you getting at?"

Matthew raised an innocent twice-gloved hand to his narrow chest. "Oh, great master, what do you accuse me of?"

"You mean accuse you of besides being a meddlesome pain in the rear?"

"Yes, besides that."

"You've been laughing at me ever since we got here, yet, for the life of me, I can't see what you find so funny."

"Don't suppose you do," Matthew murmured. He

looked up at the stone tower, his face suddenly serious. "I just find it strange that you rose at the goddamn crack of dawn from a perfectly warm bed, a bed containing, I hasten to add, a beautiful woman, and found yourself with an overwhelming desire to cover miles of snow-covered ground to see a tower that we already knew was falling down before we got here. A falling-down tower that doesn't even seem to have a door, on closer inspection. Call me crazy, but I find that extremely funny. It's either that or tragically sad."

"It's not as odd as all that," Robert said defensively.

A raised brow was all the answer he got.

"Well, you didn't have to come," Robert said, irritatingly aware that he was beginning to sound like a petulant child, but he seemed unable to be anything else.

"My boy, I wouldn't have missed this for the world. There is nothing I love more than freezing my balls off at sunrise and blistering my arse on a horse's back. It's very good for your soul, I'm sure, if of dubious worth for your manhood."

That drew a reluctant smile from Robert. "Well, if we hurry in our inspection of this tower, then the men will have got the fire started by now."

"That's another thing I find odd," Matthew continued as if Robert hadn't even spoken. "Why the hell do we need to light a fire when there is a perfectly warm Keep just over the way? A Keep that you can quite confidently call your own."

Robert shrugged his shoulders, a red flush rising up his neck, "Just seemed like a good idea if we were going to spend the whole day here we will use it to cook at least one meal."

He braced himself for the explosion, and Matthew delivered on cue.

"All day!" he spluttered. "What the hell would we want to spend all day out here for?"

"I thought we could see if anything can be done with the tower, and then perhaps we could do some hunting for the Keep's stores."

"For God's sake, Boy, I've never heard such a load of nonsense. And it's a lie. Can't you at least tell me the truth when you're so determined to freeze me to death?"

"That was the truth." Robert couldn't quite meet Matthew's eyes and was embarrassed to find himself shuffling his feet like a naughty schoolboy.

Matthew's snort was almost elegant in expressing his patent disbelief. "Robert, you've been like a bee in a bottle for two weeks. Running from sunup to sundown, longer some days, I expect, though I'm not entirely sure. I can't watch you all the time, as at my age you actually need sleep." His eyes narrowed knowingly. "It's clear as day to me that you're running from something. Today you have just managed to get a little farther than normal." Matthew stepped up and placed a hand on Robert's shoulder. "Can't you at least tell me what the hell is going on here?"

The gentleness in Matthew's usually brisk tone burnt away the last of Robert's defenses. He turned and walked a few steps away from the old man, staring unseeingly at a chunk of stone.

"The truth is, Old Man, that I don't know any longer what is going on." He threw his hands into the air and turned around. "I'm being tied in knots. Everything is so . . . complex. It used to be simple. So damn simple. I wanted land and title, so I slaughtered my way across the country to get them." His mouth twisted into a bitter smile. "And I was very good at it. No one could have been a better murderer than me."

"I always knew that you weren't a warrior, not at heart," Matthew said quietly. "A true warrior never looks on such things as murder. You always had a gentle soul underneath that rusty armor."

"You should be careful how you bandy around words like gentle, Old Man," Robert said wryly. "Another warrior might take it into his head to prove to you how gentle they aren't. It could get messy."

Matthew shrugged his shoulders. "If they would slice an old man in two for saying something they didn't like, then I hope I have the intelligence not to call them gentle in the first place."

Robert raised a brow. "There is a certain logic to that nonsense that I wouldn't dare try to unravel." He walked slowly over to one of the fallen stones and sat down, his face turning serious once more. "Gentle or no, I did what had to be done and did it damn well." His eyes locked with Matthew's. "Simple."

Matthew pulled his furs more tightly around his thin shoulders and found a boulder of his own. He grimaced as he sat on the cold, unforgiving surface, but resigned himself to the fact that it would be a while before he would be warm again.

"And, I take it, it's not so simple now?"

"No," Robert said and lifted his face to the gray and blue sky. "I have what I have always wanted, and it's not enough. Nowhere near." His hands clenched impotently by his side.

"And what will be enough?" Matthew asked, but he already had a good idea what the answer would be.

Robert's black eyes leveled to Matthew's. "I'll only know enough when I see it."

Matthew let out a low whistle through his teeth. "Boy, you have got it bad."

Robert didn't even have to ask what "it" was. "Old Man, you don't know the half of it." He paused, then surged to his feet and began to pace restlessly.

Matthew shook his head and stood slowly. "Well, my boy, it would seem that you have managed to make a simple thing complex in the extreme."

Robert stilled his pacing for a moment and shrugged his shoulders helplessly. "The complexities were there already, I'm just an inheritor of them. I manage to fight one off and another seems to grow in its place."

"So what do you intend to do?"

"I intend to keep running, Old Man, till it's time to turn and fight."

As they started off around the tower once more Matthew said gently, "Don't think much of that as a plan, Boy."

"Nor do I," Robert agreed amicably, trying to roll some of the tension out of his shoulders as he walked. "I may end up improvising and improving on it as I go." They walked on in silence for a moment and then a grin broke on Robert's face that was almost boyish. "Actually I'm beginning to find I'm quite good at improvisation. Take this little jaunt. Pure, unadulterated spur-of-the-moment improvisation."

Matthew hunched his shoulders. "And you think this a good example of your skills, do you?"

"Compared to some of the other ideas I had, I think it was a stroke of pure bloody inspiration."

"Just goes to prove, too many blows to the head really can addle a man's wits."

"It's a fine line between addled and inspired," Robert said loftily, drawing slightly ahead of the older man.

Matthew grunted. "There is also a fine line between smug and insane, my boy," he said to himself, "and, to my thinking, you are a unique combination of the two."

Robert looked round. "Did you mutter something, Old Man?"

Matthew opened his eyes wide. "Would I dare mutter in the presence of my glorious leader?"

Robert thought for a moment. "Yes."

Matthew buried his chin in his furs and muttered about a lack of respect for one's elders and Robert's laughter on the wind was almost carefree.

"Careful," Gareth said as Imogen stumbled yet again. He placed a steadying arm around her shoulders. "Maybe we should stop for a moment?" he asked softly, the worry plain in his voice.

"If you say that again, I may decide to poke one of your eyes out," she said through labored breaths. She knew she was behaving like a shrew and for a second it felt good. Unfortunately, guilt quashed the slight triumph to be found in being horrible.

"Sorry, Gareth," she mumbled. "I guess Mary was right when she said I'd gotten too soft and lazy for this."

"She actually said that?"

"Almost."

He gave her shoulders a little squeeze. "Soft, maybe, but a very nice kind of soft."

"Flirting won't make me feel better," she said briskly. "I was well past being enamored with your repartee over an hour ago."

"But I wasn't flirting," he said innocently. "I was merely stating cold, hard facts." He laughed at her snort of disgust. "Oh, Imogen, you're being far too serious. This is the most fun I've had in a long time."

"What can your life have been before this little . . . excursion?" she asked dryly.

"Perfect," he said with a wave of his hand. "I just have the good taste to prefer this."

"It would seem I've been sent abroad in the world with a man who has gone moon-mad."

"A madman *and* a sick little guide." Gareth looked behind them to where Lucas brought up the rear, dragging the nearly empty basket behind him. "And you have only yourself to blame for the illness of your smallest protector. You did say that he could eat anything that tickled his fancy."

"How was I to know that he would take it as a challenge?" Genuine concern crept into her voice as she leaned closer to Gareth and whispered, "Is he starting to look any better?"

Gareth cast a critical eye over the small, dejected figure. "Well, since emptying his stomach behind a tree, he has stopped looking green." Imogen began to chew on her bottom lip in concern and Gareth said soothingly, "Really he's fine."

"Are you sure?"

"Look, when a boy eats his body weight in food in less than fifteen seconds flat he's bound to feel a little unwell. After a bit, the effects will wear off enough for him to do it all over again." He ran a critical eye over her pale face. "It's you we should be worrying about. Are you sure you don't want to stop for a rest?"

"I warned you what I would do if you asked me that again," she said sternly, then she sighed, her easy mood evaporating. She ran a weary hand over the bridge of her nose. "How much further do you think?"

Gareth looked critically up to the sky, painfully aware of the shadows that were forming already. Soon it would be dark and they still had a long way to go. "Not far," he hedged.

She nodded her head silently, too tired even to reply, concentrating instead on the putting of one foot after the other.

The next time Imogen stumbled Gareth wasn't quite quick enough. She fell on her knees into the snow. She clenched her fist in the icy slush, her breath coming in ragged bursts.

Gareth fell into the snow beside her immediately and gathered her close. "I knew we should have stopped," he said angrily to himself, then reluctantly he loosened his hold and slowly drew her to her feet.

He led her to a relatively dry rock and knelt in the snow at her feet, chafing her hands back to life. His breath caught painfully in his chest at the sight of a solitary tear falling slowly down her smudged cheek.

She tried to wipe it away, but others quickly followed. "Damn! Damn! Damn! Damn! Damn!"

"Oh, Imogen, it's not that bad," Gareth whispered, his voice catching in his throat. He grabbed the corner of his woolen cloak and began clumsily wiping her tears away with the coarse fabric.

Her sightless eyes looked disconcertingly beyond his shoulder, fighting with shadows only she could see. "I so wanted to do this, so wanted to stop him ignoring me," she said brokenly. "I wanted to prove, oh, I don't know, wanted to prove that it didn't matter that I was . . . am blind. I wanted to prove that I was still a normal woman." Her jaw tightened painfully. "But I'm not. I am some oddity who should be locked in a room for her own good, just like Roger said. I knew I couldn't do it. I knew it, but for just the smallest of moments it seemed so, so *possible*."

No longer caring about the rights and wrongs of it, Gareth gathered her into the warmth of his embrace once more.

Lucas staggered up to the rock and plopped himself down into the snow near them, rolling himself up into a ball. He didn't care about the snow or cold or the strange sight of Lady Imogen crying into Sir Gareth's surcoat. All that mattered was that they had finally stopped and he could die in peace.

Gareth began rocking Imogen back and forth, trying only to comfort her, but he couldn't seem to stop himself from greedily storing up the memory of holding her slight body close. He had never before counted himself a fool, but no matter how often he told himself sternly not to be deluded by the sweetness of holding her and that she wasn't his, he couldn't stop his heart from filling with her, even as he knew it was all an illusion. She didn't want him. She never would be his, not when every word she spoke was of another, for another.

Even if she didn't yet know it, for her there was only Robert.

Gareth felt that truth almost like a physical pain, but he had to close his mind to that pain for now, concentrating instead on the way even her chaste embrace burned through his body.

As if she could sense the tumult inside him, Imogen gently pushed herself free from his embrace. She quickly wiped her face on the back of her hands and tried to smile. "I must look a mess."

"Yes," Gareth confirmed softly, his voice a mere husky whisper.

She let out a watery chuckle. "Not very gallantly said, but the truth, I suspect."

Gareth cleared his throat uncomfortably, trying to sound as normal as possible. "I think we should rest before proceeding," he said firmly.

"But—"

"No buts. The tower isn't going anywhere and can certainly wait a little longer for us. Besides," he continued forcefully, "our young companion was so bored by your womanly display of tears that he seems to have gone to sleep and I certainly don't plan on carrying his dead weight the rest of the way."

Imogen hesitated a moment before nodding her head. "We'll stop if you think it's for the best. I don't particularly want to be seen by Ro . . . by anyone . . .

looking all red and blotchy." Not again, she added silently.

Gareth stood briskly, carefully putting some distance between himself and temptation. "I'll see if I can find some dry wood for a fire."

"But we won't be stopping that long, surely," she protested. "And I barely feel the cold."

"Ah, but it is not for you. I'm the one that isn't used to this cold land. It will only take a moment, and it might slow down the freezing of my body a little."

She didn't believe him for a moment. She had just been close to the heat of him and not for a moment could she believe that he was suffering from the cold. "I'll wait here," she murmured and wrapped herself more firmly in the cloak as she settled herself more comfortably on the rock.

Within seconds she was asleep.

Gareth's face softened as he looked at Imogen's small sleeping form. For the moment she was his alone to protect, he thought with an unsettling sense of satisfaction, and he decided in that moment not to investigate this strange emotion too closely. Instead, he went off in search of wood, determined to simply enjoy the fleeting pleasure it brought him.

It was all he would ever have.

It was coming on dusk and Robert could look back on a successful day's hunting.

While the men had been more than a little perplexed by their seemingly pointless excursion, they had all stopped grumbling at the mention of hunting. Matthew, however, hadn't been so easily impressed. Muttering that if he was going to waste a day, he might as well be warm doing it; he volunteered to stay near the fire to keep it alight till the last of the hunt parties returned or until two hours before dusk. Then he would return to the Keep to grumble there.

Robert had barely hidden his smile of relief. He needed to spend time alone with his thoughts and the last thing he needed was Matthew's all-too-knowing presence. There were so many things that seemed lodged in his soul with nowhere to go that he needed to sort them into a comprehendible order before he crumpled under their weight.

Matthew might have a ready ear for confidences, but there was so much that Robert couldn't tell the man he thought of as a father. How could he describe all of the strange new emotions that boiled inside him, that burned in his once-frozen heart? How did he speak of this new sense of belonging, the feelings of owning and being owned? How could he explain, even to himself, nights spent chastely holding the one woman he had ever needed more than he needed life itself?

Just thinking of it made him uncomfortable, made him realize just how low Imogen had made him sink.

It was beyond even his comprehension, but each night he found himself lingering over his cups to give Imogen time to get to sleep, and yet each night the disappointment was sharp and new as he stood beside their bed and looked down on her as she slept.

In the light of day he could tell himself sternly

that it would be wiser and certainly less painful for him if he slept in the chair and waited for her to call him to her bed and into her life, but each night wisdom was lost to darker desires. He couldn't seem to stop himself from shedding his clothes and crawling in beside her. And each night he felt a near fulfillment as she curled herself trustingly into his arms as if she belonged there.

It was an exquisite, addictive torture.

It was impossible for him to have her so close and not touch her; not kiss her soft skin; not bury his face in the fragrance of her hair. He stopped only when his arousal became too intense to be endured. Then he had to be content just to hold her close, to watch over her as she slept in his arms. And each morning he forced himself to leave her before she awoke.

Matthew's right, he thought grimly. He was mad, or at least soon would be.

He hadn't meant it to be like this. On waking beside her that first morning, he'd had no thought other than wooing and winning his wife. He had watched as she slept beside him and ran his thumb over her soft lips with something akin to wonder. It was that very wonder that had made it impossible for him to stay idle in bed waiting for the sun to rise, but he had soon found an excuse to be by her side again.

He laughed at himself as he ran up the stairs two at a time to tell her of the arrival of Gareth and the horses, all the while knowing that it was only a feeble excuse to be with her again. He had rushed into her room and been stopped short as the cold hand of reality had slapped him in the face.

Reality was the elegant gentlewoman who had sat staring blindly at the clumsy oaf who had dared to barge his way into her life without her consent. The world of togetherness that he had been able to construct in the darkness crumbled into nothingness.

How could he even begin to tell her about the strange feelings inside him when he wasn't sure that he was worthy to breathe the same air as his lady?

He'd run away rather than face the cold, harsh realities. Damn Matthew to hell for being right, Robert thought darkly.

A rustling drew his mind from his hopeless contemplations. Instinctively he dropped into the undergrowth while his eyes scanned the forest around him, trying to find the source of the sound, his bow slipping easily into his hand.

A deer nosed its way cautiously forward, its hide glistening as it moved majestically through the undergrowth. Suddenly, it stood absolutely still, presenting a perfect target, but Robert lowered his arrow from the bowstring. With twenty men out on the hunt for the better part of the day, this one animal would not be missed from the table, and something about its fragile bravery reminded him of Imogen.

It stood still, seemingly staring directly at Robert's hiding place with an idle curiosity, then suddenly it turned its head to the south. Robert watched its delicate nostrils flare as it caught the scent on the wind of something it didn't like. It paused tensely for a moment before bounding off in the other direction, agile despite the snow.

Robert drew his brows together as he slowly stood

and he too lifted his face to the wind and inhaled deeply, the faint scents of smoke tickling his senses.

It was in the wrong direction for the tower fire and far too strong to be from the Keep's distant chimneys. As Robert's men would know better than to light a fire to warn the prey of their presence, it could mean only that there was someone else in his forest, and Robert intended to find out who the invader was.

Walking softly, he began stalking this new prey.

It took half an hour for him to reach the fire. He remained crouched low in the undergrowth, as he cautiously scanned the scene before him. His eyes narrowed as he recognized the man feeding the fire. Gareth had been told to guard the Keep, Robert thought with growing anger, and he had better come up with something brilliant to explain such flagrant disobedience of a direct order.

He stood swiftly and strode over to the fire, the light of battle clear in his eyes.

A twig snapped, and Gareth looked up immediately from his solemn concentration on the flames. He seemed remarkably unsurprised at seeing Robert. Instead, his face registered only a strange, melancholy acceptance.

Robert opened his mouth to speak and was mildly stunned when Gareth lifted a hand to hush him. Gareth stood up in one easy, catlike move and motioned Robert over to a group of trees just in view of the fire.

Robert's brows rose, but he followed.

He crossed his arms over his muscular chest. "Well, I hope your explanation for ignoring my instructions is good," he said, his voice vibrating with his irritation.

Gareth smiled winningly. "I must admit to quite liking it. I think it might be one of my better efforts."

Robert remained stonily silent, refusing to be cajoled. He wanted answers.

Gareth let out a deep sigh. "Actually, I think that, technically, I haven't actually disobeyed you."

Robert's eyes widened, disbelief patent on his face. "I believe I asked you to protect my home. I don't remember mentioning that you could go and play in the woods if you felt like it. Of course it is entirely possible that I'm wrong," he said sardonically.

"You are, as it happens," Gareth said with a small smile. "You actually asked me to keep Imogen safe, and that is exactly what I'm doing."

"Imogen?" Robert asked dangerously, not quite liking something about the way Gareth said his wife's name. "Explain yourself."

Gareth smiled properly for the first time, totally unintimidated by Robert's open jealousy. "Easy done. That bundle of rags on the rock is your wife and I'm gallantly keeping this wet wood alight in a vain attempt to stop us all from dying from exposure while she takes a well-needed rest."

"You dare jest," Robert shouted, but found his eyes eagerly turning to the bundle anyway. At first he could barely discern any kind of human form under the rags, much less identify it as Imogen. It was only when she, disturbed by the shouting, stirred restlessly in her sleep, spilling her hair over the rough edges of the rock, that he recognized her. No other person alive could have hair like that,

Robert thought reverently, the air suddenly trapped in his lungs.

"How the hell did she get out here?" he hissed.

Gareth shrugged his shoulders with deceptive casualness. "Apparently, the allure of your own sorry hide was so great that she decided to give both you and the tower a personal visit." His voice dropped, as he smiled fondly at her. "She was so determined to get to you that she walked herself into exhaustion because you and your men had taken the only decent horses."

Robert turned from the tempting sight of Imogen sleeping, just in time to catch the look of open admiration on Gareth's face.

Something started a slow burn in Robert's gut, a something that felt disconcertingly like jealousy. His eyes narrowed again. "You mean you have dragged my lady wife halfway across the country in winter, unchaperoned." He wasn't even really sure which was the point of protest, but he'd be damned if he'd try to make sense of it. Gareth had just better come up with the right answer.

"Oh, it all sounds so salacious when you put it like that," Gareth said with a mock leer, enjoying deliberately baiting Robert.

"Well, it better only *sound* salacious," Robert muttered, his fists clenching ominously.

Gareth sighed theatrically. "Sadly, if you look a little to your left you will notice the second bundle of rags less discerningly curled up in the snow. That was, and is, our chaperone."

Robert walked directly over to the previously unnoticed second sleeping form, finding himself not quite trusting Gareth for the first time in their long acquaintance. His brow rose. "Lucas?"

Again Gareth shrugged his shoulders. "Best I could do, I am afraid."

"What's wrong with him? He looks a little pale."

"You should have seen him a couple of hours ago; he was as green as grass. I've never seen anything like it before." Gareth looked dispassionately down at Lucas. "As to what is wrong with him, greed is his complaint. He ate too much and is suffering the rather colorful consequences."

Robert walked over to the fire, staring blindly into its depths as he thought, his mind full of the knowledge that she had come to find him.

"It is nearly dusk," Robert said softly so as not to wake the sleepers. "You can take the child and head back to the Keep."

Gareth grimaced. "Nothing like ending a long, cold day by being thrown up on," he said wryly. "And while I'm facing such grave danger, what will you be doing?"

"Oh, I don't know," Robert said, a smile of contentment dawning on his face. "Feeding the fire, I suppose."

Gareth sighed silently, unable to stop himself regretting that it wasn't his right to wait on Imogen. "Do I send men if you aren't back at the Keep in a couple of hours?" he asked quietly.

"No. We will make our own way back."

Gareth started at him hard for a moment before he turned and scooped up the slightly damp Lucas, who barely protested the disturbance. He hesitated visibly for a moment, then quickly turned back to Robert, his face darkly serious.

"Be worthy of her," he said fiercely. "Be worthy of her, or I'll cut your heart out." Then, embarrassed by his display of unexplainable emotion, he quickly turned and disappeared into the forest.

Brows drawn, Robert crouched down by the fire. He threw on one of the small green branches Gareth had gathered and watched as it spluttered for a moment before sluggishly catching alight. A rational part of him supposed that he should awaken Imogen so they could head for the Keep and the warmth it offered.

He watched as the dying sunlight touched Imogen's cheek, making her skin look translucent and fragile. He lowered his gaze and knew that he couldn't wake her now any more than he could in their curtained bed. Fortunately, he was getting good at watching over her while she slept, he thought wryly, as he pulled up the log Gareth had been using as a seat, and got himself comfortable.

This wasn't how he'd envisioned ending the day, but he couldn't seem to prevent the grin of satisfaction that worked its way to his lips.

He could honestly think of no place he'd rather be.

Consciousness came to Imogen all at once. As she went from slumber to wakefulness, her senses suddenly came alive to the smells and sounds that surrounded her.

Her heart nearly stopped.

Instead of her familiar chamber, a strange world greeted her, and it was a moment before any rational memory filled in the strangeness.

"Gareth?" she called quietly as she sat up, trying to

control her panic. "Gareth, are you still there?"
Please don't leave me alone in the dark, she pleaded
silently, but was too afraid to say it out loud.

"Not quite," came the hushed reply.

The relief that flooded over her at the sound of
Robert so near left her no room to pretend cold in-
difference. Her face broke into a tremulous smile,
and she found herself saying the first thing that
popped into her head.

"Oh, I was just dreaming about you," she said,
barely recognizing the breathy voice as her own.

She felt a finger trace the line of her cheek,
starting a small tingle that fired through her nerve
endings.

Walking for miles was almost worth all this pain,
she thought dreamily, as she threw her arms
around his neck when he moved to hold her. It was
worth it, if it meant that she was in his arms at the
end.

Where she belonged.

Chapter Seven

Robert closed his eyes and, just for a moment, let himself savor the feel of her body close to his own. It seemed like an eternity since he had held her, inhaled the scent of her warm skin, heard the pounding of her heart in time with his own fevered pulse.

Without any conscious thought his lips sought hers. She opened her mouth to meet the heat of his and he felt his desire rise till it consumed all rational thought. Her tongue met and mated with his, first sliding along his almost timidly, but soon staking a bold claim to him.

A groan started low in his chest and rumbled up and into her mouth, causing a delicious shiver to run down her spine, spreading like a liquid flame through her body. When his hands moved up from her waist slowly, his fingertips just grazing the underside of the swell of her breasts, her heart stopped beating entirely. It started again only when his warm palm rested tensely against the side of them, then it raced as she waited for him to touch her properly.

With an almost unhurried desire, he slowly moved till he covered her softness completely.

She had never been touched with such gentle passion before and she gave herself over to it. She tore her lips free from his and threw back her head as a soundless moan escaped, waves of longing pulsing low in her abdomen.

His lips, now free, began to explore the soft skin of her neck, branding her with their moist heat. That heat, as it moved down her neck, seemed to find an echo in every fiber of her body, her nipples hardening almost painfully under the rhythmic pressure of his hand. Her breath caught, but she did nothing to stop him from deftly undoing the brooch that held her cloak closed. He trailed open-mouthed kisses along the neckline of her gown, dragging them over the fine fabric of her simple bodice, dampening it where he lingered. As his mouth moved relentlessly on, the damp fabric turned cold and Imogen shivered with delight as the sensation brought her deliciously to life.

He paused for a moment, before claiming one of her nipples through the fabric. Her head dropped to his shoulder with a shudder, her lips grazing the soft skin of his bent neck.

He drew back to look hungrily at the darkened patch of fabric and the peaking nipple evident beneath it. "You're so beautiful," he said thickly. "So goddamn beautiful."

He lifted her chin with one finger, his eyes moving over her face. Her fine skin was flushed a gentle rose and her lips were open and inviting him back.

He closed his eyes and lowered his head once more, the frenzy of raw desire replaced with an almost aching tenderness. Where before there had been a war, now their lips mated as if part of the same being. Imogen curled her arms around his neck and buried her hands deep into his hair, holding on to him as if afraid he would leave.

He had absolutely no idea of leaving, although he should, he thought foggily. He tried to ignore that sensible voice, but he couldn't seem to make it go away.

He held her tightly, his hands moving to cover the gentle swell of her bottom, drawing her ever closer to the aching heat of his erection for a moment, then he slowly pulled away again with small, nipping kisses. She groaned in protest, her lips clinging to his, begging his return. His jaw clenched with frustrated want, but he forced himself to lift his head from hers.

"I don't think this is the place to continue this," he said after drawing a shaky breath.

She made a whimper that sounded to him like pain. He rested a comforting hand over her cheek, which she covered with one of her own hands, and something inside him clenched at the simple gesture. Time and place ceased to matter. All he wanted was the warm woman he was moments away from making love with. He looked up into the sky, desperately trying to cool the inflamed heat of his mind and body, but when he looked back down she was still there, in his arms.

"Night has fallen. We should move quickly," he murmured softly, trying to stop himself from giving in to the temptation of her lips once more.

His words chilled her to the core and the aching limbs and blistered feet that she had momentarily forgotten in the haze of desire returned to her with a vengeance. She let her head fall against his chest to hide the embarrassment that stained her cheeks. "I don't think I can make it all the way back to the Keep, not without falling over," she said stiffly, hating her helplessness.

Robert's brow creased with concern. "But there is nowhere else that we can go. I don't like being out in the open at night in the snow."

"Gareth said that we were quite near to the tower," she said slowly after a moment. "I'd like to visit it, if we could go there."

"A pile of rocks with no door won't be doing us much good," he said dryly, trying to ignore the jealousy that flared at the sound of the other man's name on lips he had just possessed so thoroughly.

"There is a door."

"Ah, actually, there isn't. Matthew and I walked round the thing this morning and the only holes to be seen were windows near the top and they are no good to us unless you know how to fly."

"Just because you didn't see one doesn't mean one doesn't exist." Her chin shot up defiantly. "The door to the tower is twenty strides to the east of the tower itself, beside a stone marker. The trapdoor is obscured by brush and it covers a stone staircase."

Robert's brows shot up. "Good lord!" he muttered. "Not that it does us any good. The bloody thing would fall down around our ears if we tried to shelter there. The whole structure is dangerously unstable."

She shook her head. "I don't think so. It should be safe enough."

"You wouldn't be so sure if you had seen the stones lying about everywhere."

"I can't see stones, be they lying or part of a hundred-foot wall," she muttered darkly, making Robert almost glad she couldn't see, and was therefore ignorant of the dark flush that rose up his neck.

She sighed.

"I'm not trying to say you didn't see what you saw," she said slowly as if to a simple child, "but that I think you've misinterpreted it."

Robert felt his jaw tighten. "Oh, yes, and how would you interpret it?" he asked with mock politeness.

She smiled, and leaned closer to whisper confidingly in his ear. "Well, Robert, I'd draw on my still-functioning memory and recall someone saying that the rubble around the tower wasn't from stones coming down so much as from having them never gone up in the first place."

Robert stared at her blankly for a moment.

"Hadn't thought of that," he admitted sheepishly. "So, my lady, in your informed opinion, do you think the tower will be safe enough for us to shelter there for the night?" Robert asked simply, seemingly impervious to the chaos he created inside her.

She felt as if her brain was going to explode with confusion. She had gone through so many emotions in such a short space of time that she now couldn't seem to adjust to Robert's strange, calmly accepting behavior. She hadn't expected him to actually admit that he could be wrong. Roger certainly would not have. It bewildered her so much that she didn't quite know how to react. Her world had suddenly shifted and she no longer knew what was expected of her.

"Probably," she said frowning.

He leaned over and dropped a small kiss on her frown. "Well then, we had better be off if we don't intend being eaten by wolves."

He helped her to her feet, went and stamped out the embers of the fire after making a torch to light the gloom. Imogen tried to take a small step, but the pain from her badly blistered feet was so intense she could have screamed with it. Pride, however, demanded that she keep her inadequacies to herself and she quickly made her face blank.

"Are you all right?" Robert asked, his voice tight with concern as he appeared suddenly at her side.

He sounded sincere, but she couldn't stop herself from reaching up a hand to feel if he meant it. His face muscles were tense, his soft lips pressed in a firm line of worry. He really was concerned about her, she realized with some astonishment.

"No, I don't think I am," she said slowly, frightened by her own honesty.

"Damn," he swore softly, then broke into a boyish grin. "I left Dagger quite near here. I had thought to send someone back for him to save you walking further away from the Keep, but how would you like a moonlight gallop? You're not afraid of horses, are you?"

She caught her bottom lip in her teeth as she shook her head, trying to hold in the delight that swamped her. A horse! How long had it been since she had sat on a horse and felt its muscles strain as it worked to make them fly?

"I'd love to go for a ride," she said and couldn't stop her voice from squeaking with excitement.

He lifted her effortlessly into his arms and nestled

her against him. "Well then, my lady, your steed awaits. We have no time to waste."

She smiled and said almost to herself, "Oh, Robert, if only you could comprehend just how much time has been wasted already."

She ran her hands gently over the velvet of the horse's nose. Dagger blew softly into her palms, then moved his head to nudge her between the shoulder blades, causing her to stumble. She laughed softly.

"Oh, so now you have forgiven me for waking you from your sleep, have you?" she murmured. "Somehow I don't think Sir Robert is going to be quite so forgiving." Her smile broadened as the sound of Robert's frustrated swearing carried to her clearly on the breeze.

It was strange but she found herself unafraid of Robert's temper.

Her bewilderment hadn't gone away by any means, but one thing was becoming increasingly clear to her: Robert was like no man she had ever met before. The rules that she had needed to live by for so long just to survive no longer seemed to apply. She was, fortunately, learning new ones, fast. She was learning that for all the power Robert had over her as her lord and husband, he could be infinitely gentle, he didn't like harming her, and he actually seemed to care for her.

She was learning that he alone had the ability to melt the hard darkness inside of her.

She nuzzled her face into the horse's neck, inhaling deeply the nearly forgotten scents of the animal, hoping that in the memories of that long-lost innocence she would find an escape from the tantalizing hope that was beginning to burn into life inside her. She, of all people, should know that hope was a fool's gold. She should know that gentle people didn't survive in her world and that hope was only a dangerous weapon that was used against you. Somehow, though, Robert was destroying all of her carefully constructed walls. With him she could almost believe in a world filled with light and hope.

Mind you, judging by the cursing that colored the air, hope alone wasn't going to get them into the tower, she thought with a small smile.

"Are you sure you don't want me to help?" she called over to him, but a grunt was all the reply she got.

A momentary silence fell, and suddenly the night was filled with the sharp sound of timbers snapping, followed by a low, masculine whistle of admiration.

In seconds he was by her side, giving her an enthusiastic squeeze of excitement.

"You were bloody right. Under that decrepit trap-door there is a stone staircase." Enthusiasm and energy radiated from him. "It's damn ingenious."

"Don't sound so surprised," she said with mock ferocity, trying to ignore the thrilling feel of his arm around her, "or I might find myself thinking that you thought I was lying."

"Well . . ." he murmured provocatively, then moaned dramatically as she aimed a blow at his stomach. He easily restrained her fist and gave it a squeeze. "No, not lied, but you could have very easily been misinformed."

She raised a skeptical eyebrow but changed the topic.

"Well, if you've managed to open the door, then perhaps we should enter it." She tried to keep the excitement out of her voice but failed, just as she failed to suppress the fear that was also rising inside her to match the excitement.

I'm here, Roger, she called out silently, her light-hearted mood turning pensive again, I'm finally here at your tower despite all of your threats and taunts.

I'm here, but I am so afraid.

She touched the wall as they walked down the steep steps and into the small passageway, feeling the rough edges of the stone grating along her skin. A shiver ran down her spine as the cold from the stones settled in her bones.

It was almost as if Roger was in every stone.

"I'm here, Roger." She whispered the words aloud this time, using them like a prayer to ward off evil. "I'm here."

Robert slanted a curious look down at her tense, pale face, but all emotion seemed to be carefully hidden behind a wall of stiff courage.

His jaw tightened and his hand instinctively reached for his sword hilt. He wanted so badly to ask why all her early confidence had so suddenly evaporated, why she was so afraid. He wanted to ask why just being here made her look suddenly so fragile that the act of holding her hand put him in fear of breaking her into a million pieces.

He wanted to ask, but found himself saying instead, "How old is the tower?"

She shrugged her shoulders. "It was built the second summer after I came here. More building was planned but . . ." Her voice fell away as visions of those early days of her hell rose up before her. She could almost catch the faint whiff of her past terrors in the stale air of the passageway. The tower had been such a vital part of that hell that she couldn't stop her hand from flinching away from the cold stones.

Robert had to bite his tongue, knowing that if he pressed her, she might retreat to that place in her mind where he couldn't reach her, but even knowing that it was for the best, the act of patience sat uncomfortably with him.

He silently pulled her possessively close, as they walked slowly up the stairs.

"Hold this," Robert said as they reached the top, curling her hand around the torch. He began to feel around the wall, searching for a door. The solid thump of flesh hitting unyielding stone told Imogen of his lack of success.

"To the left of the door there should be an engraving that looks like circles within circles. Press first the inner circle, then the third from the inside, then the fourth and then the second," she said softly, her face eerily blank.

He threw her a worried glance, but did as she told him. He found the faint circles quickly, pressing them in sequence. He couldn't stop himself from being fascinated as each dipped ever so slightly under his gentle push. As he pressed the last circle, the passageway echoed with the sound of rusty gears grinding into life.

"Damn me," he said as the door swung open, "I've never seen anything like it."

"Roger hired a Moor to design it. As I recall, he

was quite pleased with the results." She shivered
again. Her stomach clenched. Now just mentioning
his name in this place of his creation seemed a little
like conjuring a devil.

She thrust the torch toward Robert. "Here, take
this thing. I hardly need it," she said harshly.

He moved back quickly as the flame came a little
too close, but not quickly enough, judging by the
smell of scorched hair that filled the air, he thought
wryly. He carefully took the torch from her trembling hand. He watched her face closely, not able to
quash the concern that was now churning though
his gut. He could feel the tension that radiated
from her, smell her fear. It made the locked tower
a sinister place, a place of dark secrets, and he
didn't like it, he realized grimly.

Tension entered his shoulders. He was a veteran
of too many wars not to know the folly of ignorance
and right now he knew so little he felt like he was
fighting an unseen enemy with one hand tied
behind his back.

He set his jaw and curled his free hand around
Imogen's before stepping into the tower room.

What his torch illuminated caused him to stop
stock-still in shock. He wasn't really sure what he'd
been expecting in Imogen's dark tower, but he
knew that this wasn't it.

The place was a treasure trove!

Along one wall a staircase curled around and up
through the ceiling. Every other spare inch of
space seemed to be taken up with a jumble of objects that filled the chamber to overflowing. Furniture sat beside rolls of fur rugs and tapestries.
Wooden crates were packed one on top of the

other. Some had toppled over and revealed flashes of silver and gold.

One of the fallen boxes even revealed a pile of valuable books that had been scattered carelessly over the stone floor; their jewel-encrusted leather covers gleaming in the light of his torch.

"Mother of God!" he breathed out. "What the hell is all this stuff?"

Her smile was both bright and brittle. "My life." She let go of his hand and started to feel her way forward. Robert paused only to light a candle that had been placed in a holder near the door and put the makeshift torch into a wall sconce before following silently behind her.

She touched one of the rolled tapestries and ran a shaky hand over the back of the tiny stitches.

"What's the design?"

Her voice was quiet, and Robert could hear the pain that reverberated through it. He carefully placed the candle on a nearby box and dragged the tapestry off the stack. He clumsily unrolled it and gave it a shake, showering them both with a fine layer of dust. He looked carefully at the simple tapestry, uncomfortably aware that in normal circumstances he'd barely have noticed it.

"It's a forest scene of some sort." He gave an awkward shrug. He'd never felt quite this inadequate before. "There is some kind of flower border. In the top right-hand corner there seems to be a group of hunters, and at the bottom a group of ladies and minstrels are feasting and they are being watched by an odd horse."

She ran her hand over the stitches, the picture rising from the darkness of her memories. "Not a horse; a unicorn. It hung in my father's armory. Mother hated weapons of war in her home and would only tolerate them if the room could be made to look as little like an armory as possible." A whisper of a smile filtered over her face. "When Father wasn't looking, she would get the servants to cover the swords and bows with cloth, and when she wasn't looking he would have them removed again.

"I'd almost forgotten about that," she said, a sad acceptance etching itself on her face.

Robert's hand clenched tightly around the fabric and he had to force himself to let it go.

"Can you see the books?" she asked, unaware of his rising anger in her eagerness for more reunions.

"Yes," he answered quietly.

She felt for his hand and held on to it tightly. "Take me to them."

He helped her pick her way through the boxes, furniture and rolls of fabric. They knelt in front of the disorderly pile of books. Robert could almost feel her excitement inside himself. She held out her hands expectantly.

Robert hesitated a second, then placed the first volume carefully in them.

She ran her hand over the surface and lowered her nose to inhale the scent of leather, parchment, glue and gilt. This time when she smiled, it was almost luminous with its intensity. Robert had to fight off the feeling that he was intruding on a personal moment, but he watched her intently as she gripped the book tightly to her chest, his anger burning hot. He had to clear his throat before he could speak. "Imogen, why?" he asked tightly.

"Why what?" Her voice sounded remote as her hands moved lovingly over the old leather.

"Why aren't these things that you clearly love so much at the Keep near you?" Robert's voice pulsed with repressed anger. "Why weren't you surrounded with things that were familiar to you when you lost your sight? Why, Imogen?"

"Ah, that 'why.'" She turned to him, her smile bittersweet with pain. "Because that would have made it too easy and Roger didn't want to make it easy. He wanted to bleed me till I was obedient. He wanted me to give in and he thought that this"— she gracefully gestured to encompass the room— "would encourage that obedience."

She sat down, curling one arm around her knees, while the other held the book tightly to her chest, and began to rock gently back and forth. "Every visit he tells me of all the things he has locked in here, tells me how to get in here. Each time he leaves knowing that the information is burning into my brain. Sometimes as a refinement he brings me something, lets me hold it before stealing it away again, saying I can only keep them if I—"

"If you what?" Robert was abstractly surprised at how calm he managed to sound when everything inside of him demanded violence.

Now wasn't the time. That pleasure would have to wait; now he needed information. Information Imogen was deliberately withholding from him in her silence. He watched as she drew subtly away from him into those parts of her mind to which he had no access. Fear of losing her to her demons galvanized him into action. He tore the book from her grasp and threw it heedlessly onto the floor, ignoring her gasp of protest. He grabbed hold of her shoulder and shook her.

"If you what, Imogen? Tell me."

She raised her hands and held on to his biceps to steady herself. She could feel the iron of his muscles under his tunic. He was so strong, she thought dazedly, but that strength was protective instead of threatening. Suddenly she longed for the safety Robert represented, longed to lean into it, to never have to be alone in the dark again.

"Kiss me." Her voice was just a husky whisper, surprising herself as much as him. The silence that followed was deafening.

When Robert made no move, need drove Imogen to press a chaste kiss on his warm lips, but she realized with frustration that it wasn't enough. She leaned up and kissed him more boldly. His mouth remained firmly closed until he felt her tongue flick along it with small, butterfly movements, then he groaned and pulled her close, claiming her lips as his.

She snaked her hands over his arms, along the contours of his broad shoulders. It wasn't enough. She moved her hands down his sides, playing along the muscles, muscles she longed to touch, skin to skin. She pulled ineffectually at his tunic.

He pulled his lips free of hers and searched her passion-flushed face. "Is this what you want?" he asked fiercely, but all she heard was his gentle concern. It was that gentleness that made up her mind.

She was going to be daring and grab the elusive happiness her instinct told her this moment was going to give her.

In this place built for her torment she was going

to, once and for all, destroy all of her memories of Roger violating her soul, if not yet her body. They were going to be replaced with the cleansing memories of this man, who gruffly waited for her to give him permission to do what they both wanted, to become her husband in deed as well as word.

"Take your tunic off," she murmured, her hands moving desperately to the offending garment's hem.

He carefully moved her hands up to his clothed chest and covered both of them with one of his. "I'm serious, Imogen. I'm only a man, and if we don't stop now, I won't stop till you are my wife in every sense of the word."

She seemed to look him straight in the eye. "I don't want you to stop."

A rational part of him counseled caution, but it was drowned out by the desire that burned him clear through to his soul. He lifted his other hand and pulled off his cloak. The tunic followed.

She leaned forward and placed a kiss on the center of his bare chest. He closed his eyes for a moment as the air in his lungs turned to fire. He brought her face to his and captured her lips in a devouring kiss, and set about freeing her of her garments. He lifted his head briefly to see his handiwork.

The bodice of the dress had slipped off her shoulders, exposing her breasts to his hungry gaze, their alabaster perfection peaked by rose-pink nipples that tightened in the cool air.

"You're perfect," he said as he lifted a calloused finger to trace the faint blue veins under her white skin.

A nervous giggle caught in her throat. "I'll have to take your word for it."

"Oh, no, don't just take my word for it. Let me show you just how perfect."

He lowered his head and she nearly levitated as his mouth followed his touch. She threw back her head to moan her ecstasy and thrust her breasts out closer to his touch. He lifted both of his hands to frame her soft beauty and lifted his head so that his breath scorched her moist flesh.

"See, perfect," he said tightly as he lowered his head, once more trailing kisses from one breast to the other, quickly finding her other aching nipple.

He was right, this was perfection. And it was only beginning. Whenever she had dared to think about this moment, she had thought only of the pain and darkness she had known before, but with Robert she felt only wanted and cherished. When he reached round her and pulled one of the furs onto the floor she found herself clumsily trying to help him, wanting this precious moment like she had never wanted anything before. Carefully Robert covered its dusty surface with his cloak before gently laying her back against it, divesting her of the rest of her clothes.

The beauty of her naked body stole his breath away. From the white swell of her hips to the delicate curve of her instep, it was all beyond anything his lurid imagination had been able to create. He quickly shed his leggings and joined her, reveling in the way she greeted him with open arms.

She couldn't stop herself from flinching instinctively as she felt his manhood press hot, hard and naked against her thigh, her bravery deserting her for a moment.

Robert frowned, carefully watching her face closely

for any sign of fear. Gently, he moved her hands to that part of him. "I would have you know me," he said roughly, guiding her hands along his arousal.

With curious fingers she moved slowly over the length of him. She ran a fingertip over the satin of his shaft, touched the pearl of moisture at the tip and buried her hand in the coarse hair at the base. She encircled him completely and gently squeezed.

He groaned out loud, and she smiled, realizing for the first time that in this, she too had a power, one that went far beyond mere physical strength. Teasingly she moved to pull her hands away but he stopped her.

"No. Stay," he said raggedly and he withstood her exploration until his passion reached a fever pitch that could no longer be denied. He needed her.

With shaking hands he removed hers, wrapping her arms around his neck as he covered her body with his own, snaring her lips in another drugging kiss. His hands played over her body to tangle in the moist curls at the juncture of her thighs and with the pad of one calloused finger he gently felt her readiness for him in her scalding heat.

Lifting himself, he spread her legs and fitted his body along hers, touching her intimately with the heat of him. A groan rose from her throat as her body opened to receive that part of him that she could feel throbbing intimately against her.

Her breath came out raggedly. The need she was feeling was painful. Need rode her, making her move herself against him frantically, blatantly inviting him to ease her aching. Instead of giving in to her silent demand, he held back and teased her to a new peak of desire, driving her mad.

Finally, he slowly braced himself on his elbows and kept his fevered eyes locked on her face as he began to rock forward. She grabbed on to his arms, caught in a sense of wonderment and destiny as her body stretched to accommodate him. She moved her hips, silently encouraging him to take all she had to give, to take it all now.

Sweat pooled at his temples and trickled down his back, as the restraint required to stop from burying himself in her began to fracture. He was stopped completely, however, by the fragile barrier of her maidenhead.

"Imogen, there is going to be some pain. Oh, God, I wish there didn't have to be, but it won't be for long."

The cords on his neck strained with the effort he was exerting to stay still. She could feel that tension as it radiated down his arms and through his body, could feel it in the slick layer of sweat that covered him despite the chill.

She lifted a hand to the tense line of his lips. "I trust you," she said simply.

It was the most erotic thing he had ever heard and it broke his control completely. With a helpless groan his hips thrust mindlessly forward.

The sting of pain made Imogen gasp in surprise, but within moments the pain evaporated, as she became accustomed to the strange new sensations of completeness. Now the pain was gone, her need burned even brighter than before. She wrapped her legs around his hips, pulling him close to the heart of her and to the ache of her clamoring desire.

Robert's last tenuous hold on his restraint snapped as he felt her moving against him, beneath him, around him. He held her lips in a fierce kiss as he began to stroke powerfully in and out of her body, driving them both relentlessly forward to completion.

Wave after wave of sensation trembled through her body as the satisfaction of just holding him close was overtaken by her need of him. She met and matched Robert's thrusts, joining him as an equal partner in their desire, urging him forward, urging him to teach her about completeness.

She gasped in desperate desire, moving her legs up till her knees were under his arms, as close to him as she could be. She bit his shoulder, then soothed it with her tongue, all the while inarticulately urging him to take her to greater heights.

Then, suddenly, those heights were inside her. Every muscle in her body convulsed with the pulse of release. She screamed her satisfaction as wave after wave of pleasure crashed over her.

And still it wasn't finished. His body ruthlessly took her further, driving her beyond herself.

Robert buried his head in her hair as his own satisfaction was wrenched from his body. Her body held his tight, her internal contractions drawing his seed from him with the same ruthlessness as he had just shown. He held taut for a moment, then slumped as every last muscle in his body turned to boneless flesh.

She took the sweet weight of him and held him close.

"Don't think you can distract me," he said severely, but he couldn't even begin to hide the satisfaction in his voice. What he had meant to sound resolute and demanding came out sounding like lazy curiosity.

He lay on his side and held her close to his heart. He'd covered their cooling bodies with the other cloak, cocooning them in their own world.

"You didn't find that distracting?" she asked with a satisfied sigh. "Perhaps I will have to practice it."

"Consider my body at your disposal, for educational progress only, of course."

She chuckled and nestled herself a little closer, trying desperately to hold on to this precious moment before the real world took it all away from her again.

"But I'm not distracted," he said more seriously. "Why?"

She couldn't pretend to not understand him.

"'Why' doesn't matter," she said quietly.

"Tell me, and *I'll* decide if it matters or not."

"And if it matters? Then what will you do?"

"Then I'll pull his bowels out through his throat."

She wrinkled her nose in distaste. "That's not actually possible, is it?"

"I don't know, but I'm prepared to find out." He ran a finger up and down her arm, absentmindedly comparing the brownness of his hand against the whiteness of her skin. "Tell me."

"No."

Robert was momentarily nonplussed. "Am I entitled to know why I'm to be kept ignorant?" he asked tersely.

She twirled her fingers through his chest hair, wanting to tell him, wanting to share the darkness with him, but found she couldn't. This was so new when compared with Roger's silky threats and dark promises that echoed in her mind despite her attempts to quash them. "I can't tell you. It's that simple. I just can't," she said sadly.

"But I'm your husband now, in every sense." His hold on her tightened almost painfully. "We have just shared our bodies. There can no longer be any room between us for secrets."

She simply shook her head, her lips pulled into an unnaturally thin line.

He saw the defiance on her face and longed to break down the walls of secrets and memories that had suddenly sprung up between them. His jaw clenched painfully.

"So I'm good enough to sleep with, good enough to marry, but I'm presumptuous to think I have a right to know what's going on, is that it? I'm not trusted to share your fears, only your body!" he finished with open disgust.

"You're really angry," she said dully, instinctively bracing herself for the blow that was sure to fall.

He let out a groan of pure frustration. "Of course I'm angry, goddamn it! I'm also hurt and frustrated." He held on to the back of her head with the palm of his hand, looking angrily into her face. "You're locking me out, deliberately building walls between us. If I don't know what the hell I'm fighting, how do I defend you against phantoms and memories I can't see?"

He buried his head against her ear and whispered fiercely into it. "But understand me well, Imogen Beaumont, even if I don't know what I'm fighting, even if you won't trust me with the enemy's name, I'll fight off all threats as best as I can. I'm your sword arm against the world for the rest of my life. Do you understand?"

"No," she whispered, and his arms tightened around her compulsively for a moment.

"It doesn't require understanding. It is enough that it is so," he said arrogantly, his breath hot on her neck.

And she couldn't seem to stop her arm from wrapping around his back and resting her hand on the dimple at the base of his spine even though she knew she couldn't give him the comfort he needed, that she was the one causing the pain.

He loosened his grip on her slowly as he finally got back control of his frustration and anger, but he didn't let her go. He drew in a deep, shaky breath. "Now we sleep."

"You're being dictatorial again," she said with a small smile.

He snorted bitterly. "Well, if I'm not to be given the names of the demons unseen, I might as well protect you from the things that I can see. You've had an exhausting day and need your rest."

"As my lord and master says," she said meekly.

He grunted and closed his eyes. In moments he was asleep.

She snuggled her cheek against the side of his head where it was buried in her hair. She hadn't told him anything because years of harsh lessons had warned her against trust. Yet she couldn't stop reliving the thrill she had felt as he had pledged to protect her always. If he spoke true, she'd never again be alone in the dark unable to defend herself.

Strange, she thought drowsily, she believed his pledge.

And that sounded an awful lot like trust to her.

Chapter Eight

Robert winced when he saw that people were beginning to fill the courtyard as the sound of Dagger's hooves on the compressed earth rang out through the early-morning silence. "So much for sneaking in before dawn," he murmured softly into Imogen's ear.

She smiled lazily. In his arms she found nothing to fear at the sounds of the growing crowd. "Apparently you're not supposed to sneak in on a horse."

Robert's laughter rumbled through her. "I'd rather fail at a sneak on a horse when I have miles to cover, than to succeed on my feet."

"Amen!" Imogen said with a ferventness that made Robert laugh again as he swung down from Dagger's back.

After giving the openly gossiping crowd a stern look, daring them to comment, he turned and clasped his hands around Imogen's waist, lifting her to the ground. He felt the by-now-familiar sliver of desire knife through him as he held her close, but with a resigned sigh he forced himself to step away from her.

"Are you ready to face the hordes, Little One?" he murmured softly, and she drew a deep, steadying breath before nodding her head slowly. Robert gave her a reassuring squeeze as he drew her nearer to his side. He turned to face the crowd. A frown wrinkled his brow a little as he watched Gareth push his way to the front.

"We were just arguing over who was going to get the Keep if you two were eaten by wolves," Gareth said with a broad smile, all of last night's strange tension now absent, though when he clapped Robert on the back it was a little too hard to be entirely friendly. "So, just where did you two get to?"

Robert didn't even try to hide the smugness of his smile. "Into the tower."

Gareth's eyebrows rose. "What, *in* the doorless tower our garrison has been laughing so hard about all morning?"

"Not entirely doorless," Imogen said abstractly.

Gareth cast her a puzzled look, then shrugged his shoulders. "It matters not, so long as you're home."

Home? Robert looked over the motley hoard in the dawn light, the Keep's inhabitants mixing freely with his knights, and felt strangely as if the missing part of a puzzle had fallen into place. Home.

There was an unexpected satisfaction to be found in that realization, but his smile of pleasure soon changed to a frown of consternation as he noticed that his knights scarcely wasted a glance at him. No, they were all too busy gawking at the Lady of the Keep for the first time.

The plain jealousy that flared, fierce and intense, staggered him. His hand flexed into a fist as he fought the urge to snatch Imogen away from them and barricade her in the tower. With him.

"Lady Imogen's tired," he said tersely, and began hustling her through the crowd, trying to escape before he did something to embarrass them both. He ignored the startled look on her face. He might explain it to her later, if he could ever find the words to explain the emotions roiling inside him. Perhaps. All that mattered now was removing her from the other men's gaze. Once he reached their chamber, he slammed the door loudly behind him and leaned on it with relief. Of course, now he would have to face his very irate wife, and he wasn't at all surprised to hear the indignation in her voice.

"Just what was that all about?"

He moved to the fire and started stoking it back into life, relieved that she couldn't see the smug smile on his face. "I don't know what you're talking about," he murmured neutrally.

"I'm talking about your mad dash to this chamber as if you were being chased by a pack of hounds," she said through clenched teeth. "I'm talking about my nonexistent tiredness; I'm talking about this sudden impulse you seem to have developed to hide me away." Robert looked up in surprise at the sound of raw emotion in her voice. "For God's sake, if you're ashamed of me, just say so. I can hide away. I'm good at it and I can almost accept it, if it must be so. But not this. You can't be kind and considerate one minute, then brisk and rude the next when you can't stand people seeing your blind . . . wife."

Robert let out a tortured groan as he quickly stood. He pulled her into his arms and buried her face in his chest, holding her tightly to his heart. "Oh, Imogen it wasn't that! It was . . . I can't explain it."

"Try," she said in a defiant, if muffled, voice.

He sighed and rubbed his chin along her hair, bathing his senses in the scent. "The men were looking at you like they liked what they saw," he said lamely, rolling his eyes at how feeble it was. It sounded even worse out loud, he realized with a feeling of resignation.

He waited for the explosion that such an asinine announcement deserved but when nothing happened, he risked a glance at her face. If his jealousy hadn't still been hot inside him and riding him hard, he might have openly laughed at the incredulous look on Imogen's face.

"You were jealous of men looking at me?"

"Maybe," he muttered grudgingly.

Her eyes widened, a slow smile curling into life on her face. The smile turned into a delighted laugh and she held her sides as they began to ache. "You can't mean it?" she spluttered. "You can't actually be jealous of your men looking at Lady Deformed." Just saying it set her off into another peel of laughter.

"Imogen . . ." he said warningly.

She raised her hands in supplication, and gasped for breath. "Sorry, sorry. I forgot about not being able to say that, but you have got to admit, it is a little ludicrous, being jealousy of Lady De . . . me."

"You will also notice that I'm not laughing," he said through gritted teeth.

"I had." She smiled, trying to get control of

herself. She very nearly succeeded. "But you will understand if I find it amusing. I mean, who would have thought that it was even possible that you would feel jealousy? What are the chances of it happening?" She held herself for a second, then broke into unholy laughter.

Robert pulled her ruthlessly to him and smothered her laughter with his lips.

He ran his tongue along her delightfully full bottom lip, and Imogen immediately opened her mouth, drawing Robert deeper. He buried his hands in her hair, trying to draw her closer yet, trying to brand her indelibly with the heat of his moist breath.

Amusement had turned to desire and as Robert steered her to the bed Imogen tried to remove his clothes. They fell onto the covers in a tangle of limbs and unfulfilled passions.

Panting, Robert lifted his head and looked into Imogen's flushed face. She was caught up in the web of desire he'd spun relentlessly around her, but it wasn't enough, he thought grimly. He wanted her need for him so hot that the world ceased to exist for her.

He began mercilessly to seduce her body.

His hand moved over her soft skin, lingering here, tantalizing there, and tormenting everywhere. Where his hand went his mouth followed, drawing whimpers from her as her hands grabbed the furs, helpless.

But it wasn't enough.

He brought her closer and closer to the edge, drawing her higher and higher. He relentlessly pursued his torment of her till her body was a taut bowstring

under his calloused hands, her head tossing helplessly
on the pillow, an inarticulate jumble of frenzied pleadings escaping her lips. When his mouth found the
center of her need amongst her moist curls he tormented her with his knowing tongue.

And still it wasn't enough.

He pushed his way deep into her slick, welcoming body, reveling in the heat and moisture that
greeted him as he began to mercilessly drive them
both into a frenzy.

Imogen's body clenched around him as she
came, wave after wave of the fathomless desire
crashing over her senses. And yet her pleasure
didn't stop. With each powerful thrust, her body
convulsed around his shaft with increasing frenzy.
It was beyond her control. She could do nothing
other than wrap her legs tightly about his slim hips
and give herself over to the rule of Robert's body in
hers.

Only when he felt her absolute surrender did
Robert let his body lose control, roaring with the
sheer power of it. For a moment his body was a
rigid mass, then it turned to water, and he feared
that he might never be able to move again. Not that
it seemed such a bad fate when his face was buried
in the waves of her hair, and his softening manhood was buried deep inside her. It seemed an eternity before he could find the strength to roll off her
and gather her into his arms, holding her tightly to
his pounding heart.

And still it wasn't enough.

His jealousy continued to eat at him. Logically
he knew that he couldn't justify it, but a primitive
part of him longed to be able to hang any man who

dared to look at Imogen. But if he did that, it would mean that Shadowsend would be left without any male inhabitants fairly soon, he thought ruefully. That it was his own men he was fantasizing about destroying only made it worse. After years of implicit trust, could he not now trust them to even look upon his wife without him going mad with jealousy and lust?

He really was going insane.

He was more than a little unnerved by the sheer force of the emotions Imogen inspired in him. He ran a gentle hand through her hair and pressed her head close to him and knew with a sinking certainty that without her, he had no life.

She had somehow managed to burrow herself so far under his skin that no amount of scratching would ever remove her. Not that he wanted to dislodge her, he realized with a grimace of disgust. He could scarcely conceive of a life without her now, much less a time when he might long for her to be gone.

That was why his jealousy burned so fiercely and doubt plagued him. How could he find peace when he knew she was under his skin but he wasn't so sure that he was under hers?

What if she could all too easily conceive of a life without him? He could hold her body as close as he liked, make love to her till they were both too exhausted to stand, but it all amounted to nothing if she could leave him without a backward glance.

Her spirit was like a mirage. He had only to get too close to it and it disappeared on him again, leaving him holding a hollow nothing and it was that nothingness that frightened him to his core. He buried his face into Imogen's hair, trying to banish cold fear in the warm realities of his Imogen.

She reached out a hand and ran it over the morning stubble on his jaw, feeling the way his muscles clenched under her gentle caress. To Robert, it felt almost as if she knew he was drowning in fear and jealousy and was trying to comfort him even though she was the cause of his tumult.

It served only to confuse him all the more. He had never before associated gentle touches with the animal passions that were easily satisfied. Never before had there been any tenderness in lovemaking, and he couldn't honestly say that he had ever marked its absence before. Yet Imogen was unable to be with him and not touch him, and he couldn't imagine now how he had ever lived without it.

"I've been thinking," she whispered, flinching a little at the sound of her voice in the silence that surrounded them.

He lifted his face out of the mind-easing softness of her hair and leaned up on his elbow. He looked down into her face, and found his breath caught once more at the beauty of her. He felt just as he had the first time he had beheld her in the glare of the winter sun.

But what amazed him more was the fact that it wasn't her beautiful face that ultimately held him so ruthlessly to her side. No, it was the fragile strength of her blossoming spirit that had him so entranced that he no longer had any desire to be without her.

"Should I be worried about you thinking while I make love to you?" he asked lightly, deliberately keeping his confused emotions from her.

Her smile was wicked. "Perhaps you will have to practice more to make sure we get it right," she purred. She lifted her hand to him again, grazing the gentle smile on his lips with the tips of her fingers. He couldn't resist giving them a nipping kiss and she gave a small squeak in protest, but left them there for him to sooth with his velvety tongue.

A small shudder went through her body. "Actually, if we get this any more right, I might expire. When you touch me, there is never a thought in my head beyond that touch," she breathed.

"I must remember that," he murmured.

"By all means," she said as she snuggled a little closer to him, "but you should also remember that afterwards my thoughts come back louder than before. Hence the, 'I've been thinking.' And what I've been thinking is . . . that I'm all out of excuses, aren't I?" Her smile turned rueful. "I've scuttled my own boat, so to speak. How can I now hide away in my room when I've rather neatly proved that, with a little help, I'm more than capable of navigating the big bad world?"

He gathered her close and kissed the top of her head, expressing silently the compassionate understanding that he couldn't speak of out loud.

"I suppose I should start with the evening meal?" she said tentatively.

He watched as her teeth bit down on her bottom lip and began to worry it as she concentrated on the conundrum.

"If you helped me with the food, I might be able to stop myself from making a complete fool of myself."

"Of course I'd like to help, but perhaps it is not the best of ideas." His lips curved at the look of embarrassed dismay that flushed her face and he ran a soothing hand up over her naked back. "If you remember the last time I tried to help you eat I was so overcome by lust that I nearly ravished you on the main table," he said gravely.

Her blush was swift but she smiled wickedly at the same time. "Actually, as I recall, it wasn't lust that overcame you but a severe outbreak of tyrannical behavior. And you didn't ravish me. You settled for telling me what to do for a bit, then, and I think this is important, ended up bedding down in the chair. So much for lust," she finished tartly.

Smiling, he leaned down and nipped her bare shoulder in punishment for doubting his lust for even a second. "Actually, if we are going to be one hundred percent honest, I ended that night in this bed," he whispered huskily against her skin. "Remember?"

"A mere detail." She grinned even as she shivered with the delightful feel of his words against her shoulder. "I'm sure you can help me eat dinner without suffering from too much lechery. Besides, I don't want to be fed like a child. I was thinking you could help more with the food navigation. I can always find my own mouth . . ."

"So can I," he murmured, and was unable to resist demonstrating that skill by finding it with his mouth. By the time he lifted his lips from hers, they were both struggling for air.

"Well, so you can," she said with a tremulous smile, and he couldn't stop himself from bending down to catch that smile as well. She forestalled his predatory move this time, placing her small hands on his chest and giving it a shove, but she couldn't stop herself from tangling her fingers in the soft hair, enjoying the small contact a little too much to give it up. "Be that as it may, what I was saying before I was rudely interrupted . . ."

"My lady, I can really show you rude if you like," he growled, but she ignored him, intent on her plans.

". . . is that I have no real problem with the eating. It's the food that often goes rogue on me. Mind you, I have improved. I nearly starved in the first six months, but I managed to subsist off the stains on my clothes till I got better at it." Her tone was light, but Robert felt the pain that hid behind her levity. "And it has gotten better, but . . ." She shrugged as her other hand began fiddling with the edge of the blanket. "If you helped, perhaps—"

"What do you mean 'if'? Of course I'm helping. As if you had to ask," he scolded gently. "What kind of husband would I be if I let some bad table manners stop me?"

He spent nearly two whole days proving just what kind of husband he was.

They closeted themselves in their chamber. Surrounded by congealing food, they tried to devise a way to solve what Robert had jokingly come to call her nourishment annoyance. Imogen had laughed at that and so much else besides. It surprised her just how much laughter filled those days. Something Imogen had thought of as a torture had become an occasion for open joy.

Not that it had started out being quite that easy.

She had felt Robert's intent gaze on her like a physical touch and it had made her nervous. Instead of things getting better, the nervousness made it all that much harder.

By noon on the first day she had almost been crying with frustration but instead of giving in to tears, she had thrown her spoon across the room. Some part of her had hoped desperately that the childish display might drive Robert away from her once and for all, leaving her alone with her mortifying incompetence.

That was what it should have done anyway.

Instead, he knelt in front of her and ran a gentle hand down over her cheek. "What is it, Imogen?"

"I think it is called blindness," she said snidely.

"That display had nothing to do with blindness. It was a temper tantrum, plain and simple, and I think you will find that the sighted also have them every so often."

She crossed her arms over her chest. "And your point is?"

He made a frustrated sound in the back of his throat and stood up, leaving Imogen obtusely bereft. "You're right, Imogen, I don't have a point. I was just trying to work out what was wrong with you. Sorry, I shan't do it again."

She hung her head, ashamed by her behavior. "You're looking at me," she muttered grudgingly.

"What?"

She threw her hand in the air and stood up. "What's wrong is that I can feel you looking at me, and when you look at me I can't seem to function," she all but shouted.

He was silent for a second, then she could hear a chuckle start softly and the rumble grew till he was roaring. "All that because I was looking at you!"

he spluttered. "Good God, woman, I'll always be looking at you, given half a chance."

She put her hands on her hips and began to tap her toe, which set him off again. She heard the air rush out of the cushion as he collapsed into a chair and began gasping for air.

"When you're finished . . ." she bit out, her fury rising steadily. He didn't seem to be that afraid, snaking out a hand and wrapping it around her hips, tumbling her onto his lap in a sprawl.

"Oh, Imogen," he breathed, holding her close.

Slowly she could feel the tension begin to drain from her as her body bent itself around the warmth of his.

They sat in a silence broken only by the crackle of the fire on the grate.

"I suppose I was being a bit silly," she said slowly, and Robert had to smile at the resentful admission.

"Well, I think throwing cutlery because I'm looking at you might be seen by some as a bit that way, yes."

She sighed and absentmindedly nuzzled his neck. "I hate this feeling of helplessness. It's the knowing you can see me being unable to do things any four-year-old can do that upsets me." She smiled ruefully. "That is only fitting, I suppose, as it also seems to make me *behave* a little like a four-year-old. I don't think I will ever manage to do it."

"Of course you will do it." He covered her mouth with his hand to forestall any protest. "Not instantly, no, but you will have to trust me when I tell you that you will do it."

She lifted his hand away with both of hers. "You really think so?"

"Well it's either that, or I spend the rest of my life ducking your cutlery."

She'd smiled at him, rather enticingly, he thought, but as he went to kiss her, she clambered off his lap and went back over to the table.

She sat herself regally in the chair and raised her eyebrows at him. "Well, shall we begin again, or will it have to be a knife this time?"

"No, not the knife!" He spoke in mock horror, but his smile was real.

They worked on the problems, and in the absence of tension the time flowed easily between them. They laughed and teased, kissed and made love. In the warm glow of their togetherness, Robert felt some of his fears dissipating and he threw everything he had into the project. He longed desperately for Imogen to conquer all of her demons, no matter how small.

Only after much food had fallen, and the odd piece of cutlery thrown by both parties, did a solution come to Robert. A doubtful look filtered over Imogen's face as he explained to her what he had superiorly called his stroke of genius.

"Just put the food on the plate in a certain order?"

"Yes." He started heaping things in neat little piles on the plate. "Like the furniture in this room. If you know where the meat is, where the bread is and so forth, and it's the same every time, then as long as you can locate the plate, you should be able to eat neatly enough."

"But I won't be able to set up my plate like that."

He placed the plate precisely in front of her and then sat down in the chair next to hers. "Don't be slow-witted! I'll fill it for you. Now, the order could be like this." He carefully explained how the food was arranged. Giving her the spoon, he sat back and watched.

She scowled as she began to carefully navigate her way around the plate. He watched with growing pride as a confidence began to appear in her movements. And he had helped give that to her. He could feel that hard, dark place in his soul start to melt a little more.

When the last morsel of food made it cleanly to her mouth, she put down her spoon carefully beside the plate and sat there primly for a second, then let out a whoop of pure joy. She was laughing and crying at once as she threw herself into Robert's arms. He was unable to resist kissing her, tasting the sweet laughter on her lips.

But that elation swiftly changed to anxiety when she had to dress for her first meal in the main hall.

She fidgeted and fussed over her gown and, no matter how often Robert tried to reassure her that she looked stunning, nerves ate away her confidence. After the third change of clothes he began to seriously doubt whether his sanity would survive this excursion.

"We don't have to go down if you don't want to," he said in desperation. "I'm more than happy to eat up here with you."

"No. I won't hide, even if you're willing to hide with me." She took a large, shuddering breath. "Now, are you sure I look all right?"

"Imogen you are wonderful and look wonderful." He placed a gentle kiss on her forehead and looped her arm through his. "Now, let's go and stun my poor, unsuspecting garrison."

As they walked into the main hall he found himself running a finger around the suddenly too-tight neck of his tunic, starting to feel almost as nervous as Imogen, but for vastly different reasons. He hadn't enjoyed his first brush with jealousy and wasn't looking forward to it rearing its ugly head again.

A hush fell over the hall as all eyes turned to them.

Instead of the drowning blackness of earlier however, Robert felt himself standing taller as a glowing pride grew inside him at the open admiration in all the men's eyes. He felt only pride that this woman, with all the apparent serenity and dignity of a queen, was his. There was no room for jealousy when pride and love filled every available space inside him.

Every man in the hall was captivated.

Rumors had, of course, been flying around the Keep about Imogen since her appearance several days earlier, and Gareth had been busy dispelling the myths about Lady Deformed with a vengeance.

And now finally she stood there, allowing them to satisfy all of their burning curiosity.

Robert heard the unanimous sigh of satisfaction and could only smile silently in agreement. Imogen always had that effect, whether she knew it or not. They slowly walked up to the main dais and, once seated, the kitchen doors opened and the food and drink flooded in. Soon the silence was filled with the sounds of the knights eating.

Robert frowned with concentration as he filled

Imogen's dish and carefully placed it in front of her. He started to move away but was stopped by her grabbing hold of his hand with an unerring accuracy.

She hesitated for a second, then leaned over to him and whispered an earnest "Thank you" before placing a small kiss on his cheek.

He held her hand and lifted it to his lips. "Imogen, you have nothing to thank me for. I only helped you work things out that you would eventually have worked out for yourself. It's your own bravery that has got you thus far, nothing more."

She blushed and looked about to say something else when another hush fell over the hall. Robert dragged his eyes away from Imogen's face and a scowl appeared on his face as he caught sight of Gareth standing near the dais, his face split with a satisfied grin.

Damn the man! When Robert got him alone he'd . . . Robert mentally pulled his thoughts to an abrupt halt, and then sighed. It would appear that he hadn't been as miraculously cured of jealousy as he thought.

"Sir Gareth," Robert said formally, not willing to give the other man any encouragement. Not that Imogen shared his reserve. Far from it. At the sound of Gareth's name a look of pure delight filtered over her face.

"Gareth, are you there?"

Her evident pleasure at the prospect grated along Robert's nerves.

"My lady, wherever you are, I will always be, needing only a glimmer of your smile to sustain me."

It was such extravagant flattery that even Robert smiled. A little. And not so that Gareth could see and construe it as approval for his outrageous behavior.

Imogen arched her eyebrow. "Flirting still, Sir Knight?"

"Still!" Robert growled darkly, but no one heard it over Gareth's: "Only with you, my lady."

Imogen's laughter rang out over the hall. "Why is it I never get the last word when we speak, Sir Knight? Surely giving it to me would be the only chivalrous thing to do?"

Gareth said nothing for a moment, then exhaled loudly. "Sorry, my lady, I tried, but even for you I can't keep my mouth shut."

"That is no surprise," Robert said tersely, but Gareth only grinned at him.

"Lady Imogen, as much as I love being warmed by the glow of your presence, it would seem I'm making your husband restless, so, against my better nature, I'll get myself to the point." He went down on one knee with a flourish, and whipped a large bouquet from behind his back. "Whispers of you gracing us with your presence had reached me, and I thought that, as you were giving us such a gift, then perhaps I should gift you with this small"—Robert snorted loudly at the inaccuracy of that appellation—"bouquet in return."

Gareth placed the bouquet gently on her lap and, after reaching up for her hand, bowed over it.

Robert's eyebrow shot up when he got a closer look at the bouquet. "Gareth, why have you given my lady wife a bunch of leaves?"

"Because, Robert, I'm good, but not that good. Even I can't produce flowers out of the snow." He shrugged his shoulders. "Besides, I thought Imogen would get more pleasure out of richly scented herbs than gaudily colored flowers."

Imogen reached out a shaking hand and ran a fingertip over the bouquet. She gently crushed a leaf between her fingers and released the earth-rich smell of apple-scented chamomile into the air. She inhaled deeply, filling her senses with it for a moment, then she carefully placed the bouquet onto the table. The dampness on her cheeks glistened openly in the candlelight.

"Help me up," she whispered hoarsely to Robert, who instantly obeyed, as stunned as the rest by her raw emotion.

"Thank you, Sir Gareth. You were indeed right, they are a beautiful gift and I scarce know how to thank you properly." She said it all with perfectly acceptable formality, but then, as if unable to help herself, she bent down and placed a single kiss on his cheek.

Robert didn't have time for jealousy, not now. One look around the hall was enough for him to realize that he had other, far more pressing things to worry about. Looks of admiration had been replaced with ones of open worship. The sight of a lady being so overwhelmed by such a simple gift had worked its way under years of brutality to the soft place underneath that many of the knights had scarce been aware they had. Robert could barely resist the urge to groan in frustration. Thirty hardened warriors he knew how to deal with. Thirty lovesick grown men, however, might prove to be a problem.

He was in trouble.

Gareth's smile caught his eye. As Robert glared at

him ferociously, Gareth just winked at him and as he stood up whispered into Robert's ear. "With thirty men willing to kill their own mothers to keep her safe, at least you know she will never come to any harm."

Robert cast a quick glance around the hall, and grimaced. "I might come to harm, though. I'll get crushed by their mailed feet as they rush to be by her side."

Gareth shrugged his shoulders. "It will keep you on your toes."

Robert sighed and reached for the mead.

The only person who seemed oblivious to the impending chaos was Imogen herself. Entirely unaware of the furor she had inadvertently caused, she set about calmly eating her dinner, pausing from time to time to caress her bouquet of herbs.

Robert smiled despite himself. Things might not be turning out quite as he had planned, but married life was beginning to suit him. He filled Imogen's cup and placed it carefully at her hand.

It was suiting him very well indeed.

Chapter Nine

The sound of Imogen's laughter on the breeze drew Robert to the window. The courtyard below was bathed in sunlight, the snow of the long winter almost a memory, but it wasn't the joy of the new season that filled Robert with warmth. No, it was the sound of Imogen's laughter coming from the practice yard that brought a gentle smile to his face.

He'd organized the space as soon as his men had started arriving on his doorstep, and now most hours of the day the courtyard was filled with the clash of steel on steel. Today, however, instead of the sound of men practicing war, all that could be heard was the murmur of voices and laughter. Yet again, it would seem, Imogen was distracting the men from their serious business. Not that they weren't easily distracted, Robert thought wryly.

She had only to appear outdoors and his men willingly laid down their arms just so that they might have a chance to vie for her attention, like now. Robert tried to find her in the scene below his window but he could catch only occasional glimpses of her amongst the half-naked, bronzed, sweating bodies that clustered around her. Despite that, however, her presence seemed to fill the whole courtyard.

Robert shook his head at the folly of his men, but he was smiling all the same. How could he blame his men for being captured in her flame when he himself was one of her most willing victims? Her growing confidence and delight at the new world she was discovering was a rare jewel in a warrior's hard life, and Robert was loath to miss a moment of it.

She was trying to catch up on life after years of waking sleep and she was throwing herself into the small world of the Keep with a will. Sometimes it was exhausting just to watch her human whirlwind. Everything was of interest to her, and she was tireless in the pursuit of anything that caught that interest.

Robert smiled fondly as he caught the occasional glimpse of her chatting animatedly to his men. Ladies were not normally seen in a practice yard, or even showed any interest in the masculine domains, but when the lady was Imogen, it would have been impossible to keep her out.

There was nothing conventional about his lady.

Robert leaned on the window's edge and watched the men reluctantly return to their work as Gareth entered the yard, their departing bodies revealing fully to his eager gaze a blooming Imogen and a clearly wilting Mary. The old woman was obviously struggling to keep up with the newly revitalized Imogen.

A part of Robert was more than willing to lift the burden from Mary's shoulders and in fact he longed to be Imogen's eyes in the exciting new world she was discovering all around. But he didn't, his logic ruthlessly reminding him that to do so would be like giving her the last piece of his soul. Pride demanded that he didn't give her all of himself unless he knew for certain he had all of her in return.

That he didn't was like finding a dark corruption in paradise.

Every time he was near her, he could feel her hidden truths standing like unbreachable walls between them, he thought with a frown as he watched the two women disappear into the walled kitchen garden and out of his view.

It was only when he was no longer distracted by the beautiful puzzle that was his wife that he spotted a man in the shadows of the wall, watching Imogen as she passed.

Robert's frown only deepened when he recognized the watcher as the priest who had married them. Ian. That was what Imogen had called him. Roger's friend.

His initial dislike for the man had crystallized into something firmer. He hated the way the man always seemed to be where Imogen was, watching her every move, his pale eyes following her. Robert dearly wanted to get rid of the man, but something stayed his hand.

He feared how Imogen might react if she realized just how closely Roger was having her watched. He refused to upset the fragile balance they had found, but at the same time he made a small mental note that the second he could get rid of the man without Imogen being aware, he would do so with great pleasure.

The loud knock on the door drew him from his brooding thoughts with a start. "Come in," he called, and sat down quickly at his desk, vaguely embarrassed at the thought of being caught staring longingly into the practice yard. It seemed better to pretend to be busy at the Keep's ledgers than mooning after his own wife. When he looked up from the meaningless numbers, the sight of Sir Edmond holding a protesting lamb gave him pause.

The young knight looked uncomfortable but also strangely proud at the same time as he held the wriggling bundle with his arms outstretched.

Robert rested his elbows on the table, steepled his hands and raised his finger to his lips.

"And just why exactly have you brought me a sheep, Sir Edmond?"

The young man flushed a deep red and lowered his eyes with patent embarrassment. "It's not for you," he mumbled.

Robert laughed out loud but knew he shouldn't be amused. After all, this kind of thing had been going on for weeks and surely he shouldn't be encouraging the lunacy? It was Gareth's fault, of course. His gift of aromatic herbs had started an unofficial competition amongst the men. Every man jack of them seemed to be battling hard to earn themselves a kiss of their own and there seemed to be no length to which they wouldn't go in the pursuit of their goal.

Even the normally sane Matthew had entered into the madness, Robert remembered with a rueful grin as he met the baleful stare of the lamb.

Only that morning, the old man had proudly presented Imogen with a soft duck's feather, his knees cracking outrageously as he had knelt gallantly on the stone floor in front of the main hearth.

Robert had wanted to laugh at the old man's foolishness, and he suspected it was a desire shared by all who were witness to the folly, but Matthew's fierce glare had forestalled any such reaction. Imogen, however, hadn't noticed the suppressed amusement as she reached out and helped the old man to his feet. She had scolded him harshly for his foolishness. But she had smiled and her cheeks had been clearly flushed with pleasure at the chivalrous gesture from the usually crusty old man.

She had given him a hug and asked him if he would act as her escort on her inspection of the storeroom, to checked the freshness of the spices.

The blissfully smug smile on Matthew's face as he had taken her arm and led her away had killed all amusement, dead. And it had apparently inspired a new wave of creativity in the Pleasing-Imogen Tournament, Robert realized as he dispassionately observed the sheep that Sir Edmond was trying to hold begin to wriggle its way to freedom.

He didn't blame the men entirely. Robert himself had been more than a little inspired by the sight of Imogen caressing her cheek absentmindedly with the feather as she had walked away.

Robert's body heated as he imagined presenting her with a feather of his own.

Of course, he would give it to her in the privacy of their chamber. They would both be naked and lying on the rug before the fire. He would then run the feather over the gentle swell of her breasts, over the hollow of her navel, over the moist silk of her inner thigh and, reaching ever higher . . .

Robert closed his eyes for a moment and tried to breathe deeply. His fevered imaginings were having an instantaneous, and painful, effect on him. His groin was now full and aching and he was grateful that the table was hiding his erection from Sir Edmond's gaze, as the young man looked like he was suffering enough trying to control the sheep, without being confronted with his leader's insatiable lust.

Not that Edmond didn't have every right to look embarrassed, Robert thought sternly. Knights weren't shepherds and, as far as Robert was concerned, shepherds were the only ones who should have anything to do with sheep. Judging by the increasingly pained look on Edmond's face, he was fast coming to that conclusion himself.

"So that's not my sheep, then?" Robert couldn't seem to stop his lips twitching at Edmond's almost frantic head shaking. "So, if it is not my sheep, then why have you brought it in here?"

Edmond shrugged, his face filled with desperation. "I . . . I thought—uh, I thought . . ."

"Somehow I doubt that," Robert murmured but, taking pity on the boy, continued. "Let me guess what you think you thought. You were thinking that if you were to give that vaguely smelly beast to Lady Imogen, *my* wife," he emphasized, "she might be so overwhelmed by the—uh, magnitude, of the gift, that she might just bestow on your unworthy person some small favor. Am I close?"

Edmond dropped his head, and nodded dejectedly, a lock of his blond hair falling forward over his forehead. Was I ever that young? Robert thought with bewilderment. Somehow it just didn't seem possible.

"Well, why then hasn't my lady been presented with this unusual token?"

"Couldn't find her," Edmond mumbled, his misery now absolute, and Robert's side began to ache with suppressed laughter.

"Ah," he breathed out carefully and, once he was sure of his continued composure, he added, "would you like me to take you to her?"

Edmond looked up and his grin was radiant. "You would actually do that?" he breathed with awe.

Robert could no longer contain his laughter as he stood. "Of course. Far be it for me to deny my wife such a delightful gift. She was heading to the kitchen garden, I believe, if you care to follow me."

As they walked through the Keep's hall and into the courtyard, everyone guessed who the sheep was for, and Robert had to grin at the frankly jealous looks the men were throwing Edmond. The poor boy was beginning to walk so tall that Robert feared he might trip over something if he didn't cast the odd glance down at his feet. His new dignity was only marginally dinted by the protesting bleat of the sheep. It had to be some sort of enchantment, Robert concluded with amused awe. It was the only possible answer for the insanity that seemed to have descended over them all.

And Robert was as caught in Imogen's spell as were his men, even as he tried to fight it. He was just more discreet about his.

Not many might know it, but every few days he rode over to the tower to bring back some small thing from the horde that Roger had hidden there.

He would have brought everything over to the Keep at once but Imogen had been emphatic that it should all be left where it was. She had been coldly emotionless as she had mouthed the denial of her past, but the memory of the lingering touches she had bestowed on the covers of the books was burnt into his brain. He'd had to grit his teeth to stop the roar that had almost escaped as he had watched her surreptitiously slip a small paperweight into her cloak pocket just before they had left, when she thought he wasn't looking. That she had tried to hide it from him cut into him like a knife to his vitals, but it was only in the dark of the night, as he watched over her as she slept, that he let himself dwell on the helplessness betrayed in that small gesture. A helplessness she refused to share, dark memories she carefully shielded from his gaze. It was his primal fear of losing her to those memories that stopped him from bringing it all out into the open by tearing down the tower stone by stone and giving her back her childhood, but the anger still filled him.

Anger that it was fear of her brother and his power that made her insist that the tower should stay as it was. Anger that she doubted him and his ability to stand between her and any danger, especially the threat posed by her reptilian brother.

If only she would talk to him! If she but asked him, he would vanquish all of her demons, Robert thought, smiling savagely as he imagined the pleasure to be found in grinding Roger to dust. But she didn't tell him. She held her enemies and their secrets close to her, denying him.

Still, in his own way he fought them. He fought

them every time he presented her with a small piece of her past. Each piece of the puzzle that he returned to her was a silent pledge that he would protect her, to the last breath in his body, from all who might harm her.

He could only hope that she would understand and, in time, let him in.

Until then, he would settle for the smile she gave him each time he gave her back another relic from her youth, would settle for the warmth of her body along his as she silently thanked him at night in the privacy of their chamber.

Robert looked at the jubilant Edmond and had to smile.

If only Edmond knew.

Imogen buried her hands deep in the warming soil. The winter seemed to have lasted forever, but at last it was finally taking flight. The sun was getting slowly stronger, the winds steadily sweeter.

After years of cold, lonely isolation, Imogen couldn't help but feel that it was a glorious time to be alive. Just drawing breath and smelling the scents of spring was a gift. To be contributing to it, well, that was almost a miracle. There was much she still couldn't do, but she had also come to realize that there was so much else she could if she tried. Each day she was working harder than she had ever done before and she loved it.

Today, old Duncan was teaching her to weed, and while Mary might grumble that gardening was no job for a lady, she also enjoyed the chance to catch up on her sleep too much to pass on the opportunity.

Grudgingly, she allowed the small social abomination to continue.

Imogen smiled with satisfaction at how everything had turned out. It was good for Mary to have some time to herself after all these years of devoted service, but it was also good that Imogen was finding a place in the world. With Duncan watching over her, there was no longer any excuse for her to be idle.

He had given her a garden bed to weed in preparation for the seeds he had collected last autumn. It was amazing to know that as long as she was methodical about her work, then her hands were nearly as useful as Duncan's gnarled ones.

No, it was more than amazing. It felt like she was being let back into the human race after many long, dark years of exile. It felt like magic and Robert was her personal magician who had brought her back to life.

Her smile broadened at the absurd thought of her strong, simple warrior of a husband as a manipulative conjurer of tricks, although she had to admit that in him, there was a certain enchantment to be found. She knew she must be blushing as memory after memory filled her mind with the exact details of the magic that he created in her with his body. She had never known such joy as there was to be found in Robert's arms.

She couldn't help but shiver a little. Joy. Even to think of it seemed to be tempting fate, or perhaps it was Roger she was afraid of tempting. He was the one who had brought Robert to her, and she should never forget that. It was a surprisingly hard thing to remember, especially when it was inconceivable that any action of her brother's could be the source of so much joy.

Her hands clenched in the soil as her sunny day seemed to lose some of its warmth all of a sudden and she hated Roger for that. Damn, but he was always there, waiting at the fringes of her life to destroy everything. And as much as she tried to deny it, a part of her feared that all she was feeling right now might just be another move in his game. Perhaps he knew that if she lost this life, lost Robert somehow, she would be absolutely destroyed. If he knew that . . .

She turned her mind from the darkness and stopped thinking altogether, concentrating instead on the pursuit of weeds. She willed her soul to be soothed by the sounds of the early spring. She listened intently to the sound of birds building nests and finding mates, the sound of bees returning, the sound of sheep bleating . . .

Sheep? In the courtyard?

"Sheep?" She turned to where Duncan had been digging. "Do you hear sheep, Duncan?"

"Yes, my lady," Duncan said, scratching his forefinger along his nose as he leaned on his shovel, "and I can see one too. Sir Edmond seems to be holding it."

Startled, Imogen turned to the sound.

"Didn't mean to stop you working, Little One," Robert said laconically, "but Sir Edmond couldn't wait to give you a small . . . something."

"Something? You can't possibly mean a sheep?"

"Actually, I think it might technically be a lamb, but I could be wrong. I am not exactly *au fait* with agricultural matters."

"Aye, sir, you have the right of it." Duncan's face wrinkled into a broad smile. "That is most definitely a lamb."

"I defer to your greater acquaintance with such things, Duncan."

"Thankee, sir."

"Not at all."

By this stage, Edmond was wishing the earth would open up and swallow him. He started shuffling noisily from foot to foot, longing for what was becoming the most embarrassing moment of his life to end.

"Stop it, you two, can't you tell you're embarrassing Sir Edmond?" Imogen scolded as she got clumsily to her feet.

"Don't blame us," Robert snorted, "any embarrassment he feels is the sheep's fault."

"Lamb, sir."

"Lamb. That's right. Thank you again, Duncan."

"Ignore them, Edmond, they are just being silly," she said dismissively, giving him a large smile of encouragement, unaware that she in fact managed to dazzle him. "Do you really have a lamb?"

"Ye . . . yes, Lady Imogen," he stumbled.

"Can I pet it?" She stepped forward a little. "I've never touched a lamb before."

Edmond almost fell over himself in his rush to gain her side. With a sad, resigned shake of his head, Robert watched another of his men fall. They were all like sailors drowning under a siren's spell.

Imogen smiled tenderly as she groped to find the lamb in Edmond's arms. The lamb, perhaps also under her spell, went silent and leaned its small head closer to her touch.

"Oh, isn't it a dear," Imogen cooed, then she bit her lip earnestly. "May I hold him?"

"Of course," Edmond yelled with almost indecent relief, causing Imogen to flinch a little.

Her brow furrowed with concentration as Edmond awkwardly placed the lamb into her willing hands. The lamb settled itself peacefully in the arms of its new protector, resting its head on her forearm and closing its eyes trustingly.

"It would seem you can charm animals just as easily as you charm grown men." Robert shook his head with disbelief as he moved to her side and slid an arm around her shoulders. He couldn't help relishing the way she instinctively leaned into him although all her concentration was focused on the lamb.

"Oh, Robert, may I keep him? He is such a dear and won't be any problem."

"Now Imogen . . ."

"I promise, you'll barely know he's here. It will be no more painful than having another dog around the Keep. I promise."

"But Imogen, a *sheep* . . ."

"Please," she whispered pleadingly and Robert knew he was sunk.

"All right, it can stay," he sighed, slightly belligerent in his resignation, "but it can't stay in our chamber. You'll have to find somewhere else . . ."

His stern lecture was cut short by Imogen's squeal of delight as she threw an arm round his neck and kissed him. For a second he pulled her closer and deepened the kiss, but the lambs' wriggling protest made him pull back long before he wanted to.

Robert looked up from Imogen's flushed face to cast a quick glance at Duncan, and was relieved to see that the wise old man had returned to his digging. Edmond, however, wasn't as quick. He was staring slack-jawed at the couple when Robert's eyes met his. Robert smiled at his look of embarrassed devastation, but decided to take pity on the poor boy.

"Edmond is looking like a slapped puppy," he whispered into Imogen's ear. "He seems to think I stole his reward."

Imogen's renewed blush almost rivaled Edmond's.

"Of course, I'm so sorry, Sir Edmond." She turned and, with the unerring judgment that always amazed Robert, reached on tiptoes and placed a kiss on Edmond's heated cheek. "The lamb is absolutely wonderful and I don't know how to thank you."

"You could always name it after him," Robert said wickedly.

"No!" Edmond yelped, forgetting all manners in his distress. Robert watched with amusement as the younger man cleared his throat and started again. "No such thanks are necessary, Lady Imogen." He touched his cheek reverently. "None at all. Well, I'd best get back to work. Can't stand around talking all day."

He lifted Imogen's hand and bowed over it with more grace than Robert had ever seen him display before, then strode manfully away. Robert only just managed to catch the whoop of victory he let out before disappearing around the corner.

"Imogen, how the hell do you do it?" Robert asked, shaking his head with wonder.

"Do what?" she asked abstractedly as she tried to calm the now seriously squirming lamb.

"Never mind," he said with a bemused smile.

"Robert, I think it's hungry. What do I do?" she asked as she slipped her fingers into its mouth and it began sucking on them aggressively.

"Don't ask me. I'm a warrior, not a farmer."

"A good lord should be a little of both, sir," Duncan murmured with a knowing smile. "As for the lamb, I suggest a visit to the kitchens for some milk and a bed by the fire might be in order."

The concern cleared from Imogen's face. "Brilliant." She beamed at Duncan, and moved out of Robert's sheltering arms so that she could dump the lamb into them instead.

"What the . . ."

"It's a lamb, not a sheep, and it's hungry, so you'd best feed it."

"How come I get left with the bloody thing?" he protested. "It's from one of your foolish admirers, you look after it."

"Edmond's not foolish and I'm working," she said sternly, then wrecked the overall effect by breaking into a grin as she ran a hand over the lamb's head. "Besides, as Duncan said, you can't just be a warrior. You'll have to learn about things like sheep, now you might own some. Here's a chance to get a little practical experience, so go learn about sheep while I get back to work."

Robert scowled furiously at the suddenly busy Duncan, then looked helplessly down at the frantic creature that had started to suck aggressively on one of the toggles on his shirtfront.

"I don't want to look after the sheep," Robert said

plaintively, knowing he sounded like a petulant child and not caring.

Imogen leaned up and placed a lingering kiss on his lips. "Sure you do," she whispered for him alone. "Please."

He groaned, knowing when he was outclassed and defeated. He snaked out an arm and clamped her close to his body and gave himself over to a hard, hungry kiss in an attempt to salvage something from this disaster. By the time he drew away they were both struggling for air and the lamb was protesting loudly.

He looked down at the beast in resignation. "Milk and warmth, right Duncan?"

"That'd be right, Sir Robert."

Robert nodded and, with one last heated look at Imogen, turned to leave. He was stopped by a low murmur.

"If you come and get me in an hour, I should be finished here and we can discuss . . . *that* further in our chamber."

He threw back his head and laughed. "You drive a hard bargain, but all right. One hour, and not a second longer."

As he walked toward the kitchen he was well aware that he was grinning and had a decided spring in his step. He looked down at the lamb and gave it a smug smile. "Looks like I'm getting a reward out of you as well as Edmond, and I can guarantee, mine will be the better one of the two."

The lamb met his eyes blandly and bit down on the toggle, breaking it cleanly in two.

* * *

Imogen smiled as Robert's whistle reached her on the breeze. She didn't understand the man, she thought with a shake of her head, and started to weed once more.

"If you don't mind me saying, my lady," Duncan said suddenly, "but he's a good man, that husband of yours."

"You think so, Duncan?" she asked, calmly working, pretending that the answer didn't really matter.

"I don't think so, my lady, I know so."

A good man? Did such things exist? Did they manage to live even though men like Roger seemed to be in control of the world? It seemed almost fantastic, but a part of Imogen started fervently praying that it might indeed prove to be true. She carried the hope of her prayers in her heart as she worked. She needed so badly for it to be true. The world so badly needed good men. But to hell with the world, she thought savagely, pulling up a weed, she needed them more. Needed him more. She needed him to be all he seemed to be.

Was she tempting fate by asking for so much?

Perhaps, but she also knew that she couldn't survive with anything less. If Robert turned out to be Roger's man, then her new life would turn to ashes, and her life would no longer be worth living.

Chapter Ten

When the first messenger arrived weeks later, Imogen hadn't even realized that she had been waiting for it, waiting for Roger to stop biding his time and start playing the game in earnest. He timed his little drop of poison well, filling her with it just when she had started to forget how much pain he could inflict. Not that it wasn't easy enough to forget his darkness when she was surrounded by Robert's gentle, cleansing light. It seemed that in no time at all, he had changed her world.

Under his care the Keep had slowly settled into a comfortable rhythm, everyone easily picking up the strands of their new lives. Imogen found herself intoxicated by the simple new life that now enclosed her.

Tonight she could hear the murmur of women sewing and gossiping by the main hearth, hear the men cleaning their weapons or leathers, their deeper voices a bass note in the gentle, soothing hum that now filled the Keep. To Imogen there was no sweeter sound. She absorbed it as she sat opposite Robert at the main table; a chessboard set up between them and the lamb dozing peacefully at their feet.

She smiled contentedly as she waited for Robert to make his next move.

"You're going to beat me, aren't you?" he asked incredulously.

"Of course," she murmured, her serenity tinged with more than a little satisfaction.

He looked up and grinned. "No 'of course' about it, Little One. Until I decided to teach you this accursed game, I rarely lost." His brows dropped suspiciously. "But I didn't teach you the game at all, did I? You already knew how to play before I stumbled on the idea, didn't you?"

Her face dimpled. "As much as I'd like to deny it and let you believe that you have been repeatedly beaten by a complete novice I have to confess that my father and I used to play." She reached out a hand and consolingly patted his. "It has been a while between games, though."

She grinned at his loud grunt of disgust and couldn't help adding smugly, "Pity, really, as I seem to still be good at it."

Robert ignored her gloating, turning his attention back to the board. "It's not the losing I really mind," he muttered, "so much as the fact that I have only to tell you my move once and you remember it. You seem to hold the whole game in your head and I don't care what you say, that can't be natural."

She shrugged her shoulders delicately. "Maybe it isn't natural, but you have to admit that it's very effective."

"Witch!" he growled, and her delighted laughter brought more than one masculine head up. Even the lamb lifted his own head for a moment. Curious, he eyed his humans with a mild interest before returning to the more important business of sleeping on his mistress's foot.

Robert continued to scowl as he made the only move she had effectively left him and read out the coordinates for her grudgingly. He leaned back in the great chair and watched as her brilliant little brain analyzed the move, her thoughts scarcely discernible on her face. It took a depressingly few seconds for her to come up with her countermove, Robert thought dourly, as she rattled off the coordinates with all the confidence of a woman who knew she had won, and won decisively. Her "Checkmate, I believe," was almost endearingly smug.

Almost.

Robert moved the piece as ordered and knocked over his king in surrender.

He narrowed his eyes and looked intensely at the game, trying to understand his abject defeat, trying to work out where exactly the game had gotten away from him. He didn't lift his eyes from the board when one of the men from the first watch whispered in his ear but his face darkened ominously. He noisily dragged back his chair, disturbing the lamb once more, who let out a small bleat of protest and slowly stood.

"Excuse me for a moment, Little One," he said as he stood, "but I must attend to a small matter."

"Running from your defeat, Sir Husband?" she asked, smiling up at him with deliberately sweet innocence.

"No, that would be far too cowardly for a brave

brother, my lady?" the boy asked politely as he handed over the parchment also. Imogen could only dumbly shake her head. The messenger sketched her a quick bow. "Well then, I must return to my master. Farewell."

She stood numbly in the center of the room, her mind twisting through all that Roger had said and, more importantly, all of the things he had left unsaid.

That he had spies in the Keep was obvious, but then she had always known that, known she was surrounded by people more than willing to do his dirty work, no matter what that might be.

No, that wasn't the real corrupting poison in the message.

The real reason that the message made her feel sick to her soul was Roger's sly insinuation that Robert wasn't all he seemed to be. Roger had hit with an unerring accuracy, ruthlessly drawing to the surface the cold fear that she still somehow carried despite all of Robert's apparent kindness. It was his knowledge on just how to destroy her fledgling trust that made Roger's poison all that more deadly, and even now she could feel it spreading through her.

He was an expert at destroying a person from within, Imogen thought bitterly, admiring his skill even as it slowly chilled her. Her mind could logically see the game he played but there seemed to be nothing she could do to stop it. Doubt was eating her up, destroying the whole structure of her fragile new life and Roger had only to lift a pen to do it. A part of her despised herself for making it so easy for him, but then, Roger, the man who had destroyed all of her trust along with her sight,

had known that it would take no more than a pin-
prick to destroy her burgeoning faith in Robert.

It was as simple as it was deadly. She saw what he
did but couldn't stop it. She had been waiting for
it, knowing even while she was enjoying it that hope
was only an illusion.

And that was why Roger would always win,
Imogen thought bitterly. He always seemed to know
his enemies better than they knew themselves. He
exploited their every weakness and no matter how
clever they were, there was nothing they could do to
save themselves.

Her hands clenched impotently by her sides and
the metal of the ring seemed to burn its way into
the flesh of her palm, branding her with memories.

She carefully loosened her grip and let the finger
of her other hand run over the cut stones. She
could almost see it in her mind's eye, see the deep
red of rubies and the green fire of the emeralds.
She could feel the engraved words on the inside,
and knew with her heart the words that were
burned there: Love without measure.

Despite the bitter-cold pain that had lodged itself
inside her, she smiled sadly. Love without measure,
her family motto. A bittersweet feeling of painful
joy filled her. It was strange to finally be reunited
with this small part of her past. There was an un-
deniable joy in a memory being returned to her
from so long ago, but at the same time she knew
that it wasn't for old time's sake that Roger had
given her the ring.

It was a message.

Roger knew that she would identify it instantly
even though she couldn't see it. He knew exactly

what memories it brought with it. Memories of youth, happiness and love. She gave a brittle laugh that ended in a sob. That was what the ring had always meant to her. Love without measure.

As a child she had often begged her mother to be allowed to hold it and then, when that small liberty had been allowed, she would beg to be allowed to actually wear it.

Her mother would sit with her as she played with the sunlight in the stones, holding it first this way, then that, entranced by the colors and determined to wear the small fires on her own finger but, despite Imogen's pleadings, her mother had remained firm.

"It's too large for you to wear yet, Genny dear"— her mother would smile as she gave her a hug as a consolation—"but when your hands are as large as mine, then, I promise you, you will wear it."

"But Mama," she always protested, "my hands are ever so big. They must be your size by now." She would hold up her small dirty hand as proof of its enormity. Her mother would place her own elegant hand against it and murmur, "Soon enough, Genny. Soon enough. Until then, I will wear it to keep it safe for you."

And she had. Her mother had been wearing it that day when she and father had ridden out for the last time.

It had taken all of Imogen's persuasion to convince them to go. It had been months since Imogen's accident and her parents hadn't left her side for a moment, frightened to leave her alone in the dark. It had taken her hours to persuade them that she would be okay, that she was getting used to the world without colors, that she really would be fine for just one afternoon by herself.

Eventually they had agreed, but her mother still hadn't been able to stop herself from fussing around Imogen, issuing an endless stream of last-minute instructions to anyone who would listen.

In the end Imogen had clumsily reached out her hands to grab for her mother's fluttering ones. She had felt the cold presence of the ring and been re-assured even as she had said forcefully, "Mama, I'll be fine. There are plenty of people here to look after me. You and Papa just go and enjoy your-selves for an afternoon."

It had been a lie. She hadn't been fine, had hated being alone, but Imogen had felt a small easing in her guilt as she had listened to the two horses galloping out of the courtyard and receding into the distance.

It had taken two days for their bodies to be found. They had been thrown into a ditch beside the stream, seemingly the victims of bandits as their bodies had been stripped of everything of value.

The ring had been stolen along with everything else, but that had hardly seemed to matter.

As Imogen had sat in vigil in the small chapel be-tween her parents, she had been so numb with her grief that she had been able to do no more than sit there holding their hands in the darkness. She hadn't cried. She had wept so much and so bitterly after the accident had robbed her of sight that there seemed to be no tears left for the beloved parents that she had blithely sent to their deaths.

But the numbness hadn't lasted forever. The pain had then become almost beyond enduring.

In her dark agony she might have found some comfort in the ring and the love it represented, but it had seemed to be lost to her forever.

Her hand clenched tightly around the ring again. It should be lost forever. Roger shouldn't have had it all these years. He hadn't even been there when their parents had died. When Imogen had been found unconscious at the bottom of the stairs, it hadn't taken her parents long to put together what had happened. Their father had been so furious, he had flogged Roger to within an inch of his life, then banished him forever from the family estates. Roger had slunk off to London willingly enough.

He was able to return only after the death of their parents, when he was master of all.

He shouldn't have even known that the ring was missing. The cold reality of the ring in her hand killed the smallest part of her, that part that had been foolish enough to have hope.

There was no hope for her now, not when her parent's murderer had now set his sights on her. Giving her the ring, Roger had known that he was giving her evidence of his darkest deed, but he had also been declaring that she would never be able to use it against him. He would make sure of that.

Imogen clamped down on her sudden need to expel the bile from her stomach. Her fingers loosened around the ring till it rested gently in her shaking hands as she fought the desire to hurl it as far away from her as she could.

Instead, she lifted it to her chest protectively.

She would keep it, just as Roger had known she would. The game had changed, had become deadly, and that was what Roger wanted her to remember every time she felt the ring. He wanted her to know that she was in mortal danger, and there was not a thing she could do to save herself.

A cold sweat beaded on her back and slid down her spine. She clenched her teeth to break off the scream that rose in her throat. It would do no good, she realized bleakly.

She heard Robert's strangely hesitant "Imogen?" behind her and her spine straightened instantly, as if pulled up by an invisible string.

She quickly slipped the ring onto her finger, not once questioning her instinct to hide it from Robert. She barely noticed that it fitted perfectly as she stuffed the parchment into her girdle and ran a trembling hand over her cheeks. She dreaded the thought of finding them wet with memories. She would hate to give that weapon to yet another enemy.

She need not have worried. They were as dry as her heart was cold.

"Imogen?" Robert repeated softly. "Is all well?"

She could hear his annoyance, but he quickly got himself back under control. What a clever man, she thought wildly, able to stop being the king's butcher at will.

She turned to him and her smile was as bright as it was brittle. "Yes, why wouldn't all be well? Did you really think that the poor little messenger might harm my person?"

"What exactly did your brother want?" he asked calmly enough.

He wanted to tell me he now had a partner, Imogen thought cynically. She shrugged her shoulders with a careful negligence. "Not much, really. I'm surprised he wasted the good parchment on such frivolities." She couldn't seem to find control and her voice rose shrilly. That wouldn't do, she thought with numb panic. She couldn't let him know just how much she was hurting and she tried to draw herself back under control, but she wasn't as good at it as Robert was. "He just wrote to ensure my well-being. And yours, of course. That is all. I didn't bother with the expense of more parchment for a reply."

She heard the rustle of his feet through the rushes as he began to pace the length of the room, perhaps trying to expend some of that ever-present restless energy she had come to know so well.

For a moment she envied him that energy, envied him the release that mindless movement would give. She seemed frozen to the spot. In the absence of that release, the pain grew until it was almost too great for a mere mortal to support. She was being suffocated by her absolute stillness.

"Damn him," Robert swore suddenly, causing Imogen to flinch when he reached out and grabbed her shoulders in an almost-painful grip. "He is nothing to us, has no power over us, do you understand me? Believe me when I tell you that you have nothing to fear."

Imogen found herself cringing away from the contact.

Roger had won. He had tainted it all, tainted her life with Robert. She couldn't stop her shiver of revulsion at the corruption that she could feel growing deep inside of her and yet some part of her mourned as Robert dropped his hands quickly to his side, stung by her blatant rejection.

A silence stretched between them and it grew

into a chasm, a chasm Imogen knew she could now never bridge, even if she had wanted to.

"Obviously there was more to this message than you have said." Robert's kept his voice carefully neutral. "I think I might just go and have the message read to me."

Imogen shook her head jerkily. "I wouldn't bother. There is nothing in it to cause any excitement." She felt no triumph in the knowledge that she wasn't lying. The poison wasn't to be found in the words but in the bitter memories they evoked.

Robert's silence spoke eloquently of his skepticism, but Imogen didn't have the strength left to try and convince him otherwise. Let him read it, she thought listlessly. It would change nothing. The life that had filled her for months disappeared all at once and without it she barely had the strength to hold up her strangely hollow body.

"Do what you will. I think I will retire for the night," she murmured in a faraway, world-weary voice.

"I'll join you when I've got everything sorted down here. I'll just go and get Mary to take you up."

She waved him away. The thought of being close to anyone just now, even the loyal Mary, made her skin creep. "I can manage the stairs by myself." She walked slowly to the door, trailing a hand along the wall.

"It doesn't matter, you know" Robert's voice sounded strangely hoarse.

"What doesn't?" she asked lifelessly.

"Whatever he's said and done; it doesn't matter. He has no power over you or I. Not here, not anymore."

She nodded her head obediently, but her heart knew that he was lying. Roger held her still, held her so tightly that she could scarcely breathe. He would continue to hold her, no matter where she went, no matter how far, he would hold her until the day he killed her.

Robert lied.

The next morning she woke to the feeling of bile rising from her stomach. She only just made it to the chamberpot in time and seemed to spend a lifetime emptying the entire contents of her stomach and much more besides.

She slumped down onto the floor beside it and rolled herself into a ball, waiting for the nausea to end, waiting for the room to stop spinning. She rocked herself slowly, trying to absorb the silence and emptiness of the bedchamber into the chaos of her mind.

Robert was already gone and if she hadn't lain awake all night in their bed listening to the regular sound of his breathing, she might never have known that he had been there at all. He had risen silently long before dawn and dressed without a sound. She had listened to the sudden stillness that had filled the chamber moments before she had heard the door quietly close behind him.

Only then had she dared to allow herself sleep.

To have woken up with this all-consuming sickness was a perfect end to a perfect night filled with Roger and the cold fear he had mercilessly brought back into her life, she thought listlessly. There was no longer any room left in her heart for anything else, no room in her mind for thoughts that weren't tainted by that fear.

She even feared to sleep. A part of her longed for the oblivion that it promised but, as she knew all too well, the second she sought its refuge, the nightmares would take control.

More than anything, it horrified her to think of what she might do in their power. In that place of perfect weakness she might try to climb into Robert's arms in search of his strength. She longed for the strength to be found in his embrace.

It was a strength she could no longer afford to count on.

The uncertainty Roger had fed her with such relish was spawning its dark fruit, she realized, with a nearly hysterical giggle that ended in a final dry retch into the chamberpot.

She closed her eyes for a moment, moving seamlessly from black to black, but even in that darkness, the dawn had to be faced. It took a great act of will to drag herself from off the floor and away from the stench of the chamberpot.

She had no idea how to live in this strange new day. It was entirely alien. Gone was the light and energy that had been slowly penetrating her darkness. She barely had the will to move one foot after the other, but somehow she managed. She moved quietly through the day, and the only satisfaction to be found in it was that she survived.

She even managed to survive the cold formality that had descended between Robert and herself.

She knew that the walls between them were of her own construction, but she lacked the strength to even attempt to tear them down. Not that Robert seemed prepared to scale them either. He retreated behind them, silently waiting like a predator in the shadows.

The evening meal had been a torture of courtesy and politeness. Gone was all laughter and tenderness. In their place stood a cold nothing, and it was a coldness that was infesting the whole Keep, subduing all of the occupants. They all watched their lord and lady warily, puzzled by the sudden rift that had sprung up between the couple overnight. They all went about their duties as if there had been a death.

In a way, there had been. Imogen felt as if she was dying, disappearing a little more with each passing day.

Even the escape of sleep was now denied her. Each night they lay only inches apart and she did nothing to bridge the gap and very quickly the inches became miles. She was alone, just as Roger wanted her to be, and surely he gloated over it with increasing relish in each new message that arrived at the Keep.

The second one arrived not even twenty-four hours after the first, Robert bringing Roger's messenger up to their chamber midmorning. Imogen had been propped up in bed, trying to swallow a few mouthfuls of bread to stop her stomach's strident protests. The little bit she had managed to ingest turned to lead when Robert had ground out bitterly, "This idiot refuses to give me the message even though I have solemnly promised to have it read to you."

"I have my orders, sir," the messenger said stiffly, obviously offended by Robert's belligerent attitude.

This time, the messenger was an older man, and

Imogen wondered dispassionately what had happened to the child of yesterday as she heard Robert's growl of, "Well, get on with it, then!"

"Robert, if you would leave us," she said softly, smiling bitterly as she realized she was now as eager as Roger to banish Robert.

Not that Robert seemed to mind.

He left without even a token protest this time, Imogen realized absently. Roger had been right. The loving husband had been an act. A faultless, unbelievably tempting act. She was almost grateful for that insight, as it helped to numb her. She listened to the messenger's light voice with a growing fatalism:

My dearest first love,

I hope you have enjoyed the small token I sent you. Giving it to you now seems almost like completing the pledge I made to you all those years ago in the tower room at home. Do you remember that tower, Sister, dear?

I had thought to come for my normal visit, but have decided to wait till Robert has had more of a chance to do his job. Is he still suiting you, dearest one? I think of him as my little gift to you. I watch the two of you with much anticipation and I'm sure neither of you will disappoint. It wouldn't be a good idea to disappoint me. Remember, the king stands with me. Lies with me as well, which I find terribly convenient.

I shan't tell you how close to you I am at the moment. I do not want to deprive you of the pleasure you will get out of trying to guess, though here is a small clue: I am as close to you as your last breath.

This time he claimed to be her "loving brother."

She quickly dismissed the messenger, wanting to be alone with her self-disgust. He knew he'd won. His gloating was clear in the anonymous voices of the messengers he was sending her, and she was letting him. There was nothing she could do about it. All of the battles she had won in the last months came to naught if they could be lost so easily.

And there was *nothing* she could do about it.

She had always known it would come to this even as she had tried to deny it, had always known the happiness she had found with Robert was an illusion designed to crush her utterly. It had all been part of Roger's plan. It was this certainty that chilled her to the bone, freezing the scepter of hope that had till then been staying tenaciously alive.

It was like losing her sight to those cold stone steps all over again. Just as Roger had known it would. That damn man knew her too well, Imogen realized as she leaned over the bed to retch the pieces of bread into the chamberpot. He knew her so well that her destruction was a certainty, and he planned to kill her with memories and tantalizing glimpses of what could have been.

She sat bolt upright in bed as she realized with a dawning horror that he had told her that years ago, although she hadn't understood it. He had told her not with words but with stone. The tower. She had always assumed he had built a replica of the stone tower that had claimed her sight as a cold testament to his power over her, as a cold memorial to all of her pain, but it was more than that, she finally understood. It was the key to her ultimate destruction,

Roger's macabre way of letting her know the method of her own demise.

He was always going to win, and Imogen couldn't help but admire his skill even as she felt herself ceasing to exist. He played an amazing game, and played to win.

Always.

_____

Chapter Eleven

Robert swung the axe violently down, barely noticing that the log obediently split in two as he mechanically reached for another. Then another, and another.

At some point he had absentmindedly discarded his tunic and the sweat ran down his exposed torso, glistening along the ridges of muscles on his abdomen. A dark lock of hair tried to fall over his face, but sweat held it in place at least for a moment, until he impatiently swept it back, then he hefted the axe over his head once more.

He barely noticed the heat of the midday sun beating down on his exposed head, concentrating instead on each muscle as it stretched and shifted to do the repetitive work, relentlessly seeking oblivion in physical labor. Perhaps, if he worked his body till it was exhausted, he could achieve a state of numb bliss.

It wasn't working, he admitted grimly to himself as he brought the axe down. His mind refused to be silenced, ruthlessly following the

well-trod circles of fear and anger, just as it had
been doing ever since the arrival of Roger's first
message. With each note Imogen received, the
clamoring inside him grew louder.

He watched helplessly while she seemed to fade a
little more each time. He couldn't reach her. No
matter what he did or said, the essence of her had
somehow slipped through his fingers. She had disappeared into her nightmares where he couldn't reach
her, and it frightened the hell out of him. He had
never felt so impotent, so unsure of what to do, and
he hated it. He seemed to be sitting idly by while his
whole world fell apart silently around him, but there
was nothing he could do to stop the decay. That
bitter knowledge invoked in him an unholy desire to
break things. Lots of very large, human-sized things.

The axe sailed through the air and found its
target easily. Lifting the blade quickly he settled a
new log on the block and with a fluid movement
brought the axe down again, but the violence of
metal slicing through wood was nowhere near
enough to appease the rage that roiled in him. He
had only to think of the hollow, brittle shell that
surrounded Imogen, and once more he felt the
battle rage fill his every particle.

He ground his teeth as visions of the farce that had
been the last month filled his mind like taunting
shades. He was slowly sinking in a leaden sea of
politeness, damn it. Imogen treated him absentmindedly, as if he was some kind of half-remembered acquaintance. Really, she did it so well that
even Robert was sometimes hard-pressed to recall
that they were husband and wife, friends and lovers.

Robert deliberately brought the axe down harder, enjoying the pain that shot through his arm as beguiling memories taunted him, memories of what had very nearly been his. Memories of Imogen as she had almost become.

Almost.

Gone was the glorious woman he had watched learning to embrace the world. In her place existed a mere shadow, barely able to sustain enough life to smile. It was an endless torture. Not only did he have to watch her spirit dying before his eyes, but he also had to stand by as each day her body became a little frailer, faded that little bit more.

Sometimes, Robert wasn't sure which frightened him the most, although he suspected it would be the slow suicide that would be his ultimate enemy. If she willed herself out of existence, he would lose her forever.

She had always been an ethereal being, but now her physical fragility had become a macabre effigy with an eerie appearance of life in death. Her pale skin had taken on a bruised translucency, her eyes dull, lifeless nothings rimmed by gray circles. In bed at night he didn't dare touch her, frightened that she might just shatter in his arms.

Or, worse still, pull away from him.

To lie next to her and not be able to touch her was a pain beyond pain. He longed with every fiber of his being to pull her close, longed to hold her against his heart again, but her icy withdrawal frustrated all such longings. It left him restless. He prowled around the Keep more like a caged animal than a man. He was beginning to notice the wary glances from his men. They were treating him like he was a wild beast, and a wounded one at that.

He grinned bitterly at the description. It was disturbingly accurate. He *felt* like a wounded beast deprived of its mate, and that primitive part of him would have liked nothing more than to howl his pain to the endless skies.

He could only hope that his men would understand and could forgive him this display of human weakness.

Of course they understood, he thought with a wry twist of humor. Most of them were feeling something very similar themselves. He had already noticed the worried concern that appeared in their eyes as they too watched Imogen's transformation into a lifeless mockery of what she had been.

And they had every right to be worried, Robert thought darkly as he moved yet another block into place. Hell, Robert was so filled with fears and torments that he thought he would explode, but at least he could find some small consolation in the fact that he knew who was to blame. His enemy had a name: Roger.

That alone wasn't enough. Robert had long since stopped trying to intercept the bastard's messages. Imogen's cold demand to hear each new note alone stilled his hand. So instead, he was forced to stand aside and wait to find out just how much collateral damage had been inflicted with each one.

The axe whistled through the air and landed with a satisfying crack.

He was seriously considering slaughtering the next of Roger's toads who dared to darken his doorstep.

He was only barely managing to hold off doing just that by the merest thread of sanity. Instinct might demand that he protect the woman he loved, but logically he knew the messengers were not his real enemy.

Sadly, Roger was no fool. He stayed comfortably out of reach, hiding behind the king. The cunning little rodent knew that there he was safe from Robert's anger and could continue to play this little game with complete impunity. There was just no way to get at the man without bringing the full force of the monarch's anger on his own head.

No, Robert had to wait and see exactly how the game was being played, wait until the prey dared to reveal itself out in the open before he could extract his revenge. It had to happen eventually and hopefully before Imogen was broken entirely. When it did, Robert would remove every last trace of the man from the face of the Earth.

All threats to Imogen had to be annihilated utterly and this sick little game ended absolutely.

He rolled his eyes in disgust when he realized that they had got him doing it now, calling this abomination between brother and sister a game, when it was nothing of the kind. Games didn't take live hostages, didn't have body counts, didn't leave behind victims. That was war, a deadly war that Imogen was losing and there was nothing he could do about it.

His hands were tied till Imogen trusted him enough to tell him what the hell was actually going on here.

Robert lifted the axe high and brought it down with all the force at his disposal.

"You do realize, of course, that you have a veritable army of people whose job it is to chop your wood?" Gareth asked lightly enough.

But Robert's teeth were bared as he lifted his head. His eyes narrowed as he caught sight of the man leaning casually against a wall.

"What do you want?" Robert spat out tersely.

"Tsk, tsk, tsk. Those are not the words of a happy leader," Gareth murmured, levering himself off the wall and ambling over to the woodpile. "And need I ask whose head you envision as you abuse those poor, innocent logs?"

Robert's smile was almost feral. "They're messengers. Each and every bloody one is some liveried bastard's head." He brought the axe down again, imagining that instead of wood, the cutting edge was burying itself into flesh, sinew and bone.

Gareth's brow shot up. "Well, you had better not mention that to the bandy-legged man who is uncomfortably standing near the main fire as we speak. The poor man is of that unpopular profession and might lay an egg if he had a glimpse of your—uh, wood-cutting frenzy."

Robert groaned as he leaned wearily on the axe handle. "Good God, won't that man ever run out of parchment? That would make it four in five days." Robert shoved his hair out of his eyes again, feeling heartsick at the thought of losing yet another piece of Imogen. "Have you sent for Imogen yet?" he asked quietly.

"No, can't say I have," Gareth said nonchalantly, reaching up a finger to scratch his roughened cheek. "It wouldn't be the sensible thing to do at all, especially when you consider that the messenger isn't for her."

"It's not?" Robert asked blankly.

"Nope."

Robert waited a moment before grinding out in exasperation, "Well then, who the hell is it for?"

"Why, just for novelty value, the messenger is actually for the master of the Keep, not our little mistress."

"Well, why didn't you just say so?" Robert asked without heat, too busy absorbing the relief that washed through him. Strange, but it almost felt like a reprieve. He buried the axe blade in the cutting block and grabbed his tunic off the pile of logs where it had landed.

"Any idea where this messenger comes from?"

Gareth's smile was devilishly amused and Robert almost groaned, knowing from long experience that could mean only bad things. Gareth's humor was always at its best when it was at someone else's expense.

"Well," Gareth drew out, "judging by the livery and our man's general air of pomposity, I'd have to most certainly say that this one comes straight from the king himself."

Robert stood still midstride. "You're kidding!"

Gareth shook his head, his smile only growing.

"Well, what the hell could he want?"

Gareth leaned closer and whispered, "Well, I thought you might ask me that, so I asked him, and he said that our beloved monarch has been so lonely without you, he has decided to recall you to court."

Robert stared openmouthed for a second, hoping

against hope that this was one of Gareth's perverse jokes, but it wasn't.

"Shit!" he said succinctly.

"So when do you leave?" Imogen asked politely.

"Early tomorrow morning," Robert said stiffly, but he couldn't seem to stop himself from drinking in the sight of her even as he mouthed mindless pleasantries. "We will have to travel hard if we're to be back before planting, and I certainly intend to spend as little time as possible on this folly."

She smiled and nodded, but her expression remained blank. It was like she had already dismissed him from her presence and from her mind.

His hands clenched at his sides. She was so close, yet she might as well have been one hundred leagues from here for all the good it did him. He could no more touch her than he could the moon. He watched the early spring breeze ruffle her hair as she stood by the window, her hands held tightly together, her spine resolutely straight. His eyes saw her serenity, her apparent regal acceptance, but that wasn't what his heart knew to be true.

In his heart he heard her soul's endless screams of pain. He had only to look at her to know that for all her apparent strength and resolve, she was slowly being crushed by a great weight. It chilled him to the core that she might be so easily destroyed. In all his life he had never seen anything that frightened him more than Imogen's living death.

It hurt him just to look at her, hurt to see her passiveness in the face of her own destruction. It hurt so much that it angered him. He wanted to slap her, shake her, kiss her or perhaps all three at once—anything that might bring her back to life, back to him.

His hands remained by his sides.

She sat bathed in sunlight and it harshly illuminated the suffering that had started to dig its way into her face. Her eyes were sunken in the sharp bones of her face, her once gently rounded cheeks were harsh angles that stretched her skin till her cheekbones were angry slashes across the sides of her face. The black-violet shadows under her eyes were the only color. Even the rose-pink of her lips seemed now to be just another shade of white.

It was a face that haunted him even as he searched his brain for some way to draw her away from the demons that were eating her alive; draw her toward him.

But he had no answers. He had to look away from her before he could find his voice.

"You're not eating enough," he said gruffly. "That dress looks like its hanging on a corpse, not a woman." He couldn't help but smile a little grimly at the lie. She had lost weight and it worried the hell out of him, but not for one moment did he think she looked like a corpse. She would always be the most beautiful woman Robert had ever seen.

She shrugged her shoulders carelessly. "I've not been hungry."

"I don't care if you are hungry or not," he roared, his anger igniting in a second, a grim reminder of just how close to the end of his tether he really was. "You will eat properly or I'll tie you down and force-feed you myself."

"How very husbandly you sound. Roger would be pleased," she said sneeringly, her smile darkly amused.

And that was the ultimate problem, Robert realized with sudden certainty. She thought he was Roger's man and nothing he said or did would penetrate the shell she had built around herself while that viper whispered his poison into her ear. He began pacing, his hands clenched helplessly by his sides.

"I don't just *sound* husbandly, Imogen, I am your husband, your lord and master, if you prefer. As such, I want you to eat more than the sparrow portions you have been subsisting on. By my return, I will expect you to have put on all the weight you've lost. No, I want you to have put on more than that. I want you to be so fat that I will never have to worry again. Am I being understood?" His anger reverberated around the room.

"Of course," she said silkily and Robert knew she hadn't heard a word. She was set on going to hell her own way and not a thing he said would make one jot of difference to her.

He paced back to the fire.

"I'm only taking Matthew with me," he said tersely. "Gareth will be left in charge of the garrison."

She nodded her head mutely and they lapsed into an uncomfortable silence. He longed to say something. Or perhaps he just longed to hear her say something voluntarily to him or even longed for her to come over to him and let him hold her in his arms for a moment.

But longings were not reality, Robert thought

hollowly, as she serenely dismissed him with a quiet, emotionless, "God speed, Sir Robert."

He should have been used to it by now; her rejections should have long since lost their sting. They hadn't. A fresh flash of pain struck him deep in his gut as she cast him aside once more. He bowed formally over her hand. Her skin felt icy cold under his warm lips, her face carefully blank when he looked into it, drinking in this last sight of her before turning and leaving the room.

Once the door closed behind him he couldn't stop the fury that built up inside him like an inferno, demanding an outlet. A volley of swearing filled the hall.

"I'll take that to mean that you two haven't sorted anything out," Mary said dryly as she walked toward him.

"There is nothing to sort out, apparently," he snorted derisively, knowing it for the lie it was. "I can't remember a time when I have ever been subjected to such politeness before."

Mary's brow dropped in concern. "Aye, but there is a wealth of pain behind that politeness." She shook her head. "I'm worried sick, I don't mind telling you. I have never seen her like this, never this bad. Oh, he's hurt her before, but this time"— she shrugged her shoulders helplessly—"it's like he's destroying her."

Before Robert could say anything, she poked a finger into the center of his chest. "And what I would like to know is: what are you going to do about it?"

Robert gave a shout of bitter laughter. "Mary, you seem to have mistaken me for an active player in this farce. I'm just a very bewildered member of the audience, like you." He shook his head and rubbed a tired hand over his eyes, trying not to notice its slight tremble. "Quite frankly, Mary, I don't have a clue as to what I should be doing."

"Neither do I, but I'd like to suggest that running to London ain't the answer," she said stoutly.

"I've been summoned, and there is sod all I can do about it," he muttered, feeling strangely defensive in the face of Mary's righteous indignation. He would never understand how this one old woman always managed to put him on the defensive.

"Well, take her with you, then. I don't want her left alone, not while she is this fragile."

"Hardly alone," he said wearily, but Mary just ignored him.

"She was alone in this Keep for years," she said earnestly, "regardless of how many people lived here. She was like a sleepwalker. Till you came along. *You* made her alive. She was starting to return to what she had been before she lost her sight and it did my old heart good to see it. If you did it once, surely you can do it again, if only you would try." She grabbed his arm. "Please try."

He looked down at the old woman's determined face as he gently extracted his arm from her tight grip. "There is nothing I can do. Imogen won't let me help, and I have been summoned to London by the **king**. I must go." He awkwardly put a hand on her shoulder, trying to comfort her. "Perhaps it is for the best. Perhaps the distance will help Imogen deal with all that she needs to deal with," he finished lamely. The platitudes lacked conviction even to his own ears.

She shook herself free from his hand and glared up at him accusingly. "I don't like it, and no good will come of it," she muttered darkly, then, with her head held high, walked into Imogen's chamber.

Robert felt his own shoulders slump wearily.

"I don't like it either, Mary," he whispered into the darkened hall. "I don't like any of it."

"Can you think of anything I might have left out?" Robert asked as he looked to where Gareth lounged in a comfortable sprawl on the chair by the hearth.

"Well, you did fail to mention anything about exactly how many logs should be on the main hearth at five in the afternoon, but other than that small oversight, I must say I found you disturbingly thorough." He gave Robert a lopsided smile. "I shouldn't have to think for the entire time you are gone."

Robert grimaced. "A bit over the top?"

"Only a shade. Don't worry, it is only an old Saxon Keep, it will be fine. You have left me to look after entire armies with fewer orders so I'm sure that I can manage one small Keep with such a wealth of information at my disposal."

Robert stood and walked to the window. "I never felt quite like this about any of my armies." He clenched his fist and thumped it down on the ledge. "Damn. I don't like this, Gareth. It just doesn't feel right."

He looked out the window at the land that had come to mean so much to him, and couldn't shake the terror that had lodged itself inside of him, that somehow he was in very real danger of losing it all. It wasn't rational, but everything suddenly seemed under threat.

He took a deep breath. He had to concentrate on countering any threat, not on his fear of losing everything.

"You think that the summons is part of some kind of plot against you?" Gareth's voice might have sounded reasonable and calm, but Robert could well hear the thread of steel that ran through it.

Robert shook his head. He turned and leaned his hip against the window ledge, crossing his arms over his broad chest. "Who knows? It might just be as entirely innocent as it sounds. Perhaps the king is preparing for more wars and simply wants to hire me and my men as mercenaries."

"Are we still for hire?"

Robert shook his head decisively. "The only battles I'm going to fight from now on are going to be for the express purpose of protecting what is mine, not to help our greedy little monarch grab more of this island."

Gareth smiled faintly. "You make him sound like a fat little boy chasing after sweetmeats."

"Well, you must admit there are certain similarities."

"An impressive boy."

"The sweetmeats aren't exactly insubstantial either. Any child would have to be a little impressive to want them."

They both smiled for a moment, but their smiles faded quickly as the ever-present worry returned.

"And if the summons isn't just an innocent request for a pet warrior?" Gareth asked quietly.

"Then there is going to be some serious trouble," Robert said grimly, visions of looming disaster crowding his head. "That's why I have left you in charge."

Gareth lifted an eyebrow sardonically. "Well, I suppose I am more than amply qualified to deal with trouble. After all, I've spent a good deal of my life making it, so spotting it shouldn't be hard. Your home will be safe with me."

"That isn't what concerns me now. Everything I've said thus far boils down to one solitary task, and if you don't succeed at that task, then I'll kill you, even if I have to come back from the grave to do so."

"I almost believe you would too," Gareth said with a dry chuckle, "and that can only mean one thing: Imogen."

Robert's jaw tightened painfully. "She is all that matters to you from now on. You protect her, you keep her safe, and to hell with the rest of the world. Is that understood? I don't care what you have to do, or how many heads you have to break to do it, just see that it's done."

Gareth let out a low whistle of admiration. "You really do love her, don't you?" he forced himself to say, deliberately ignoring the pain he had no right to be feeling about another man's wife.

For a second, Robert almost forgot to breathe. He had never heard it said out loud before and it seemed strange to hear it now. Strange, but so right at the same time.

He had to clear his voice before he could speak.
"Yes, I love her. I love her more than life itself."

Gareth looked down at his hands. "If it's any consolation, I think she also loves you."

"Then keep her alive so that she can tell me herself someday," Robert said harshly, his emotions too
raw to say anything more.

"Nothing would give me greater pleasure." A
sudden wolfish grin flashed over his face. "I might
even make her life a little more comfortable by disposing of a messenger or two. There seem to be
enough of them about at the moment that one or
two less of the little buggers will hardly be missed."

Robert smiled faintly. "Be my guest."

"I'm going to enjoy myself." He paused for a
moment, a thoughtful look on his face. "Actually,
while you're in London you could stop the messengers entirely by destroying the source. After all,
Roger Colebrook is a creature of the court. He's
bound to be slithering around our monarch somewhere if you look close enough."

"I could put his head on a pike to give her as a
present," Robert said wistfully.

"Sounds perfect. The castle you intend to build
will need the odd head on its walls as decoration."

"Tempting, isn't it?" Robert's eyes gleamed with
the possibilities.

"Well then, go and be tempted, my friend."

The morning air was brisk and the sun not quite
risen when Robert walked Dagger into the courtyard. Despite the earliness of the hour, the Keep

was already starting to wake, the sounds of life filling the air. Matthew waited for him in the courtyard, mounted a magnificent dappled warhorse. He sat slumped in his saddle, a look of belligerent resignation clear on his face.

Robert couldn't help but feel the familiarity of the scene. Things seemed to have come full circle, here he was leaving the Keep and Matthew was in almost exactly the same spirit as he had been five months ago.

Robert shook his head. Five months didn't sound right, somehow. It seemed at once like forever but also the merest blinking of an eye. Still there was no denying that in five months, everything had changed. He had traveled north with dreams of mortar and land, but he was leaving it without his heart. He was now more owned than owning.

Home. It was hard to remember how simple his ideas of home had been. To him it had meant only an abode, a roof to shelter under, but now the word was a rich tapestry woven with all the joy, fear, helplessness, protectiveness and desire that had come into his days.

His entire being was now entwined inexorably with the existence of this simple little Keep. He couldn't explain it, but over the past months he had become a part of all the souls that found their shelter within his walls, especially with the fragile lady who unknowingly held his heart in her hands.

Not wanting to waste his last night at the Keep on sleep, he had lain in bed and watched over Imogen as she slept, but he hadn't been content merely to look. No, for the first time in weeks, he allowed himself to reach out a hand and touch her. He had gently traced the sweep of her hair, ran a finger down her delicate nose, rubbed his thumb over the swell of her bottom lip. He had touched her so lightly that he had only just been able to feel her. It hadn't been enough. His body had burned to do more, but he had been loath to disturb her. She had finally, after weeks of nightmare-filled nights, managed to find sleep and he wouldn't wake her from that temporary escape from life.

Though perhaps she hadn't slept that deeply.

He had seen the solitary tear glittering in the firelight as it slipped from under her lashes, watched as it slid silently over her temple and lost itself in her hair. He had wiped its path gently away, hating to think that she cried even in her dreams. The sense of helplessness seemed to have lodged itself permanently in his chest, and he couldn't say that he was developing much of a taste for the emotion. It was also more than a little frightening to realize he would have been quite content to spend a lifetime just watching over her.

It had been hard to find the willpower to leave, but somehow he had.

He had leaned over and placed a chaste kiss on her forehead, whispering, "Be safe, Little One, and know that I love you."

While the rightness of his love made him whole, it also left him exposed and vulnerable. He had risen swiftly from the bed and quietly got dressed. He had denied himself the luxury of looking back, knowing that if he did he might never be able to find the will to leave his home and his love.

"Well, are you going to actually get on that horse, or are you going to waste the whole day mooning about?" Matthew asked testily, breaking into Robert's brooding thoughts.

"I thought age was supposed to make a man more patient," Robert said with a smile as he ran a hand along Dagger's mane.

"Hardly. There is a very limited time left to me and I have absolutely no desire to spend it frivolously watching you stare into space."

Robert laughed as he mounted. "Well, come on, then," he said, and spurred his horse forward and out of the courtyard, not once looking back.

There was no need, when he carried it all in the space where his heart had once been.

Chapter Twelve

Robert prowled around the room, the frustration that boiled restlessly inside him demanding a physical outlet. A week spent as the king's "guests" and he felt like he had been static for an eternity. His muscles now demanded work, even if that work was only this pointless wondering.

As he paced, his mind seethed with an uncomfortable mixture of memories and questions.

No, that wasn't honest. It wasn't questions, plural, that haunted him but a single, solitary question. All of his curiosity could be rendered down to one simple, pure droplet of puzzlement: exactly what the hell was going on here?

Robert strode from one side of the room to the other, then back again as his bewilderment went round and round his mind with a dizzying speed, but still he could find no answer. Not that it should have surprised him. Nothing was as it should be.

In the time it had taken the king's summons to reach Robert and for him to make his way down South, the king had decided to remove the court

from Westminster Palace. Apparently, on whatever
idle whim guided him, William had felt an overwhelming urge to inspect one of the many
fortresses he was having built along the South Eastern coastline above the line of London.

Robert's jaw clenched in frustration. God save
him from the whims of monarchs! He had wasted
valuable time in the pointless trip to Westminster,
and had then been forced to make his way through
the ever-busy eastern roads, chasing after the court.

When finally he had managed to track down the
wandering king, his sole ambition had been to get
it all over with and start for home at the earliest
opportunity.

As distasteful as it was, Robert had even been prepared to play the courtier if it would hasten the
process. After all, with the correct amount of sub-
servient drivel administered, even the most recalci-
trant monarch could be rendered pliable.

Then Robert could have got to his very important point.

He knew he would enjoy telling William firmly
and succinctly that he was no longer for hire. He
was retiring from the life of a mercenary and the
king would have to find himself some other fool to
come running when he beckoned. If William
didn't kill him after that outburst, Robert thought
wryly, well then, he could start planning the rest of
his life.

The first thing he would do with his retirement
would be to start looking under some of England's
most aristocratic rocks to find out exactly where Roger
was skulking these days. Beyond finding the little scum,
Robert hadn't quite decided what precisely he would

do to him, but whatever he chose, it would be deliciously and irrefutably permanent. With that pleasurable little job done, he could return home and, if all went according to his schemes, he would never again leave it.

That had been the plan, simple yet effective. Just the way Robert liked things, but everything remained strangely elusive.

Elusive be damned, he hadn't yet even managed to clear the first hurdle. Thus far he had been denied even an audience with the monarch. With a truly exasperating politeness, Matthew and he had found themselves imprisoned in two small rooms, ostensibly awaiting a royal audience. Oh, they had placed the most discreet of guards on their door and didn't once mention the word arrest, but that was just a small political technicality and everyone knew it.

So he was forced to wait.

Day after long day passed while he awaited an audience that he had never wanted in the first place. Really, it was enough to cleave a man permanently from his sanity, Robert thought with a grim smile. God knows, he could feel his own slipping away a little bit more with each successive day of enforced inertia.

Inertia was a grim punishment for a man used to action. It was leaving him with far too much time for thinking. The more he was left to his thoughts, the more he dwelled on how everything had got so messed up, and it wasn't a very edifying exercise. No matter how he tried to sort it all out into some semblance of rational order, it came back to one certainty that haunted him: he should have stopped this torture before it got started. He should have stopped Roger from getting his talons into Imogen's soul.

If he had managed to do that one small task, then perhaps he could have prevented his world from collapsing around him.

He should have simply run all of the messengers through with the point of his sword and burnt their parchments into so many pounds of ashes. Granted, it wouldn't have been very friendly, but at least it would have left Imogen untouched by the soul disease that was even now eating its way through her.

Or he could have taken Imogen away from this cloudy island and let her find some peace in the sun of southern France far away from her brother.

Robert gritted his teeth and closed his eyes in self-disgust. Should haves and could haves all boiled down to one sickeningly solid reality: he should have done everything in his power to save her from the nightmare world that was slowly crushing her into nothing, and the only way he could have done that was by making her tell him exactly what the hell was going on between her and her brother. Then he could have put an immediate stop to it, bloodily, if that was what the situation required.

Strange, but from this distance it all became clear. It really had been as simple as that. But something had stilled his hand.

No, not a nameless something, he thought with a disgusted growl, but pride. It was his own cocky, foolish pride that had stopped him doing what needed to be done. What else but pride would demand that he wait for her to come to him? It was

his pride that had desperately wanted her to admit
that she needed him as much as he needed her.

Now, all his pride was gone, burnt away by the
shame that almost overwhelmed him. What did his
pride matter in the face of love?

A love he had never declared when she could
hear.

And that was another thing that he should have
done. He should have gone to her on bended knee
and told her that he loved her. He should have
taken her into his arms and held her tightly and
never let her go. Damn, but he didn't like being so
far away from her, not when he had left so much
unsaid between them. It ate at him.

What if she wasn't safe? What if she had stopped
eating entirely and had even now faded away? What
if she was being stalked by her nightmares with no
one to hold her in the darkness?

He paced to the window and stared into the sunshine without seeing. He was being tortured by
what ifs, he thought with a derisive snort, and
began pacing once again.

"If you don't stop that, I may be forced to kill
you," Matthew said amiably, the sleepy expression
on his face at odds with the violence of his words.
He lay on his side in the cot that had been pushed
hastily against one wall to accommodate the old
man in Robert's makeshift prison. A half-drunk jug
of wine sat on the floor beside him, the major con-
tributor to Matthew's amiability.

Robert tried to quiet the stalking demons that
possessed him, sitting down on the floor and
leaning his head back against the wall, but his feet
still tapped on the stones and his fists rhythmi-

cally clenched and unclenched in time with the churning of his thoughts.

Matthew looked over to him balefully. And that was Robert trying to be restful, Matthew thought with a silent sigh. Still, it was an improvement on the incessant pacing Robert had been doing for the past week, so Matthew just closed his eyes. He couldn't help grimacing as he felt the motion sickness—caused by the cheap liquor and Robert's prowling—roll through him.

He opened his eyes quickly and lifted the jug to his lips once more. "To the king and all who sail in him," Matthew slurred, and tilted the jug in a mock salute.

"You're drinking too much, Old Man."

"Of course I am," Matthew agreed with a lip-smacking slurp. "It's not as if there is anything more pressing that I should be doing. I might as well enjoy the king's hospitality to its full extent." He looked balefully at the ruby liquor. "Although, I do think that the king could afford to at least buy some wine that doesn't taste like vinegar."

"Not that taste would stop you," Robert murmured and sighed with resignation as Matthew's Adam's apple bobbed with each long swallow, but still he couldn't help but envy the old man's ability to lose himself in an alcoholic fog. God knows, he would have tried it himself if he had even half believed for a moment that Imogen's pain wouldn't follow him into his stupor. At least sober he was in some kind of control. Drunk, he might just disgrace himself with tears.

Robert shifted uncomfortably and started to get

up to resume his pacing, but quickly sat back down when he caught sight of Matthew's raised eyebrow.

Silence descended but Robert's mind roared with his impatience and guilt even though he knew that, for now, there was nothing that could be done. He took a deep breath, trying to calm the swelter of emotions. He needed to forget, needed to numb his mind. He closed his eyes and willed himself to feel no pain. He might have actually slept for a moment, because the bang of the solid wooden door hitting the wall brought him jarringly back to consciousness.

He stood quickly, instinctively wary of any change to their monotonous routine. Matthew, however, didn't seem to be all that interested. His drunken face reflected only the most mild curiosity.

Robert didn't recognize the guard who couldn't quite look him in the eye.

"The king commands Sir Robert's presence in the throne room," the man said formally, and Robert narrowed his eyes. This wasn't an invitation to dine with a benevolent monarch. This was serious.

"Finally," Robert murmured steadily, but a cold chill settled low in his spine, warning him of impending danger. He reached for the sword that rested against the wall.

"Sorry, Sir Robert, but I've been told to make sure you are unarmed before you go into His Majesty's presence."

Robert's hand hovered over the hilt for a second, then dropped to his side.

He was reluctant to leave it behind when every nerve in his body screamed that danger was threateningly close. He might as well be naked as leave the relative safety of these rooms unarmed, he thought grimly. The presence of his sword hanging low on his left hip would at least give him a chance, but apparently it was a chance that was being denied him.

He had never before been unarmed in the king's presence.

Strange. William had never been squeamish about weapons before and those with any sense went armed when close to a throne. After all, absolute power produced a lethal violence that was equaled only by the violence produced by extreme poverty.

Casting a rueful glance at his sword, he turned to the guard and shrugged his shoulders nonchalantly. "Well, in that case, I'm ready."

The other man nodded and, with a formal "Follow me," left the room. Robert turned quickly to Matthew, painfully aware that his time had run out.

"Get out of here if you can, Old Man. Get to Shadowsend and tell Gareth to move Imogen out of the country as fast as he can. There should be enough gold in my strongbox to buy you all a new life somewhere else. Tell him to also pay the men and then they can scatter."

Despite all of the alcohol in his system, the older man's eyes were clear as he nodded his head once. Robert longed to say more, but the guard waited with visible impatience in the hallway just out of earshot. Robert gave Matthew a crooked smile and followed the guard from the room.

"Give the king my love," Matthew called after him,

"and tell him not to be so cheap next time. He could at least buy some decent wine for his prisoners."

Robert's smile broadened and he just shrugged at the clearly scandalized guard as he casually followed him along the halls. His smile slowly faded as the strange quiet of the castle penetrated his consciousness.

Things had certainly changed in the six months Robert had been absent from the court. Gone was the easy air of debauchery, replaced by the heavier atmosphere of suspicion and fear. As they passed down passageways the silence became oppressive. Voices that had once risen in dissipation and revelry seemed to have been unnaturally stilled. It was disconcertingly like the hush of a tomb.

A well-protected tomb, at that.

The guards appeared to have trebled in number. They stood guarding who knew what at regular intervals along the halls. Robert suspected that more likely than not it was their presence that had suppressed the normal babble of the court. It had even infected the servants. They scurried about in a terrified muteness, never once letting their eyes rise higher than the floor.

Robert's eyes narrowed speculatively. William's debauched, merry court seemed to have died and on its corpse was growing a fungus that reeked of fear.

They passed clusters of noblemen whispering in corners. Every now and then Robert recognized a face of someone who had been if not a friend, then at least an ally, but whenever he tried to meet their eyes they slid their gaze away quickly, as if he no longer existed.

Robert didn't take it personally. Judging by the

level of fear that was trapped in the stone walls of the castle, they were probably wishing themselves out of existence at the same time.

It didn't take a genius to realize that there was something wrong here, very wrong.

Robert felt himself preparing for battle as they waited outside the throne room, to be announced to a monarch who had always waved aside such formalities. The apprehension lodged like a solid block of ice in his stomach as the realization dawned that he would be very lucky to ever leave this place alive.

Robert closed his eyes and took a steadying breath. Unbidden an image of Shadowsend filled his mind, its dark rooms and unsteady stairs suddenly a comfort. Thoughts of the Keep were swiftly followed by thoughts of its lady. In his imaginings she smiled at him and, strangely, the tightening in his gut started to ease.

Slowly he opened his eyes and straightened his shoulders. He was ready. William might be a dangerous opponent but, for the first time in his life, Robert had something worth fighting for.

He walked with quiet confidence into the throne room behind the guard, his gaze sweeping over the scene carefully, all the while assessing the situation.

He was startled to see the blond, almost feminine beauty of Roger Colebrook lounging comfortably against the throne and then for a moment Robert was almost blinded by the cold rage that boiled to life at the sight of the other man's triumphant smile. The urge to go and forcibly remove that smile was almost overpowering. For an instant Robert's mind came alive with images of the kinds

of death that he had witnessed, all the deaths he
himself had inflicted, but now, every half forgotten
face was replaced with Roger's.

There were really so many very messy ways that
man could die but none of them quite messy
enough to suit Robert's mood. He couldn't help
but feel that Imogen's life of pain deserved a spec-
tacular justice, and he itched to give her just that.

It was an enormous act of will that kept him from
striding over to the man and strangling him with
his bare hands and he mastered his dark desire
only by reminding himself that it would be a futile
attempt. The guards protecting the king protected
Roger by default. They would stop him long before
justice had extracted its due.

Robert gritted his teeth in frustration and promised himself silently that justice would still happen
soon. Roger couldn't hide behind the king forever
and the second he was alone and unprotected
Robert would make him pay for every drop of pain
he had brought into Imogen's life.

Robert dragged his gaze away from Roger; he
had to if he was to stay in control. He couldn't
afford to let the murderous rage consume him. He
shifted his concentration to the man who sat
slouched on the throne and was taken aback by the
changes that six months had brought about in
William. If it hadn't been for the red flame of his
hair and face Robert doubted he would have recognized him at all.

William's eyes, once expressive and, often as not,
angry, were now empty and cold, sunken into a
face pulled taut by unseen stresses and marked by

new lines. The man appeared to have aged twenty years in mere months.

Even more surprising was the way that he visibly carried arms and even wore a heavy hauberk, despite the fact that he had an ample supply of guards to protect him. William looked like a man in mortal fear for his own life and Robert didn't think he was going to enjoy finding out exactly what this had to do with him. He fell on one knee slowly and lowered his head. "Your Majesty," he said formally, and awaited permission to arise.

It was a permission that didn't come. Keeping his head down, he heard William get heavily to his feet.

"So the bastard returns at last," the king said slowly, coming to stand directly in front of him.

"As Your Majesty ordered," Robert said quietly.

William gave a hollow shout of laughter. "Oh, Robert, you almost sound like a loyal subject when you talk like that." He paused before adding tightly, "Almost."

Robert didn't flinch when he felt the cold edge of a sword touch the back of his neck, but the chill spread through him.

"You see, Robert, you sound loyal only to those not privy to your machinations and, unfortunately for you, I am all too aware of what you've been getting up to." Robert felt the sword blade move slowly over his skin, and the sharp flair of pain as it drew blood. It trickled slowly down his neck and was absorbed into the weave of his tunic.

"My loyalty is not feigned," Robert said with a deliberately bored voice. "I have no plans other than to live in peace and quiet on the lands you have graciously given me."

The blade was suddenly gone and Robert quickly lifted his head. There was no point in fawning any longer, he decided, refusing to grimace at the pain the gesture cost him. William leaned on the hilt of the sword with the point pressed into the rushes. His eyes glared narrowly out of his red face as he shook his head wearily.

"Now, now, Robert, I don't like being lied to. Your plans have come to naught because I now know everything. I know all about your bargaining with my brother, Henry. I know you plan to assassinate me so that he can claim my throne as his own. I know it all, and it is all treason!" He lifted the sword and slammed it hard against the stonework of the throne steps. Sparks flew and the sound of it rang out around the room like a bell.

Robert didn't flinch and his level gaze served only to infuriate William further. He raised the point of the sword up to the center of Robert's unprotected chest. "The only thing I need from you," he ground out, "is the name of every other traitorous cur on this accursed isle so that I may then destroy them at my leisure. If you tell me, I might even relent and let you die quickly."

And that was that, Robert thought with a detachment that didn't surprise him. This was how his life would end, not on the battlefield but in the deadly viper pit of court intrigue. He was found guilty of crimes he hadn't committed and had now only to await a certain death. Well, that being the case, he would be dammed if he'd kneel subserviently a moment longer.

He rose gracefully to his feet, noticing with amusement that William took a hasty step back, his eyes darting around the room. Robert shook his head. It had actually come to this. William was truly afraid of an unarmed man. If it wasn't so bloody sad, Robert might have laughed aloud at the absurdity of it.

"Sir Robert, I didn't give you permission to stand," William yelped, his red face blossoming into an alarming shade of purple.

"I didn't ask for your permission. I find I can no longer kneel before a man who thinks me capable of treachery. Besides," Robert added dryly, "I don't believe you have given me permission to assassinate you either, but I'm believed capable of that."

William quickly retreated to the relative safety of the dais, then stood up stiffly, trying to regain some of his dignity. "You have just proved by your own actions that you do not respect my throne."

"The throne's fine," Robert mocked softly, "it's you I'm finding hard to respect at the moment."

William's jaw tightened and Robert felt a small satisfaction at the other man's anger, as he glared and grimly continued with his pronouncement. "Therefore you leave me no choice but to strip you of all your titles and possessions. You will be held prisoner, under sentence of death, at my pleasure."

Robert closed his eyes for a second, surprised by the pain that shot through him. Shadowsend receded into the realms of distant memory. He had been allowed to live a precious dream, but now he must wake to the harsh realities of life.

He had lost everything, yet oddly it felt almost like none of it had been his to lose.

He opened his eyes and gazed narrowly as Roger stepped forward and confidently reached out a hand to touch the king's arm. That Roger lived was the one regret he would take with him to the grave and beyond.

William covered Roger's hand with a beringed one of his own and nodded his head. "Oh, and while you await execution, the running of your estates will revert to my beloved Roger, as will the guardianship of your wife."

The blood flew from Robert's face. "No!" he yelled as he took a hasty step forward, not caring that the guards unsheathed their swords.

William raised a brow. "I don't see any other possible solution. You should be grateful. Most traitors' wives are not treated so well."

"Your Majesty, you can't just hand her over to her brother," Robert said, able to plead for Imogen where he hadn't been able to do so for himself. "She is of an age and the lands were left to her in her own right. Do with me as you will, but give Imogen her freedom. It is all I ask."

Liar, an insidious voice whispered in his ear. You would also ask for her happiness; you would have her given freedom and light.

But those things were not even the king's to give.

For the first time in his adult life, Robert found himself praying blindly to a God he had never believed in: God, let me go to my grave knowing that my love is living a life free of fear and pain. Let me know that she is smiling and strong.

The King smirked. "What? Give Lady Deformed freedom from her own brother on the say-so of a traitor? I think not. She will have to be kept under close watch just to make sure that you

haven't polluted her with your treason. Who
better than her own, loyal brother?"

"I wouldn't leave a dog in Roger's protection,"
Robert said through gritted teeth. "Imogen has suffered enough at this . . . this . . . thing's hands. She
deserves better now, goddamn it."

"Such ardent devotion," Roger said with a sly
smile. "Anyone would think you had fallen in love
with Lady Deformed."

"Don't call her that!" Robert roared and
searched his mind frantically for some way to shield
Imogen from these evil men. He stepped toward
the dais without really knowing what he was going
to do, but knowing he would do it well.

His eyes blazed with murder and saw nothing but
the object of his hatred smiling mockingly down at
him. He didn't notice William's frantic call for the
guards to restrain him, Robert's only focus cen-
tered on Roger.

It took five men to stop him stalking toward the
throne, six to bring him back to his knees. He struggled only because they stood between him and his
goal. His mind didn't even register the pain that
flashed through him as a mailed hand slammed into
his jaw. They eventually subdued him, holding his
arms tightly behind his back so that he couldn't
move.

"Remove him to the dungeons." William smiled
tightly and his hand clenched around the hilt of his
sword.

Robert started to struggle with renewed vigor.
"William," he bellowed, ignoring the king's shout
of outrage, "don't be blinded by lust. Roger may be

your lover, but he's only using you in his sick, twisted games. The man's a snake. William—"

One of the guards aimed a blow at his stomach, knocking the wind out of him but he couldn't let it stop him.

"William, set Imogen free. Don't bind her to that sniveling, twisted little bastard. He will hurt her. Don't hurt her anymore, for God's sake . . ." He had never before begged for anything in his life, but for Imogen he was not surprised to find that he had no dignity left.

He never saw the sword hilt that rose and came slamming down onto the back of his head. He barely even felt the pain as unconsciousness claimed his mind.

As the floor seemed to rise to meet him, all his awareness was focused on the fact that he had failed. He was abandoning Imogen to all she feared and he realized, his heart weeping with despair, that there wasn't a thing he could do about it.

He had failed her.

Roger watched with satisfaction as the guards dragged Robert's unconscious body from the throne room.

It really had worked out far better than he could have hoped.

It was clear for all to see that the fool had actually fallen in love with Imogen. It was too perfect! Why, Robert had even been prepared to abandon the dignity he wore so well, to plead with the king on Imogen's behalf. That bespoke love in any language.

And such devotion must surely be returned.

Imogen's heart must have opened wide to let her warrior in, and that left her more vulnerable than she had ever been before. That was all Roger needed.

She was now his.

He had only to tighten the chains a little and he would have her on her knees begging, promising him anything, everything he wanted. All to save her beloved warrior.

Perfect.

She would finally be in his absolute control. She would be humiliated, just as he had been for all those years as his parents' forgotten son. She would be forced to submit to his will. She would obey him, regardless of what she may think, feel or want.

And that was the perfect revenge he had spent long years working toward.

He suddenly felt William's gaze on him and he forced his lurid fantasies to the back of his mind. There would be time enough for him to indulge in them later. Right now, he needed to concentrate on pacifying the man who was central to all of his plans, who guaranteed their success.

He couldn't afford to become overconfidant. A frown briefly marred the perfection of his face as he looked at Robert's retreating form.

His plan would need a little tweaking, it would seem. As satisfying as it was to see Robert brought low by a woman, his extreme level of passionate devotion might prove to be something of a problem. It was that kind of devotion that removed chains and defied kings.

So he would have to die. Soon.

A pity, really. Roger had intended to keep him alive for a while yet. The mere threat of his death dangled in front of Imogen would soon bring the bitch to heel. However, it would seem that alive, Robert might create more problems than he was worth.

No, he would have to go, and that didn't really present a problem, Roger thought with a small, satisfied smile. Imogen was now under his own benevolent guardianship, so her husband's life or death was a formality.

"I told you he was dangerous," Roger murmured as he leaned toward William's side. "The sooner he is dead, the safer you will be. And I want you to be safe." He dropped a teasing kiss on the strong column of William's neck.

William narrowed his eyes thoughtfully, for once entirely unmoved by Roger's seductions.

"There is something not right here," he growled suspiciously.

"The only thing not right is that he lives to threaten you." Roger shuddered dramatically. "I for one won't sleep easy till we are rid of that man. When will you give the order?" Roger didn't bother to hide the gloating tone in his voice.

"After I work out what the hell is actually going on here."

Roger's eyes narrowed irritably. Now wasn't the time for William to start thinking. The last thing Roger needed was for William to actually work out what was going on.

Still, he knew better than to press too obviously, so he just shrugged his shoulder indifferently. "Your decision, I suppose."

William turned and pinned him with a hard look. "My decision always." A thread of steel ran through his voice. "Never forget that I'm your king and your master. Confine your manipulations and games to others. I would be more than a little displeased if I found you taking advantage of my preference for you."

"As if I would," Roger said with an almost-credible wide-eyed look of innocence. Then he deliberately flashed an engaging smile.

"Sometimes I wonder why I put up with you," William grumbled, but drew Roger into his arms nonetheless.

"Because no one can make you feel like I do," Roger murmured huskily and then pressed a passionate kiss on William's lips.

As the kiss deepened and lusts flared in William, Roger's mind detached itself and began coolly considering his situation.

He needed to destroy the least bit of suspicion about his motives for desiring Robert's death. William's compliance was vital if he was going to succeed. He had to succeed. There was no room for failure now.

Imogen was his.

Consciousness returned to Robert all at once. One second he was sinking weightlessly in the painless dark, the next every cell of his being was screaming in pain.

Obviously, the guards had gone about their job enthusiastically, he thought wryly with a sharp, painful intake of breath. He lay as still as possible in the straw that scarcely covered the cold stone and began to rationally calculate the damage, trying to stop himself from passing out again with the pain.

Judging by the fire that engulfed him with every breath, they had fractured a few of his ribs, so they must have kicked him; and the relentless pounding of his head no doubt came from its violent encounter with that sword hilt. The other pains were only minor in comparison. He glanced down at himself, stripped bare but for a cloth to cover his loins, and grimaced at the sight of the bruises and cuts that now decorated his body.

Nothing fatal.

All in all, he supposed he should be grateful that it was only superficial damage. He felt only a little worse than the time he had been run over by a herd of stampeding warhorses, he thought with a dark smile, then winced as the cut on his lip reopened.

He struggled into a sitting position, then, with a deep, steadying breath, tried to stand up. He was quickly forced back to his knees with a thump by the chains on his wrists. The bastards had deliberately shortened them. It was impossible for him to stand to his full height.

He clenched his jaw tightly and waited for the pain to pass.

Brilliant, he thought bitterly, William really was determined to keep him on his knees. He eased his legs out and tried to settle down in the straw. He wrapped his arms tightly around his ribs to hold them still, and then leaned his head back against the cold walls.

He closed his eyes to see if he could find some comfort in sleep, but the taste of failure was still too bitter on his tongue. Despite all his best efforts he had delivered Imogen directly into the hands of her enemy. He allowed himself only a few short minutes to dwell on self-pity, guilt and regret, letting them consume him, then he carefully shook himself free.

It did Imogen no good, and her safety was the only thing he would allow his mind to dwell on. That was all that mattered now.

Matthew might even now be free and heading north to mobilize Gareth and the other knights. Imogen could be safely out of the country before Roger could do her any more harm. Gareth would see to that. He would get her out of this country, hide her away so that she could be safe. He would look after her, would make sure that she was free.

Perhaps he would even marry her. He would, of course, wait politely for her to forget her husband of such a brief time.

Robert gritted his teeth as jealousy consumed him, but he couldn't let that emotion deceive him. He had seen a little of his own love for Imogen burning in the other man's eyes. It made sense that if they were brought together, then love would have to declare itself eventually, and Imogen would be a fool to deny herself a chance of happiness.

It was only natural.

Jealousies burned bright and clear in his chest at the thought of any other man claiming Imogen for his own; of any other man but himself guiding her through her days; of any other man holding her at night as she gave in to the passion that burned in her soul.

He longed to cry out. Don't touch her, she's mine!

She's the other half of my soul, my reason for living, my love and my life. Mine.

But it was a cry in the wilderness.

"Imogen," he sighed, and knew it was an unachievable prayer. The only place where she was unquestionably his was in his heart and mind. He closed his eyes and conjured her from his memories, re-creating what he needed most.

He proved to be too good at imagining. He had to clench his hand to stop himself reaching out and trying to touch the vision of her that his mind had produced to torment him. If he did that, she would disappear and he needed her like he had never needed anything before in his life.

He saw her as he liked to see her best.

She stood naked and happy, her face glowing with peace. Her hands rested pertly on her hips, her head held at a saucy angle as she seemed to regard him. She was so achingly real that Robert could have almost sworn that the scent of her perfumed hair drifted through the cell to tantalize his senses.

He watched transfixed as her lips soundlessly whispered the words his heart longed to hear.

"I love you."

He smiled gently and murmured aloud, "I love you too."

This time, when he slipped from consciousness he was surrounded by memories of Imogen and dreams of the life that they might have built together at Shadowsend. His last conscious thought was that the mad must truly be happy men, if they were all greeted by such visions once their sanity had been dismissed.

Then he thought no more.

Chapter Thirteen

Matthew sighed and lowered the wine jug to the floor, more than a little reluctant to actually sober up, but Robert needed him. That meant Matthew would do everything in his power to help.

Well, try to, anyway.

He stared at the ceiling and had to smile wryly as he acknowledged the folly he had committed himself to. Of course he would do what Robert had asked of him, just as soon as he worked out how the hell it was to be done. Sure, Robert had made it sound easy enough. Escape and warn Imogen. What could be simpler?

Pulling your bottom lip over the top of your head for one, Matthew thought with a derisive snort that echoed in the silently empty room. No, it was no simple thing the boy asked, and Matthew had years of painful experience to compare it with.

But difficult or not, he still had to do it.

Slowly he moved his legs over the edge of the cot and eased his feet onto the floor. A raspy groan escaped him as he sat up, his stiff legs protesting his sudden desire to move. He narrowed his eyes and took a deep, steadying breath. At least the room remained stationary. That meant he wasn't drunk, despite all of the cheap liquor he had ingested over the past days, which was only fair at his age.

He deserved to have a hard head. It compensated for the rheumatic pain that seemed to fill every joint in his body as he tried to lever himself out of the sagging cot. Now, however, wasn't the time to indulge his pain, not if he was to drag his sorry carcass across England again. He just couldn't afford to let the aches and pains of an old man stop him.

No, that wasn't quite right. He would have to drag his sorry carcass across England not once but twice. He buried his face in his hands as he remembered that Robert also wanted him to get Imogen out of England. He shuddered. Out of England meant a ship. He hated ships. He had traveled only once on an accursed sea devil, and had sworn then that if he got off the damn thing alive, then he would never again defy the laws of nature. As far as he was concerned, if the Almighty had wanted men to travel the oceans he would have given them gills.

He shuddered again, then lifted his head resolutely. Boats were in the future. His more immediate problem was getting out of the castle and, really, the boy had been damnably vague as to how he thought that feat was going to be accomplished.

Matthew might be too lowly to have as many guards placed on him as Robert had, but that was hardly the point when one guard prevented him leaving the castle just as effectively as ten. Getting out of the castle was the linchpin to any plan he may have to rescue Imogen as Robert wanted.

The boy was an idealistic dreamer despite his rough edges, Matthew realized with a rueful smile. For all his training as a warrior, Robert was still a wide-eyed boy in so many ways. Oh, he might hide it well enough beneath the bluster of knighthood and few guessed that it was so, but Matthew had known the boy too long to be fooled.

It was the idealism and hidden vulnerability that had called him to Robert's service in the first place. And how he had paid for that sentimental folly! He had spent years trying to make sure Robert wasn't killed by one of his own chivalrous gestures, those self-same gestures that Robert denied existed, and now here he was, at his advanced age, about to commit one of his own. Until now it had always suited Matthew to deal with the practical side of things while Robert dashed around doing knightly things, and he did it well.

Too damn well, it would seem, if Robert thought he could single-handedly save the beauty from the circling beasts. He snorted in self-disgust as his mind began sifting through his situation, trying to find a way to do just that. He smiled with satisfaction as a solution began to formulate.

Certainly, the plan he devised was crude and lacking in a certain finesse, but for all that, it would work perfectly. That was one of the joys of being low-born, you didn't have to muck around with such frivolities as style. If a thing worked, it worked.

And this would work, he hoped, as he finally found his feet.

He waited patiently beside the door for the guard

to bring in his usual bowl of slop for supper. When the man finally arrived Matthew took full advantage of his surprise at finding the cot empty to bring the chamberpot down on his head, hard.

The guard grunted very satisfactorily as he fell to the floor with a muted thud. Matthew quickly dragged the dead weight of the man farther into the room. He closed the door and began to remove the guard's clothes. Once the man was naked, bound and gagged, Matthew hauled him onto the cot and threw a blanket over him. In the ill-lit room one drunk man covered with a blanket looked very much like another, Matthew thought with a smile of satisfaction as he began to remove his own clothes.

That fact would hopefully buy him the time he needed.

Matthew couldn't help a grimace of distaste escaping as he began slipping on the other man's sweaty clothes and leather armor. Obviously the guard in the cot didn't value personal cleanliness, Matthew thought with a fastidious shiver, but dressed quickly anyway.

He gave himself a once-over and nodded with satisfaction. He would pass easily as a member of the King's Guard and the smell that lingered in the unconscious man's clothes would surely prevent any closer inspections.

He left the chamber calmly, locking the door with his stolen keys. If he was in luck, it would probably be several hours before anyone thought to check on the drunken old man, and the guard he had knocked out wouldn't be coming to any time soon to raise the alarm. That should give him the extra time he needed to not only get out of the castle but also to find out exactly what kind of trouble the boy had got himself into this time.

He slipped the keys into one of his pockets, straightened his shoulders instinctively after a quick check of the corridor. Several guards loitered down at the far end but none of them was paying him any attention.

He headed straight for them. These were the very men who would best know what had happened to Robert.

Fortunately for him, the King's Guards were the same as bored men everywhere, they loved to gamble and gossip in equal measure. It took him no time to find someone willing to answer all his questions in return for a few rolls of the dice and soon he was crouched down in a dark niche with a guard, the younger man's face filled with chagrined wonder.

"Damn your eyes, Old Man. You can't have won again!" he muttered as he picked up the dice suspiciously. A close inspection revealed nothing amiss and reluctantly he began counting out the coins he had just lost. "I've never seen luck such as yours," he growled darkly.

Matthew shrugged his shoulders and rolled the dice from one hand to the other. "If I was truly lucky, my boy, do you think I'd be guarding empty rooms in this half-built castle?"

The younger man snorted in companionable agreement. "These days, there are very few lucky men wearing the king's livery." He stood and leaned up against the wall next to his pike, looking broodingly out over the deserted corridor. Matthew quickly stashed away the money in his pocket, knowing that reminding the man of his recent fleecing might not make him all that forthcoming with the information he needed. He stood up stiffly and grabbed his stolen pike to lean on, shaking his head in commiseration.

"Aye, things have certainly changed. This used to be a fine enough life, but now . . ." He shook his head again and sighed, for good measure.

The guard took the bait and leaned forward conspiratorially.

"You know how the king has become obsessed about his security?" He dropped his voice. "Well, they are saying that he isn't all that wrong to be. I've heard whisperings that there are important people trying to make certain that he doesn't live all that much longer. One of these days, mark my words, he's going to wake up with a knife wedged between his ribs."

Matthew nodded his head, his agile mind quickly adding the new facts to the old. "And that prophesied dagger belongs to Robert Beaumont, right?"

The guard grinned. "Not now it won't. He won't live long enough to be anyone's assassin."

Matthew joined the boy's laughter, but his stomach clenched tightly. Robert had finally managed to get himself into a situation that even Matthew didn't know how to get him out of.

Trying to sound only mildly interested, Matthew scratched his thumbnail over his nose. "I fought with the man once on the Welsh borders. I find it hard to imagine he would have anything to do with treason."

"Ah, but that was before they forced him to marry Lady Deformed. Marrying that one would be enough to change anyone, to my way of thinking. I mean I've heard that she is missing her nose and at least one arm . . ."

Matthew had to grit his teeth and hold on to his pike very tightly to stop himself from planting his fist right in the middle of the boy's face. The thought of breaking his nose became strangely satisfying as he listened to the seemingly endless litany of Imogen's imagined defects. He didn't bother to remember that five months ago he had thought much the same thing himself. What mattered now was that he knew different. He knew her, liked and admired her. It was a hideous barbarity that one small detail had taken on such grotesque proportions.

When he couldn't bear to hear anymore he cut the boy short. "But surely marrying Roger Colebrook's sister couldn't be all bad, regardless of how, uh, ugly the lady might be. I mean, it almost puts you in bed with the king himself."

The man chuckled. "Ain't that the truth." He sighed and shook his head before adding, "I don't think those two men want to be in bed together, not in any sense. There ain't much love lost between them. After all, they say it was Colebrook himself who denounced his brother-in-law." He shrugged his shoulders. "Beaumont probably said too much in front of his ugly wife and she passed it on to her brother. Families can be such queer things. I mean, I knew this one man who . . ."

Realizing that they were straying from the point, probably forever, Matthew said something vague about needing to be elsewhere and walked quickly down the hall. As soon as he was out of sight he set about finding the most discreet way to leave the castle.

Once in the courtyard he strode toward the stables as if he had every right to do so.

Amongst the king's vast selection of horseflesh, it took him some time to locate Dagger's stall. The horse whinnied in greeting when he recognized this new intruder.

"Shut up, you idiot, or you can explain to the groom just what the hell I'm doing saddling a traitor's horse. That'll be just before they turn you into so much hound's meat," Matthew growled darkly but gave the horse an affectionate pat on the neck all the same.

He saddled the horse quickly and swung stiffly up into the saddle. Back in the courtyard Matthew continued his show of bravado, reckoning it would be all that would get him out of this hornet's nest. Not that the sentry on the gate seemed all that interested in checking the credentials of an old man on an elderly horse. They waved him on as soon as he claimed to be on an important mission for the king.

They might have been more questioning if they had seen the speed that Matthew took off with when he was far enough away from the noisy wooden drawbridge. He didn't waste time questioning his luck. He leaned over Dagger's neck and coerced him into a faster gallop. He had to get Imogen on that boat out of England as quickly as possible. There was no time to waste, because after he had achieved that, he was going to have to come back here.

He might have promised Robert that he would make sure Imogen was safe, but to Matthew's way of thinking that wouldn't be at Robert's own expense. It was becoming sickeningly clear that Robert desperately needed his help.

His mouth settled into a grim line as he rode away from the castle. It didn't sit well with him that he was leaving the boy, especially not when he was up to his neck in trouble. He didn't like it at all, but there was sod all he could do about it until he had fulfilled his other obligations. Once they were completed, then he could try to help Robert.

Not that he had any idea how he could help, but maybe, after he had got the wife out of the country he could come back and do what could be done for the husband.

Even if it was only to see he got a decent Christian burial.

Imogen turned her face full into the sun, but she couldn't seem to feel it. She had a solid core of ice wedged inside of her and even the intense rays of the sun could not melt it. She doubted she would ever be truly warm again.

Not that it mattered. All sensation and feeling were frozen inside her and there was nothing she could do to shake off the numbness. She felt as if she had ceased to exist, but her body hadn't been informed and mindlessly it continued with the automatic business of living even when there was nothing alive left inside.

The strange sensation was only compounded by the fact that everyone surrounded her with a conspiracy of concern, hemming her in from all sides, acting as a suffocating buffer between her and the real world. They all did it. They tiptoed around her as if she might break if they dared to raise their voices.

And she didn't have the strength to stop it.

There just seemed no reason to. Let them make all the decisions just so long as they left her to her numbness. Nothing mattered anymore.

When Mary had suggested Imogen might feel a little more like herself if she sat outside for a spell, Imogen had agreed, although she had no desire to sit outside in a chair like an invalid. But Mary was wrong. She didn't feel better. Her hollowness was entirely portable and had joined her in the cold sunshine.

She sat on a hard chair borrowed from the main hall in sunshine she couldn't feel, looking at things she couldn't see.

Her hands clenched tightly together in her lap, her fingernails driving into the soft flesh of her palms, but she didn't feel the pain. All sensation had stopped from the moment Robert had ridden away.

Strange, but even as she had come to fear him, he had still taken with him the last vestige of hope. She couldn't understand it. How could she have given him so much of herself when she didn't trust him? How could it be that without him she ceased to exist, that she could no longer even feel her own pain?

It wasn't possible, unless she had come to love him. And she couldn't love him. How could she when she knew he was playing on Roger's side? Playing Roger's game, was Roger's man.

But if it was true, if despite all logic she actually

loved Robert, then Roger had won, just as he had always told her he would.

She drew an unsteady breath, smelling Roger's gloating satisfaction in the air. When he caught up with her this time it would be worse than it had ever been. This time he would no longer have to wait. This time, he would stop only when there was nothing of her left.

This time. Would it start like it always did? Would she wake from her tortured sleep and know he was there? She knew the answer.

She would wake and find him waiting. There would be no warning, no time to plan. There would be nothing she could do to protect herself. "Run, Little Sister, I want you to run." His voice would sound so normal that it only made what he said, what he was about to do to her, with her, all the more grotesque.

She would run. Her hands would be sweaty and she would struggle frantically with the bar on her chamber door. Eventually it would lift. It would be in the passageway that the walls of panic would press grindingly in on her. She would be slumped in a cowering heap when Roger found her.

His excitement would be a tangible presence as he touched her, hurt her. "Beg me, Little Sister. Beg me to take you. Beg me and all of this will stop." She had heard his calm voice caress over those words so often that even though she was safely away from them for now, she covered her ears. It didn't work. His voice was trapped in her head. "Well then, if you won't beg, we will have to play a little more."

And he would play, but this time he wouldn't

stop. This time he wouldn't wait for her to beg. He would take her utterly and at that moment she would cease to exist altogether. That was the only way this torturous game could end. She had always known that.

But for a short, wonderful moment, she had dared to let herself forget that. That was why she hated Robert even as a small, traitorous part of her thought she might be in love with him. She hated him for showing her hope. She had actually dared to believe that at last the nightmares were truly over. But they weren't and she was too weak to fight them now that they had returned.

Roger's win would be pathetically easy, she realized listlessly, but instinctively crossed her arms over her middle. It was a gesture that proved she wasn't yet as entirely resigned as she needed to be. She couldn't be if she was actually trying to protect, however feebly, the heart that now beat under her own.

That small, living secret was the one thing that repeatedly managed to penetrate the fog that surrounded her. Under her cold palms there lived another soul struggling its way into life. It seemed impossible to imagine such a thing, but this unborn child would not be denied its existence just because it seemed impossible. It did exist, even if she didn't.

That knowledge was startling in its newness. She had been standing like a lifeless doll as all of her gowns were altered to fit her changing shape. Her waist seams had to be let out, as everything else had to be taken in. Even then, she hadn't seen the truth. It had taken Mary's flat "You're pregnant" for her to understand the changes taking place in her own body.

She had yelled at Mary, told her that she lied, that she had got it wrong, that she wasn't to tell anyone, but even as she had denied the possibility, a growing sense of wonder had consumed her. For a moment, she had actually felt a quickening of life and hope in her own soul.

Of course, that died the moment she recalled that her child was not only a living symbol of just how close she had come to actually believing in Robert, but also another living hostage to fate. Roger was circling ever closer now and any child of hers would be destined to suffer her fate.

She couldn't save it, any more than she could save herself.

Sometimes she felt disgusted that her body had betrayed her utterly and at other times the knowledge that the baby would experience her fate was a cold pain in her chest. But there was nothing she could do, so she ignored the child, ignored Mary's concerns. Or, at least, that's what she tried to do.

The contrary child seemed to take every opportunity to remind her of its existence, as if it was refusing to be denied out of being. Already, the child was too much like its father. She clenched her hands on her lap and bit down on her bottom lip. No matter how she hated it, hated him, all of her thoughts kept returning to him. The worst of it was that she couldn't stop herself from softening a little as memories assaulted her.

She could almost hear the deep rumble of his infrequent laughter floating all the way from London to warm her as sunshine never could. She

remembered his rough kindnesses and clumsy
gentleness. She had even caught herself smiling at
memories of his flaring temper. It was a smile that
died as those harmless memories brought more
dangerous ones with them, memories of the
cleansing depths of their passion. In Robert's arms
she had felt herself washed free of all her brother's
corruption.

For a time she had actually dared to believe that
somehow he had given her back all that she had lost
when she had looked into Roger's eyes that day in
the tower and seen his perverse desires for the first
time. But such beliefs were dangerous. They burned
away a little of her numbness and no matter how she
tried to fight it, Robert intruded. He had taken possession of her dreams. Each night, she dreamed
dreams of once more being held securely in his arms
as he woke her body to all the desires of the flesh.
She half-remembered, half-imagined, the feel of his
large body as it covered hers, his turgid erection
scorching her with the intensity of his desire. When
she woke she felt aching and hollow, her arms
clutching nothing but cold, empty bedding.

It was a torture to know that her body and soul
called out for a man who would betray her, but no
matter what she did, hope kept sneaking under her
guard.

It was hope that was going to kill, doubtlessly just
as Roger had planned it would. There was nothing
she could do to stop it.

Nothing at all.

* * *

She was dragged from a dreamless sleep by the sound of Mary breathlessly calling her name.

"What?" she managed to mutter groggily, trying to free herself from the hands that were ruthlessly pulling her into a sitting position as if she had no more substance than a lifeless doll.

"My lady, you must come at once!" Mary yelled frantically as she threw a robe over Imogen's shoulders and began pulling her to her feet. "It's an emergency."

Imogen was hustled out of the chamber's doorway before she even had time to protest.

Not that protesting would have done her any good, she thought sleepily as she was propelled barefooted over the Keep's cold floors. Mary had obviously run mad.

She held on to Imogen's hand tightly as they ran down the stairs, but even as Imogen's dazed mind screamed that this was madness, weeks of mindless acquiescence had robbed her of any ability to fight it.

Mary dragged her into the silent hall, then let go of her hand, leaving her stranded and bewildered. For the first time in an age she felt rage boil sluggishly to life inside her. She straightened her shoulders, and tried to marshal the calm that she wasn't quite feeling right at that second.

"Just what the hell do you think you're doing, Mary? Why, exactly, am I not in my bed?" she asked through gritted teeth.

"I'm afraid that is my fault, my lady. Gareth didn't think it was a good idea for me to present myself to you in your bedchamber. He seemed to think it might be compromising somehow. God knows why,

I don't think I remember even how to compromise a lady anymore."

Imogen quickly pulled her robe more securely around her shoulders before turning to the decidedly masculine voice she couldn't identify through her confusion.

"Who's there?" she demanded, her voice rising to a squeak on the last syllable.

"I'm deeply hurt, my lady. I've only been gone a relatively little while and already you seem to have forgotten me. How fickle art woman!" the voice chided softly.

"Matthew?" she asked hesitantly, then a warm rush of welcome filled her as she felt her cold hands being held in his arthritic ones. "Matthew!"

Robert had come home, she realized with bewildered confusion. She hated him, she told herself sternly, but even as she thought it, her foolish heart skipped a beat.

"My lady," Matthew said solemnly as he placed a kiss on her knuckles and she could tell by the cracks of his protesting joints that the old man knelt before her.

She reached out a hand and groped for his shoulder. "No, no, please don't do that," she said, hauling him back to his feet.

"We don't have time for this folly," Gareth ground out with exasperation. "We have to get her out of here as quickly as possible."

Imogen's brows furrowed in confusion. "Gareth, you're here too? Just what is going on? What are you talking about? Are you here, Robert?"

An embarrassed silence was her only answer.

Gareth looked quickly to Matthew, who shook his

head to the unspoken question, then cleared his throat uncomfortably. "Matthew can explain it all to you."

Ignoring Matthew's ironic "Thanks very much!" Gareth walked quietly over to Imogen and, placing his arm around her shoulders, he guided her over to a seat near the hearth. The embers of a fire still glowed gently and Gareth made sure she was settled comfortably before moving to stand behind her. He barely resisted the urge to place his hands protectively on her shoulders, but to do so wasn't his right.

His jaw clenched and he folded his arms over his chest instead. He would have given everything he owned for Imogen not to have to face the blow that was coming. He would have taken it himself if he could have. She looked so fragile, sitting there, lost in the large chair, and he couldn't stop from worrying that perhaps she didn't have enough strength left to survive this after she had survived so much else.

"Well?" Imogen asked hesitantly. "What is going on?"

Matthew dropped stiffly into the chair opposite hers with a small groan and he stared deep into the embers, trying desperately to find the words to say what had to be said. How did you tell a woman that her husband had probably already been executed for treason? A quick, clean cut seemed to him the best way to inflict such a cruel wound.

"Your brother has accused Robert of treason and the king believes him. He has been imprisoned and is now awaiting execution." The old man sighed before gruffly adding, reluctantly, "For all we know the deed has already been done."

"No," she whispered, her horror dawning. Her face became a mask of confusion. "No. He can't be dead. That's not the way it's supposed to happen. That isn't the way of it at all."

As Matthew listened to her strangely stilted, un-shocked reaction, the guard's blithe words about Imogen's probable complicity in Roger's schemes suddenly reappeared unbidden in his mind.

"Care to explain to us, lass, just how much of this you already knew?" he asked darkly, his voice cold with suspicion.

Gareth took a protective step closer to Imogen and glared warningly at Matthew, but she didn't even notice the threat inherent in Matthew's words, her mind too absorbed by the devastating implications of what they had just told her.

It was unbelievable!

In her agitation, she got up and began pacing the room, words tumbled out unchecked. "Roger wouldn't do this. It just doesn't make sense. It's me that's supposed to be destroyed by his games, not Robert. For God's sake, Robert is his man in this. He can't destroy Robert. Why would Roger do that? It just *doesn't* make sense ... unless Robert was innocent, unless Robert never meant to hurt me. If that's so ..."

If that was so, then it was she who had betrayed Robert, not the other way round. If that was so, then the world Robert had shown her, the laughter and smiles he had shared with her, the passions he had built in her, they had all been real.

And she had thrown it all away, thrown him away. She had hidden behind her fear, her hate, her pain, and closed herself off from the one good thing to enter her life. She had sent him into danger and not once given him the only thing he had ever asked of her, although he had never put it into words. All he had ever wanted was her love and she had held herself back. It didn't matter that she had every reason to doubt, not when none of those reasons had anything to do with him.

And that was Roger's ultimate victory, she realized bitterly. She had been in his dark games for so long that she had not even been able to reach out and take the hand of the man who had wanted to do nothing more than take her into the light.

Now that loving man was going to die and that too would be her fault.

She buried her head in her hands, her thin shoulders visibly shaking.

"I can't let him die for me," she whispered, her voice breaking.

Matthew's suspicions dissolved as his agile mind quickly began to make sense of her garbled ramblings. "It's not your choice to make," he said gruffly, trying to ignore that part of himself already grieving for the man he would have been proud to call his son. "What's done is done and we must move on and start planning for the future. Robert told me to get you out of England, and that is just what I intend to do."

"Did he say where he wanted us to go?" Gareth asked, his voice thoughtful as he quickly began sorting in his mind all that needed to be done before they abandoned the Keep.

Matthew shook his head. "He didn't have time to go into specifics. Anywhere out of the reach of the king of England should do the trick. Somewhere warm and Mediterranean, I think."

Gareth narrowed his eyes. "We could do that. My

brother has lived in Italy for the last five years, fighting for a Florentine nobleman. I'm sure he would be able to take us in, help us get Imogen established."

"Sounds perfect."

"What will you do about money?" Mary asked practically, already doing mental inventories of everything in the Keep, trying to work out just what Imogen would need. "And I doubt whether either of you realize just how much time it will take to pack up a household this size."

"We will be able to take only the bare essentials. Anything that can't be carried on a horse can't come." A small smile filtered across Gareth's face. "I know it will be hard, Mary, but you have to remember that we are fleeing, not going on a pleasure jaunt, and pack accordingly."

"Well, as I'm too old to go to some damn foreign country, Sir Knight, I don't think I will be either fleeing or jaunting anywhere. There is a convent a day's ride from here that will take me in." Mary's brow furrowed. "But what about the rest of the household? What do you expect them to do?"

Gareth thought for a moment, his fingers running restlessly through his hair. "Some of the men will take you to your convent, and as for the rest of the household"—he shrugged his shoulders—"they will have plenty of time to pick over the corpse of what is left behind before the king confiscates it. Then they can disappear into the landscape."

Matthew grinned. "After they have finished with their job, the king probably won't be able to find enough evidence left to prove that anyone at all had ever lived here."

"We will have to get started now, if we are to get to the coast before the king starts closing down the ports on us," Gareth said thoughtfully.

"Which port do you have in mind?"

"One far enough away from London for safety's sake that will also get us to Italy by the most direct route. I've got a map somewhere . . ."

"I'm not going to Italy," Imogen said suddenly, cutting ruthlessly across the babble of conversation, taking a grim satisfaction in the dumb silence that immediately followed her declaration before pandemonium broke out.

"What are you talking about? Of course you're going." Mary said, aghast. "As the wife of an executed traitor and sister to an all-too-powerful madman, fleeing is the only thing for you to do."

"Well, I'm not going to do it." Imogen's voice was filled with calm certainty.

"If you intend to remain here, then I don't doubt for a second that you have separated yourself entirely from all sanity," Matthew said testily, then added in a slightly calmer voice, "and may we be so bold as to enquire what it is you *do* intend doing if not to flee sensibly?"

"I intend to do what any other loyal wife would do. I intend to prove my husband's innocence."

Another gratifyingly dumb silence filled the room.

"How?" Gareth growled in confusion. "We have no proof of his innocence!"

"Not that they have a hell of a lot of proof about his guilt," Matthew said darkly.

"Oh, don't you worry, I have proof." Imogen said

with grim satisfaction. "The proof has been steadily streaming north for months."

Gareth narrowed his eyes. "I love Robert like a brother, but I won't have you put in any form of jeopardy even for his sake. I promised Robert that I would keep you safe and that is just what I intend to do."

"This isn't your decision to make. It is mine, and my mind is already made up."

He looked as if he would like to protest, but instead he nodded his head in reluctant agreement. "Fine. We will travel to the king instead, but I'd like to have a boat held in reserve, just in case you can't save the world as completely as you seem to think you can."

Imogen bit her bottom lip nervously. "Then you will come with me, even though I'm not doing what you want me to do?"

Gareth's face gentled for a second. "Lady Imogen, I'd follow you into the mouth of Hell and tweak the tail of the Devil if you asked me to."

"There is a certain similarity between the two follies," Matthew said with evident disgust.

But Imogen ignored him as she groped for the chair and sank into its depths gratefully. Everything inside her was confusion.

Robert truly was innocent of wishing her any harm.

He really was the man who took time to teach his wife chess, the man who took in a lamb on his wife's whim, the man who had patiently returned to her pieces of her past even when she was afraid to receive such gifts. He too had felt the passion that had burned so brightly and shared in the tenderness that had grown between them as he held her close after passion had spent itself. He had loved her when he had whispered those words to her when he thought she slept. They had actually come from his heart, not Roger's twisted mind.

He had given her his love and all she had managed to give him in return were the twisted fears Roger had created in her. She could no longer hide behind her numbness. Emotions clamored to the surface and they were almost painful in their intensity. The guilt and fear for his life burned so brightly that they made her want to cry.

But there was also something else.

A something that she didn't quite dare name.

He had said he loved her. Love. It had been so long since she had been free-hearted enough to either give or receive it. She had lived with Roger's dark games so long that she had thought all the love had been frozen out of her, yet suddenly she knew that it hadn't. Deep under the shell of her cold fears she could feel it sluggishly coming back to life.

She loved him in return.

Inside of her a dam released and tears welled in her eyes. She wanted to cry for all the lost time, for the miracle of Robert's love and hers for him, but most of all she wanted to cry because she could lose it all even as she found it.

She didn't cry. Instead she lifted her chin defiantly and made an instant decision. She would be damned before she let Roger take from this world the only thing that meant anything to her. For Robert, she would fight, for the first time in her life.

She drew a deep, steadying breath.

"We can't stand around here all night," she said shakily, "there is much we must do."

Gareth looked into her face and smothered the small thrill of sadness that filled him as he saw life in her face once more. It was like she had finally woken up after weeks of sleep, but that life wasn't for him. Not that he'd ever expected it to be any other way, not really. But to judge from the pain he now felt, some part of him had been fool enough to love her a little and ached to know that she didn't love him in return.

He straightened his shoulders and prepared to fight for the lady who would never be his.

"Well, Lady Imogen, where shall we begin?"

Chapter Fourteen

And to think the journey had sounded so simple from the comfort of the Keep, Imogen thought ruefully. She tried to stretch the nagging pain out of her spine, but nothing she did would shift it, not when the relentless plodding of the horse's gait undid all her good works. Really she shouldn't have expected anything else. It would seem that she was finally, truly comprehending that nothing in this world was easy. Imogen snorted quietly at the understatement. Easy, hell, this was almost impossible.

It seemed so silly to think about it now, but "getting to Robert" had sounded like the easy part of the plan back at the Keep. All it really seemed to require was for her to throw her leg over a horse's back and make a quick dash down south where the real work would begin.

This going south was neither quick, nor a dash. It was tortuously backbreaking and it was taking so long that Imogen was becoming increasingly afraid it was to be a never-ending journey.

She was starting to forget she had ever lived a life

that didn't involve some horse's all-too-uncomfortabl
back. The rough hide of the beast had become he
whole world, and what a tediously slow world it was
Her humor wasn't improved any by the knowledg
that their lack of speed could be laid squarely at he
feet. Her blindness now served to slow them all down
If she couldn't see, then she couldn't really ride. Be
cause of that she had to have her horse led by eithe
Matthew or Gareth, like a child on a pony.

She tried to find some consolation in the fact tha
as slow as their progress was now, at least they wer
going faster than they would have been if Garet]
had got his way. He had thought that the only saf
way for Imogen to travel was in a litter. He had beer
so pigheadedly determined on that point and sh
had only got her own way by declaring, with grea
sincerity, that she would rather walk all the way t
London on her knees rather than suffer the indig
nity of traveling thus. She had won herself the righ
to ride a horse, but she wasn't so sure now whethe
that was a real victory or not.

To make matters worse, each night, when she wa
finally released from her equine prison, she had t
face the night terrors that awaited her.

She hated it, hated the fear that filled her ever
time Gareth called halt for the night. She tried t
hide it, not wanting to show such feebleness o
spirit, but that denial didn't stop the panic from
stealing her breath away each night when she wa
finally curled up in her blankets. Each and ever
evening she was held captive by morbid fears tha
were brought to life by the sounds of the endles
night. She lay trapped in her terrifying imagining

till she could stand it no longer and had to cover her ears or risk losing her sanity.

But blind silence held its own terrors. With her ears stopped, she knew she had not even the slightest chance of saving herself, and that knowledge was more frightening than any night monster her mind could conjure.

And when she finally found sleep in exhaustion, she then had to face the waking. She couldn't see her strange new environment, and in that moment of waking she felt a terror that was almost beyond her ability to endure.

But endure she did. Each morning, she waited in terror for it to ease. Managing to live through those endless moments of pure fear revealed depths in herself that she had never dared believe existed.

It surprised her. She was finding a discipline she hadn't even known she possessed. She didn't scream or cry. Not once, no matter how much she wanted to.

It was primitive, but it was survival and she found a grim pride in it, and she would keep doing it. For Robert.

For him alone she kept putting one foot after the other. She couldn't let herself forget that the evidence she carried in her saddlebags was the only thing that might save him. She had to be strong at least till her task was done. Only then, when he held her in his arms again, could she indulge herself and fall apart.

And he would hold her again. It had to happen that way. She couldn't dare think anything else.

She took a deep breath, and whispered, "He is safe. He is waiting for me. All will be well."

She had to believe it, had to be brave. Unconsciously, her hands moved to cover her slightly curving stomach, drawing confidence and quiet from the still incomprehensible knowledge that even now Robert's baby rested safely under her heart, then she quickly dropped her hands and took hold of the pommel to stop them from giving her secret away.

She wished Mary was with them. At least she would have had someone to share her excitement with. The girl who had come along as lady's maid just wasn't designed for confidences. Imogen smiled a little at the absurdity of even contemplating talking about anything important with the grumpy woman.

If Imogen had had her way, they wouldn't have been burdened with their reluctant maid. When it had become clear that Mary was too old to even contemplate such a journey, Imogen had assumed that only Gareth and Matthew would travel with her.

Gareth, however, had other ideas.

He had insisted that they take one of the Keep's younger maids. "For appearances' sake," he had said with evident embarrassment, clearly hoping not to be drawn on the finer details of chaperonage. Mildryd had volunteered for the duty and Imogen had to admit that she was proving interesting, if nothing else. Why she had wanted to come along when she so clearly hated traveling, disliked horses and detested work of any kind, however, defeated Imogen.

Although, there was an entertainment to be found in the way Matthew exploded every time he had to deal with the disinterested servant.

"It's good to see you smiling again, Imogen," Gareth said warmly as he drew his horse beside hers, startling her out of her thoughts.

Her smile dimpled a little deeper. "I was just trying to recall some of the new words that Matthew—uh, taught me last night when he was trying to get Mildryd to cook dinner. I think they were ever so impressive, don't you?"

"They were." Gareth grinned. "Some even I hadn't heard before, though I think it might be better if you tried to forget them."

"Better, but nowhere near as much fun. Besides, I have to remember them if I'm going to ask Robert what they all actually mean."

Gareth let out a soft chuckle. "And I would just love to hear how he manages to explain them to you." He grimaced a little. "In fact I imagine he will yell more than a few of them at me when he realizes just how much we have managed to broaden your . . . er, horizons, while he's been gone."

Imogen laughed as she tried to imagine the sophisticated Gareth trying to explain away her suddenly advanced education in curse words.

Gareth watched the joy on her face, transfixed as always by the radiance of her laugh. A companionable silence grew between them as their horses walked on slowly, Gareth holding the leading rein tightly. It was pleasant, but it couldn't entirely distract Imogen from the seriousness of their journey. "How much longer till we are there, do you think?" she asked softly.

Gareth squinted at the sun for a moment, his mind swiftly making calculations. "I'd say that we have another good five days of travel ahead before we reach the fortress, presuming then that the king is still in residence there. If not . . ."

Imogen sighed in frustration. "That long!" She shook her head. "It's my fault. You two would be traveling a lot faster if you weren't being slowed down by a blind woman." Her hands clenched so tightly onto the saddle pommel her knuckles whitened.

Gareth shrugged his shoulders philosophically, reaching out a reassuring hand to cover hers. "If it wasn't for the determination of our blind woman, we wouldn't be traveling with any hope of saving Robert. Instead, we would be fleeing to the nearest port. Without the evidence you carry, I wouldn't give much hope for Robert's chance of surviving." His voice stopped suddenly and he quickly looked away.

Gareth didn't say aloud that he feared they might be traveling only to retrieve Robert's body parts from the king's castle walls. He didn't have to. Imogen heard it all the same.

The silence that now descended was heavy with their grim thoughts. After a reassuring squeeze, Gareth lifted his hands from hers and pulled out in front once more, and Imogen purposely loosened her grip on the pommel, trying to think of nothing. She refused to let herself dwell on the possibility that Roger had already won, but no matter how hard she tried, fear and worry stalked her.

That evening Gareth set up camp in a clearing off the road near a small stream. Imogen gratefully slid off her horse, having been more than a little afraid she finally might have melded permanently with the beast.

She wanted to groan as she ran her tired hands over the nagging pain in her back, trying to shift all the kinks out of her tired muscles. She turned her head as she heard Matthew walking toward her, grumbling hotly under his breath.

"Have you been arguing with Mildryd again?" she asked sweetly, smiling up at the irritable old man.

Matthew let out a long snort of disgust. "One doesn't argue with a cow, one yells at it in the vain hope that something of sense will penetrate its thick skull."

"And did it?"

"What do you think, my lady? I've been trying to get through to her since we started this ill-fated journey but nothing gets in. All I am doing is wasting perfectly good air and I still end up being your nursemaid."

"Well, I think you make an entirely wonderful nursemaid. You seem to anticipate my needs even before I realize what they are. Why, I bet that even now you're making plans to walk me over to that stream I can hear bubbling so brightly, so that I can freshen up." She dimpled up at him and lifted out her hand, which he threaded through his arm with a shake of his head.

"You see far too much sometimes," he said with a rueful laugh, which broke off suddenly. He cleared his throat in discomfort. "Well, you know what I mean," he said gruffly.

"Of course I do. You are accusing me of being too clever for you," she said serenely, "and I have absolutely no objection to being thought of as such.

In fact I think it is very insightful of you to have realized it at last."

He was laughing once more as he slowly walked her over to the stream. He helped her kneel down on the grassy bank and carefully placed one of her hands in the cold rushing water.

"Now, I'll just be right over here. I'll give you as much privacy as I can but . . ." he finished lamely and stood stiffly.

She nodded her head understandingly. "But not enough of it to get me killed, right?"

"Right."

She listened to his departing footsteps to make sure he had left the immediate area before quickly and efficiently setting about washing her face, neck and hands. The stream was freezing; its banks swollen with the first of the snow melt. The intensity of the cold caused Imogen to catch her breath and she couldn't help shivering as she splashed the icy droplets over her skin. She had got very good at this sort of thing, she realized, with some satisfaction. She didn't need as much help as she had at the start, much to Matthew's relief, no doubt, she thought with a grin.

As the day's travel started to disappear from her skin she let out a long sigh of satisfaction.

It felt so good to be somewhat clean again, but she couldn't stop a wicked part of her mind longing for a proper bath. As she lifted her heavy hair off the back of her grimy neck she indulged herself in the tantalizing fantasy.

She inhaled deeply and could almost believe that she smelled the scent of warm roses. She heard the ghost of a large crackling fire in the babbling of the stream and it seemed to warm the skin of her shoulders and face. So real was the fantasy that she was sure that she could feel the hot water all round her, moving over her naked body in lazy, sensuous waves.

The image was so seductive, she found herself doing something that she hadn't done in some time. She tried to draw on her dwindling store of visual memories to create a proper vision to go with the imaginings of her other senses.

Those memories were now graying and faded, but it was so much like being able to see that it hurt eyes accustomed to the dark. She closed them instinctively, going from black to black.

It was nonsensical, but it seemed to work. Suddenly her mind glowed with pictures of an intensity that would never have existed in the real world.

The fire was vibrant with all of the shades of red and orange she had ever seen. It illuminated the room of her memory with the penetration of sunlight. It was a strange room, a mixture of childhood memories and fantasies of her bedchamber at Shadowsend.

She saw herself in the bath, and was surprised that in her mind's eye she was no longer the girl she had last seen. No, she was seeing herself as the woman she might have become.

If in her mind she was a woman, then it was only right that in the shadows of her memory there stood a man. Even though, frustratingly, he stayed just out of reach from the fire's glow, Imogen knew it could only be Robert. The light of the fire played oddly over his naked body, darkening his pale skin till it blazed like polished bronze. Her brow furrowed as she struggled to create a body she had never seen, but she couldn't seem to bring him into focus. She might know him as she knew no other soul, but her mind lacked the memories to draw him for her. He belonged to her darkness.

Everything she knew about him had nothing to do with how he looked.

She knew the smell of him, the taste of him on her tongue, knew the sound of his laugh, knew the feel of his body as it moved over hers, knew the feel of his skin under her palm, knew the shape of his face under her fingertips. She knew all of that and more but couldn't begin to imagine what his face looked like. She just didn't have the memories to imagine what she had felt so often with her hands.

A feeling of exasperation filled her as she realized that she didn't even know the color of his hair, didn't know if the soft waves on his head matched the springy mat that covered his chest or whether it was a slight shade darker, like her father's had been. She didn't know if the love of her life had laughing blue eyes or forest green ones.

She let out a small groan of frustration as the vision began to break up under the weight of her ignorance. She had to grit her teeth against the foolish urge to call back the Robert of her visions. She wanted to demand that he step into the light so that she could at last see the face of the man she loved, but it was too late. He was gone and once more the shadowed fog filled her.

She wrapped her arms around her waist, trying to hold on to the warmth as long as she could. She sighed shakily, trying to draw some consolation from the fact that what she hadn't been able to see

with her memories, she had known with the touch
of her hands and lips. Even at this distance, those
memories were able to light in her a desire that ac-
celerated the beating of her heart. She caught cold
rushing water in her cupped hand and splashed her
face, hoping to clear her head, wanting to freeze the
lingering desire that could have no conclusion.

She crawled carefully back from the edge of the
stream before standing slowly and drying herself on
the corner of her cloak. She had already called to
Matthew that she was finished when the babe suddenly started to move. She stood absolutely still,
caught by the wonder of the strange, new feeling of
another life moving inside her.

That wonder must have manifested itself on her
face, because Matthew's voice was threaded with
concern when he reached her side.

"Imogen, what the hell is it?"

The words to explain the sensation escaped her,
so instead she grabbed his hand and placed its
gnarled strength over the fluttering movement.

For a moment his brow crumpled in confusion at
the strange action, but that confusion quickly
cleared when he realized what he could feel.

"My God," he whispered in awe and moved his
other hand to the center of her back, holding her
body still, but he was still barely able to feel that
small, miraculous movement. Suddenly he lifted
his hand away as if burnt. "Damn," he whispered
angrily. "Damn, blast, Holy Mother of Christ and
shit."

It was only then that Imogen realized that she
had inadvertently told Matthew her secret. She
winced as he continued to swear with increasing

creativity, but she couldn't help the relief that flooded her. It was good to finally share the joy with the man who'd come to mean so much.

"How long have you known?" Matthew asked flatly, the anger gone from his voice as his mind quickly started to search out the practical way out of this suddenly increasingly difficult situation.

"A month or more."

Matthew growled with exasperation. "And just how far along do you reckon yourself to be?"

"I'm not entirely sure," she admitted with a small shrug of her shoulders. "Mary guessed that I was four, maybe five months."

"Damn." Matthew ran an agitated hand through his thin hair.

"I believe you are starting to repeat yourself at last," Imogen said dryly, then added cajolingly, "it doesn't really matter, does it?"

"Doesn't matter, she asks!" Matthew exploded. "Doesn't really matter? Of course it bloody well matters. What kind of idiot do you take us for? Do you really think we would have dragged a pregnant woman halfway across this godforsaken country if we had known? Imogen, why didn't you tell us about your condition when we were planning this ill-conceived mission?"

Imogen felt herself flush. "Would telling you have really made any difference?" she asked quietly.

"Of course it would have made a difference. You wouldn't be here arguing with me, for one thing. Instead you would be safe on a boat destined for warmer climes."

"What I meant was, would it have made any difference to Robert's situation if I had told you about this?

You need me to save him. The king has to listen to a woman of noble birth, no matter how much he might dislike it." She smiled coldly as she pulled herself up straight. "As much as he might like to, I can't be ignored. You and Gareth, on the other hand, well, you can all too easily be dismissed as mercenaries prepared to lie and connive to save your leader." She drew a shuddering breath. "I didn't think it ultimately mattered, because whether I'm pregnant or not won't save Robert, but me seeing the king might."

"Have you considered in all your scheming that Robert might be long past saving?" He watched Imogen blanch at that possible truth but continued ruthlessly, "What if Robert is already dead and all your noble sacrifice actually achieves is to put you and your baby in danger? Did you think of that before you started on your foolish quest?"

"Of course I thought about it," she said softly, her hand moving instinctively to cover her womb. "But I have also thought about my child growing up without a father. I think of me, living the rest of my life without the man I love. I think about how he must be suffering now, and I think about how I am the cause of that suffering. You think I don't know that if it weren't for me, Robert would have been safe? Strangely, I find I can think of little else."

Her face tightened with determination. "But I do not think about being too late to save him. I will not think of it. Robert lives and he waits for our rescue. If I thought anything else, I just might run mad."

Matthew stared at her in silence, admiration warring with fears across his weathered face.

"I didn't mean it," he muttered finally. "I don't believe Robert is, well . . ."

"Good, because it isn't true. I'd know if he was no longer with us." She grabbed his hand and placed it on the slight curve of her stomach once more. "We'd know."

Matthew might have forgiven her, but no matter how hard Imogen tried to convince him otherwise, he felt he had to tell Gareth about the baby. And the other man's reaction turned out to be everything Imogen feared it would be.

After his initial stunned amazement, Gareth's anger had known no bounds. He had stormed over to her and yelled at her about the stupidity of her actions. She kept her peace, waiting hopefully for his anger to blow itself out. It didn't do so for some time, but when the first wave of his fury was spent he stormed off into the night, saying that he needed time to think. The supper that night was such a silent, strained affair that Imogen was actually relieved to retire to her furs.

It was midnight before Gareth returned to the camp.

He was no longer roaring like a wounded lion, but as Imogen lay by the fire listening to him moving about the camp, she could still feel his anger simmering below the surface. After a while he sat down with some cold supper on a plate and began eating it halfheartedly.

"Do you feel better now?" Imogen asked quietly.

Gareth paused a moment to swallow before answering. "You should be asleep," he said quietly.

She pulled herself up onto her elbow, not noticing that the blankets had slipped down a little.

Gareth did, and his hand clenched painfully around his trencher.

"I tried, but I just couldn't when I was worried about you."

"I thought pregnant women slept all the time."

"Some do, I'm sure, but not me. Not right at the moment. Sometimes I think I will never sleep properly again."

Gareth was quiet for a moment, then, as if he couldn't help himself, he ground out, "Why didn't you tell me?"

Imogen could hear the hurt from her betrayal in his voice and she searched desperately for something to say that wouldn't upset him further and would make him feel better.

"It wasn't like that, Gareth, I didn't tell anyone, until Matthew. Mary guessed. I didn't want to know about it myself. It . . . the baby disgusted me somehow." She sighed. "It's so hard to explain."

"Try," Gareth said with stony determination, and Imogen realized that there was going to be no easy escape for her.

She drew a shaky breath.

"I thought Robert had betrayed me. It seemed to me that my body had joined that betrayal by harboring his seed. Then, when I realized Robert was innocent, when I learned that loving him and bearing his child wasn't an act of betrayal, everything was chaos. I needed to do this so badly . . ." She shrugged her shoulders helplessly. "I knew you would try to stop me if you found out about the child."

"Try? Hell no, I wouldn't have tried. I would have

bloody well succeeded, even if that meant I had to tie you bodily to the bed."

"And he has to ask me why I didn't tell him?" she murmured with a shaky laugh and Gareth frowned, not wanting to understand.

"Perhaps you may have a point," he said grudgingly at last. "I see that, but I hope you can also see my point." He stared at his trencher, not seeing his congealed meal. "You shouldn't be doing this. I thought it was a frighteningly dangerous folly even before I knew about the baby. But now, my God! You are not just putting yourself in jeopardy but also your child, and I'm responsible."

"But if I don't put me and my child in jeopardy, I will lose Robert and that's something I am unwilling to contemplate." She pulled the blanket more securely around her shoulders to ward off the chill. "That makes it all my responsibility, my choice, not yours."

"My God, you can be unbelievably stubborn."

"Thank you."

He laughed despite himself. "I didn't mean that as a compliment, trust me."

"I know, but fortunately for you, I'm quite prepared to take it as one."

With that, an uneasy truce grew between them.

Imogen tried to put up with his excessive fussing with as much grace as possible, and in return Gareth tried to keep his worried disapproval to himself. Neither was entirely successful.

But they tried.

"When will we get to the fortress?" Imogen asked tightly, not able to bear the silence a moment longer. She held on to the cup Matthew had given her but her throat was too tight to even try to swallow the contents.

"If we break camp at dawn, we should reach the fortress around midday," Gareth said neutrally.

"So close," she murmured.

"So close that I can almost hear Robert complaining about how long it has taken me to get out of there and back again," Matthew said bracingly as he moved to stoke the fire. He caught Gareth's gaze and raised a meaningful brow in Imogen's direction.

Gareth followed the look, then lowered his eyes to stare into the fire for a second.

"I hope they have him chained up well," he said musingly.

Imogen moved her head in his direction sharply. "Why?"

"Because it should slow him down a bit. Once they unchain him, he's going to kill me. And that is before he finds out that not only have I put his wife through this ordeal, but she is also pregnant. Yes, I think I would definitely like some iron holding him in place when I tell him that."

Imogen chuckled but once she settled into her furs for the night, all her worries and fears returned to her in a rush. She was haunted by what ifs.

What if Roger had already won? What if . . .

No, it couldn't be so. She wouldn't even try to imagine her world without him. She tried to block all such dark thoughts by conjuring up memories of Robert, of loving him, of laughing with him, of being held by him.

Just before dawn she found herself desperately praying for just one chance to put everything right.

They were all so caught up in their own thoughts, no one noticed as Mildryd slowly stole from the camp and disappeared into the night.

Ian paced up and down in front of the well-lit altar, his impatience to have it all done with reaching screaming point. Roger was already an hour late and there was every chance it would be several more hours before he bothered to arrive. That was how the game was played and Ian had no choice but to keep waiting if he wanted to have even the slightest chance of finally being free of it all at last. A life entirely free of Roger and his dark webs of intrigue? It was almost impossible for him to imagine, he realized with a disgusted snort. In his experience, the webs that Roger spun were endless. No one ever escaped them, and struggle against them seemed only to entangle the victim further.

Ian had found that out so long ago, he could hardly remember a time when he wasn't bound to Roger.

There were distant memories of having a normal life, but they were so hazy and remote that they no longer meant anything. He could remember the first time he ever met Roger, however, with a vivid intensity.

He had been so young, so full of pride and purpose. He had waited so long to begin his knight training that he could scarcely believe that the day had arrived at last. It was that enthusiasm that had made him such pathetically easy pickings for Roger. Even back then Roger had been able to mesmerize and charm when and whomever he wanted.

He had always enjoyed collecting souls.

Ian had all too quickly and easily fallen under the spell of the older boy. It was infuriating now to remember that he had actually been flattered when Roger had included him in his exclusive circle of friends. It had taken him too long to realize that the Roger he had admired was just an illusion, something conjured to fool the world.

And when he did realize, it was too late. When things started to go so terribly wrong there had been absolutely nothing he could do to stop them, but he had been so frightened by it all that he had actually abandoned his dreams of becoming a knight. He had turned to the church instead and in the monastery he actually found some peace. It had protected him from Roger's dark schemes and offered him some forgiveness. He mightn't have been a very good priest, but being one was good for him.

But in the end even the great and powerful church hadn't been able to protect him from Roger, Ian thought with a bitter smile.

Roger had found him and, smiling charmingly, had threatened him with that unique blend of truth and lies that would see him destroyed unless he became Roger's spy in Imogen's household. There had been no choice. He gave up his new-found peace and once more lost himself in being Roger's man.

Ian slumped onto one of the cold, hard benches and buried his head in his hands.

His soul was Roger's, and he couldn't help but hate himself for that.

"I hope I haven't left you waiting too long."

Ian's head shot up and he quickly found his feet.

Roger ambled into the light of the candles, the gold thread on his doublet twinkling gaudily. He looked around at the newly completed chapel and shuddered slightly. "I can't say I am that enamored with your choice of meeting place"—he smiled at Ian knowingly—"but I suppose that there is no better place than a church to meet one's priest."

"You told me to tell you if I heard anything else about the Lady Imogen," Ian said abruptly, anxious to get this final betrayal over.

Roger seemed to be in no such hurry. He wandered up to the altar and idly picked up one of several candlesticks and began to consider it carefully as he spoke dispassionately. "My dear Ian, if I had my way, you would still be in Shadowsend. I'm still not entirely sure why you are here at all."

Ian crossed his arms over his chest, trying to resist the urge to snatch the candlestick from his hands. "I could not stay there, abusing people's innocence and trust by pretending to be their honest priest. With Lady Imogen gone the whole purpose of the deception was lost."

"But, Ian, you are a sanctified priest."

"That couldn't save me from you, could it?" he spat out bitterly. But when he saw Roger's smile harden he drew a deep, steadying breath. "Tonight I have heard from the woman I had traveling with the Lady Imogen. She has told me that the party is camped only hours away."

"So close," Roger said softly as he carefully returned the candlestick to its position. "I never realized that my little sister could be so resourceful."

He stood for a second, staring at the cloth covering

the altar, then turned quickly as if to leave. Ian stepped in front of him, his face taut with outrage.

"Is that all, then? Is that all you have to say?" Ian searched the serenely beautiful face in front of him for a moment, then quickly looked away before he could begin to actually believe in it. He shook his head in disbelief. "Because of you, I have just thrown away my last piece of self-respect and here you are treating it as if it all means nothing to you, as if this is just a tidbit of gossip I have collected merely to entertain you. If you don't care, why have you made me act a Judas all these years?"

Roger raised a brow questioningly. "My dear Ian, calm yourself. Priests don't have any need for self-respect. That is what their God is for, after all." He smiled brightly, but it didn't reach his eyes. "And don't forget that you also have me and my eternal patronage."

"I'd be better off with the patronage of the Devil himself." Ian turned from Roger then, no longer able to abide being so near him and for once not caring if the other man saw his contempt.

"Careful, or I might just remove that patronage." Roger's cold eyes raked over Ian. "Till now, I have been very generous and let me assure you, you will miss my generosity if I decide to withdraw it."

Ian's hands clenched impotently at his sides. He knew that there was nothing he could do and his silence was an admission of his own weakness.

Roger smiled approvingly. "Good. I'm glad that you have managed to see sense. Now, if you will excuse me, I have a very important appointment with the king. Thank you for the information, but

I would prefer in future if you confined our contact to messengers."

Ian watched him stride confidently from the chapel and had to resist the urge to cross himself. The deed was done and there was nothing he could do to undo it.

He turned and walked slowly toward the altar, staring at the glowing crucifixion. Suddenly he sunk to his knees, impervious to the cold that radiated from the stones and, for the first time in months, found inside of himself enough of the priest he had once been to be able to form the words of a simple prayer.

But he didn't waste this small miracle on his own tattered soul.

No, he prayed for the young woman whom he had been systematically betraying for years, and who was even now throwing herself into the very mouth of Hell itself. It was a last desperate act, and he knew with a sinking certainty that it would be futile, just as everything had been since the long-ago day he had meet Roger Colebrook.

He knew Imogen well. He had watched her from a distance, had watched her grow and blossom over the months of her marriage and had even been a little proud when she had found within herself the courage to confront Roger, a courage he himself lacked.

Admiration, however, couldn't blind him to the facts. The chances were she wouldn't survive the game Roger was playing with her, few did. But still Ian prayed.

He prayed for a miracle.

Chapter Fifteen

A shiver ran down Imogen's spine as the high walls of William's fortress cast them into the shadows. She hunched her shoulders, trying to steel herself against the darkness of this desolate place. It seemed impossible to comprehend that somewhere within this stone menace was the man who had brought a little sunlight back into her life.

It was all so alien to her, yet if her life had been all it should have been, she would have belonged to this cold darkness, it would have been so much a part of her that she would have long since stopped seeing the suspicion and hate that had built those thick stone walls. She would have seen nothing wrong in destroying an innocent man to satisfy another's dark desires. With eyes that saw, she would have been blind to the gentleness and love that lurked under Robert's armor.

And that would have been a tragedy indeed.

Imogen's hands tightened compulsively as she heard the horses' hooves strike the fortress' stones. Suddenly, there was no room to retreat. She was now committed to do all that needed to be done. She stiffened her spine, and felt her chin rise aristocratically. It was as if generations of breeding were suddenly manifesting themselves inside her after years of absence.

That breeding was the only chance she had. It might not give her an ability to beg, but it would hopefully give her the confidence she needed to make demands of a king.

They halted, and Imogen's horse pranced several times before being subdued by Gareth's firm hand on the leading rein.

"Halt. Who seeks admittance to King William's fortress?"

Gareth sat stiffly in his saddle and for a second allowed himself to indulge in the fantasy of turning tail and getting Imogen the hell out of here. Only the certain knowledge that she would never forgive him if he did so stopped him from making realities of fantasies.

Grudgingly he called out, "It is Lady Imogen of Shadowsend and her retainers who seek admittance into the king's presence."

His voice sounded calm enough, but he also made sure that it was injected with just the right amount of confusion, as if he was asking how anyone could question Imogen's right to approach the king's gates.

Imogen smiled tightly at Gareth's display of arrogant confidence. It was a side of the laughing man she had never noticed before, but to judge from the stunned silence that descended, it was very effective, for all its infrequent use.

She silently wished he would share a little of that

arrogance with her. She was painfully aware that every eye in the castle's outer bailey must now be trained on her. She knew she would be the center of their rapt attention, but she couldn't let herself be cowered by it. Instead she sat serenely as if it all meant nothing, but that only served to titillate their audience further. The sound of many voices murmuring scandal started low and spread like wildfire. Imogen felt her face flush as the words Lady Deformed reached her ears.

"Sir Gareth, why am I waiting? We have declared ourselves, surely that is enough," she asked imperiously, deliberately pitching her voice well over the rumble of the crowd. A hush fell, no one wanting to miss one moment of this surprise entertainment.

"I'm not sure, my lady," Gareth said respectfully, but Imogen could hear the smile in his voice as he too began to play to their audience. "Perhaps you have stunned the poor guards with your beauty."

She shrugged her shoulders, as if such extravagant flattery was only her due. "Surely they can be just as rapt when I'm inside the castle as when I'm outside in all of these draughts." She knew by the sigh of satisfaction that rose around her that she was playing her part well.

If only she could believe the part, but it was all bravado and went only skin-deep. She was terrified that someone would shake themselves free of their surprise and recall that she was the wife of a would-be assassin.

Fear was becoming an all-too-frequent companion, she thought abstractly, her every sense straining to try and gauge if their bluff was working. When she heard the clank and rasp of the guards stepping aside to let them pass, Imogen thought she might actually faint from the relief that flooded through her.

She allowed her muscles to sag with it instead, but only for a moment. She quickly straightened in her saddle. They had overcome only the first obstacle and there were many more still to come.

Gareth brought the horses to a halt near the large oak doors of the main entrance, slid swiftly from the saddle and walked to Imogen's side. He reached steadying hands around her waist and gently lifted her to the ground. Taking her arm, he nodded stiffly to the groom taking their horses to the stables, while trying to hide the sinking feeling in his gut as he watched their means of escape disappear around the corner.

His attention was brought back to Imogen as a shiver went through her body. He gave her arm a reassuring squeeze. "You are doing well, Imogen, you acted just like a princess," he whispered admiringly, then added with a sad smile, "Robert will be proud of you."

"Thank you," she said softly.

Matthew slowly walked over to join them, looking around the courtyard in disgust. "And to think I had to work so hard to get out of here! I should have saved myself the bother if I was only going to throw myself back into the Devil's teeth."

Gareth flashed a grin at Matthew. "I'm glad you didn't see fit to mention your recent adventures to the guards. If they recognized you as an escaped prisoner, all the hauteur in the world wouldn't have got us in."

"We would probably still be trying to explain it as they walked us to the scaffold," Imogen murmured.

Matthew snorted derisively. "No chance of that. These idiots wouldn't recognize the end of their own nose, much less the reappearance of an escaped prisoner." He shook his head. "They are a rabble of ill-disciplined old women. Give me a month and I might just be able to whip them into a vaguely capable group of scullery maids, but only if the hard work didn't kill them all first. It would take a lifetime to turn them into soldiers."

"Should you be complaining about their lack of discipline when it was that self-same lack that let you escape in the first place?" Gareth asked with a raised brow.

"It is the principle of the thing," Matthew said loftily and Gareth laughed out loud.

Imogen's smile was tight and preoccupied, her mind working at a furious rate as she tried to decide how to proceed. "Attack and surprise," she said quietly, and for a moment it almost seemed as if she was once more in front of the Keep's hearth, listening to Robert explain to her the intricacies of chess.

Gareth only just caught the softly spoken words, but he understood what she meant. He slipped his arm through hers and began to guide her up the main steps. Matthew followed behind more slowly, glaring at the gathering crowd in what he knew was a satisfyingly threatening manner.

Imogen flinched as the main doors closed behind them, but she continued to walk beside Gareth with the appearance of calm confidence. She knew only too well that if they were to succeed, they had to move so fast that no one noticed that they were, to all intents and purposes, laying siege to the king and his fortress.

Any hesitation on her part and it would mean doom for them all.

Their luck held, with the guards too stunned to challenge them. They were all shocked at finally seeing for themselves the infamous Lady Deformed. Word of their arrival had spread quickly, and the halls were already filling with people eager to catch a glimpse.

Gareth cast a concerned glance down at the small form walking close to his side. The serenity of her face didn't fool him for a moment, not when he could feel the death grip she had on his arm. He would have done everything in his power to shield her from these cruel, prying eyes, but there was nothing he could do.

It didn't help his temper any that he knew the curiosity of the crowd was being fed by their need to see Imogen's infamous deformities for themselves.

Even unseen, Lady Deformed—the misbegotten sibling of Roger the Angel Courtier—had titillated the court's jaded curiosity, but this was just too good an opportunity to be passed up. That there was no damage to be seen on the proud figure that walked with such graceful dignity excited them even more.

Excited, titillated and aroused, Gareth thought grimly.

He felt his brows draw tightly together as he noticed the lust that flared to life on more than one man's face. Their amazement was quickly turning from something a little less innocent, and into something a little more carnal. He tried to glare them all down, but for every man who lowered his eyes at the ferocity of Gareth's raw anger, there were another ten that became more intrigued by the fragile beauty who managed to inspire such fierce loyalty.

Loyalty at court was even rarer than innocence.

His irritation communicated itself to Imogen in the sudden tautness of his body. She gently squeezed his arm, trying to reassure him. "Don't let it worry you, Gareth; their rude curiosity doesn't hurt me. It is no less than I had expected."

Gareth gritted his teeth, but if she could stand it, then so must he. Tolerance didn't mean acceptance, however. Payments would be extracted later and he silently began committing each leering face to memory.

He was so busy at it that they almost ran into the guard who suddenly stepped out from the crowd and halted their progress.

"The king demands the attendance of Lady Imogen Beaumont in his chambers immediately," the man said formally, but he also gaped openly at Imogen, not at all deterred by her glaring companions.

"Excellent," Imogen said loudly for all to hear, "lead on."

"Ah, my lady, I'm sorry but the king has requested only your presence. I'm afraid your retainers will have to wait for you elsewhere." He gave Matthew and Gareth a pointed look, expecting the men to immediately obey the royal edict, but neither made any move to abandon their lady.

Imogen's arm tightened around Gareth's.

"I'd hate to appear to be disobedient to my sovereign, but I'm afraid that one of my people will have to come with me. I am unable to see and I need their help. Surely the king does not expect me to abandon my eyes?"

Imogen's voice was soft, but everyone in the room heard her simple pronouncement and it created a minor uproar.

For a moment, the guard's eyes clouded with confusion, but he recovered quickly. He stepped toward her and bowed gallantly. "It would be an honor, my lady, to act as both your escort and your eyes if you would allow it."

She hesitated for a second but knew that there was no other way. A royal command was a royal command. She didn't dare disobey.

She slowly removed her arm from Gareth's.

"Wait for me," she murmured.

"Forever, if need be," Gareth said fiercely as he bowed respectfully over her hand.

Matthew moved quickly to do the same, his creaking joints protesting their ill use loudly. It was all the reassurance she could take with her.

She felt the stranger link his arms through hers, and found herself walking stiffly beside him as she left behind her last link with the familiar.

The guard walked slowly, careful to guide her around every obstacle, but it seemed to Imogen that in no time at all they were outside the king's chambers, waiting to be formally announced. She listened intently to the faint sound of her name being spoken, and the curt, rumbling reply it got. An absolute terror settled over her as she gracefully walked into the chamber on the guard's arm.

All was silent in the room except for the rhythmic, agitated tapping of a fingernail on wood.

Imogen loosened the guard's arm, and dropped into a faultless curtsy. "Sire," she murmured, her early training returning to her in an instant.

She remained in a low curtsy and while she couldn't hear anything over the loud beating of her heart, she managed not to flinch when she felt a meaty finger smooth along her jawline and lift her face to the light.

King William's eyes narrowed dangerously as he looked into the face of Lady Deformed for the first time. Courtiers had almost killed themselves in their rush to get to his chambers with the news, each eager to be the first to tell him that Lady Deformed was a beauty without equal. They had all wanted to see his reaction, wanted to be the first to know whether the king would treat this innocent beauty as his lover's sister or as a traitor's wife.

Their descriptions had varied wildly, but the central astonishment had remained true in every telling of the tale. Each of them had said in their own way that Lady Deformed was even more worthy of the title "angel" than was her brother.

William had gritted his teeth and refused to let them know that he was as genuinely astonished as they were. He couldn't let it be known that he was as ignorant as everyone else of the truth. He hated the thought of people knowing that Roger had never once seen fit to tell him that the rumors about his sister had been no more than a tissue of lies. Never once had he tried to tell William the truth, not even in the relative privacy of the royal bed.

In fact, until Roger had unexpectedly suggested

the marriage between Imogen and Robert as a vicious joke, he had never once spoken of his sibling, and William had foolishly assumed that the silence was the result of discretion. Now that he could see for himself that there had been no need to hide this lady, however, he had to also admit the unpleasant truth that he had never really known what deep game Roger had been playing.

He dreaded finding out, but this woman was going to make it impossible for him to hide from the truths that would tear apart his life.

He dropped her chin suddenly and moved over to look out the window. "So, why exactly have you decided to invade my fortress, Lady Imogen?" He paused, then added bitingly, "I doubt your brother requested your presence after all this time."

"Like any other dutiful wife, Your Majesty, I have come to be with my husband." As she said the dangerous words she kept her face carefully lowered. "I have also come to prove him innocent of the gross accusations that have been leveled against him."

William turned toward her and leaned against the windowsill, crossing his arms over his stocky chest. "You would dare plead for the life of my would-be assassin? It is a very dangerous thing to do in the circumstances," he said coldly, but was unable to hide a faint flicker of admiration. He watched her lift her chin slightly when most men he knew would be cowering at such a display of royal disdain.

"Robert is innocent," she said simply, her voice clear and strong with her conviction.

"There are many who would say otherwise," William muttered darkly.

"Like my . . . brother?" She spat out the last word as if it was poison.

William narrowed his eyes and couldn't help but recall that it was on Roger's insistence that Robert had been held prisoner.

"Perhaps," he murmured cagily, dark suspicions already starting to find a home in his mind.

"Well, Your Majesty, I hope you won't be offended if I tell you that you are a fool if you believe Roger over Robert."

"It is not normally considered entirely intelligent to call your king a fool," William said with a faint smile.

"I'm sure a king needs to be told the truth just as much as any other man," she said before she realized what she was doing. "Sorry, I forgot myself," she said stiffly.

William tut-tutted. "I'll have none of that now, my dear. I like it much better when you spit fire. It's more honest, if not entirely pleasant." He contemplated her for a moment and then reached a decision. He gently raised her to her feet and guided her over to a chair. "Now, I think it is time for you to tell me all the . . . uh . . . truths that you know."

With her hands clenched tightly in her lap she began. She stammered as she started her story, but slowly her voice strengthened. She told him of Roger's strange obsession, told him of his act of violence that had led to her blindness, told him of the isolation and fear that had held her all but captive. The king's strangely understanding silence gave her the confidence to tell of her dark fears concerning the truth about her parents' death, of

Robert's arrival in her prison, of his kindness. Her voice rang with certainty as she pledged his total innocence in any of Roger's schemes, but when her story finished she found herself holding her breath. She could hardly expect to unravel Roger's coils in a mere hour and she couldn't help but fear that somehow, by coming here, by telling all she knew, she had managed only to play into his hands.

"And you have the messages that prove this?" William asked slowly.

She nodded and pulled the small bundle out from the hidden pocket in her cloak.

She waited silently as William carefully looked over each and every one, her nerves stretching steadily thinner.

"I knew that there had to be more to this than there seemed," he murmured absentmindedly to himself. "And you still have in your possession the ring that belonged to your mother?"

She ran a light finger over the cold metal, then slid it slowly off her hand, glad to be rid of its sad weight. William took it and placed it carefully on top of the letters, his face turning grim when he recognized it as the ring Roger had often worn on a chain round his neck.

"Well, Lady Imogen, you have given me much to think on. I thank you for your bravery and for daring to tell the king about these truths."

She could hear cold anger in those words, and couldn't help but shiver, realizing too late the extent of what it was she had dared to do.

Unexpectedly he changed the topic, asking her what her immediate plans were. It took her mind a moment to put together a coherent reply, answering numbly that she hadn't made any plans beyond this interview.

"Excellent," he said smoothly. "I will have chambers put at you and your people's disposal till I have sorted this matter out to my satisfaction." He placed a heavy hand on her slight shoulder. "It shouldn't take long."

She had to swallow past the lump of cold fear in her throat before she could speak.

"May I . . . May I ask where exactly my husband is?" she stammered.

William smiled sardonically. "It will no doubt relieve you to know that Robert is languishing rather romantically in the dungeons, awaiting my pleasure."

The rush of relief that washed over Imogen left her feeling so light-headed that she barely noticed as William helped her from the chair and handed her over to the guard he had summoned.

"Rest," he suggested awkwardly. "It will help the time of waiting to pass."

"Thank you," she said huskily.

William cleared his throat uncomfortably, signaling frantically for the guard to get this weeping woman out of his presence, and he let out a sigh of relief as the door closed behind her. He hated women who cried. Not that he saw them doing it all that often; he made sure of that.

He turned from the door and couldn't stop himself from walking over to the table and picking up the ring. It was only a simple piece but beautiful in its own way.

He hated it.

The cold metal seemed to yell for the entire world to hear that King William, son of the great

Conqueror, had been taken for a lovesick fool. His hand tightened compulsively around it, pressing the ring's smooth edges deeply into the flesh of his palm. But, even hidden, he couldn't seem to stop its cold weight from whispering that the man he loved didn't love him, and never had. Roger had been attracted only to the power inherent in being the king's lover, not the person beneath the crown. It was a truth that left a bitter taste in his mouth.

Not that it was completely a revelation.

He had always been a little skeptical about the depths of Roger's passion, had always known that kings were rarely loved for themselves alone. Despite that, he had actually dared to hope that Roger felt something beyond lust for power when he surrendered his body intimately to the demands of his monarch. He had even believed that it hadn't been self-interest alone that had led Roger into the royal bed.

William snorted derisively as he threw the ring carelessly back on the table. He had been deluding himself and it was time for him to stop acting like a fool in love.

He reached for the tankard of ale that was never far from his side and drained the contents in one long swallow and called for another. While he waited he stared broodingly at the letters, letters that were clearly written in Roger's own hand. They were damning. In them Roger actually dared to gloat about his power over the king. Their very existence mocked him and he longed to consign them to the fires of deepest Hell.

When the second tankard arrived he drank it more slowly, all the while staring at Roger's damnation.

By the fifth he had to close his eyes, no longer able to bear it. He leaned back his head against the chair and smiled sullenly at his own folly. Tonight he would get drunk and tomorrow he would face harsh realities. Tomorrow he would have to be king.

"Leave the jug and bring me another," he said harshly to the servant who waited patiently near the door. "Then, after that, I don't want to be disturbed." He opened his eyes and pinned the man with a steely stare. "Not by anyone, is that understood?"

The man nodded frantically, anxious to get out of the king's explosive presence.

William smiled savagely at the sight of the man scuttling off in fear. Tonight he would grieve in private. Tomorrow he would face the laughing eyes of his court.

Tomorrow, and for the rest of his life.

"What the hell do you mean you can't let me in?" Roger roared. "I always have access to the king's person."

"I'm sorry, my lord, but the king's instructions are clear. He was not to be disturbed." The guard's eyes didn't quite meet Roger's. "By anyone."

Roger glared in frustrated anger, but knew that he was temporarily beaten. He turned on his heel and marched back to his chamber, struggling to ignore the gloating stares that followed his progress, but unable to stop the dull flush that flared on his pale face.

He dismissed his attendants and sat down on the bed.

It was all that bitch's fault, he thought angrily. Ian

had warned him, of course, but he had failed to comprehend just how much damage his sister could do in such little time.

Perhaps he should have listened to Ian. He'd said that her marriage had changed her, but Roger hadn't taken the priest seriously. He had been confident that he had the king, body and soul, and nothing his little sister could say would change that.

It was a mistake. In just a matter of hours, Imogen had managed to turn the king's mind against him. What else could explain the king's unprecedented refusal to see him? When he had his hands on his little sister, nothing would save her, he thought savagely.

He tried to feed his anger, tried to let it consume him, but it couldn't disguise the panic that was eating into the pit of his stomach. Somehow, everything was going terribly wrong. For the first time in his adult life, he was losing control of a situation. It left him with the overwhelming desire to break things.

Like Imogen's sweet little neck.

His eyes narrowed as a vision of her filled his mind. His palms itched to break her, to sully her perfection, to make her his alone. The bitch! This was her fault. She had somehow managed to insinuate herself into the king's confidences, and undermine all of Roger's perfect schemes, but even while his mind was screaming with the bile of his hate, he couldn't stop his body's arousal.

To know that she was within reach ate into him, like a cancer in his brain. She had actually come, actually dared to confront him. It was beyond comprehension. It was not supposed to happen this way! This wasn't part of his plan.

She was supposed to have been so frightened that she could scarcely breathe. She was supposed to be still hiding under the covers of her bed, waiting for him to come and claim her. She was supposed to be so without resources that she had no other choice but to accept her fate.

And her fate was to become his absolutely. There was to be no escape for her. The victory would be all his. That was the plan.

Instead, she had managed to leave her secure prison and come to the king like some avenging angel. All that courage and strength just to save some bastard who had been forced into her bed. Roger clenched his teeth.

No, Little Sister, he thought darkly as he stood up and instinctively began to straighten his clothes. *you might yet manage to save your husband, but there will be nothing you can do to save yourself. I will win.*

He always did. He would crush her completely and no one and nothing would stand in his way this time.

She was his.

Chapter Sixteen

Gareth stepped quietly into Imogen's chamber only after he had made sure no one had seen him skulking in the corridor outside her room. He gently closed the door, making no sound. He turned slowly, letting his eyes adjust to the dark room.

He found Imogen standing by the open window, her profile bathed in moonlight. The dark waves of her hair hung like raw silk in the silvery light, lifting gently in the warm spring breeze, filling the chamber with its perfume. Gareth closed his eyes and inhaled deeply.

"I see you not only managed to give your own guards the slip, but have also got past mine," Imogen said softly. Startled, Gareth opened his eyes and responded to the slight smile on her face with one of his own.

"And here I was thinking I was sneaking about most discreetly," he said with a chuckle.

She shrugged her shoulders elegantly. "Men who spend their days in heavy armor aren't able to achieve the level of discretion required for a good sneak." She smiled gently at him. "Their rather forthright odor tends to do all their announcing for them, I find."

"My lady, are you trying to, very politely, of course . . ."

"Of course . . ."

". . . to say I need a bath?" He tried to sound offended, but Imogen could hear the grin in his voice.

"I would never dare to question a gentleman about his bathing habits. I'm far too well brought up for that, but you have to admit that it wouldn't exactly hurt if you splashed some water and soap around at the end of the day." She spoke lightly, but already the smile was fading from her face. Her expression became pensive as her mind returned once more to the maze of intrigues they now had to pick their way through.

Looking at Imogen, Gareth felt his own face turning grim.

"What did William say about Robert?" he asked quietly.

"A whole lot of nothing." She sighed and folded her arms tightly around her middle. "He very politely told me that Robert is alive for now, but would give me no assurances beyond that. He listened to all I had to say, took the letters and dismissed me, telling me to get some rest, like some concerned host." She snorted. "He doesn't seem to realize that it's not very good manners to put guards on your guest's door. All I know for sure is that we now await the king's pleasure."

Her eyes filled with tears, but she refused to let them fall.

"While Robert is still alive, there is hope, Imogen, don't forget that," Gareth said quietly. "That William is at least considering our evidence is the best we could have hoped for."

"But if the king decides to side with Roger, by morning we could all be dead."

Gareth scowled. He racked his brains to find something to say that could be at once both a denial and the truth, but there was nothing he could say. Well he had never let that stop him before, he decided. "Imogen . . ." he began, but she cut him off.

"I want to see him. I want to be with Robert."

Gareth's eyes widened in shock and he let out a long, low whistle. "And just how the hell do you think we are going to achieve that?"

"It can't be all that difficult. If you can manage to get past your guards and mine, surely you can get me into the dungeons. It couldn't be all that much more challengeing, surely." Her mouth twisted into a wry smile. "Don't tell him I said so, but Matthew was right. The guards here are less than impressive, as you have already found out tonight."

Gareth paced to the window and scowled out into the night. "I suppose, with a few well-placed bribes and a lot of skulking, it could be done. Possibly," he admitted reluctantly. "But to do so is madness! If we get caught by anyone with half a brain, all of the goodwill you have managed to foster with William will evaporate in an instant."

Even as he gave the warning, he knew he was wasting his time. The determined look on Imogen's face told him that her mind was already made up. She was going to do it whether Gareth liked it or not.

He grimaced as he all too easily foresaw how Robert would react to Imogen materializing in his cell. Robert would strangle her for even contemplating such a thing. He would then strangle Gareth for going along with her insanity. And he was going to go along with it, he realized morosely. He had only to see the radiant smile that bloomed on Imogen's face to know he was already committed to this folly.

He would never be able to fight her when she bestowed one of those beautiful smiles on him.

"Grab your cloak," he said coldly as he walked briskly to the door and stood there tapping his foot.

As soon as this unholy mess is sorted out, he vowed silently to himself, he would get as far away from Imogen and her siren's call as the size of their frighteningly small planet allowed. Perhaps he could go on a crusade. Surely Jerusalem would be far enough away from her for him to reclaim his soul from her gentle hands.

While he was reclaiming his soul he should try to find out exactly where it was he had lost his backbone, he thought with a dark oath.

Imogen walked carefully forward, and linked her arm through his. She leaned up and whispered, "Thank you" in his ear, and Gareth began to worry that he would never get Imogen out of his soul, not even when he was six feet under.

He turned to her and tucked a strand of hair behind her ear. "It would be very easy to love you," he said softly, a self-deprecating grimace passing over his face as hers filled with confusion and concern.

"But Gareth, I love . . ."

He placed a finger over her lips. "I know. You love Robert." Wondering at his own masochism, he added gruffly, "And I also know that the mad behemoth loves you in return. No, Imogen, I know that your love is otherwise engaged and I wouldn't try to change that. I just wanted you to know that no matter what happens here, I . . ." His voice faded, mere words seeming entirely inadequate to express all he felt.

She raised a shaky hand to his cheek, her eyes bright with unshed tears. "That is not love, Gareth. You don't love me." She quickly shook her head to still his protestations. "You care for me, as I care for you, but love doesn't grow with only one person tending it. Not true love. Love cannot exist in the misery of unrequited feelings. True love is something that happens between two souls. When they find each other, they will both see in the other the missing parts of themselves. True love isn't the sad longing of just one person. Someday, you will find true love. A dear soul like yours was never meant to be alone."

Gareth's vision blurred and he had to clear his throat before he could find his voice. "You are a very wise woman, you know." He tried to smile, but managed only a shaky imitation. "Wise, that is, when you're not running around like a madwoman, trying to break into royal dungeons."

"And you're a very special man, one whom I care for deeply, when you are not being an overprotective ogre."

"I will try to be content with that."

Gareth saw her grin and take a deep, steadying

breath, and knew that his moment had passed. He wasn't entirely sure that he was at all sad to see it go.

But then, there would be time enough for regrets later.

"Well, let's see if I can use my specialness to get you into His Majesty's dungeons." He wrinkled his brow. "Although I can't say I like your choice of venue for your liaison."

"I'll have you know that no less a person than the king said that his dungeons were very romantic," she said with mock hauteur.

Gareth snorted dismissively. "Not much of a recommendation when you consider that our beloved monarch also finds your brother romantic."

She was still giggling when Gareth returned after checking that the coast was clear.

"Right, let's get to it," he whispered, and hustled her unceremoniously out of the room.

The sneaking proved to be all too easy. William might have guards everywhere, but that quantity did not translate into quality. Most of them seemed to spend their time clustered in dark corners, gambling away their meager wages in the pitiful hope of increasing them.

As they slipped into the dungeons Gareth found himself in complete agreement with Matthew's early disgust at the discipline in the king's service. It hadn't even been a challenge. It was only when they reached the door of Robert's cell that they encountered the kind of professional guard who had to be well paid to look the other way.

Gareth stood outside the cell and haggled deftly with the man, but in the end they had to pay the exorbitant amount the guard demanded. The man smiled toothlessly as Gareth grudgingly counted over the gold pieces.

"Well, thankee, sir," the guard said, not trying to hide his glee. "Don't forget that me replacement will be arrivin' just before dawn, so you had best have done your business by then." He gave the money a gloating jangle, before walking away, whistling.

"How long will that give us?" Imogen asked quietly, but even so her voice still seemed to echo around the empty stone passageway.

"About four hours. I'll knock three times to let you know that it is time to leave."

He quickly used the key and pulled the door ajar, maneuvering Imogen so that she was in front of it.

"Take two steps forward and pull the door," Gareth murmured and held on to her shoulders for a moment, then stepped away.

Imogen hesitated. "Thank you doesn't even begin to explain how grateful I am to you for doing this," she said shakily.

Silence was all the answer she got. She took a deep breath and pushed open the door, walking carefully into the unknown.

"Be happy," Gareth murmured before disappearing into the shadows to await the dawn.

At the sound of the door closing Robert's eyes opened, his mind instantly awake and wary. He tried to keep every muscle relaxed so that it would appear as if he still slept, but every sense was alive to any threat that might come out of the darkness.

"Robert?" she whispered.

His eyes flew open in shock. "Imogen," he mouthed silently, rolling over on the straw pallet, careful not to get himself tangled up in the chains yet again.

The sight of Imogen standing hesitantly near the closed door made him fear that he had finally lost his mind. He could only just make her out in the dim light that radiated from the guttering candle they allowed him at night. That single candle was the one concession they made to his erstwhile rank and he had never been as grateful for it as he was at this moment when it revealed Imogen's face to his hungry gaze. It was a lifetime since he had last been able to feast himself on the sight of her and even in the imperfect light, she made his soul replete.

"Robert, are you there?" she whispered again, her voice tense with fear.

"Yes," he said hoarsely as he pushed himself carefully into a sitting position. He cleared his throat and continued in a voice more like his own. "What the hell are you doing here?"

She hugged herself tightly as a tremor of relief flooded her at the sound of his beloved voice. Until she heard him a part of her hadn't quite believed that he was actually safe. "I came to be with you," she said gently.

"What?" he all but bellowed. "You traveled halfway across the country for a . . . a social call to a cell?"

"Oh, I thought you meant . . ." she stammered in confusion. "No, what I've actually come to do is to get you out of here, to prove to the king that you are innocent, to . . ." Her voice stumbled to a halt

as she felt the growing anger that radiated from
Robert and filled the cell.

"Are you mad? I told Matthew to get you out of
the country, told him to get you the hell out of this
mess. So what do you do? You throw yourself into
the middle of it." He let out a strangled sound of
disgust and buried his head in his hands, lifting it
again instantly, his eyes narrowed with suspicion.
"Who brought you? You can't have traveled all this
way by yourself, so who the hell helped you in this
folly?"

"Gareth and Matth-Matthew," she stammered
again.

"I'll kill them," he growled furiously. "I will kill
them with my bare hands. I'll tear them apart strip
by strip."

Imogen's relief at finding him safe began to give
way to a vague sense of being ill-used. She had
come so far, braved so much . . . certainly not so she
could stand there and let him vent his spleen, she
thought indignantly.

"That isn't fair. It's not their fault. It was all my
own idea," she said with dignity, but ruined the
effect by biting her bottom lip worriedly. "Are you
angry because I'm trying to help you?"

"No, you fool," he ground out precisely. "I'm
angry because you have put yourself in danger. I'm
angry because I feel guilty that it is for me that you
have done so. I'm also bloody angry because there
is not a single thing I can do to help or save you. No
while they have me chained to a goddamn wall." He
pulled hard on the chains, which clanked as if to
emphasize his point, and he inhaled sharply as th

iron manacles dug into the bruised and bloody skin of his wrists.

"You're hurt," Imogen gasped and instinctively moved toward the sound of his pain. She had taken only two steps when her foot snagged on a raised stone, and before Robert could shout a warning, fell down. Pain shot through her knee as it struck the stone floor, but she scarcely noticed. It seemed irrelevant when Robert was suffering so much for her.

She crawled to close the distance between them, only stopping when her hand touched the warm strength of his thigh. Robert watched with disbelief as she rested on her knees and started running anxious hands over him to check for hurts.

"You've lost so much weight," she moaned as her hand moved over the bare skin on his torso.

"William isn't much of a caterer." He tried to sound carelessly flippant, but it came out in a husky murmur.

She whimpered as her hands moved up to his face and felt his nearly healed wounds through the beard that had grown during his captivity. "Pain," she whispered. "So much pain."

Her voice wavered as if she was the one in pain, and Robert's anger evaporated in an instant. Without pausing to consider the wisdom of his actions, he found himself dragging her onto his lap and into his arms, wanting to comfort her. It comforted him as well. To hold her again was a miracle that he hadn't dared even to pray for.

He held her as tightly as he dared. Reverently he buried his face in the perfumed waves of her hair and gritted his teeth as desire bit deep into his body and soul. The feel of the soft skin of her neck through her hair was like a call to his soul and he couldn't stop himself from rubbing his face against her, his bearded cheek rasped quietly.

Imogen hesitated, terrified that she might hurt him, then slowly wrapped her arms around him burying her hands into his hair.

"Oh, God, this has to be a cruel dream," he choked out as he began to trail kisses with fervid haste along the line of her throat.

"If it is a dream, then may we never have cause to wake up."

"Amen," he sighed, and pulled her head down to his and smothered her parted lips in a searing kiss.

It was a kiss where spirits met.

Imogen knew in that instant that life and love were too precious to be wasted on the meaningless frivolities of doubts and fears. The only thing that mattered was right here, in the meeting and mating of their tongues, in the hands that tried to pull each other so close that she no longer quite knew where her body ended and his began. She let out a groan of raw desire, and Robert answered it with one of his own.

He would go mad if he wasn't part of her. Now. Here. In a dungeon.

The thought froze him. It was impossible to think of savagely taking his beautiful Imogen on the straw pallet that was the only bed his meager cell had to offer.

He dragged his mouth from hers and drew her head against his chest, his breath coming in ragged bursts as he tried to gain control over his raging body. That control would have been more easily found if every inch of Imogen's body wasn't pressed against his, but he lacked the willpower necessary to put her away from him entirely.

He was only a man and even as his honor demanded he let her go, his achingly aroused body could no more put her from him than it could fly from William's fortress.

When he thought he might be able to see her without falling on her like some ravaging beast, he gently allowed the tension in his hands to ease, and dared to look into her flushed face, her lips bruised from his kisses.

"Sorry," he growled. "I didn't mean for that to happen. Not here."

"Why . . . why did you stop?" she asked in confusion, her mind still numbed by the raw desire that filled her to overflowing.

"I thought it was for the best."

"You thought . . ." She pushed herself away from him and grabbed his head between her hands. "Why is it that you get to make all of the decisions? Why is it that you never ask me what I think, or never even think to ask me what I might want?"

Robert ran a finger over her cheek and along the damp fullness of her swollen bottom lip.

"Forgive me, but I don't want to take you like a dog in heat on the stone floor of His Majesty's dungeon." He saw her flinch at the coarse expression, but he continued determinedly. "Imogen, I'm chained to a wall so that I can't stand, or even crawl to the other side of the room. I'm not fool enough to believe that you can want to be with me like this."

She lifted her face and placed a lingering, searing kiss on his startled lips.

"I love you. I want to be with you," she murmured against his lips, her breath burning his skin as her words fired his heart. "I want to be held in the arms of the man I love. I want to be able to forget about the outside world, even if for only a moment. I want to forget that there might not be a tomorrow for us." She groped for his manacled hand, lifted it to her breast and held it there by force when he made to move it away. "The only thing I care about is that you hold me as close as you can in the precious time we have managed to steal. Please hold me," she whimpered, her voice breaking.

Robert groaned as he pulled her into a crushing embrace, not able to reject her generous gift. "I suppose I should be grateful that William saw fit to imprison me in a new fortress. Compared to the filth of Westminster's, this is a paradise," he muttered as he fumbled with her skirts so that his hand could touch the warm satin of her thighs. He groaned helplessly and closed his eyes as his hand ran adoringly from knee to hip. "You do know that you are entirely mad, don't you?"

The cell filled with her sultry laughter. "Well, that would just about make us a matched set, then . . ." Her words were cut off by a gasp as his long fingers moved along the skin of her inner thigh and brushed the curls that protected her feminine core.

That protection proved entirely inadequate and Robert's fingers found the treasure that they sought, sending shivers of ecstasy through her body. His hand resting under hers tightened around her breast, sending a shaft of pure fire to her lower abdomen.

"Oh, Imogen," he murmured as he lowered his

lips to capture her moans and whimpers of pleasure. He no longer dared to question the fate that had brought this woman to him and made her say that he was the man she loved, but he let out a growl of frustration as he tried, and failed, to pull her body under him. His chain clanked noisily as they tangled around them.

He dragged his lips reluctantly from hers. "Damn things," he groaned as he tried to untangle himself, only seeming to tangle himself further.

Imogen pulled herself to one side, listening impatiently to the sounds of his struggle, trying to determine how they had him chained.

"Can you sit against the wall with your legs out in front of you?" she asked hoarsely. Taking Robert's aggravated grunt as an affirmative; she placed her hand in the center of his wide, bare chest and gave it a gentle push. "Then do it."

Robert hesitated only a second before complying. Imogen waited till everything was near silent and the only noise to be heard was the sound of his ragged breathing. She had to try and steady her own before she felt ready to do what she wanted to do for him.

She was going to show him just how much she loved him; she was going to show him the woman she had become because he loved her. She was a woman who was no longer so completely crippled by the past that she barely existed. Because he loved her.

Reaching out, she ran her hand up the length of his calves, the hair bristling under her fingers, creating an enticing friction. She smiled a little when she heard his sharp intake of breath as she placed a kiss on the rough skin of his knee, then one on the more-sensitive area on the inside of his thigh.

"I don't have the stamina for this torture," he said gruffly.

"Well, I have enough stamina for both of us," she whispered, placing another kiss higher up. Her heart ached as she realized the truth behind his jest. The deprivations he'd suffered in the time they'd been seperated had changed him. He was leaner, not as strong; though the feel of him under her hands still made her ache with want. It didn't matter. What she had planned required him to do nothing more than love her.

She lifted herself so that she sat astride his lower legs and, with an unembarrassed naturalness, she drew her simple dress up over her head.

"Good God!" Robert breathed out slowly, the air starting to burn in his lungs. He realized then just how inadequate his memories had been. Nothing could compare with the sultry angel who was bending over to kiss the base of his manhood. Her hair fell forward, moving over his skin in exquisite torture.

Imogen hesitated for a moment. After so long spent dwelling on the pain Roger had brought her, she expected to feel fear but instead of memories of her brother and his perversion, her mind was too full of Robert to be distracted by the past. Robert had freed her from it all.

His love had made her clean and whole.

There were tears in her eyes as she placed a kiss on the moist tip of his straining need. Robert found he couldn't look away from the sight, and of their own volition, his hips lifted from the floor as a groan was torn from deep in his chest.

"Shhh," she whispered soothingly, lifting her head to smile at him tremulously. "I will make it all better."

Cupping him in her small hands she sat up and carefully guided him into the moist heat of her. The feel of the long, hard length of him pressing up against her almost sent her over the edge and for a moment she wasn't sure she was going to be able to control herself. It took all of her strength to slowly lower herself till she was completely full of him.

She was so profoundly moved by the joy of their joining that it was a second before she could find her voice. Her hands were shaking as she lifted them to frame his face. Gently she rubbed her nose against his.

"Robert Beaumont, I love you with everything I have," she whispered huskily. "You have taken all of my pain from me, made me whole. You gave me love, even when all I had to give you was my fear and hate. And, for all of that, I owe you more than I can ever repay."

"Imogen . . ." Robert ground out through clenched teeth, but Imogen put a shaky finger on his lips to still them.

"But all I do have to give you—my life, love and body—are yours. Forever."

Robert felt his heart expand till he wasn't sure if his chest could contain it. He lowered his head and claimed her sweet lips in a kiss as he lifted his legs till his feet were flat on the floor. The movement brought the center of Imogen's desire hard against the base of his erection. She gasped at the sudden change in sensation and Robert smiled hungrily against her lips as he shifted in her again.

"That's right, Imogen, let it go. Let me watch your face as you come apart for me."

She threw back her head, her hands curling into the hollow on his shoulders, as her body undulated against him. The long line of her throat beckoned to Robert in the candlelight and he lowered his lips to the pulse that beat wildly just under the skin. With a nipping kiss, he sent her over the edge, her moan sounding like music to his ears.

The silken wall of her sheath convulsed around him and it was then his turn to groan helplessly as his own desire was drawn from him. His large hands moved to cover her hips, sealing her against him, as wave after wave of his seed filled her.

They were both held suspended for a moment, then in a rush Imogen felt her heart start to beat again.

Robert's head dropped back bonelessly against the wall and his arms moved around her damp back to hold her steady against him. Her ragged breathing played over the heated skin of his chest as she nestled her cheek against him.

She didn't even mind the cold chains that trailed from his wrists over her back and buttocks. Just so long as she could feel him breathing underneath her, feel his big, capable hands moving softly over her back and his shrinking manhood still buried deep inside her, then she was happier than anyone had a right to be.

"I love you," he growled softly and instantly found the peace that had eluded him for years. He was now doing what he had been born to do. He was loving Imogen.

She turned her still passion-flushed face up to his, her hand reaching up to trace the sensual softness of his lips.

"I love you too."

Robert tightened his arms around her, trying to keep her close and safe from the rest of the world. It was a futile gesture, but for the moment it almost seemed possible.

If Imogen loved him, then anything was possible.

The three sharp knocks rang out but Imogen just held on to Robert more tightly. She didn't want to leave. In this cell she had found love and for a few precious hours she had been able to live a dream.

Mostly, they had just talked. They had talked about silly things, about their childhoods, their dreams and mistakes. Robert had told her a little about his life as a mercenary, about its hard, unforgiving days and cold, lonely nights. She had tried to tell him a little about Roger's games, but she had quickly stopped. He wasn't ready to hear, and Imogen couldn't help but be a little relieved. She wasn't truly ready to bare all the secrets of her soul, especially not if they hurt him.

For similar reasons, she hadn't wanted to tell him about the baby. She knew it would only give him one more thing to worry about when already he was trying to protect the world. But now she couldn't hold it in. She frowned as she tried to find the words to tell him. "Robert, there is something I must tell you before . . ." she started, but he cut ruthlessly over the top of her with an urgent growl.

"You have to be safe, Imogen. Regardless of what happens to me, you must be safe. Claim complete ignorance; throw yourself at William's mercy; run away. Do whatever it takes to make sure you stay safe. You are all I care about and if you let anything happen to you, I will . . . Well, I don't know what I will do, but trust me when I say you don't want to find out! Do you understand?" he finished furiously, making the dear words sound like a threat.

He shook her gently till she managed to choke out a startled, "Yes."

"Excellent," he breathed with a satisfied sigh, then stole one more heated kiss. Even after making love once more after their first heated coupling and having held her tightly in between, Robert still hadn't had enough of her.

This time it was Imogen who ended the kiss.

"But I won't abandon you," she said with fervent determination, wanting him to understand. "I will only do what I believe to be right."

Robert let out a rush of frustrated cursing at her obstinacy. "I should tie you up and give you back to Gareth stuffed in a bag," he muttered with disgust, painfully aware of how powerless he truly was.

"I love you too," Imogen smiled softly as she stood, quickly finding the dress she had discarded earlier and shaking the straw from the skirts.

Through worried eyes he watched as she pulled it over her head, enjoying the sight of her easy movements, but feeling sick to his stomach with the knowledge that in a cell there was nothing he could do to protect her. Even when he tried to stand up and pull her close he was defeated by the chains that held him. Hearing his struggle, she reached out a hand and clumsily found his bare shoulder, gently pushing him back to his knees before he hurt himself. She then tenderly touched his face in farewell, lingering as tears gathered in her eyes.

Robert grabbed her hand in both of his and placed a string of heated kisses on her palm. "I love you too, Wife, with all my heart, body and soul," he said hoarsely. "That's why I'm as worried as hell for you and ranting like a madman. I need you to be safe."

Imogen pulled her hand away as the three knocks came again impatiently.

"I know," she said, tears now falling freely down her cheeks. When she heard his moan of distress and the sound of his chains rattling as he tried to reach for her again, she knew she had to leave before it became too painful for them both. She turned quickly and felt her way to the door, opened it quietly and left without another word.

Imogen closed her chamber's door on Gareth's almost silent retreating footsteps, leaning her hot forehead against the cool wood. She was incapable of stopping the seemingly endless stream of tears from falling. She could feel the dawn breaking on the morning Robert might be taken from her forever and she grieved for herself, for him and for the precious child their love had produced.

That she hadn't told him about their baby saddened her, but she knew it was for the best. He was already tormented with worry for her, if he knew about the baby as well, he would only suffer more. It was selfish to burden him further.

A baby shouldn't be a burden, but a joy, a joy Robert deserved to have to its full extent. She would wait and tell him at a time when it would bring only happiness. The baby had waited this long to know its father, it could certainly wait a little longer.

She bit her lip as the horrendous possibility occurred to her that there might be no more time left to them. What if this new day brought only death and darkness? What if that darkness consumed Robert, consumed them all?

She turned from the door and wrapped her arms around the slight swell of her stomach to protect the life that sheltered within. It was a futile gesture. She couldn't even protect herself from what this day might bring.

"So, sister of mine, just what is it that you have been up to?" Roger asked silkily behind her, and she froze at the sound of the all-too-familiar voice in the darkness.

A shock of cold panic slipped down her spine as she felt his hand grip the back of her neck and his soft lips touching the side of her face as he ran his thumb slowly over her full bottom lip. To have Roger touch her lips, still bruised from Robert's kisses, felt like a defilement and, for the first time in her life, she turned her head away from him.

He only laughed.

"You have managed to ruin everything, Imogen," he said mildly. "Because of you, William won't see me. I don't think I have long to wait before the axe falls and it is all your fault."

He suddenly applied a painful pressure to her neck, forcing her chin into her chest as she slowly sank to her knees. "You have meddled where you shouldn't have, Sister dear, and I am afraid that you now must pay the price."

Lifting his hands and releasing his hold on the back of her neck for a moment, he casually backhanded her, sending her sprawling to the ground.

"But don't worry," he whispered. "I have already come up with the most perfect way for you to apologize . . ."

Chapter Seventeen

Robert was wide-awake and staring broodingly at the stones when the cell door opened. He didn't bother looking up, his mind and soul still too consumed with Imogen to worry all that much about this new intrusion. Robert barely acknowledged the guards as they told him that they were taking him to the king's private chamber. They removed the chains from his legs and wrists, one of them tersely ordering him to stand up.

He stood stiffly, finding it difficult to get his back straight. The guard threw some clothes in his direction, which he caught clumsily. A small smile filtered across his face as he slowly dressed, the absurdity of the situation amusing him despite his worry. "Five guards?' he enquired with a raised brow.

"Surely William can't be that worried. What sort of trouble does he really think I am going to cause while half-starved and unarmed?" He slipped on his boots, then tried to roll the strain out of his shoulders. "I suppose I should be flattered he thinks that even with all of that, I'm thought to have enough strength to be a serious threat."

Not that he had any trouble finding all kinds of reserves of strength last night with Imogen in his arms, he thought dryly, and tried not to laugh out loud at the memory. He suspected that these men mightn't get the joke and in Robert's experience there was nothing as dangerous as an armed man who didn't get the joke.

He contented himself with being safely ignored as the men manacled him and marched him out of the dungeons, but it was only when they reached the king's apartments that Robert found his mind focusing on the situation at hand, instead of the brilliant memories of the night just past.

It was an unusual situation, to say the least. Condemned men didn't normally have meetings with the king. William tended to keep his slaughter well away from the royal person. Despite the strangeness, however, Robert didn't doubt for a moment that this odd social visit was merely a postponement, not a reprieve.

His eyes narrowed thoughtfully. Death had never held much fear for him. He was a knight for hire. He was a giver of death and destruction and knew that he would one day be a receiver of it. Life was never meant to be forever, and the life of a knight was often brutally short. He had long since made his peace with that but, now, for the first time in his life, he felt his skin break out in a cold sweat at the thought of his own mortality.

And his fear had a name: Imogen.

She had brought a value to his life that he had never had before. He hated knowing that he would

be leaving her behind unprotected in this danger
ous world, and the longing to have more time to
hold her in his arms was almost unbearable. Some
how, though, he suspected that there wouldn't be
time enough in eternity for him to have his fill of
her.

He had to free himself of these morbid thoughts.
He would achieve nothing by dwelling on this new
fear, especially not when it had the power to para
lyze him. Sunken in self-pity he would be of no help
at all to Imogen. He drew a deep breath as he
walked into the king's chambers surrounded by the
Royal Guard.

He didn't bow to the man standing near the
window even as the guards around him did so with
energy. Instead, he stood passively, his manacles rat
tling as he crossed his arms defiantly over his chest.

William didn't seem to notice this impertinence.
He barely seemed to notice that his privacy had
been invaded at all. Instead he stared morosely out
the window and, even from the door, Robert could
see that his eyes were badly bloodshot, and that his
hand trembled slightly.

"Remove his manacles, then leave us," William
said, not even bothering to look round as he spoke,
his voice alcohol-roughened. The guards quickly
removed the iron rings and bowed, eager to leave
the room.

I'd like to have half their luck, Robert thought wryly
as he began rubbing blood down into his hands
gritting his teeth at the pain caused by the sudden
return of his circulation.

After a long moment, William turned from the
window and moved to sit down in a nearby chair

Robert hesitated a second, then decided that in this strange scene, bravado was everything. He sat down in a chair across from William's.

Robert only barely suppressed the groan of pleasure that rose in his throat as he stretched himself out full length in the chair. Tired muscles started unwinding and returning to their natural position. As the pain slowly eased he found his curiosity increasing as to what was actually going on. He had sat only as an act of defiant bluster and had never expected William to let the insult remain, but he did. None of it tallied with what Robert knew to be fact. Hell, even before this mess, William had wanted to convert Robert to a dismembered form as quickly as possible. Now that William had the perfect excuse, he seemed to be too distracted to focus his anger.

Robert didn't like this strange behavior and found himself automatically bracing himself.

"Your wife is certainly a most unusual baggage," William said suddenly.

"You could say that," Robert said, carefully keeping his voice neutral. But if the king dared to threaten Imogen in any way, Robert was more than ready to kill him with his bare hands.

"I believe I did say that," William said testily. "Most unusual. I don't think anyone has ever called me stupid to my face before, not and lived to tell about it."

Robert winced and tried desperately to think of some mitigating circumstance to explain away Imogen's undiplomatic statement, promising himself at the same time that if he ever got the chance he would have a very long discussion with the woman about how best to stay alive when playing games with kings. "She has been under a lot strain lately and . . ."

William nodded his head and waved away the excuse with a dismissive, "Yes, Yes," grimacing slightly as the sudden movements sent pain raging through his raw head.

Robert waited with coiled preparedness for William's next move, but the man seemed quite content to stare at the floor, as if he was trying to divine answers from the stonework. Robert found his patience growing dangerously thin.

He needed this to end. Now.

"Just what the hell is going on here?" Robert asked bluntly.

A ghost of a smile played over William's face as he lifted his eyes to meet Robert's, his brow rising sardonically. "What a truly excellent question." He sighed and ran a shaky hand over his face before continuing wearily. "As near as I can make out, you and I have been dragged into a rather nasty little family argument. We are nothing but bit players in a larger drama, it would seem." William's voice was filled with a brooding bitterness, his eyes narrowing with sober anger. "You are no assassin, are you?" he finally asked accusingly.

Robert smiled lopsidedly. "One would think you are almost saddened by that."

William stood up abruptly and began to pace the room before answering. "Aye, I would damn well prefer you to be an assassin. If you were the treasonous dog they told me you were, I could have you executed on this very day and could be rid of you permanently. If nothing else, it would make my world less irritating. I have always liked the idea of seeing your arrogant carcass dangling from a noose."

"Thank you," Robert murmured.

But William didn't seem to notice the interruption, as he was too caught up in his vague feeling that somehow Robert had cheated him on purpose by not being guilty.

"I've never liked you," William continued. "You're smug, conceited and entirely without respect. You insult me just by living. You dare to patronize me, and dare further to do it in my presence, damn you, like I am just some squire instead of your king." He swung round and pinned Robert with a glare. "But you damn well don't plan to kill me, do you?" he roared.

Robert pretended to consider it for a moment, daring to believe for the first time that there just might be any number of tomorrows in his future. "No," he said finally, unable and unwilling to hide his grin.

William seemed to deflate and age before Robert's eyes.

William then carefully averted his face, moving to look out the window once more. "I've been an absolute fool," he said with soft disgust. "I have somehow managed to give myself over to an evil illusion." William needed no reply to that statement; too consumed dealing with sad truths that Robert knew nothing of.

When suddenly he turned around, all visible grief was gone. "So what exactly do you know of Lady Imogen's past?"

It took a second for Robert to catch the abrupt

change of topic, and then he just shrugged his shoulders.

"Very little. She holds her truths very closely, like a talisman to stop any further evils. She has let only small parts of her past escape. I do know, however, that she has been kept a virtual prisoner by her brother and that that bastard has deliberately hurt and terrified her. At the same time, he has bound her to him in some way that I just cannot seem to unravel—yet." Robert looked down at his white knuckles. "In all, I know enough so that if you leave me alone with your precious Angel Courtier for even just a few minutes, I will send him straight back to the Devil."

William smiled darkly. "Sounds perfect."

Robert raised a brow questioningly and William met his look blandly. "Let's just say that Roger has become something of an inconvenience. I hope your wife continues to keep her own counsel concerning her brother, as I would rather the world remained ignorant of my own folly in this drama."

And with that Robert had to be content. William was clearly going to say no more. Not that the details mattered now, Robert realized slowly, not when the king was all but telling him that he was removing the dark cloud of threat from their lives.

Robert felt strangely reluctant to grab this reprieve with both hands after the initial jubilation passed. He was too cautious to trust something he didn't entirely understand and his instincts were warning him that it couldn't really be this simple. "So, where exactly does that leave Imogen and I?" Robert asked, his muscles tensing as he awaited the reply.

William shrugged his shoulders. "It leaves the pair of you as far away from me as humanly possible," he said succinctly.

Robert let out a surprised laugh. "Can I have that in writing?" he asked, elated, but not letting that blind him to the particulars.

"If that's what it costs me to get you gone, I'll do it right away." He went to the door and bellowed for his secretary. The poor man scuttled into the room and quickly scribbled down William's formal notice of exiling Robert and Imogen to Shadowsend.

Robert slowly got up, wincing only slightly with the pain of the movement. "I may have to beg a little more of your hospitality. Just time enough for some rest." He looked down at the borrowed clothes. "And a bath."

William grunted his affirmative as he heated his own sealing wax in a spoon, moving it slowly over the flickering candle. "Well, I suppose I owe Lady Imogen at the very least one rested husband. She might faint if you go to her in that condition. I'll have one sent to your chamber now," he said, and flicked a disgusted look over Robert's unkempt figure.

"She is made of sterner stuff than that," Robert murmured enigmatically as he took the paper from William's outstretched hand.

With a small bow, Robert turned to leave. But William halted him and reached down to the table, picking up a small ring. "Give this to your lady." William stared at the simple band intently. "And tell her that justice will be done."

Without comment, Robert took the strangely

warm ring and walked quickly to the door, eager to tell Imogen the good news about their exile.

William's disgusted mutter of "I really don't like you" reached him as he opened the door.

"Don't worry, Your Majesty," Robert said with a smile as he looked over his shoulder, "I've never been none too fond of you, myself."

William's startled laughter followed Robert down the hall as he left the room a free man.

"If you don't stop humming, Robert, I may have to actually leave this bed so that I can kill you," Gareth said through gritted teeth, "and at the moment, I find the thought of leaving this bed truly perverted."

"You never were a morning person, were you?" Robert asked with a good-natured smile, feeling very happy to be alive as he stepped into the copper tub that the servants had brought to the chamber Gareth and Matthew had been sharing. His impatience to be with Imogen raged inside him, but when he saw her this time, he wanted it to be without the least vestige of the dungeons clinging to him. This was the start of the rest of their lives and he wanted to do it properly this time. Still, he raced through his bath, not wanting to waste any more time away from Imogen than he had to.

"How very observant of you," Gareth said sarcastically. "I am certainly not a morning person, not when that morning is separated from the night by only a few moments of sleep. I also find it does my humor no good to be confronted by a disgustingly happy madman asking me whether he can have a bath and borrow some clothes so that he can go and seduce his wife. Again." Gareth yawned and pulled the blankets up to his chin. "I'd say I'm actually displaying remarkable tolerance by not strangling you."

Robert chuckled as he began to scrub the soap into his scalp, groaning with happiness at the sensation. "You should be grateful that I haven't taken your head off your shoulders for daring to bring Imogen to the court and then letting her go down into the dungeons last night," Robert said with a smile as he enthusiastically lathered the suds. "I left you to look after her, not to give her an education in the king's justice system."

Gareth rolled over and shrugged his shoulders. "Sorry about that. I knew you wouldn't be best pleased but, at the time, I was more afraid of her than I was of you. Since you have been gone, the woman's turned into a complete harpy." He shuddered delicately. "At least they had the good sense to chain you to a wall. Her, they left free to terrorize the populace, and I'm man enough to admit that she frightened the hell out of me."

"Wise man."

"I thought so," Gareth replied modestly.

"Spare me," Matthew said flatly, his gaze never wavering from his hands as they expertly sharpened Robert's sword.

Robert only laughed again as he ducked his head under the water to get out the last of the soap. He stood up once he was finished and casually wrapped a cloth around his hips, letting out a deep sigh of satisfaction. "God, that's good. I feel almost human again, which is novel after so long spent living like a caged animal."

Gareth opened an eye and gave him an assessing once-over, taking in his faded bruises and weight loss. "Well, I don't care what you think you feel like, you look a starved mess." He closed his eyes and rolled over onto his back. "And that is no mean feat when you consider the obscene amount of food you forced me to watch you put away when you first got here."

"Well, you had better keep your eyes averted as I intend to eat a lot more before this day is over. I aim to take full advantage of the king's erratic hospitality after so much time spent in his less-than-inviting dungeon." He smiled teasingly. "You're getting squeamish, Old Man."

"Old man?" Gareth murmured without opening his eyes. "I'm younger than you."

"Only by twelve months," Robert reproved as he began hunting for some clothes. "And as for how I look, a bit of good food and soft living should see that off nicely."

"I wouldn't get too ready for that soft living just yet if I were you, Boy." Matthew's face, when Robert spared him a glance, was the picture of gloom and despair.

"Why ever not? Surely I have done enough hard living for the time being?"

"Aye, that's as it may be, but there seems to be one little detail you have overlooked." Robert raised a questioning brow, his attention caught. Matthew looked down at the sword blade, its length glowing in the early-morning sunlight. "You seem to have forgotten that the brother still lingers on the scene."

Robert laughed with relief and grabbed a deep blue tunic, pulling it over his head. When his face reemerged, his eyes glowed with an almost feral light. "You have got it wrong, Old Man. I haven't forgotten that bastard for a second. I'm looking forward to sending him off to Hell with his head under his arm, but that's not my idea of hard living. It will be a pure, unadulterated pleasure."

"Will you want any help?" Gareth asked conversationally.

"No, the disposing of the big brother is a pleasure I intend to keep for myself. I am going to enjoy reaching down the son of a bitch's throat and pulling off his balls."

"Graphic," Gareth murmured appreciatively.

"I liked it," Robert demurred with false modesty.

"Like small boys playing at war," Matthew said in disgust as he leaned the sword in the corner.

"You don't like the plan? I kind of thought that he deserved it." Robert paused a moment. "And worse."

"It's not a question of whether the worm deserves it or not," Matthew growled with barely restrained impatience, "but what I'm questioning is why his painful demise hasn't already been achieved. I happen to think you're underestimating your enemy, and that is always a fatal mistake in my experience. Do you think he is now blithely waiting in his room for you to come and play creative executioner? Knowing that pond scum, he is already making plans while we speak."

Robert shook his head. "It doesn't matter what

he is planning, I will beat him. He is not playing mind games with a terrified orphan anymore and, at the moment, that self-same orphan is my priority. Roger can wait his turn and, when the time comes, his opponent is going to be a grown man, not a child."

"I was just saying it as I see it," Matthew said with a quiet conviction that temporarily rocked Robert.

"You really can be an old woman sometimes, you know," Gareth said with another yawn.

"Better an old woman than a dead hero."

"Play nicely now, children," Robert said with a slight smile, enjoying the familiar sounds of the two men arguing again. It was strange to confess, but he had actually missed it.

He sat on the end of the bed and put on Gareth's boots that he had found near the hearth. As he moved his feet away quickly, he blithely ignored Gareth's disgusted mutter: "Well, make yourself at home, do."

Robert stood and spread his arms wide. "Well, I think I'm ready to go and tell my lady wife about her exile." He smiled with relish. "And I even have it in writing and sealed by the king himself."

"Well, you just toddle along and do that, but for God's sake do it quietly. Some of us actually need sleep if we are to function normally." Gareth cast a disgusted look at the glowing radiance on Robert's face, then pulled a pillow over his head.

"And Roger?" Matthew asked quietly.

"I'll see to him before we leave in the morning, never fear. But right now I need to be with my wife just to reassure myself that we are both alive." He gave the old man a beatific smile as he left the room.

"Idiot," Matthew muttered.

"Not an idiot, but a man in love," Gareth said, his voice muffled by the pillow.

"That is the worst kind of idiot of all."

Robert's good humor lasted till he found Imogen's chamber empty, then it evaporated as if it had never existed. A cold feeling lodged itself in the center of his heart as he took in the silent barrenness of her room and he knew in that instant that something was wrong. Terribly, utterly wrong.

He didn't question for a second his certainty that Imogen was in grave danger. She was the other half of him and he could almost taste her terror as if it was his own. His hand went for the hilt of his sword before he remembered it was leaning against the wall where Matthew had put it.

He narrowed his eyes grimly and, acting on pure instinct, went in search of Roger Colebrook.

When Robert found his chambers were also empty and that all of his servants had been summarily dismissed last night, he found out the true meaning of fear. It filled his chest till he almost ceased to breathe; but even so, he refused to let panic cripple him. He knew that, great though his own fears were, they were nothing compared with what Imogen must be feeling.

She would be terrified.

He ground his teeth together as he tried to imagine how she was surviving her worst nightmare, *if* she was surviving. He had to get to her before

Roger succeeded in destroying her utterly. He deliberately calmed down and methodically set about finding his wife. One of the guards on the gate thought that perhaps he had seen them leave on one horse, and he seemed to be under the impression that they had been heading toward the north.

Toward Shadowsend.

It was logical, but if he was wrong, valuable time would be lost, time Imogen would have to spend trapped in her worst nightmare. With that thought, Robert made the conscious decision to stop thinking. Every time he thought, he became paralyzed and he couldn't afford for that to happen.

He had to act.

Robert tried to get an audience with the king, believing that at the very least William owed him something. He waited outside William's chamber for what felt like a lifetime, pacing and sending message after message.

Silence was the only answer he got.

Now that William was sure of Imogen's continued silence and Robert's exile, he simply wanted them gone from his mind and from his castle. After three hours of frustrated waiting Robert realized that there would be no royal help forthcoming. He would have to act alone.

Strangely, that suited him, he thought grimly as he returned to Gareth and Matthew's chamber, preparing mentally for the most important hunt of his life.

He didn't spare Gareth a glance as he found his sword belt and slung it around his hips, welcoming the familiar feel of its cold weight.

Gareth sat at the bench and had been throwing

dice idly until Robert's abrupt entrance. He watched in surprise as Robert carefully slid his weapon into its sheath and mechanically adjusted the belt to the correct position.

"Am I to take it that the second reunion didn't go according to plan, then?"

"There was no reunion," Robert said emotionlessly as he reached for a dagger and slipped it into a band he put on his arm. "Roger has taken her out of the castle and seems to be heading toward Shadowsend."

There was no need to add that he was preparing to follow them.

"What . . . how?" Gareth yelled, not even noticing the chair he knocked over as he stood.

"He must have been waiting for her when she returned this morning. The guard on the gate thought he saw them ride out about an hour after dawn." Robert gritted his teeth. "The idiot actually had the balls to tell me that he thought that the lady had looked a little distressed. A little distressed, and he just let her go?"

"How many teeth did the man have after he told you that?"

"I left him his teeth. I broke the fool's nose instead. Next time he sees a lady in distress, I can guarantee he will make further enquiries."

Gareth suddenly had a horrible thought and he swallowed loudly. "You haven't mentioned it, but did Imogen tell you anything important last night?" he asked earnestly.

"I fail to see what was said last night has anything to do with this," Robert ground out, not wanting to think about the happiness he had found last night, not now.

"Damn! She didn't, did she? If she had, you would see only too clearly what I am trying to ask." Gareth took a deep breath. "Robert, Imogen is pregnant."

Robert suddenly stood still, transfixed.

"How . . . ?" he started stupidly, struggling to get his mind to function properly.

"The usual way, I suppose," Gareth said with faint amusement.

Robert suddenly slumped down on the bed. It was too much for his mind to deal with rationally.

"I didn't tell you about that to make this harder." Gareth placed a hand on Robert's shoulder. "But as you're going after them, you need to be prepared for anything you might find." He dropped his hand and stared into the distance, his voice filled with self-recrimination as he continued. "Coming all this way exhausted her, no matter how hard she tried to hide it and even before that, well, you know she had been struggling. I don't know how much more stress her body can take. To be put through this now . . ." Gareth shrugged his shoulders helplessly. "I just don't know."

For a moment Robert hid his face in his hands, then he lifted it and he stood up, his face scrupulously free of any expression as he finished dressing.

"Do you want me to come with you?" Gareth asked quietly.

"No!" Robert cleared his throat uncomfortably. "No, this is personal. I will hunt him down myself. What I do need you and Matthew to do is to get your sorry hides up to Shadowsend as quickly as possible. Gather up the men there and get them ready for war."

"What war?"

"If I don't find Imogen within a fortnight, I will go to Shadowsend myself, get the men and then tear this island apart stone by stone till I have found her," Robert said grimly.

"William is not going to like that."

"His likes and dislikes are no longer any concern of mine."

Gareth nodded his head. "Well then, my friend, I can only wish you good hunting."

Chapter Eighteen

Imogen couldn't escape him. He was everywhere. He had effortlessly consumed her entire world till all that existed for her was his touch, his smell surrounding her with cold menace. He held her in front of him on the horse, like she was a child, enclosing her ruthlessly in his world so that she knew there was no escape.

Her hands clenched together tightly and she drew a deep, stilted breath, trying to close herself off from reality.

If she didn't exist, then she would no longer have to feel the body that pressed hard against her back, trying to absorb her. But she did feel it and nothing she did was going to make it go away.

A shiver of revulsion raced through her body before she could stop it. He felt it and she knew sickeningly that he enjoyed it. He pressed her so close that she feared she would shatter and be merged into him forever, the very thought making her shiver again.

And that excited him more.

She could clearly feel the heat of his erection where it throbbed against her hip. His arms tightened painfully around her.

"Was that a shiver of anticipation? Can't wait till I have you completely either? Well, we will just have to try and be patient. I have plans that I won't let you ruin with haste," he whispered insinuatingly near her ear, and chuckling deeply as she instinctively tried to move her body away from his. "Imogen, dearest, this is a saddle. There is nowhere for you to go."

He casually dragged her back ruthlessly against him. "You will have to stay right here. With me."

She struggled not to throw up as she felt him burning against her once more.

A single tear slid down her face and she hoped that he couldn't see it. The last thing she wanted was for Roger to know of her weakness. If he knew, he would only get stronger, be able to destroy her outright.

Worrisomely, she wasn't as frightened of that as she should be. If she let her body die, her spirit would be released from this dark world, but even as she longed for it, she turned her back on the peace it offered. She couldn't give up, not this time. There was too much at stake. She didn't move, fearing that Roger would guess her secret, but mentally she wrapped her arms protectively around her baby.

For the sake of Robert's child she must survive this terror.

Every time the babe moved, Imogen held her breath, afraid that Roger would sense that movement, afraid that if he knew of its existence, then

nothing on earth would stop him from tearing i
from her.

He hadn't yet noticed and she would do every
thing in her power to keep it that way, she though
fiercely. She would let nothing harm her baby, even
if that meant her own desires had to be ignored.

Robert's child kept her alive just as she kept i
alive, and she smiled faintly as it occurred to he
that already the child was taking after its father. I
seemed that the pair of them were both conspiring
and plotting to protect her in their own ways.

Her throat tightened painfully as memories of
Robert filled her, and with those memories came
guilt. She had left him while he was in danger.
Roger had taken great relish in telling her that
while he might have fallen from royal favor a little,
Robert had never had any favor to start with. Roger
had laughed as he had prophesied that, regardless
of the truth, William would take advantage of the
situation to remove Robert while he could.

It might have already happened; he might already
be departed from this world. She mentally flinched
and pulled her mind away from such evil thoughts.
They would destroy her if she let them, and Robert
wouldn't want that for her or their child. He would
want her to survive and to remember always that he
loved her and teach their child about that love. She
knew that with a certainty that defied distance and
time, life and death.

She deliberately filled her mind with memories
of the love Robert had given her in the prison cell
and the love she had given him in return, and of
the strength Robert had radiated even as he waited
to die. It awed her that even at the point of death

his only concerns were for her own safety and that she loved him.

No, she realized with amazement, more than merely loved. He completed her, was the other half of her soul, and so she had to live, to keep that part of him alive. He would always have existence in her memories and in the face of the new soul that their love had created.

For those reasons she must endure.

Another tear fell unchecked down her cheek.

She flinched as Roger wiped away the tear with the pad of his thumb.

"If you cry, my dear, I will be bound to think that you don't want to be with me and might find myself taking offence." He kissed her neck. She shuddered again, and he chuckled as he sucked brutally on the tender flesh as if he was trying to draw her fear inside of him. "And we wouldn't want that, now, would we?" he asked tauntingly as he lifted his head.

She shook her head stiffly.

"Not good enough," he whispered, his hand moving insinuatingly up her body. "I find I have a longing to hear you say the words. I have always found your voice most . . . soothing." His hand moved to her breast. "Sooth me, Sister."

"No, Roger, I wouldn't want that," she said jerkily and reached to snatch his hand away from where it clenched her breast painfully.

Roger chuckled and let his hand drop for now. "Much better."

This time she managed to suppress the shiver of revulsion that started in the pit of her stomach, then carefully made her mind a blank nothing. She surrounded herself in an empty fog where she didn't exist, Roger didn't exist and pain didn't exist.

She didn't know how long she stayed like that, but so successful was she in constructing her emptiness that it was a moment before the fact that they had stopped moving registered in her mind. Roger lifted her down from the horse and she listened to him move around in the now-familiar routines of establishing their nightly camp as if it was all happening to someone else, not her.

She didn't try to run away. She had nowhere to go.

She heard him move toward her and knew he bowed ironically before her with a courtly flourish before gripping her elbow and propelling her forward. "My lady, let me take you to the stream."

She stumbled clumsily but soon recovered. She had quickly learned to do whatever he told her. He would enjoy too much suppressing a revolution and Imogen refused to give him any more pleasure.

He let go of her arm when they reached the stream and took a step back, but he didn't leave. He never did.

He watched and waited as she relieved herself. She felt her soul shrinking under the weight of her humiliation. Her hands were shaking as she awkwardly followed the sound of running water and reached to wipe her face, her tears mingling invisibly with the water.

Her misery was so absolute that she didn't even protest when Roger unexpectedly swung her up in his arms and carried her back to their camp.

He held her close, his breath a hot brand over her face as he slowly lowered her to the ground. He didn't let her go. He held on to her upper arms with a bruising firmness as he watched her narrowly.

"You have put on weight," he said blandly. "Haven't you?"

She tried not to flinch but knew that her face drained of all color and betrayed her.

"I only just noticed," he said as he carelessly removed her cloak and threw it on the ground. "Most strange," he murmured to himself as his eyes raked her figure assessingly.

His hand moved down her arm and over to her breast. "You're fuller here," he said as his hand moved to the swell of her abdomen, "and here."

Her mind fragmented. He knew! How had he worked it out? And when? Had he noticed as he had carried her, or had she done something at the stream that had alerted him?

Had she somehow betrayed herself?

Neither of them said a word as his hand continued to move over her. Words were not needed between them. They both knew what the other thought, knew what was going to happen. She knew he would not stop now until she was destroyed. He had no choice. The rules of the game had been decided so long ago that her betrayal had sealed her doom regardless of what either of them now might want.

Imogen was oddly relieved when the silence was broken by the sound of flesh hitting flesh, and actually welcomed the pain of his hand hitting the side of her face.

"Bitch," he said through gritted teeth. "You let that bastard into your body, into *my* body, didn't you?"

"He was my husband. You gave me to him," she said calmly, despite the throbbing pain of her face. "What else could you expect?"

"I didn't expect you to enjoy it." His hand made

contact with her face again, splitting her lip, filling her mouth with the metallic taste of blood. "You opened your white thighs and welcomed him into your body, greeted him with wet warmth, let his seed find a place in you. You're a whore," he spat out angrily.

The next blow brought her to her knees, but he couldn't stop the laugh of triumph that boiled inside her. "You lose!" She threw back her head, and tears streamed down her face. "You lose because you thought everyone was a twisted half human like you, incapable of real emotions. You actually thought you could bring another person into your game and not lose control."

She slowly got back to her feet. "But you did. You lost control at that moment, didn't you? Robert wasn't what you thought he was, was he?" She spread her arms wide tauntingly. "He had me, and I welcomed him. He came into my life and gave me back all of the laughter and light you had taken away from me. And, you know, the funny thing is, because of you I was almost too blind to see his goodness. Can you believe it? I almost let it slip through my fingers because you had destroyed my ability to recognize love. Almost."

Her laughter rang out.

"In the end, however, he is stronger than you. You are nothing compared to him. So, yes, I let him into my body; yes, I loved him with all my heart and soul and strength. And you know what that means don't you? No matter what you do, I win." The smile on her face was radiant. "I win because despite you I have loved and been loved in return."

This time the blow knocked her to the ground her head hitting a rock and stunning her.

"Don't believe that for a moment, bitch," he spat out, and aimed a furious kick at her prone body. "A baby is an easy enough thing to remove and once it's gone, you will soon forget these futile notions of love. I won't let that bastard's spawn survive long. Your body is mine, will be mine again. That I can promise."

He turned from her dismissively with an angry curse and she rolled herself into a protective fetal position, listening in silence as he started a fire and boiled the salted meat he had brought with them. He didn't give her any when it was prepared, but began to eat with a noisy relish. Imogen didn't care, too full of the truth she had yelled at him.

She had won. Despite all of Roger's dark games she had managed to become a complete human, capable of love, not just a pawn in his twisted rituals and desires.

She truly had won.

Robert's knees cracked as he knelt down to feel the ashes, their coldness mocking him. Damn! He was no closer to catching up to them than he had been yesterday; or the day before, or the day before that.

No matter how hard he pushed himself, Roger continued to remain ahead of him because he was not slowed by the need to track down his quarry. Robert was hunting them, using all of his skill and experience to follow them as they traveled slowly north, but that very hunting was slowing him down and every day that passed was another day Imogen spent living her worst nightmare.

Visions of just what Imogen might be suffering rose

to torment him yet again. He clenched his hands in impotent rage and stood up quickly. He couldn't let his anger consume him, not now, when Imogen needed him and all the skill he could muster.

He carefully submerged all emotion and cast an expert eye over the camp. They still had to be at least a day ahead of him, but with two people on one horse they weren't moving as fast as he could if only he knew for certain where they were heading.

Though there was no sign of it, there was now no doubt in Robert's mind as to their intended destination. It was only an unprovable gut instinct, but he was certain they were heading to Shadowsend, heading for the tower Roger had built all those years ago for just this purpose.

Years of hard-learned experience wouldn't let him rely on instinct alone, but with each mile farther north, his certainty grew. He knew enough about Roger, from the little Imogen had revealed, to know that for Roger, rituals were important. Things had to happen in a certain way for him to enjoy them to their full. Roger wanted it this way, had been living for this moment for years.

But Robert couldn't let what he *thought* he knew lead him astray.

He ground his teeth in frustration and was turning to mount his horse when something else caught his eye, a small detail he had almost overlooked. Written in the dust were signs of a physical struggle. A body had fallen to the ground while someone else stood by, a small dark spot, evidence enough that some blood had been spilt.

Imogen's blood.

Robert's teeth clenched and a muscle started to twitch in his cheek.

There was a cold purity to the anger that burned to life inside him, that turned to dust the last of his doubts. He climbed on to the horse's back and galloped away from the scene of Imogen's humiliation, not once looking back.

He was done with following. If he stopped trying to second-guess himself he could get to the tower before them.

Then he would wait.

The rational part of his brain warned him that if he was wrong, if Roger wasn't heading to the tower, then Imogen would be lost. But he chose not to listen. It was time to put complete trust in his instincts. They alone would get him what he wanted most in the world: Roger Colebrook's blood all over his hands. Never before had he ever been so grateful for his ability to inflict death. It made all of those dark years of the sword worthwhile.

He ignored the pressure he felt building behind his eyes and the thickening of his throat as he thought of Imogen. There would be time enough for emotions later.

If he was lucky, all the time in the world.

"Do you know where we are?" Roger asked as he drew the horse to a halt.

Imogen could barely hold up her head. She had been slipping in and out of consciousness for days, but Roger's voice always seemed to effortlessly penetrate the fog that surrounded her and bring her ruthlessly back to his world.

"The tower," she managed to get out around the swollen pain in her throat. It was still unbearably bruised from were Roger had throttled her the night before. Or perhaps it had been the night before that. Time had blurred and now shifted fluidly around her.

"Very good," he murmured approvingly, effortlessly swinging off his horse. Once on the ground he crossed his arms over his chest and waited. This was a new ritual. He didn't assist her, gaining a perverse pleasure from watching her helplessness.

Imogen half-climbed, half-fell off the horse, holding tightly on to the pommel till she was certain she wouldn't fall over. She stood unflinching as Roger slipped the rope back round her waist, tying it firmly in place. He gave the lead a sharp tug, and Imogen stumbled forward.

Roger didn't slow his pace as he went down the steps that led to the tower. Imogen barely managed to stay upright as Roger navigated the cool underground passageway and into the ground room of the tower.

"There seems to be some things missing, Little Sister. What have you been up to?" he asked politely as he tugged her along after him.

"Robert . . ." she managed to say before Roger pulled her up to his side and closed his hand around her throat, his fingers covering the bruises neatly as he began to casually squeeze the air out of her.

"Of course, the late, unlamented Beaumont." He shook his head as he said smoothly, "The man was a fool."

He dragged her up the stairs, his hand held tightly around her throat, intent now only on ending the game and destroying the last of his uncertainty as to its outcome.

It seemed to Imogen that in no time Roger was opening the door to the topmost room.

"Damn," he muttered, "something's blocking the window." He dropped his hand from her throat, but still held on to the rope as he carefully walked into the room, feeling for a lamp and flint. Finding them on a small table in the center of the room Roger quickly lit the lamp.

The light revealed a large, menacing figure standing with lethal casualness by the blanket-covered window.

In the candlelight, Robert's face looked like an avenging angel and he smiled evilly at Roger as he reached for his sword.

"Good God," Roger gasped in shock.

"No, Colebrook. Not God, but justice," Robert said, his smile broadening as he struck out with the flat of his sword, sending the other man reeling.

The blow jolted Roger out of his shock and he tried instinctively to back out of the room, but he ran into Imogen, who was standing behind him. He impatiently shoved her out of his way, smiling slightly as she stumbled backward.

She barely had time to comprehend the unbelievable fact that Robert was here. Her feet caught in her skirts as she lurched from the tower room and slammed into a cold stone wall. Confused, she pushed herself off the wall, and her heart stopped when suddenly all she felt under her left foot was air. She had stumbled to the top of the stairs, and suddenly her mind flashed back to the other tower in Cornwall, to those other stairs that had claimed her sight. The tower Roger had replicated at Shadowsend to torment her. She panicked and tried desperately to find her balance in the swirling darkness that surrounded her.

She flailed out her hand, but couldn't find anything to grab hold of. She tried to step away from the sickeningly long fall she knew was in front of her, but Roger's reversing body blocked any retreat. As she stumbled she realized with a sinking certainty that the only thing between her and an endless fall to the bottom of the stairs was the rope that dug painfully into her waist.

A rope that was in Roger's hands.

She was unable to stifle the scream that tore through her throat as she felt Roger jerk the rope sharply, deliberately keeping her off balance.

Roger held on to the wall of the passageway for support, his head still ringing from the stunning blow. Robert stood in front of the lamp, his body casting Roger into shadow. Roger pulled the rope tightly and Imogen stumbled again with a terrified squeak. "I had hoped you would be dead by now, bastard. I can't help but find it inconvenient that you aren't," Roger said through clenched teeth, wiping the blood from his lip with his sleeve.

Robert pointed his sword at Roger's throat, smiling broadly as it nicked the skin. "You're not that lucky, Colebrook, and I'm not that easy to kill. Not when William has turned against you." Robert smiled. "He has even given me permission to kill you."

Roger pulled suggestively on the rope, enjoying Imogen's moan of fear as she stumbled blindly down a step. Robert narrowed his eyes angrily but kept his attention focused on Roger.

"Kill me, Beaumont," Roger said with relish. "And I'll take your whore to Hell with me."

"You dare threaten her?" Robert asked incredulously. "When I hold a sword at your throat?"

"Oh, I dare anything, Beaumont. That's why I always win."

Robert was so fast that Roger didn't even see the thrust that pushed the sword deeply into his belly, not stopping till the blade cut through to the other side.

Roger looked down in amazement at the hilt that protruded from him, his hand reaching instinctively to pull it out even as he knew it was too late. He looked up at Robert and smiled. "But I still win bas—" He was cut off by the gurgle of blood that trickled from his lips. He let go of the rope and, with his last burst of strength, gave Imogen a surprisingly powerful push before slumping to the floor, dead.

Imogen's scream was piercing as she felt herself start to fall. It was so sickeningly familiar that her body was already anticipating the pain of flesh hitting unforgiving stone.

"No!" Robert roared and he sprang over Roger's body to try and catch her. He saw her falling as if in slow motion and flinched when he heard her fragile body make its first contact, feeling it as if it was his own pain. He leaped down the steps, trying to get to her, but her fall was broken only when she stopped with a sickening thud on the first landing.

She lay eerily still when Robert reached her and fell to his knees beside her. He lifted a shaky hand and gently swept her hair from her face, gritting his teeth helplessly as he looked into her pale face.

"Imogen, oh, God, Imogen," Robert pleaded brokenly, not even noticing the tears that fell unchecked down his cheeks. He hauled her battered body against his chest and began rocking as he pleaded with her to wake up, pleaded with her to live because he loved her more than life itself.

Her silence was like a dagger in his heart.

He looked into her bruised and bloodied face, flinching inside at the deathly paleness of her translucent skin; its stillness taunting him.

"Please, Imogen," he whispered huskily. "Please stay with me."

Her silence echoed in his heart like a death knell.

"For God's sake, man, sit down. Your pacing is giving me a headache," Matthew said gruffly, but wasn't surprised when Robert ignored him, keeping up his fevered walking from one side of the room to the other.

"Two days!" Robert burst out in disgust. "For two days she has been laying there like death and all that fool healer you got can say is that we have to give her time."

"And the woman is right," Gareth said reasonably and returned Robert's glare with a sad, understanding smile.

Robert let out an angry curse and returned to his pacing, his raging thoughts whirling around his head. It seemed an eternity to Robert since he had arrived back at the Keep in the middle of the night with a broken Imogen in his arms, not caring for a moment that his anguish was clear for all to see.

He had been like a madman after he laid Imogen onto her bed—stalking around the room and roaring at anyone who dared to suggest that he should leave the local healer to do her job. In the end, after he yelled at the woman that he would kill her if anything happened to Imogen, he had been forcibly banished from the room. It had taken three of his men to drag him away from Imogen, and the healer had bolted the door to prevent his return, only Mary being allowed in and out of the sickroom.

They managed to drag him no farther than the end of the passageway before he struggled free and roared at them all to leave him alone.

And there he had remained, not leaving for anything, refusing to eat or sleep. Instead he incessantly paced or sat with his head in his hands as despair consumed him. Gareth and Matthew silently passed the vigil with Robert but were unable to comfort their friend. Neither man said that all would be well, preferring silence to lies.

For two days the Keep held its breath and waited—while Robert paced, Matthew cleaned armor and Gareth sat throwing dice.

Those were the longest days any of them had ever passed, but Robert almost wished them back when the weary healer finally stepped out of Imogen's room just as the sun was setting on the second day. He stared at her blankly for a moment, then walked reluctantly up to her, his heart in his throat.

The harried woman barely had time to get out that Lady Imogen had just awoken before she was being shoved aside.

Robert strode into the room but stopped short when he saw Imogen lying small and still, engulfed in furs. He swallowed the lump in his throat and let his eyes devour her for a moment. Her eyes opened slowly and turned to meet his with an unerring accuracy. She smiled and the beauty of it looked out of place on her pale, bruised face.

"The healer said that you were awake," Robert growled awkwardly, then flushed at the foolishness of the statement.

Her smile grew larger. "Aye, more awake than I have been in my life," she whispered.

Robert's brow furrowed. "So you are all right?"

"Better than best." She lifted her hand slowly and covered her stomach, a satisfied smile curving her lips. "It is amazing, but our little one's heart is still beating. It didn't seem to mind being thrown around too much."

Robert didn't realize that he had moved forward until he dropped to his knees beside the bed. He lifted a trembling hand to cover hers, his eyes wide with astonishment as he felt the firm, round mound for the first time. "When Gareth told me, it didn't seem real." His hand caressed her gently, wonder dawning on his face. "We are going to have a baby," he murmured in awe, hardly believing that moments ago he had been afraid that he had lost her and now here he was holding his hand atop the life they had created.

She pouted. "I should slap Gareth. I wanted to be the one to tell you." Then her face cleared quickly and the radiance returned. "But I still have one secret that Gareth can't spoil. I didn't even tell the healer."

Robert dragged his eyes away from where his large hand covered hers and looked at her questioningly.

She bit her bottom lip, unsure of what to say. She reached out her other hand slowly and ran it through his hair. "I had wondered what color your hair was after you left, but I had never asked, so I couldn't imagine," she smiled shakily, "but I should have known that your beautiful, brooding face could only be surrounded by midnight hair." She turned her head to the side carefully regarding the face she was seeing for the first time, although she knew it as intimately as she knew her own, her finger moving along his cheekbone. "And midnight eyes."

It took a second for him to understand. Stunned, he raised his hand to cover her eyes wonderingly, feeling her lashes against his palm as she blinked.

"You can see?" He scarcely recognized that unsteady voice as his own as he removed his hand and saw the truth radiating from the liquid depths of her brown eyes.

"Yes." She pulled his palm to her lips. "I really did find justice in that tower, just like you said. Roger gave me back what he had taken from me all those years ago. I will now be able to see for myself if our baby has your eyes or mine."

Robert felt a tear fall on the back of his hand and didn't know if it was his or hers. They stared at each other in wonder and then slowly moved into each other's arms. Robert buried his head in her breasts as his shoulders heaved with tears of joy and relief. Imogen just wrapped her arms more tightly around him and held him close as her own tears fell.

Now was the time for tears both happy and sad, and neither tried to stop them.

Their tears healed them, made them whole.

Made them one.

Epilogue

Robert swung easily down off Dagger's back and handed the reins to the waiting groom. He looked around the bustling courtyard and smiled with satisfied pride. His improvements had come along nicely while he had been away and there was no reason why they shouldn't be finished within the year if all went well.

The speed could at least in part be attributed to the fact that they hadn't had to quarry stone straightaway. Robert had derived great satisfaction in pulling the tower apart block by block and, because of that ready supply of good stone, his home would be as well defended as any of the king's castles.

Not that stone fortifications had been enough to save William, Robert thought with a slight frown. A man couldn't live behind fortifications forever, it would seem, and away from their strength even a king was vulnerable. William had found that out while hunting in New Forest on a hot August day when a stray arrow had ended his troubled reign.

News of the king's death had spread like wildfire, and Robert had heard many different stories. Some said Walter Tirel had shot at a stag, aimed poorly and hit William instead. Some said that Henry, William's younger brother and part of the hunting party, had paid Tirel to shoot William deliberately. The church said that God had reached down a hand and redirected the arrow with careful precision to hit the king's black heart.

Whether it had been a hunting accident, an assassination or the final judgment of an angry God, publicly, at least, most accepted the official view that it was simply an unfortunate accident with a fortunate outcome. Robert wasn't so sure.

Henry was something of an unknown quantity, and Robert was wary but had cautiously joined the new king's many supporters at the recent coronation.

In fact, that was the one definite thing he had against the man. Because of the coronation he'd had to travel to Westminster to pledge his allegiance to the new reign. He would much rather have stayed at home with Imogen and their little baby, Kathryn, than spend a month in the murky confines of the court.

He inhaled the sweet air of home and let it sooth his tired soul. Now all he needed was to hold his wife close and he would feel human again. He cast a searching glance around the courtyard but didn't find Imogen running to meet him.

The groom grinned at Robert. "We weren't expecting you for a couple of days yet, Sir Robert, and I believe Lady Imogen said this morning that if she had to wait forever for her errant husband she would at least do it in the tranquility of the rose garden."

Robert nodded and strode over to the walled garden, only just resisting the urge to break into a run.

He quietly walked through the arch and hung back in the shadows, content for the moment just to watch as Imogen moved amongst the brightly colored flowers. She stopped to pick one of the blooms and lifted it to her face, closing her eyes to bathe herself in the scent for a moment, then opened them again to absorb the lushness of the color of the rose.

She gently placed it in the basket that hung on the crook of her arm, its edges already hidden with the riot of color from the varied array of flowers she had already collected. Robert crossed his arms over his chest and smiled with contentment.

Color. It was his wife's newfound addiction and consequently his life had become filled with it.

Imogen seemed determined to make up for all those years of darkness by filling every corner of her life with the brilliance of color. Sometimes the results were a little startling, it had to be admitted, but Robert didn't mind. To him it was simply a sign of health and happiness, and looking at her moving gracefully amongst her gardens he could feel both radiating from her.

The sudden sound of a sleepy gurgle drew Robert's attention from the beauty of his wife. Imogen had brought Kathryn out with her, he realized with a smile. Her little basket nestled in the shade of the rosebushes and she yawned as he watched, sticking her fist in her mouth before finally giving in to sleep, obviously impervious to the nearly fully grown sheep that contentedly ate grass nearby.

Robert's face softened as he looked at the tiny human. It still seemed amazing to him that he had a daughter, that his love had produced another life. And it was all a gift from the woman who loved him. He didn't know how he was ever going to repay her.

Somehow, Imogen had managed to give him everything he had never dared ask for.

His heart swelled to bursting as his eyes found Imogen again and lovingly followed the contours of her slender body. He couldn't help but admire the way she now moved with both grace and confidence, though sometimes that very confidence terrified him.

She seemed to have no understanding that there may be limits to her new strength and refused to let him lock her away so that he could keep her safe. Not that he hadn't tried.

After she had regained consciousness, he had been prepared to tie her to the bed if that was what it took to keep her unharmed; but, of course, eventually Imogen had balked at the idea. Even when he had, rather graciously he felt, conceded that he might let her sit in a chair for an hour each day after the baby was born. She had only smiled at him very sweetly, told him that he was a dear man and that she loved him, but he was insane if he thought she was going to play an invalid all her life just to stop him from worrying.

It seemed to Robert that in no time she was out of her bed and throwing herself into life with a will. There had been no stopping her. All he had been able to do was to follow helplessly in her wake, trying to protect her from anything that might cause her harm. He had resigned himself to the fact that the only way to keep her safe was to be with her constantly—and that hadn't been without its consolations, he remembered with a grin—but she had tolerated it only for a little while.

She had turned on him one evening and told him in no uncertain terms that it was time for him to go about his own business so that she could get on with hers. She had insisted she could no longer abide him as an overbearing nursemaid.

He had tried to tell her, calmly, that he was only being sensible, that while she seemed to be healthy, she shouldn't forget that it wasn't so long ago she had had a near-fatal fall and that she was pregnant. She needed to be looked after and he wanted to do it.

She had laughed, waved aside his concern, tweaked his nose and gone on her merry way, leaving him no choice but to do likewise.

Despite her condition and his fears, she had set a relentless pace, much to Robert's horror. It was a sign of just how bad things had become that he had actually been relieved when he was called in from the fields with the news that Imogen had gone into labor. His frazzled mind had foolishly thought that at least it would slow her down a bit and give him some peace from his near-permanent state of worry.

That relief had quickly evaporated as a night and another day passed with Imogen struggling to bring their child into the world. It had been as bad as waiting for her to awake from her ordeal at Roger's hands and, to make it worse, he had once more been banished from her side while she fought for her life, the healer already very wary of him after their previous encounter.

As time had ticked by without end, he had suffered all the shades of fear and guilt it was possible to suffer. Every time her screams reached him, he had listened with the grim knowledge that she suffered only because he had followed his animal lust and got her pregnant.

When the sound of a baby's lusty cry broke into an unnatural silence, Robert hadn't felt any ease in his dark guilt. It had almost brought him to his knees. The healer was wiping her bloody hands on her dress when she came and told him that all was well. He had run from the room before she had finished speaking, only reassured that Imogen was safe when he was able to brush her sweat-soaked hair from her forehead with a shaky hand and rain kisses over her exhausted but jubilant face.

"I'll never touch you again," he had vowed fervently between kisses. "I will live like a monk before I ever put you in jeopardy again. I promise."

She had smiled serenely and raised a hand to his cheek. "And here was me already trying to decide what we could call Kathryn's brother or sister." She had let out a tired, husky laugh at the horrified look on his face.

"Not just yet, perhaps," she murmured soothingly. "Not till I have a little rest at least."

"Not ever!" he had roared at her, and considered that the end of the matter, contenting himself with watching over her and Kathryn through the long nights.

The days that followed had been hell for Robert as he watched Imogen struggle to do everything at once. Although she denied it, the birth had drained her already stretched resources, but she still refused a wet nurse and ignored the nursery maid he had appointed, stubbornly determined to look after Kathryn herself. Robert had been bewildered as to what he should do. He couldn't just stand by and watch helplessly as Imogen struggled to balance the child's needs with her own body's need to rest and heal, and had soon found himself having to try and deal with Kathryn as he was the only one Imogen would let care for her baby.

He would have done anything if it meant Imogen could get the rest she so clearly needed, but he was a most reluctant nursery maid. The tiny, helpless scrap of humanity terrified him. He had never been around babies before, and scarcely knew where to start with his own. His hands seemed too large and clumsy to deal with such tiny limbs, but he had set his jaw and learned the mysteries of child soothing and napkin changing. In the process he found himself falling totally under Kathryn's innocent spell.

He seemed to drown in those wide, innocent eyes that were so much like his, and was totally captivated by the smile that reminded him so much of the woman he loved. Kathryn every gurgle of pleasure became for him a prize of infinite worth, her every tear an enemy to be fought off with a will.

The newly discovered joys of fatherhood had almost been enough to make up for the self-imposed chastity. In that month before Henry's summons he had found something approaching contentment, but that hadn't stopped him from burning to be with Imogen.

Kathryn was now two months old, and things

certainly hadn't become any easier for him. Even now as he watched Imogen, he found himself gritting his teeth as his blood pooled in his groin. He had been able to deal with his lust before because Imogen had needed to heal, but now that she was radiating health and well-being he didn't know how he was going to survive.

"Are you going to spend the whole day skulking?" Imogen asked calmly, without looking up. Her ability to do that always made him smile.

"I think I might skulk for a bit. After a month away, I find I'm enjoying the view."

Imogen let out a less-than-elegant snort. "He abandons us for what feels like forever, Kathryn, and then all he wants to do when he finally finds his way back, is to look." She shook her head sadly. "I hate to say it, but I think your father is a madman."

She let out a delighted squeal as Robert lunged and swept her up into his arms.

"Now, don't you go bad-mouthing me to Kathryn," he said with mock ferocity. "How will she ever grow up respecting her father if her mother casually casts doubt on his sanity?"

Imogen smiled and wound her arms around his neck. "My girl will grow up to be a clever woman and she will make up her own mind as to the state of her father's questionable sanity."

Her laughter was cut short by his lips descending to cover hers. He inhaled her laughter, feeling like a starving man let into a feast. Time stopped entirely when Imogen knowingly parted her lips, and invited his questing tongue to explore the familiar territory once more. Robert didn't have the willpower to stop, and found himself drinking deeply the taste of Imogen's passion.

The small, catlike mew of pleasure that escaped Imogen drew him back to sanity and he groaned as he tore his mouth free. "I promised I wouldn't do this," he said raggedly.

"Making all the decisions again?" she asked with a husky chuckle. Deprived of the heat of his lips on hers Imogen ran intoxicated kisses down his neck to satisfy her own need for him. "Not to do this— now that would be insane."

She lifted her gently amused eyes up to meet his. "I won't let you put me in a dark box for my own protection, Robert. I've tried that, and I can't say that I much cared for it. I'm much stronger than you seem to think." She smiled mistily and ran a finger over his full bottom lip, sending a shiver of passion through his body. "With you in my heart, mind and soul, there is nothing I can't do. Nothing we can't do together."

He kissed the tip of her finger, then moved it aside to capture her lips once more, but this time the kiss was as much about love as it was about lust. "This is still madness. We're in the rose garden, for God's sake. Anyone might see us."

"Then let's be mad together."

And they were, surrounded by light and color, with their baby sleeping peacefully nearby, undisturbed by her parents' love.

It truly was madness, but, oh, what a divine madness!